CAN YOU SEE ME

Joanna Lloyd

For my son, Matt, who makes each ordinary day, an extraordinary one.

CHAPTER 1

Sydney, Australia.

DARK COILS OF SMOKE HINTING at ugly memories seep through the walls, slink across the floor and lasso my ankles. My breathing rasps, ragged. My arms hang stiff by my side.

His low hypnotic voice nudges me past the fear and I jump into the abyss of lost time. Recollections flood my captive mind, winging me back.

"Talk to me, Layla. Is the memory there?"

My heart beat pounds, drowning his words. There are doors… not the right one…turning…

"There…over there…that door," I tell him. "Heavy…too heavy to open.

"Try again to open the door, Layla. It's important."

I tense stomach muscles and force my hand up to the handle… fear, dread…I pull my hand back.

"No. I can't go in," I whisper.

"We're nearly there, Layla. Stay strong. I'm right beside you, you're safe."

His mellow voice slows my breathing, gives me courage. I take another step. The smoke dissembles into hands inviting me to approach.

"Layla. Open the door. We need to know."

Grey vapour clogs my nostrils and eyes. Intense fear knifes through me. My mind screams. In a flash the murky images are sucked away like water down a drain and I snap back to the room, back to reality.

A reality fashioned from the darkest of nightmares.

Thing is, I know what I am now. The aberration I've become.

I just don't know how I got here.

The clock turns over. Another session wasted and my memories are still locked away—a cabinet with no key. We both know, without the key it's impossible to deal with the carnage.

Part of me is relieved to remain in ignorance, part is desperate for the truth; and another part yearns for the sweet release of slipping out of this gruesome excuse for a body. I am careful not to reveal these dark thoughts to Dr. Leighton, my psychologist. In case he has me committed and put on suicide watch. Instead, I swallow the self-revulsion and apologise for yet another failed bid to piece together the events of that horrific day.

With a sigh, he leans back in his chair, his attempt at a benign whatever-you-can-manage-is-fine-by-me expression not quite successful. The faint creases in his brow carry the responsibility of extracting my memories; information essential for my rehabilitation as well as the investigation into the fire.

"Would you like some water?" he asks.

I nod with a loose movement of my head and reach for the glass. He guides my hand around the base.

I take three greedy gulps. "I'm trying. It's so hard," I tell him. "The fear seems to block it out and … oh, God…" I bury my head in my hands. "Perhaps it's better I don't remember. Do you think?"

He straightens his black-rimmed glasses and lifts an eyebrow to throw the question back at me.

Reaching up to rub my nose, which drips as the tears build again, my hand bumps across the cratered terrain of my wretched twist of a face. I cringe, curling my hand into a fist to protect my fingers from the horror.

He leans over and lowers my wrist. "It will come when you're ready. And the day will also come when you no longer define yourself by your physical appearance. One day at a time, Layla. That's all you can do. And I'm here to guide you through this new world of yours. We'll look at the memory issue again next time."

What does he mean, *this new world of yours?* I don't want a new world. I refuse to spend my life locked in this hell. I jerk my hand away and leap from the chair, my chin quivering like a child about to tantrum.

"I want my face back. I want my life back," I cry. "That's never going to happen, is it? So why am I here? No one can help me. I hate everything. I hate this. I hate me."

I grab my bag, rush across the room, and wrench the door open, startling the doctor's next client, who drops his Reader's Digest. Before I can escape, Dr. Leighton—who has asked me to call him Jarrod—puts one hand on my shoulder, closes the door, and steers me back to the armchair. For a slim, fine-boned man, he has a firm grip.

"Let's talk about what's stopping you from going back to work. You're well enough to return as far as physical health goes. How do you feel about making that your next step?"

Is that a joke? He knows I walked out of Stein and Laverick that last day at the top of my game. Two weeks before I'd been promoted to Associate Director of Business Development. Not only had I snagged one of the hottest new clients in town, but I'd done it under the nose of our biggest rival. Brian Townsend, my vice president, toasted me with Moet and I left for the weekend believing, where my career was concerned, the sky was the limit.

I blink at him. "You say that as if it's easy. That I can walk in and go back to where I was. I saw the revulsion on their faces—the ones who visited me in hospital—and then there's the clients."

Jarrod—it feels strange to call him this—leans back in his chair, shaking his head. "I am under no illusion this will be easy for you, Layla. It might even be the hardest thing you do. You may decide not to go back, but I suspect, financially, that's not an option for you. So, it might be time for you to step out of this half-life and back into the world. Give it some thought, and we'll explore it more next time."

I know he's right on all counts, but I can't face it, yet. Thinking our session is over, I place my hands on the arms of the chair to push myself up, but again his voice stops me.

"This may help, but please understand it is a contact, nothing more at this point."

He reaches over to his desk, flips through a stack of cards, pulls one out, and copies a name and phone number onto a sheet of paper.

I take the paper and read the name.

"A surgeon?"

"A cosmetic surgeon who specialises in burn reconstruction."

I scrunch the paper and thrust it into the pocket of my cargo pants.

"Has it escaped your notice, er, Jarrod, that I have already had eighteen operations to repair scar tissue? All performed by plastic surgeons?"

His patience is admirable. Rather than booting me out the door, he closes his eyes for a moment and nods. "Yes, I am aware of that. This man is at the Mt. Sinai teaching hospital in New York; an expert on major facial reconstructive surgery. He's the best in his field."

"You really think he can do something about this?" I wriggle my fingers, at a safe distance from my face.

"If anyone can, it would be Dr. Gassner. He has an impressive list of qualifications and academic credentials, and he's renowned for developing some amazing new techniques."

I raise my eyebrows in question.

"The techniques?"

I nod.

"Well, processes like micro-surgical tissue transfers, skin expanders, laser technology. I think you may now be ready to try more than the doctors have offered here. Your specialist at the hospital agrees. However, these procedures are extremely expensive."

"How expensive?"

"Well, I can't say for sure as each case is different, but tens of thousands of dollars would not be an exaggeration. Then you have the airfare, accommodation, and other therapies which are essential to a complete recovery."

My shoulders slump in defeat. "Impossible. Maybe if I'd continued working all this time, it would be affordable. I've been living off my savings for almost two years now."

He frowns, aware I was earning a high salary before the fire.

"Investment banking is different from other jobs, Jarrod. A good percentage of any salary increases or bonuses are retained in company stock, not handed over in cash. Looks good on paper but in reality, not so much." I curl my lip. "Which means you've not given me an option, only false hope."

This time he doesn't try to stop me leaving, just hands me my cap, which he insists I remove at each session.

The lift shudders to a stop and I catch a glimpse of my face in the shiny, reflective wall. I want to punch at the reflection, scream and stamp my feet in frustration at the unattainable possibilities. But I swallow the sharp-edged anger and head to the main doors.

How I yearn to walk out of the building and mingle with the crowd. Disappear into anonymity. But those days are gone. Eyes, which before the accident, gazed through or past me, are now unable to look away; faces flinch in revulsion; children point with a hand over their mouth and grab their mother's skirts.

Each time I step outside I feel as if I've dropped into the sixteenth century, condemned and running the gauntlet. Instead of whips and clubs, my torturers wield revulsion, fear, and ridicule.

With a quick tug, I tilt the cap to the left to cover my bald patch, and hurry down Sydney's Macquarie Street. I duck into a narrow lane, and stop at the door to my latest hideout, a secret underground lair discovered last week. A place I would have run a mile to avoid in my other life. I edge open the door and descend the stairs into the dark belly of the bar, safe within the cocoon of dim lights and dark, painted walls. The sound of Neil Young's "Heart of Gold" winds through the room, giving a retro feel to the otherwise soulless space. A long, narrow bar follows the far wall, where a huge Carlton & United Breweries monogrammed mirror reflects the bottles of liquid amnesia. A smattering of regulars perch on stools at the bar. Littered throughout the room are the rejects and misfits of the city.

My people.

"Hello, beautiful, what can I get you today?"

Beautiful? An inappropriate giggle bubbles into my throat at this absurdity and I thrust a hand in front of my mouth to catch it. I look up at the obese barman as he raises an eyebrow, a slight grin dimpling his pudgy cheeks. I'd expected to see the skinny bloke with the ponytail, from last time. Not this behemoth. To my relief he doesn't balk at either my obscure humour or my gruesome face; in fact he doesn't seem to notice the scars at all. This bar is an alternative universe where freaks rule. It's the best I've felt for eighteen months.

"Thank you." I snort as another giggle threatens to escape.

"What's your name?"

"Clyde Norbert Campbell, at your service." He turns up his hands in a gesture of surrender. "And you think you've got problems."

"Clyde Norbert's not that bad." I swallow. "No, you're right, it's dreadful." I dissolve into an infantile fit of hysterics. His face splits into a wide, cheeky grin.

"I don't usually delight the ladies this much, maybe it's my lucky day. And just Clyde will do. Then you won't have to lose control every time you say my name." He places a glass of wine on the counter. "I'm guessing you're a white wine girl. Do you have a name?"

How perceptive—about the wine. Although in the last few months I haven't been very discerning about my alcohol. I pick up the glass and draw in a long, cool mouthful, closing my eyes in relief as the fruity bite of the wine drains down my throat.

"Ah. Just what I needed. And my name's Layla."

A rasping voice demands a gin, and the barman wanders to the other end of the bar.

Curiosity forces me to peer down the counter at the woman with shocking red hair and a voice like a file grinding metal. Her short skirt is pulled halfway up her thigh showing long, muscled legs and meat platter feet. There's a tattoo on one leg, but I can't make it out.

The woman spins on the stool and faces me. "Something on your mind, sweetheart? Or have you got a thing for older women?" There's a burst of appreciative laughter from one of the shadowed booths.

Embarrassed by her tasteless remark, I turn away. The woman hikes her skirt a tad higher, steps off her stool, and sashays over to where I'm perched at the bar. My stomach lurches as I prepare for the stinging remarks, the look of horror, and the drunken gasp of revulsion.

"If you look at me again like I'm something you'd wipe off your shoe, princess, Clyde here will be wiping you off the floor. Got that?"

Speechless, I blink and nod. The woman shows no sign of having noticed my face. "Thank you," I blurt, grateful to be insulted for my behaviour rather than my face.

She snarls like a dog, her lip curled over her prominent front teeth. "Thank you? You stupid bitch. Are you taking the piss?" *Crap.* Now I'm in real trouble. She thinks I'm making fun of her.

Clyde delivers a schooner of beer to a figure huddled in one of the booths and darts back at the aggressive, raspy tone of the woman's voice.

"Hey there, Lavender, that's enough. This lady didn't come in here to be insulted. That's what I'm here for. Sit down, and I'll bring you some coffee."

The woman feints at me and snorts as I jerk back in fright, then returns to her stool, tottering on leopard print Minnie Mouse heels.

Clyde flicks the switch on a coffee machine behind him, and as I drain my glass, he leans over and puts a pudgy hand on my arm. "Don't let her get to you. She doesn't mean anything by it. I'll get you another drink, on the house, to make up for Lavender's rudeness."

Nice gesture, but I'm ready to run. Contrary to my initial comfort, this is another place where I don't belong. The woman twists on her stool to stare at me; to see if I have the guts to stand my ground.

I glance at the barman who raises his eyebrows and smiles. I feel like a child in a sandpit who's had sand kicked in her face by one kid while at the same time another one offers to share his spade. I swallow and turn away from the mean kid.

"Okay, Clyde. Another wine."

Lavender scowls and reaches for the last dregs of her drink. A spark of power darts through me at her withdrawal. Now that's a sensation I've missed over the past months. Clyde pushes another glass of wine towards me. At this rate they might have to scrape me off the floor after all.

I study the glass. A victor's cup. My finger smudges condensation drips as they chase each other down the glass and onto the grubby towel strip which covers the bar. If someone had told me two years ago I'd be sitting in a seedy bar at four in the afternoon in the company of a super-sized barman, and dodging insults from a middle-aged hooker, I would have suggested they were delusional. But this is it. This is who I am now.

"Need to talk?" asks the fat barman.

"What?" I'm shaken from my moment of comfort back into defence mode. "Mind your own business." I slide forward on the stool, ready to move away from the bar.

"Suit yourself, but I don't get too many interesting people in here and I thought my day had just got better." He turns away and rearranges glasses and bottles against the back wall.

"All barmen are frustrated psychologists."

He gestures with his head at the other clientele lurking in their dark corners. "Some stories are worth listening to and some I'd crawl under a rock to escape."

"Alright, if you're so interested, I'll tell you how I got this." I point at the left side of my face and neck.

"If that's the story you need to tell, go ahead."

"Don't pretend you're not dying to know. It's this ugly mess. That's what tickles people's curiosity. They want to know how I got so horribly burnt."

Without thinking, I toss back the rest of my wine to ease the rising anger.

"Or…I could tell you how I got so horribly fat."

I stare at him in amazement. "Are you kidding?"

"You're right, it's a boring food story. More wine?"

Why not? Hell's not for the sober.

"Sure."

Clyde hands me another glass of wine. I take a sip, then another, and sit back against the small back of the stool.

"Well?" he asks.

"Well what?"

"The story. You were going to tell me how you got so *horribly burnt*."

A string of helpless despair slithers through my body. Lowering my gaze to the wine glass I mutter, "Sorry, can't."

"What, I ply you with alcohol, entertain you, piss you off, and there's nothing in it for me?" He slaps the cloth into the sink and with both hands on the side of the bar leans towards me. "Why can't you?"

His ponderous bulk invades my personal space. I shift further back on the stool. "Because I don't remember."

"What don't you remember?" he asks.

"Any of it. Not a damn thing. Total blank."

"So was it an accident?"

"I don't believe it was an accident and I've told the police that, but there's not enough evidence unless I can recall something. The investigators found a candle had ignited the curtains and think I left it there."

"But…"

"But I didn't. Why would I light a candle and put it on the floor next to a curtain? I think it could have been an electrical fault. My ex-landlord is running scared in case I decide to sue him for negligence."

"Do you think he was negligent?"

"Nothing's been found to prove he was and I can't remember anything, so investigations have hit a dead end."

I'm not sure why I'm answering this stranger's questions. But for some reason it feels natural and safe.

"Shit. So you can't even rant and rave at the cause?"

"No, especially as the unofficial suspicion is that I was the culprit. But I can rant every time I see my face in the mirror. I just don't know who to direct it at. How's that for a paradox."

He grins. "I love a good mystery. Sounds like you need someone to play Robin to your Batman; to investigate what happened. I could apply for the job."

What the hell is this guy on about? Does he think this is a game? I thrust my hand into my purse, throw twenty dollars onto the bar and stand.

"Looks like I was wrong about you. I'm just a source of amusement for you. This isn't some Marvel comic we're in. This is my life."

I snatch my bag from the back of the chair and scramble up the stairs, incensed at being taken for a fool. Like an idiot, I believed he was interested in me, Layla, not the scars and I dropped my guard. The shithead doesn't see me; he sees freak entertainment.

"Layla, wait!" He puffs up the stairs and grabs my elbow. "I was never talking to your scars. Only to you. Don't get them confused."

CHAPTER 2

I SHAKE HIM OFF AND STEP outside. Don't get them confused! What sort of a moron is he? The scars *are* me. People don't point and say, "Look, there's Layla," or, "look, at the woman in a green dress." No, you fat, insensitive bastard, they point and say, "Look at the weirdo with the grotesque face."

Since they released me from hospital, I've heard it all. The words spoken, and unspoken but audible in the shocked faces. Too angry for civility, I barge, head lowered, through the crowd towards Circular Quay. It's quite a walk, but it's better than sitting in a bus where I'm a captive freak-show exhibit. Being on the ferry will be bad enough.

What am I thinking? Going back to work would mean a ferry and bus ride every day, twice a day. Then there'll be an office full of people doing their best not to stare, to pretend nothing about me has changed.

I punch my ticket into the slot and thump with impatience at the sensor arm as it circles to allow me through to the wharf— boiling with crowds of rush hour commuters. Most will stay inside out of the mid-September wind so I head for the back deck, choose an end seat, prop my feet on the chair opposite, and close the zipper on my jacket.

Two minutes to go. A loud blast of the horn causes the stragglers to run for the gangplank, their faces scrunched with anxiety until they board. Then they smile at how clever they've been to catch the ferry at the last minute.

Despite being late afternoon, a bright glare bounces off the water, bringing tears to my eyes and blurring my vision for a moment. As I blink to focus, a streak of colour to the right catches my attention. A yacht, bright red spinnaker ballooning, runs with a stiff breeze, past the ferry.

We were all taught to sail when we were kids, in a snub-bowed Manly Junior yacht. My older sister had no further interest when she became a teenager, but my brother and I raced Laser Radials for years and then crewed on bigger yachts. Reliving the adrenaline rush of open water sailing, my eyes are riveted to the fluid beauty of the fifty-footer flying over the water, until the yacht disappears into the shadow of the Harbour Bridge, passing Milson's Point and the burlesque face of the Luna Park entrance, hidden from my view.

This memory of happy times reminds me why, against my parent's wishes, I recently made the decision to leave the family home and move, alone, into the flat in Manly. It was something I had to do. For them as well as for me.

At first, returning to my parent's home, between and after the numerous hospital stays, was a practical decision. I needed the physical assistance as well as the emotional support. But months of Mum being a helicopter mother—constantly hovering—and worse, being a social worker helicopter mother, wore me down.

Each day she brought home the name of another support group or someone else who'd "gone through almost the same as you, Layla". She expected me to rush out and bond with yet another group of strangers who sit around one night a week having a pity party. Even at this early stage of my rehabilitation, I recognised how easy it would be to settle for being *a burns survivor*. A static identity I could claim with impunity for the rest of my life.

Even when I managed to side-step Mum's well-meaning advances, there was still my dad. The person I love the most in the world. Each time I looked at him, I saw the tragedy of my accident etched into every line of his face. When he smiled at me, his eyes carried the pain of seeing his daughter maimed and broken.

I couldn't make my mangled face the first thing he saw each morning and the last thing he saw at night; or let him carry the burden of a father's failure to protect his child.

That's why I moved out.

I breathe in a deep lungful of fresh, salty air and watch the magnificent sails of the Sydney Opera House diminish as we skirt Fort Denison and draw closer to Bradley's Head.

A squeal of delight interrupts my thoughts as a small child, dragging her mother by the hand, stumbles onto the back deck.

"Please, Mummy, I want to watch the waves."

"It's too windy outside, Amy. Come on, you've had a look. Daddy will be worrying about us."

The child, ignoring her mother, dashes across the deck in front of me and trips over my bag, which I'd flung onto the floor next to my seat. She flies forward, her hands outstretched, straight towards the hard metal side of the vessel. Without thinking, I leap from my seat and catch her as a gust of wind whips the cap from my head.

The child, Amy, looks at my face and screams.

"Mummy! Mummy, get the monster away."

Her mother wrenches the child from my arms, holding Amy's head against her chest so the child won't have to see the beast. My heart hammers in my chest as panic, coated with embarrassment and humiliation, surges to my throat. Angry tears wet my cheeks, but there's nowhere to run, nowhere to hide.

The child's father appears and in a small act of kindness, retrieves my cap, hands it to me, and mumbles, "Thank you", while at the same time shepherding his family away from me.

As I swallow to quell the sick churning of my stomach, I have a perverse wish that Clyde had witnessed the exchange so I could say, "Now do you think the scars and the person are separate?"

❦

Puffed from traipsing up the hill to my flat, I stop to catch a breath. Wedged apologetically between two multi-million-dollar mansions is Hula Nights, the block of old red brick flats owned by a friend of my parents. He and his wife have not caved to the outrageous offers from developers and private home buyers to purchase the ancient building and, more importantly, the land, to make way for either modern apartments or a multi-story home. They describe this as their charity because of the four tenants who have lived here for decades. His mother, from whom he inherited the flats, left a request in her will that he allow the existing long-term tenants to live out their lives in their homes.

Two months ago one of the tenants moved into a nursing home and he offered the flat to me at a ridiculous rent. I accepted. Despite the name.

I climb the steps and give the front door an adroit kick. The salt air makes it stick. A furry ball of excitement launches from the floor into my arms as my West Highland Terrier, Bennie, mixes a yelp of joy at seeing me home with a whine of accusation at having been left to his own devices for so long. He stares at his leash behind the door, giving me an opportunity to redeem myself.

Bennie is impossible not to love, but the last thing I'd wanted when I came out of hospital was another dog. My much-loved mongrel, Danger—named for the constant accidents he caused when always underfoot—died in the fire and left me carrying survivor guilt. When I lost Danger, it was symbolic of the parts of me I also lost in the fire. They were irreplaceable and so was he.

However, my mother knew best—pet therapy had worked with her clients—and I would be forced to face the outside world at least once a day when I walked him. So I came home one day to find my younger sister, Ruby, clutching a struggling Bennie, with remnants of her favourite childhood book, *The Mysterious Benedict Society*, in his mouth. She insisted on naming him Benedict—after all, he'd swallowed the story.

With my eyes averted from the mirror above the hall table, I flick on the light and then remember there is no mirror. That was my old house, the beautiful terrace in Balmain—now a burnt-out shell. I kick off my sandals and follow the diamond pattern of the tiles down the narrow hallway into the small kitchen off to the right. In the blur of dusk, Cabbage Tree Bay and Shelly Beach are barely discernible through the old sash window, but I can still hear the gentle slap of the water on the pebbles as it sneaks up the beach.

My phone has been off since the session with the psychologist and there are three missed calls from my mother. Seconds after I turn it on the sounds of Godfather Guitar dance the phone along the counter.

"Hi, Mum."

"I've been trying to ring for hours, didn't you get my calls?"

"I needed some time after seeing the doctor, but I'm here now. Is everything all right?"

"Well, what did he say? Do you feel better after seeing him? I found a support group for you."

I put the phone on speaker and drop a capsule into the coffee machine. "A bit frustrating with the doctor. I still can't remember anything about the fire, but he mentioned a new surgeon. And I don't want another support group, thanks anyway."

"I could come to the group with you. So you wouldn't feel awkward, or like you didn't know anyone. What do you mean he told you about a surgeon? You've had every surgeon the hospital had access to."

Damn. The coffee's too hot and I burn my tongue. "This one's different, Mum. He can do things the others can't. And I don't need you to come with me to another group, because I'm not going."

"Oh, darling. Don't you think you've been through enough operations? And each time they think they can help, they build up your hopes and then you're even more distressed when it doesn't work. Where is this doctor, anyway?"

"He's in New York. He has a private clinic but also works out of Mt. Sinai Medical Centre." I wait for the inevitable response.

"New York? My God. What will that cost? Darling, you say you're not ready to go back to work, so how would you afford it?"

"Maybe I am ready to go back to work," I say, shocking myself with the words. "If that's what I have to do to pay for this."

Mum releases one of her long-suffering sighs. "I know you don't want my advice but I'm going to give it anyway."

Yes, of course you are, and I wouldn't expect anything less.

"It tears your father and me apart every time we see you go through another operation thinking everything will go back to the way it was. Darling, maybe it's time to put your hope and energy into finding a way to live with this."

I drag out the kitchen stool and sit. No one seems to understand that I will never give up, never stop trying to fix this horror. But maybe she's right, maybe there is no way out. A stab of grief pierces me. I would rather die than stay like this.

"I don't expect you to agree with me, Mum, but I'm going to contact the surgeon. Nothing more I can say. I need to go now. Give Dad a kiss for me. I love you."

My mother's voice quivers with emotion. "I understand, darling. I love you, too. Call me when you've spoken to this doctor."

Had I really said I was going back to work? It's something I've been resisting for months. If I don't go back and display my grotesque mask of a face, then my work colleagues will continue to see me as I used to be. But if I do go back to work, I can earn the money to pay for the surgeon to repair my scarred features. My logic sounds as twisted as my face, but still, maybe it's time.

The coffee ripples across the surface as I blow to cool it, and a low rumble in my belly alerts me to the need for food. Soup will be quick, easy, and might even make me feel better. But first I have to walk Bennie, then I'll eat, and call Tom. His name, even in my thoughts, elicits a physical response—an ache in my chest.

Since the accident, I hesitate before dialling his number. Our relationship has become shapeless, without parameters or definition, and I'm no longer sure of my place. Silly, I know, but it makes sense that a man like him would not want to be seen with a woman like me.

I walk over to the sideboard and pick up the only photo of myself I keep in this new flat. It's Tom and me at the company awards dinner two years ago when he received Highest Achieving Employee award. After all my photos were destroyed in the fire, Tom made me this copy. His handsome face, piercing blue eyes, and that cracker of a smile still make my heart pound. Beside him, I look wonderful in a slinky, red Rachel Gilbert gown, my thick, dark hair glistening in the light of the camera flash as I gaze up at him. The perfect couple.

❦

With Bennie happy and exhausted in a heap at my feet and Jack Johnson's mellow vibes wafting from the speakers, I slurp at my pumpkin and lentil soup. Not so long ago, Tom would have sat across from me, amused at my choice of menu, asking where the hell his steak was. I drop the dishes into the sink, fill it with water, draw in a fortifying breath, and dial Tom's number.

He answers on the fifth ring. "Layla. How was your appointment today?"

Although his smoky voice is like music to my ears, I'm annoyed his first question concerns my therapy. As if there's nothing else about me that holds his interest.

"Yeah, okay. He told me about this amazing surgeon who might be able to improve the scarring on my face and body."

The hesitation before he responds tells me he, like Mum, is sick of hearing about the next person who is going to press rewind; back to before the fire.

"That's good. But what makes you think he'll be any better than the others?"

"The cost."

No response to my attempt at humour, he tap-taps the top of his desk with a pen, as he considers my news. "So, he's incredibly expensive. What will you use for money?"

Now I wish I hadn't told him about this, but I wanted him to think I might again look like the person he fell in love with.

"Not sure yet. Anyway, it's an option at the moment. Let's leave that subject for another day. I wanted to ask you when you thought they might be open to me coming back to work."

Do I imagine another hesitation? "You'd be better to bring that up with Brian. He's been working quite closely with Kelly and might need time to shift some of the clients back to you."

"So, this Kelly. Is she doing a good job?"

"Seems to be. Brian appears happy with her progress."

"Tom, you'd tell me if Brian's unsure about me coming back, wouldn't you? I mean it will be hard for me to face everyone, but I think I have to get back to work. In fact, it's the only way I'll have the money to try this other surgeon."

"From my point of view I want you to come back when you're ready. As far as Brian's concerned, I'm sure any hesitation on his part would be to do with the whole workplace situation being difficult for you. Look, call Brian and see what he thinks. If you're sure you're okay, I've got to get back to this Request for Proposal document before I lose the client to someone else. I promised they'd have it by lunchtime tomorrow."

"Of course. I miss not seeing you."

"Me too. Sleep well. I'll dream of you."

The phone screen flicks back to the menu and I hold the memory of his face in my mind. It's hard to imagine him dreaming of me as I look now. I wave my hand as if to push those thoughts away. Not that they've been far from the surface since the first time I saw myself in Tom's eyes the day they removed the bandages. He turned away in an attempt to hide his reaction, but I saw his body lurch as he recoiled at the sight. For weeks after, he cried each time he visited, then appeared to accept it.

Until the day we tried to make love.

Enough of the morbid *can Tom love a gargoyle from a Grimm's fairy tale* lament. If I can find the money to see this plastic surgeon, the beast might turn into a beauty. I reach into the pocket of my cargoes and pull out the paper with the name and number. As I read the information and register the requirement to travel to New York, I have a flash of panic at having to endure the stares of an aeroplane full of passengers for so long; not to mention being in a closed space. Beads of sweat drip into my eyes while I breathe rhythmically—in and out, in and out. Until at last I register the voice of Jack Johnson again and bring into focus the intricate Aboriginal dot painting on my living room wall.

My older sister, Corinne, in a burst of financial generosity, bought this piece of dreamtime art for me when a treasured Aboriginal painting by Munganbanna, a gift from our parents, was lost with all my possessions in the fire. Each time I catch sight of the piece, this gesture surprises me. Corinne has always regarded me with disdain, even dislike. Maybe she thinks the fire has created a level playing field.

Whatever bizarre reason she has for showing some sisterly affection, I'll take.

With my guard up.

CHAPTER 3

N O MORE PROCRASTINATION. TODAY I'LL phone Brian Townsend and tell him I'm ready to come back to work. I pick up my phone and scroll through the contacts list, pressing Brian's name. That's as far as I go. A cold sweat coats my forehead and paralysed by anxiety, my finger freezes. I can't do it. Not yet. Maybe another week and then I'll be ready.

Bennie nudges my leg and cocks his head to the side, aware something is not right. To let him know his concern is welcome, I drop my hand down to stroke his soft, white head. Eager for more attention, he tries to leap onto my lap. His short legs don't quite make it and as his paws scrabble against my arms, I haul him up. He lands onto my right hand which still grips the phone, and activates Brian's number. I drop the dog and the phone onto the floor. *Oh crap. Please, I can't do it.*

"Hello? Hello. Is that you, Layla?" his voice booms from the speaker.

Of course, my number came up on his phone. If I don't answer, there'll be no way I can convince him I'm ready to face the office and clients. Leaning down, I pick up the phone and take a deep breath to calm the churning in my stomach.

"Hi Brian. It's Layla here." Of course it is, he already knows that. My voice is an octave higher than normal. Wiping sweaty palms down my jeans, I try to locate my normal voice. "You're probably wondering why I'm calling you."

"Well, not really. Tom gave me a quick call last night after he spoke to you."

I experience a small stab of irritation. It's as if we are kids and Tom has dobbed on me. Maybe he thought he was helping.

"How are you, Layla? I've been meaning to phone and see how

you're doing. I miss your bright, creative brain."

"If only I could send that in unaccompanied by the face." Crap, what made me say that? I was trying to act as if this wasn't a problem. Brian ignores my stupid comment. "Sorry, Brian. I didn't mean to make you uncomfortable."

"Not at all, Layla. Tom mentioned you had some thoughts about returning to work."

Straight to the point. I might as well get it over with. "Yes, I think I'm ready to give it a go. You okay with that?"

"Of course, I always said you were welcome to come back whenever you're ready. I'll need to know there'll be continuity with clients, though. Are you done with all the hospital stays?"

I wish I knew what Tom had said to him. I can't tell him about New York after that statement. If I do he won't agree to my return and then I won't have the money to go. A dilemma, but I'll sort it out later.

"I understand, Brian. Whatever happens, I'll ensure clients are always the first priority. Why don't I come in to see you on Friday and if all's well, I can start back soon after? I have an appointment at nine which will be about an hour so I could drop by after that."

There is a pause before he answers. "Yes, good. Good. Come into the office around ten thirty on Friday and we can decide when you're going to start. I'm looking forward to seeing you again, Layla."

"Me too. It will be good to be back." *Liar.*

I hang up the phone feeling like I've been locked in a cage and all I want to do is rip open the door and run. But I've made a commitment, to myself as well as to Brian. So on Friday I will name the day when I return to work.

At least I managed to make the call. Well, Bennie did. Showing no sign of guilt or remorse, he smiles his wide doggie smile at me and the anxiety recedes.

Now I need to de-brief with someone. My fingers fold around the phone, but instead of Tom's name jumping into my mind, for some inexplicable reason, I imagine Clyde, the rude, fat barman, cheering me up with his irreverent sense of humour. Of course that's a ridiculous notion. Especially when I was so rude to him. Perhaps my brain got fried along with my face. Forget the debrief.

In his self-appointed role of social co-ordinator, Bennie decides a walk is required. He trots to the door and tugs at his leash. Good idea. Fresh air and the beach beat a phone call. Besides, the phone is my current enemy, so I shove it between the cushions on the couch—that makes me feel better.

With Bennie showing off his doggy obedience school lessons, we hop down the uneven, concrete steps that lead to Marine Parade and the beach. I step down one step, Bennie trots down two. When I tug on his leash, he backs up by manoeuvring his butt and back legs onto the step above with his forelegs still perched on the step below. This is his bizarre version of 'heeling'. To the casual observer we look like we're training for an animal circus act. All I need is a red nose and baggy trousers.

At the bottom of the stairs Bennie gives two high-pitched yaps as he spies Mr. Bacik—another tenant in our flats, who swims in the ocean pool every day. He climbs out of the pool and towels himself dry. I release Bennie to leap around Mr. Bacik's legs and lick at the salt water on his feet.

"Good morning, *kochana*. So nice to see you and this scallywag dog." He scratches behind Bennie's ears sending the dog into trembles of ecstasy.

"Morning, Mr. Bacik. You're brave, it can't be more than twenty degrees out and the water's freezing."

"Gets my blood to circulate and the joints moving. Tells me I'm still alive. Although Mrs. Bacik's nagging is good enough for that." He winks as he pulls a gaudy Hawaiian shirt over his head. "Don't tell her I say this, or I never hear the end of it."

He is eighty-five years old, has a heart murmur and suffers from emphysema. None of which affect his wonderful sense of humour or the way he embraces life. Every time I see the old man he takes the time to let me know I matter to him and has never averted his eyes from my scars. I used to scorn old people as a waste of time and space, but I now feel an affinity with them. It seems that once you become old, damaged, or infirm, the young and the beautiful treat you like a blot on the landscape. My shame as I watch him is that I was guilty of such insensitivity until life turned me into one of the blots.

"A penny for your thoughts, my friend, you are somewhere else,

I think. Maybe I take advantage while you don't think straight and ask you to join an old man for a cup of coffee." He chuckles at his joke and breaks into a fit of coughing.

I take firm hold of his arm and gesture towards the Corso—the strip of shops across from the beach.

"Best offer I've had all day. Let's go."

The pleasure on his face makes me duck my head to hide my watery eyes. Since the accident an offer of my company usually elicits garbled excuses and a quick exit. I grip his arm harder and pull him close as we stroll beside the beach to the Bean There coffee shop.

The wind plays across the waves, whipping bursts of salty spray into the air, splattering surfers as they paddle their boards out to catch the next curl. I recall taking surfing lessons one summer a few years ago. In the days when I had to be sex goddess, gourmet cook, fastest gun on the trading desk, and accomplished athlete.

One morning, I caught a huge wave, stood up on the board and, heady with success, lifted one arm in a graceful wave to Tom and a bunch of his friends. The board twisted, then nose-dived into the wave, throwing me over the top. In the melee, my bikini top parted company with my breasts as the board flipped, and the wave, or, I suspect one of the hovering surfers, whisked it away, never to be seen again. The humiliation of struggling past squealing toddlers and their leering fathers with the board clutched to my chest like a lover, haunted me for months. Despite constant encouragement from Tom's shameless mates, I cancelled the surfing lessons.

A strong gust of wind lifts my cap and I release Mr. Bacik's arm to hold it down. It flicks my hair around my face and sucks at the light jacket I threw on over my T-shirt. If I'm cold, Mr. Bacik must be freezing after being in the cold surf and still wearing his wet bathers. The thought of him doubled over trying to catch his breath has me risking the loss of the cap to unzip my jacket and offer it to him. He thinks it's a great joke.

"This old man is tougher than you think. Is bracing, not cold. Put your jacket back on, *kochana*, you need it more than me." I offer once again and on his second refusal, gratefully slide my arms back into the sleeves. He gestures at my cap. "Why don't you take off your cap? You fight so hard to keep it on, as if your life depends on it."

How perceptive.

"The fire burnt my hair and I have a bald patch on this side." I lift the cap and show him. "When I wear the cap, people don't stare." I recognise the flaw in this statement. "Well, they stare but only at my face, not my hair."

Mr. Bacik flings his tanned, flabby arm around my shoulders. "You want to see a bald patch? Look up here." He taps the top of his head which is bald except for a few wisps of hair looking confused, as if the rest of the gang has left without telling them. "Now that's a bald patch."

Funny, but I still grip my cap.

We reach the coffee shop and Mr. Bacik pulls out a chair for me. "You know, *kochana*, it's an interesting thing this being stared at. When we are young we try so hard to fit in. Not be any different so people won't stare and point at us, or worse." A grim look flits across his face. There's something he isn't saying. "Then when old age comes we wish we are not so invisible. Wishing someone would point and stare, to let us know we still exist. Maybe we even do crazy things for attention like wear a Hawaiian shirt or swim in freezing temperature. Old age, such a slippery slide to invisible."

I order a soy latte and he orders a cappuccino—just because Mrs. Bacik has told him he isn't to have dairy products.

"So, in about forty years I can look like this, chuck my cap into the air, yell *yeehah* and no one will even see me?" I ask. "I think I might enjoy this old age stuff."

He pats my arm. "This is the truth, *kochana*: I would give anything to be young once more, to have courage to be different, even to have a bald patch in my beautiful thick hair and a scar on the side of my face." God, now I want to cry. But even with his kind, wise words, I'm self-centred enough to believe he can't know the pain or loss I have experienced.

Mr. Bacik leans over to mop the foam moustache off my top lip and narrows his eyes at something behind me. "I think there is someone who knows you. A big man, looking you over, Layla."

"You'll get used to that when you're out with me, Mr. Bacik. People stare because of my freaky scars, not because they know me."

"No, I'm sure is more than that," he tells me.

I half-turn my head and catch the bulky side view of a man paying for a takeaway coffee. There is something about him, but I can't place it. Bugger, now that will annoy me all day.

"He looks familiar, but not sure why. Keep talking to me while I try to place him," I whisper.

"Too late, he comes over."

"It's Layla, isn't it?" I turn to face him and then it hits me. The barman from that dive in the city.

"Er, yes. Clyde? I nearly didn't recognise you."

"No, I'm unrecognisable when I'm not surrounded by all the finery and *je ne sais quoi* of The Black Hole."

I giggle at his droll response.

"Clyde, this is my friend and neighbour, Mr. Bacik." A snout-nudge at my calf reminds me Bennie is also there. "Oh, and this is Bennie, my personal trainer. He makes sure I walk every day."

Clyde shakes hands with Mr. Bacik and, with difficulty, gets down on his haunches to pat Bennie. In an absolute overplay of cuteness, the dog decides to hold out a paw for a shake, do two clockwise turns and then rest his head on Clyde's bent knee. Of course Clyde's won over and has Bennie on his lap in seconds. These are all tricks I taught him to show Tom, but my strong-willed Westie always sniffs with disdain when I ask him to show off his tricks. Perverse little bugger.

"So how do you two know each other?" asks Mr. Bacik.

Crap! "Um, from…er…" How can I tell this lovely old man who thinks I'm such a nice girl that I know Clyde from a seedy bar, where I go to drink in the middle of the day when I can't cope?

"I work in an establishment in the city where Layla sometimes comes for a bite to eat," Clyde says.

I flash an innocent smile at Mr. Bacik.

"So, you live around here, son?" asks the old man.

"I live at Balgowlah but often come to Manly on my days off."

"Well, we shouldn't keep you, Clyde. Nice to see you again," I say.

A clear dismissal, I know, but I'm not yet comfortable with this new part of my life bleeding into the old.

"You too, Layla. Good to meet you, Mr. Bacik." He gives Bennie a last scratch behind the ear and pushes himself up. "Oh, by the way, Layla. We're having a special on the Lavender Tongue dish next week if you want to drop by."

I shoot him a daggered look which has him chuckling as he walks out with his takeaway coffee.

"Seems like a nice young man. Maybe he could lose some weight. Invite him down to swim with us old people sometime," says Mr. Bacik, watching Clyde's back view.

"I don't know him that well. And I'm not sure I'll see him again, anyway, Mr. Bacik."

☾

When we've both finished our coffee and Mr. Bacik has regaled me with stories of his beloved Poland, I lean over and kiss his cheek.

"You know what, Mr. Bacik? This is the nicest social outing I've had in a long time."

"Then my job, it is done, young Layla. Time to get me home before I disgrace myself—incontinence, you know." At the look of shock on my face, he grins. "That was a joke, *kochana*. Well, almost."

I drag him back along the Corso and up the stairs to our flats faster than I can say 'geriatric pull-ups'. I even consider a taxi, but he insists on walking, tickled by my barely-concealed anxiety over his weak bladder.

I leave the old man chatting to his tomato plants near the front steps and duck inside my flat. With no more distractions, I can't ignore the ordeal which looms before me. It's time to prepare for my meeting with Brian. Tomorrow I must enter the workplace again, but as a distorted version of my former self.

Out of habit, I turn into the kitchen and flick on the kettle. While it boils, I throw my shoes and bag into the bedroom and on the way out am stopped by the photo of Tom and me at the awards dinner. How will this be for him? My return to work. Will he be embarrassed by my appearance? Protective? Will he still send sexy comments to my computer and then wink when I look up in mock surprise? It's hard to imagine.

How I long once more for those spine-tingling days when Tom and I first met. When his lusting blue eyes and cheeky smile told me he was mine.

CHAPTER 4

AM I READY TO EXPLORE my relationship with Tom? Under the honesty drug of hypnosis? Alternatively, I can bury my vile head in the sand and pretend he just needs time. That our relationship is solid.

The nine o'clock appointment I told Brian about is with my psychologist, and these questions bounce around my skittish brain as I prepare for the day.

I arrive early and flick through a Psychology Today journal. There's an article about the power of touch. I cringe at the irony, tossing the magazine back onto the table. To avoid the stare of the woman opposite me in the waiting room, I focus on the aquarium in the corner. A blood red swordtail runs for cover, flanked by the iridescent tetra police. But the swordtail's visibility makes it impossible to hide and soon he darts out again to suck at a waving Amazon sword plant. The fishbowl drama is interrupted by a door opening, and Jarrod beckons me into his room. A shudder runs through me as I push up from the chair. Today's agenda may burst some fantasy bubbles.

He closes the door and appraises me. "You look smart today, Layla. Going somewhere special?"

Of course, he doesn't know.

"I'm actually going into my old workplace after we've finished here. To see about returning."

A tell-tale rise of his eyebrows. "What a surprise. I am so happy you feel up to taking this step. Do you want to spend some time preparing with me?"

Tempting. "No. I've decided I need to explore the changes in some of my relationships since the fire."

"I see. Any relationship in particular?"

I look over his shoulder at the Monet print on the wall. "Er, yes, I'm confused about my relationship with Tom; have been for some time. It would be helpful to have some understanding around his behaviours towards me."

He nods, tapping his chin. "Why don't we take you back to when you first met, the things you liked about him, and any behaviours you may have ignored at the time which might give you more clarity now." He watches me for a moment before continuing. "I think this will be quite beneficial for you, Layla, as you seem to be experiencing a strong sense of loss for what you believed was an unbreakable connection."

I shrug. "Sounds naive, doesn't it? If it was as good as I thought, he wouldn't be affected by what's happened, would he?"

"Let's have a look then, shall we?"

He instructs me to relax; to go where his warm fluid voice takes me. Back to when Tom and I first met. Both young and bursting with potential. Seven years ago.

At first I can't hook into a memory. I'm vacillating above my timeline, excited and nervous of what I will see. Then I drop down into my younger self. Back in uni.

Caught in the push of students exiting the lecture theatre, I press against the wall to wait. When the stream of eager bodies thins, I swing my bag of books onto my shoulder, amble out to the hallway, and pull out the list of planet units, or electives. With two days left to make a decision for the semester, I vow not to move until the choice is made.

The squeak of sneakered footsteps on the tiles distracts me from the list and I wait for the person to pass. Instead of continuing down the hall, the squeaking stops directly behind me. A subtle blend of shampoo and a woody cologne tickle my nostrils. Then a deep voice, inches from my ear, chuckles.

"I'm thinking Drugs, Alchemy, and the Quest for Immortality."

I keep my eyes on the page. "Yep, sounds enlightening, but I'm thinking Drugs across Cultures. Gets straight to the point without wafting around in other dimensions."

"Got to admit, I do like a girl who gets straight to the point."

It was then I turn. To an Adonis. The first thing I notice are his deep-set, piercing blue eyes, then my gaze roves to the sensuous lips and blazing white smile. I nearly go cross-eyed trying to appear as if I'm focussed on his face, while surreptitiously checking out his muscled arms and broad shoulders.

For lack of anything clever to say, I thrust out my hand and nearly punch him in the stomach. He sucks in a breath and jumps back.

"Oh, crap, sorry. I'm Layla. I haven't noticed you around before."

Adonis grasps my hand and holds it, long enough for a thousand darts of electricity to shoot up my arm and straight into the pit of my…stomach.

"Probably because I've just defected from Sydney Uni. Good to meet you, Layla. I'm Tom. I'm new to this campus, so I've been orientating myself with everything." He extricates his hand from mine with a grin. A grin that tells me he knows the effect he has on women. "I know you're trying to work out your subjects, but I'm trying to find the cafeteria. I've been wandering around the campus for hours and I'm panting for a coffee. You wouldn't be able to show me would you?"

I battle with playing hard-to-get but, damn, he'd stalled me at 'panting'.

"I suppose I could come back to this later."

I reach down for my backpack but it takes two goes to lift it, as my arms seem to have developed a slight tremble.

☾

The coffee could have been black, white, latte, stewed or absent, and I wouldn't have noticed. He was funny, smart, and charming. We stayed at the cafeteria all afternoon; the planet units could have orbited off the page for all I cared. I have no clear memory of the journey to his North Ryde flat, but I know we didn't last until it was decently dark before tearing off each other's clothes. The sex was great, for him; a little fast for me. But these things take time.

Afterwards, lying in his bed with my leg slung across his hard, warm thigh I have a moment of guilt. I had been sort of dating

Lyndon, a fellow student, for a couple of months. For me there is no emotional attachment, but I have to admit Lyndon wanted more. After today, though, Lyndon will be history.

Tom rolls over and runs his hand through my hair, smoothing it away from my face. His touch sends tingles through my body. He traces his finger down my cheek, neck, and over my left breast.

"Everything about you is perfect, Layla. Your glistening, midnight hair, your mysterious dark brown eyes, silky, flawless skin and luscious perky breasts…"

It's so corny, I snort. He frowns, then grins and pinches my nipple. I yelp, swipe at him with the pillow and take off into the bathroom, locking the door. I need to snavel some toothpaste and rinse my mouth.

When I emerge, he's disappeared. So I sling on my knickers and T-shirt and wander out to the kitchen. The heavenly smell of fresh-ground coffee and the even more heavenly sight of Tom, resplendent in a pair of tight, black Calvin Klein boxers, brings me to a standstill at the door. I could get used to this sort of domesticity.

"Hi, beautiful girl. I'm brewing some coffee and then we should think about food. Take-away do?"

This can only mean he wants me here for longer.

"Take-away sounds perfect." He grabs a stack of take-away menus and fans them onto the table, indicating it's my choice. "Um, I seem to have worked up a good appetite. So how about pasta?" I suggest.

He nods with approval. "Exactly what I was thinking. Marinara?"

That's the one I would have chosen. We are made for each other. Obviously.

*

"Layla, I want you to think about some early events in your relationship," says Jarrod, bringing me into the twilight zone, between my memories and the room. "Something that might have given you an indication of how committed Tom was to you as a whole person, rather than only being enamoured with your appearance."

I float back over our first few months together. And stop. We are at a dinner party with some of Tom's high school and uni friends. All affluent, ambitious, and intelligent. I'm nervous, the new girlfriend, smiling and nodding as they interact. A tall girl with a sleek helmet of short, dark hair leans over and tells me her name is Mindy, and she is Tom's ex-girlfriend. I flinch, not needing to know that piece of information, and cast a glance at Tom to see if he is equally as uncomfortable. It's obvious he's heard her comment as he winks at Mindy and blows me a kiss, before resuming his conversation with one of the blokes. I squirm, but pretend I'm interested in the number of high distinctions she has earned at uni.

Despite the obvious camaraderie between Tom and his friends, I detect a competitive undertone throughout the evening. At one point, he is exaggerating the merits of Macquarie over Sydney Uni, and tosses me a cue to jump in and support his claims. Boys having pissing contests.

The night is fun except for one thing. A number of times Tom poses the question, "Isn't she perfect?" His friends either agree or make a joke, while I wince, embarrassed.

It's a hard gig, this being perfect, and I'm not sure how long I can sustain it. Or if I want to. Darts of fear curdle the pâté in my stomach at the thought of how he'll react when he realises he's made a mistake; that I'm not perfect. Not like him. I glance over at Tom, plates balanced up his arm, as he helps serve the main course.

Before he sits down again, Mindy makes a strange comment, whispered into my ear. She tells me she hopes I can do the perfect girlfriend thing better than she did. A bit creepy; has she read my thoughts? Despite Mindy's comment, I suspect she hasn't lost hope for a rematch. Her eyes follow Tom all evening, like a magpie locked on a shiny trinket.

My mind leapfrogs over memories until four years have passed. Tom and I have graduated; both snagged positions at the same investment bank—Stein and Laverick. Dream front office jobs which involve researching new products, developing investment strategies, managing portfolios, and entertaining prospective and existing clients. We're in China Town having a celebratory dinner. I'd recently returned from another overseas trip, this time to Japan, where I'd signed a multi-million-dollar client. Over dessert he strokes my hand and says there is something we have to talk about, when the time is right. A marriage proposal. I'm sure of it. But can't remember if it happened. Then I'm in ICU.

Without encouragement from Jarrod, I skim over the horror and pain of the long days in hospital, to the morning Tom is by my bed when my face stocking is removed. The pivotal moment when everything I thought Tom and I had, including a sparkling future together, is obliterated. Not by the fire, or my injuries, but by Tom's look of utter horror when he sees my ravaged face.

A cool finger on my forehead brings me back, from the hospital room and the image of Tom's revulsion, forever imprinted in my brain.

"Did you get some insight, Layla?"

"Yes. I think I did." I glance down at my left hand. No ring. That talk never happened.

We end the session and I prepare to face the next hurdle. The workplace.

⚘

A loud blast of a horn jump-starts my heart as a taxi veers away from me, an angry finger brandished at the window. Despite what I saw during the session, I'm not ready to accept I have lost him. I replay his constant overtures to perfection in my mind. Am I exaggerating this? There was so much more to us, I'm sure. Of course there was.

A block from Stein and Laverick I shake off these thoughts. I'm being unfair to Tom and not allowing him the time he needs to make sense of the situation.

When I walk into the building, Tom meets me in the lobby. A gallant gesture of support. One which makes me doubt the evidence of superficiality I have just seen in my session. He even holds my hand as we step out of the lift and walk along the corridor to Brian's office. The feel of his strong, warm grip sends shivers to the pit of my stomach and I experience a small moment of grief at the limits of our present intimacy. Tom says he's too worried about causing me pain to do more than stroke the right side of my hair and face, put his arm around me, or hold my hand. That's on the rare occasion he's stayed overnight. In the spare bedroom. *Stop it.*

Tom knocks on Brian's office door, but when we enter he isn't alone.

"Layla, wonderful to see you back." He averts his eyes from my face as he introduces the petite, busty blonde next to him, holding a bunch of manila folders. "I don't think you've met Kelly. She's been managing your client portfolios while you've been away. And doing an excellent job, I might add." He winks at Kelly.

I have a childish urge to stick my finger down my throat.

Instead, I hold out my hand to her. She has a surprisingly strong and authoritative grip. So she isn't just a pair of big tits. I glance over at Tom to see where his eyes are focussed. Good, not at the tits—well not while I'm in the room anyway.

"Good to meet you, Kelly, and thank you for holding the fort while I've been away."

I figure I'll let her know straight up that I'm back and she doesn't have to do my job any more.

With a sympathetic tilt of her head, she gestures at my face. "Terribly sorry about your tragedy. I can't imagine how awful it's been for you. I expect it will take you quite some time to find your way again."

Touché.

"If it works for you, Brian, I can start back on Monday week." Brian nods his assent. "We can do a handover then, Kelly."

Her eyes flick back up to my face and a little frown puckers the creamy texture of her forehead. She glances over at Brian, her silence more powerful than words.

Tom makes eye contact with Kelly but avoids my stare. "I might leave you three to it and get back to my charts. Layla, let me know when you finish and I'll walk you back down." Again no eye contact.

A jolt of irritation shafts through me. His words make me feel like a child who needs a kind person to shield them from the nasty world. I'm about to retort, *don't bother*, when Kelly speaks up.

"Don't forget we're meeting for lunch, Tom." She throws me another sympathetic look. "You don't mind, Layla? Business, of course."

I hate this woman.

I fake a sweet smile—if you could call anything about my scarred face sweet—but I don't bother with a response. Tom scuttles from the room. I don't blame him for her behaviour, he's always been pursued by predatory females. Before the fire I'd never doubted how he felt about me. But with my self-esteem in my boots, she's rattled me. And why couldn't he look at me?

However, as much as it irks me, I'm going to need a game plan for this. I desperately need Brian to give me back my job, so I can fund the facial surgery. If that means sucking up the crap Kelly is going to ladle out, then I'll do it. But only as long as I need to. I swallow my resentment and gesture to them both.

"Well, what have you two decided I can get started on?"

Relief almost drips from Brian's face and I swear Kelly looks disappointed.

When we've finished, Brian doesn't wait for me to call Tom; he buzzes his secretary and instructs her to tell Tom I'm leaving.

It's petty, but when he tries to grasp my hand in the lift, I step out of reach. After all, he's about to have lunch with Pamela Anderson. It doesn't escape my notice that once we reach the front entrance, Tom makes no mention of when he'll next see me.

It's not yet lunchtime and I need something to dull the pain and doubt that ricochets around my head. My feet turn to the left and head towards an alleyway off Macquarie Street to a bar named the Black Hole.

***

Halfway down the stairs, I stop and blink to accustom my eyes to the dark. "A Horse With No Name" wafts from hidden speakers and my head nods in time with the beat. The same old man from last time huddles in his booth mumbling to himself, a glass cradled in his hand. Near the bottom of the stairs, the skinny bloke with the thin pony tail and flared denims leans back on a metal chair with his tooled cowboy boots on the table. He looks up as I take another step down.

"G'day, Layla. Nice to see you again."

He remembers me. Then again, he probably doesn't see too many faces like mine. Besides, the fat barman, Clyde, had yelled my name out as I left the last time. I have no idea what his name is, though.

"Hi, er, good to see you, too."

At my response, the grubby old man looks up and waves. I wave back and he smiles. Under the stained beanie, a glimmer of intelligence sparks in his bloodshot eyes.

What the hell am I doing here, greeting a sauced-up old alcoholic and a skinny seventies throw-back bouncer like they're old friends? I turn around and start to haul myself back up the stairs when another voice calls out.

"Don't go, Layla. Let me make you a coffee."

How did he know that was exactly what I needed to hear? A coffee is harmless enough, although I'm still not sure about being here.

I twist my body around without changing direction. "I probably shouldn't. I need to get home. I'm not sure why I even came in."

"That's a shame, I was making one for myself so I could take a break while Gavin watches the bar. I wouldn't mind some company."

That's why I'm here. To talk to someone who doesn't pity me.

"All right, a coffee would be nice, thank you. Long black." I won't even suggest soy milk.

Clyde gestures to a table away from the entrance and within minutes places a mug of surprisingly fine smelling coffee in front of me.

"Going somewhere special?" He indicates my outfit.

I look down. "Oh. I've been in to see if my old workplace can bear to subject themselves and their clients to me. I need the money."

"And can they? Bear to have their clients see you?"

God, he doesn't spare my feelings.

"Well, with Anti-Discrimination laws they don't have a choice, but I'm not sure how they really feel about it. A bit worried is my guess. The job is about using my seductive people skills to sell them our investment products. So, a lot of schmoozing."

"Sounds interesting. Are you good at what you do?"

His clear, brown eyes regard me from under thick, sandy-coloured hair.

"I used to be. Very good, in fact."

"Then that should be all that matters. Although, my own experience is that a person's appearance is as important as the product they're selling. The human race seems obsessed with how we look—with perfect."

Perfect. Yes, Tom's original description of me. It felt uncomfortable and undeserved then, but impossibly far from the truth now. What would Clyde have gone through? At the very least, he would have been teased and bullied at school. Unless he'd been the bully, but somehow I couldn't imagine that. He leans forward, hunching one shoulder as he speaks. A vulnerable posture.

"When do you start back?"

"Monday after next. That gives me a week and two days to somehow get up the courage to face over sixty people, most of whom only remember me as I was before this." I gesture at my face and arm.

Clyde scrunches his mouth and gives a thin smile.

Suddenly the enormity of what I'm doing smacks me in the face and my airways contract. I gasp for breath. Clutching my chest, I breathe rhythmically as I've been taught. *In, hold, out. In, hold, out.*

"Layla. What's happening? What can I do?"

"Just," I pant, "an anxiety attack," *pant,* "give me a moment."

He stands and moves behind me, rubbing slow circles around my back, as if I'm a child in need of comfort. It works. Within minutes the anxiety passes and without a word, he sits down again and hands me my coffee.

This level of intimacy with someone I hardly know embarrasses me. Neither of us mentions it. I'm grateful he doesn't point out, like others I have told, that a return to work may not be advisable under the circumstances. Not that he knows me well enough to have an opinion, of course.

"I think my behaviour last time I was here left a bit to be desired. I was a bit ragged and probably took it out on you. I want you to know I'm sorry."

"You're right, you were a bit rude." I blink at his blunt response. "But that comes with the territory. A shrink would say I must have a pathological need to be insulted to keep coming back to work each day."

"Does everyone insult you? I mean, some people must be nice to you."

"No, not really." He grins. "Lucky I've got my emotional buffer piled on."

I groan at the reference to his weight. "Oh, God, you really have your psychobabble down pat, don't you? Sounds like you've given this a bit of thought."

"Well, if ever I forget about it, my mother, bless her heart, likes to remind me. To make sure it's always at the forefront of everyone's mind."

"She has a problem with your weight?"

He gives an exaggerated eye-roll, head-drop response.

"Okay. Picture this. I've only seen her two weeks before and I rock up for the dreaded once-a-month family dinner."

"Oh dear, every month?"

"Every gob-spitting, bum-scratching first Wednesday of the month."

"Eew, what a description."

"I'm trying to convey the horror of it." I gesture for him to continue. "So, as I was saying, I rock up for dinner—with my brother, Tyler…"

In unison we both exclaim, "He got the good name."

"Anyway, Mum grabs Tyler in a hug of motherly affection and I move in for my allotted piece of parental tenderness. She thrusts out her arms to stop me and says, 'I see you haven't managed to lose any weight, Clyde Norbert,' then turns to my brother and walks him inside the house."

There is an element of sadness alongside the humour in his story and I feel a sudden kinship with him.

"Oh, I can beat that! My mum is a social worker and loves support groups." Clyde grimaces. "So every week she locates another support group for me. And they all have tragic names. The last one she dragged me along to was called *The Victims of Facial Disfigurement*. We walk in and there is a sea of horror masks.

People who've been in car accidents, shooting accidents—or not accidents—fires, or been physically assaulted. Honestly, it was like being on the set of the "Thriller" video. And everyone is checking out the face next to them and breathing a sigh of relief if it's worse than theirs."

Clyde guffaws, spurting his mouthful of coffee across the table and onto my sleeve.

"Oh, sorry, sorry," he says; mops at me with one of the paper serviettes, which sit at attention in a silver holder. "And whose was the worst?" he sputters.

"Well, it was a toss-up between mine and this little gnome-like fellow who'd been in a shooting accident. The skin graft had become infected and one side of his face was twice as big as the other making him look a bit like a squashed melon. But I think I won in the end."

"Good on you. A winner. I'll bet your mum was proud."

This throws us both into hysterics, until I think I might choke while trying to catch a breath. When we finally settle down, he picks up his coffee again and grins at me over the top of his chipped mug.

It feels nice, normal even.

"Oy, you're not being paid to have fun," yells seventies Gavin. "Time for your next load of insults."

Clyde pushes out his chair. "You don't have to go. You can sit up at the bar and I can shimmy up and down, chatting, serving drinks, shimmying, chatting. Might even lose some weight."

"Chance would be a fine thing," I quip.

He slaps his forehead. "God, I've known you for five minutes and already you sound like my mother."

"Your therapist would say you've obviously attracted me because you think you need someone like your mother to keep tormenting you."

"I don't have a bloody therapist."

I turn my palms upwards in surrender. "Well, there's your problem."

Gavin slams a bottle down on the counter, reminding Clyde to come back to the bar.

"Is he the boss? Little upstart."

"Owner's son, so almost. And he's not so bad when you get to know him." I grimace, not convinced. "Got to get back to it. Are you staying a bit longer?"

Pushing back from the table, I hook my bag over my arm. "No, I have to go."

"Can I introduce you to someone before you go?"

I look around the dim room and can't see anyone other than the old man in the corner, and Gavin. I shrug in assent. Clyde holds up five fingers to Gavin to let him know how long he'll be and leads me over to the dim shadows of the booths. He stops in front of the old man.

"Excuse me, Professor, may I interrupt you for a moment, please? I'd like to introduce you to someone."

Why is he talking to this sozzled old loser with such respect?

The so-called professor peers up out of the gloom and takes a moment to focus on Clyde's face.

"Of course, my dear boy. Your interruptions are always most welcome."

I cough to smother my gasp of surprise at the smooth intonation and cultured, English accent. I had expected a drawling, slurred, obscenity-laced mumble. That's how homeless alcoholics are depicted in the movies, anyway. I presume he's homeless, based on the dishevelled, soiled state of him, and the scuffed duffle bag next to his chair, saucepan dangling from a cord at the top.

Clyde steps back, pushing me towards the old man. "Layla, I'd like you to meet Professor Bainbridge. Professor, this is my new friend, Layla."

That makes it sound as if he really is a professor. Unlikely.

His hands are encrusted with dirt, the nails broken and black edged. I cringe at the thought of taking his grimy hand in mine, but as the two men wait expectantly, I know there's no choice.

"Very pleased to meet you, Professor Bainbridge."

The old man looks down, and as if he's read my mind, says, "I am a touch ashamed that I haven't yet had my daily scrub. There weren't enough beds at the shelter last night, but I'm hoping to be in luck tonight. For that reason, I won't subject your clean, sweet self to personal contact. Please be assured that does in no way indicate a lack of pleasure in meeting someone who can bring such joy to my fine friend, Clyde."

A burst of compassion for such a sweet, caring gesture makes me reach over and grasp his trembling hand with both of mine. It may have been my imagination but I'm sure his eyes fill with tears, before he retrieves his hand and returns to gaze into his glass. Clyde indicates we're done.

"I look forward to seeing you again, Professor."

He nods and a small smile twitches his lips, but the old man doesn't raise his eyes again.

At the bottom of the stairs Clyde asks me to wait, while he hurries back to the bar, grabs a small pad and a pen.

"I'm hoping you'll come back here and visit us again, regularly, in fact. Although I'm not sure why you would." He grimaces. "On the off chance, I want to give you my phone number, in case you ever need to talk, or you want to catch up for a coffee, or a bite to eat away from here."

This all feels a bit awkward and I want to tell him I have a boyfriend, but he doesn't seem to be asking me on a date, merely offering an ear if I need to talk. Besides, The Black Hole and the people in it are so removed from the world I normally live in, it's as if I'm on another planet. A planet where Tom doesn't exist.

I take the phone number. "Thank you. You never know, I might do that. Well, that is if I run out of support groups."

At the top of the stairs I half turn and although Clyde and Gavin are already otherwise occupied, the professor lifts a hand.

A sliver of shame shafts through me as I concede the sozzled old loser has a story like anyone else. Who am I to judge a book by its cover?

CHAPTER 5

WHEN I WALK IN THE red light is flashing on the answering machine. It will be either Mum or Dad, as anyone else would have rung my mobile if I wasn't home. I press the button and Dad's voice speaks hesitantly to me. He hates answering machines.

"Hi pumpkin, it's your old dad here. I'm cooking a lamb roast tonight, and we were hoping you could ditch Tom Cruise and come over for dinner."

He chuckles at his own joke—a reference to an old ad campaign.

"Not your Tom, of course. Don't ditch him. In fact, he's welcome to come as well. Yes, bring him too." *My* Tom? Is he? The million-dollar question. "Hope to see you, love. I miss you."

Luckily the stool is in landing distance of my bum as I plop down, feeling as if my heart is being squeezed by the emotion my dad evokes in his short message. Actually, it's an incredibly long message for Dad. I want to see him. I miss him, too. Perhaps I will phone Tom and see if he'd like to come with me. It's been so long since he's spoken to my family—we've tiptoed around each other for months, not sure if we're friends or lovers. I dial his mobile and it goes straight to message bank, so I leave a message and phone Dad back.

"Lamb roast sounds great, Dad. Who's going to be there?"

"Surprisingly, all the family. I threw out invitations and everyone happened to be free. Ruby will be here, of course, Matt and your favourite sister-in-law." I groan. The woman rubs every bristly hair on my body the wrong way, but I do miss Ruby and Matt. "And Corinne's able to come as well. How about that? And it's not even Christmas."

I don't react outwardly to his news Corinne will be there. Even with her recently improved behaviour, she's not my favourite sibling. For Mum and Dad, though, I can swallow my discomfort and be nice to her.

My little sister, Ruby, is only fifteen, so I see her every time I go home, but my older siblings and I haven't been together for a meal for months. I'm suddenly suspicious.

"Mum's not planning some sort of get-Layla-out-in-public intervention, is she?"

"I don't think so. Well if she is, she hasn't told me. I'm only expecting my family and the lamb roast. An intervention? I've never done one of those. Might be fun"

"Dad!"

"Just come on over. Is Tom coming?"

"I've left a message, so it might be a last minute decision, if that's okay.

"No problems. See you around six thirty?"

"Okay, but I'm warning you, if everyone starts to circle me with their chairs, I'm out of there."

"Love you, pumpkin." The line goes dead.

Bennie has his lead between his teeth. To gain my attention, he makes a feeble attempt at a menacing growl.

"Really? That's the best you can do?"

He looks away with a peeved whine and does a dog version of an eye-roll—a sideways stare through the white tuft of hair hanging over his eyes. I shove my mobile into my pocket and follow him out the door.

While he's chasing sticks at Shelly Beach, the phone rings. It's Tom.

"Hey, Layla." He used to call me babe. "I got your message. I was going to give it a miss, but that'd mean going home to cheese on toast. Lamb roast trumps that and I haven't seen your mum and dad for a while so, hey, let's do it." I feel a ridiculous surge of excitement, as if it's a first date. His voice still does that to me, as well as the thought of seeing him. "By the way, I saw your friend, Tegan today. She said to say, hi."

"Oh. She didn't say anything else?"

"Not really. She was chasing her four-year-old with the other one in a pram. Don't you speak anymore?"

"She's busy."

My chest clenches at mention of her, but I push the loss of my best friend to the back of my mind.

"You still there?" Tom asks. I mutter acknowledgement. "How about I pick you up at six?"

I return my attention to our dinner date and a shudder of excitement skitters up my spine.

"Sounds good. It shouldn't be a late night, but if it is, maybe you could stay. In the spare room, I mean. We could have breakfast, or do something in the morning," I blurt, a hot burn of embarrassment heating my neck.

I've broken my rule not to pressure him, but I can't swallow back the words. There's an awkward silence.

"Yeah, might be nice to do something tomorrow."

A lukewarm response, but I'm so desperate to rekindle what we had, I'll take the crumbs he's tossed me. And try not to torture myself with the memories of our past; when he couldn't bear to be away from me and when he was with me, he couldn't keep his eyes, and hands, off me.

I scrub my mental screen clean and remind myself of one of the many mantras I've played continuously since coming out of hospital. *One moment at a time, expect nothing.* Who am I kidding? He's coming to me after lunch with Kelly. How can I compete with that?

⟨

We pull into the circular driveway at my parents' Pymble home and park behind my father's Volvo. The two-storey Tudor residence nestles amongst the huge blue gums and stringy bark trees, secluded from the rest of the world. It's hard to imagine we're in the middle of a suburb.

I push open the door of Tom's black Saab Convertible as Ruby hurtles down the front steps, waving. She's wearing purple tights and a tiny midriff top which clings to her breasts. Good heavens, she isn't a kid anymore. I lift my gaze. There's something wrong with her face. When she gets closer I see her eyes are ringed with thick, black kohl pencil and one side of her beautiful auburn hair is shaved and patterned in crosses. She has a piercing on her top lip and in her navel. What was Mum thinking?

"Christ, look at your sister," whispers Tom.

"Rubes, what have you done to your hair? And when did you get the piercings?"

She shrugs. "Do you like it?"

"It's different." Tom raises an eyebrow. What else can I say? For years she was such a shy, nervous kid, who jumped at shadows. I'm sort of pleased she's daring to stand out. Although this is may be a bit of overcompensation.

"Thank goodness you've come. Hi Tom."

She pulls me into the house and I'm hit with nasal nostalgia: the smell of succulent, herby roast lamb, firing good memories from my childhood. Metaphors for love and comfort. Ruby screws up her nose and leans towards me. "Corinne's here and so is Matt and *Maureen*."

"Shhh, they'll hear you, Rubes. Maureen's all right; a bit stiff, that's all."

"Whatevah!"

I tug her to a halt. "What's all this about, Rubes?" I gesture at her head.

She slaps one hand on her skinny hip and rolls her eyes. "Not you, too. Dad doesn't let up. You're all just out of touch. This is tame next to most of my friends."

"Maybe you need new friends, little sis."

We follow her into the living room.

"Tom, Layla. How nice you could come," bleats Maureen.

What? This is my family home. Ruby grins pointedly and I avoid her eyes.

"Maureen, it's been so long. How's your job going?"

"Not too bad, you know. Not sure how long I'll stay, though. They simply aren't making use of my skills.

"Which skills would they be, Maureen?" asks Ruby.

I give her a surreptitious flick with the back of my hand.

"I hope you're not being rude, Ruby. My organisational skills. Matt thinks I would be a great asset to someone who needs a personal assistant or executive secretary. You know, someone to keep them organised, remind them of meetings; be a gatekeeper with difficult clients, that sort of thing."

"Matt is probably right, you'd do very well in a job like that," I say. "But they'd miss you at Myer, wouldn't they? You're in charge of the Manchester section if I recall."

The cynical remark goes over her head.

"Yes, but I think I need to spread my wings. At least until Matt and I start reproducing."

"Eeew. Not in front of the children, Maureen," squawks Ruby. "That's my brother you're talking about."

"Shut up, Ruby. Come here, Layla, and give your big brother a hug."

Matt lifts me off the ground in a bear hug, but I twist enough to ruffle his moussed hair. That makes him drop me. He hates his hair being mussed up. He's such a sweet man, I have no idea why he chose Maureen. One of the mysteries of life, I guess.

"Layla, you're looking well."

No hug from my sister, Corinne, who's the oldest of my siblings. For many reasons, some best left buried, we have never been particularly close. She's thirty-three years old, so there is the age gap of six years and then there's her unpleasant, sometimes vicious manner. I still maintain a guardedness around her—a remnant from our childhood.

Unlike the rest of us, Corinne had no academic aspirations and works in a small, second hand book store. She's had a few boy-friends, none of them worth remembering and most lasting no more than six months. This sudden and uncharacteristic interest in my health annoys rather than comforts me.

"What do you mean, Corinne? How can you tell through the scars how I'm looking?"

She blushes with either discomfort or anger at my response. Maybe being burnt has made me mean. A spike of shame heats my body.

Mum bustles out of the kitchen and kisses my left cheek. She always makes a point of kissing the side with the scar to let me know she loves that side as much as the good side. Nice gesture, but sometimes it irritates me as something too orchestrated.

"Where's Dad? In the kitchen?" I ask.

"Yes. He's giving the roast another baste and then he'll be out. Matt, how about getting everyone a drink. Tom, looking as handsome as ever. Come and give me a hug, make me feel like a young woman again," says Mum, the consummate hostess.

Tom grins and engulfs her in an embrace, then puts both hands on her shoulders and tells her how beautiful she is.

I watch the bantering between my family and Tom, and instead of feeling safe and normal, I feel bitter at how easy it is for everyone else to go on as if nothing has happened. Whereas for me, life can never be normal again. I now stand at the door of normal, looking in, with both feet rooted in my own private hell—a place no one else can enter. My mother glances over at me with a slight frown and I force a smile.

❧

We sit down at the long dining table while Dad carves the meat and Mum hands down plates of vegetables. Tom sits on my right hand side with Ruby on my left and Maureen, Matt, and Corinne opposite.

"Great dinner, Dad," I mumble, around a crispy baked potato.

"I'm trying to get a bit of fat on that skinny body of yours, pumpkin."

It's true, I'm all angles and planes now. My soft curves disappeared after lying in a hospital bed wrapped in silver foil, and then skin stockings for months. The worst scars, on my left thigh and left arm, were serious third degree burns destroying subcutaneous fat and muscle which will never regenerate, keeping those areas scrawny and shapeless. I can't look at Tom after Dad's comment.

"You're beautiful exactly as you are, Layla. As long as you're well, that's all that matters," blusters Mum, trying to fill the pregnant silence.

Dad glances at her with adoration shining in his eyes. My mother is of Turkish descent and quite beautiful. Her lustrous, auburn hair is pulled back from her face, exposing dark almond-shaped eyes and flawless honey-coloured skin. We used to look alike. Before. In fact Matt and Ruby also inherited Mum's beauty, her colouring and bone structure. Matt wouldn't be happy to hear himself called beautiful, but in a manly way, he is. Corinne, on the other hand, must have the genes of more distant relatives as she looks neither like Mum nor Dad. Although her fair skin and blocky body would more likely have come from Dad's side. Probably a throwback to his Aunt Louise, my great-aunt, who was so unattractive, she made your eyes water.

"Hey, Layla, we haven't done our Sunday brunch for ages. Why don't we start it up again?"

Mum beams at Matt, delighted at his attempt to get me out in public.

Before I can respond, Maureen jumps in. "Matt must have forgotten, but we've sort of made that our special time now, Layla. He works hard and I like to make sure he doesn't have any obligations on Sundays. Why don't you drop over to our place on the odd Sunday?"

Despite being about to tell Matt I wasn't ready to front the Sunday brunch crowd, I change my response to annoy Maureen.

"That sounds good, Matt. You'd be welcome to come as well, Maureen. We usually go to either Yum Cha in Chinatown or a great little café at The Rocks."

"We can think about it. If we decide to do it, and I'm not saying we will, I imagine Manly would feel better for you, Layla, rather than being somewhere busy like the City."

In other words, my brother's tactful wife was saying she didn't want to be seen out in public with me in a place where someone trendy might know her.

"Bloody hell, Maureen, have you got a PhD in Insultology?" asks Ruby.

"Ruby! Language, please," says Dad.

I look down to hide my grin at the fact he didn't pull her up for telling Maureen off, only for swearing.

Mum and Corinne simultaneously shove back their chairs, clatter plates on top of each other, and request dessert orders.

I want to hug Matt when he continues our conversation as if Maureen has said nothing.

"Sis, how about you and I have brunch this Sunday? You choose the place." He turns to his scowling wife. "I know you won't mind, Maureen." The look on her face tells us all it will be a dry week for poor old Matt.

After muttering a non-committal response, I follow Mum and Corinne into the kitchen and before Mum can say anything about Maureen, I bail her up about Ruby.

"What on earth has happened to Ruby's head?"

"It's her new way of expressing herself. It's important to let her spread her wings and find her own identity."

Corinne looks at me and shakes her head. "Mum, do you know any of the kids she's hanging out with?" she asks.

Good question.

"I've met a couple of her friends. A mixed bunch. And there seems to be a boy she's keen on too."

"The fact Ruby states she looks tame compared to her other friends would make me a bit worried, Mum. I think you ought to check out her friends. Especially the boyfriend," I add. "And have you had the sex talk?"

"Good heavens, Layla. She's fifteen. She probably knows more than we do."

"I certainly hope not," says Corinne. "She seems to have had a physical and attitudinal transplant since I last saw her."

My mother continues scooping trifle into round glass bowls. "It's all very normal. Young people have to reject the values of their parents by rebelling, so they can formulate their own values to take them into adulthood."

Corinne and I look at each other in resignation—a rare connection. You can't argue with Mum when she leans on her years of social work experience to make a point. I only hope she's right and Ruby's not in any danger.

"Well, at least she's stopped wetting the bed," says Corinne.

Mum and I stare at her. This is a subject we never raise as it upsets Ruby so much: the fact she was still wetting her bed at twelve. Luckily Ruby isn't in the room. Without another word, we grab the bowls of trifle and walk back into the dining room.

Tom picks up his dessert spoon, but before mining his trifle, he catches Dad's eye. "Did Layla tell you she's going back to work?"

I want to kick him in the shins.

Every head jerks up, but Mum has the words out first.

"Really? You've made the decision to do this? Do you think you're ready, darling? We could try to help you if it's only for financial reasons."

I glance over as Corinne, exasperated, rolls her eyes. She thinks I consume Mum's attention. Funny, I feel the same about her.

For once, though, we're in agreement. I don't want the attention. If I can steer the conversation away maybe the doctor in New York won't be mentioned. I flash my eyes at Tom in warning and shake my head at Mum.

"It's time," I say, "and my psychologist thinks it would be good for me." I hold up my hand as other mouths open to speak. "Please leave it. I need to make my own decisions about this."

"Yes, that's true," says Dad, with a quick wink in my direction. "You let us know how you go. Now eat up everyone." He finishes a mouthful of trifle and gestures at me with his spoon. "What if I see if the other accountants will make a spot for you at the firm?"

Dad has wanted me to work with him since I first enrolled ten years ago to do a double degree in Applied Finance and Economics at Macquarie University. At the time, I tried to let him down gently, explaining I fancied the hurly burly clamour of investment banking; of predicting market sentiment, hunting down clients, and building their portfolios to dizzying heights. I also yearned to travel to exotic locations, where I would seduce big corporations with my sharp intellect and astute knowledge, perfumed with a dab of feminine wiles. He got the picture. He conceded defeat and cancelled the nameplate for my office door.

I blow a kiss across the table at him. "It's okay, Dad. Thanks for the offer."

Throughout dessert, Ruby's phone—banned from the table—pings with messages and she almost quivers in her anxiety to gobble down her trifle and get to the phone. I would so love to see those messages.

By the time we have coffee, I've pinned Ruby down to spend a couple of nights with me next weekend. If Mum isn't going to check out what she's up to, then I will.

With groans and chair scrapes, everyone gets to their feet and we say our goodbyes.

"You have to stop working so hard, Tom, and come and visit us more often," says Dad.

"I'll do my best, Robert."

Tom shakes Dad's hand, hugs the women, and lands a friendly punch on Matt's shoulder.

I watch the gestures which were once commonplace, and the

familiar grief hits like a hammer into my chest. It's not true that time eases pain.

𝕮

To my surprise, Tom decides to stay the night and although I expect he'll take the spare bed, I'm as nervous as a virgin on her honeymoon at the alternative possibility. For many reasons—some mine, some his—we've not had sex since I left the hospital. I crave intimacy with him and cling to the hope tonight's warm family connections might act as a catalyst, stirring the passions shared before the fire.

Tom uses the bathroom first and then I go in to clean my teeth. I stare at the apparition reflected in the mirror; at the loathsome, puckered scars which mar my face, deform one ear, and twist the side of my mouth. By some miracle both eyes escaped damage.

I could audition for the role of the Phantom in *Phantom of the Opera*. Although one side of my face is horribly disfigured, the other side was hardly touched by the fire. Sometimes I'm grateful to at least have half a face, but mostly it's a reminder of what I've lost. And the truth is no-one looks at you with one eye closed. Their gaze covers the whole face and is stopped by the contorted, freaky side. Closing my eyes, I finish cleaning my teeth.

Enough of the self-flagellation. I turn away from the mirror and consider the positives. Tonight was a good night for a number of reasons: the unconditional love of family and even a tenuous connection to my sardonic sister. Perhaps her uncharacteristic gift of the painting marked a shift in our relationship. It's as if this damaged version of me is more palatable to Corinne than the original Layla. Whatever it is, I'll take what I can get; it's a relief not to be protecting myself from her, and tonight we even agreed in our concerns about Ruby.

Then there was the pleasure of seeing Tom back in the bosom of my family, where he belongs. Contentment swelled in my chest as I'd watched him tease Ruby, banter with my mother, and discuss politics with my father. I want to freeze-frame the evening and tuck it into a treasure box to be pulled out whenever I feel vulnerable, unloved, and insecure.

I open the bathroom door and turn into the bedroom. Tom is in my bed. My heart pumps with an equal measure of thrill and dread. Unaware of the clamour in my body, he raises his eyes and smiles. An uncertain smile, I'm sure of it.

Once a clear breath cools my lungs again, I note the oddest detail. Tom is on the wrong side of the bed. He's on my side, the right side. I am a bit confused until I remember he hasn't shared my bed since I lived in Balmain, where he always slept on the left side. Oh well, variety and all that. And then the cynical thought hits me: from that side, he only sees the good half of my face.

Enough paranoia. I climb into bed, my heart still drumming against my ribs. Do I spoil the moment with a question about why he chose that side of the bed? Or do I cut him some slack. Let him use whatever coping mechanisms he needs to do this?

While my rational side wars with my insecure side, my mouth leaps in.

"How come you've swapped to the right side of the bed?"

"What do you mean? Don't I always sleep on this side?"

"No. When I lived in Balmain, you slept only on the left side. Same in your flat."

"Have you got a point, Layla?"

My stomach churns and I feel slightly sick. I glance away as a freshening breeze lifts the curtain, carrying the distant cry of a cuckoo and the smell of seaweed. I counsel myself to let it go. Like the prayer of Grace from my childhood, 'to be grateful for what I am about to receive.'

Alas, I was never one not to finish what I start. Besides, my therapist told me if people answered a question with a question, it was often to avoid the answer.

"I wondered if you'd changed sides so you can't see my scars."

"Do you really think I'd do that? You must have a very low opinion of me."

I sit on the bed, my legs curled beneath me, ashamed at my accusation and perversely pleased it's the right side of my face he sees.

"I'm sorry, that came out wrong. And it's not your fault. It must be awful to be attracted to a person, only to have them change so completely overnight. I understand if you can't feel the same. I guess you need to do whatever you can to make it easier."

I wait to give him the opportunity to say I haven't changed, that I am still the same person.

Without responding, he turns off the light, plunging the room into thick darkness, and pulls me towards him. Then he quietly and gently makes love to me as if I might break. The only thing breaking is my heart, but I can't blame him. Not when I love him so much.

I cling to him afterward, wanting the intimacy to go on forever, but his gentle snoring tells me we're done.

CHAPTER 6

A SHARP, PEPPERY JAVAN AROMA BITES into my senses and draws me from a restless sleep. When I force my eyelids open, Tom is holding out a coffee mug, his hair dripping from the shower. He looks delicious and I want to reach out and pull him back into bed. But I'm shy, awkward with our new intimacy. With one hand, I push the pillow up to cushion my back and grasp the mug with my other hand, breathing in the mix of coffee, salt air, and the scent of my coconut shampoo in Tom's hair. A slight breeze rattles the bamboo wind chimes and through the window I see a flock of seagulls swoop over the water to snatch at a school of fish. An idyllic moment. The mattress dips as Tom lowers himself back onto the bed, wrapped in only a towel and I turn my head, enough to see him.

With an evil grin, he lifts his firm butt into the air, whips the towel away, and drops it on the floor beside the bed. My heart leaps pathetically, as if someone is about to bestow a great gift of benevolence upon me. He whispers my name and I turn my face, a little more, to display my unscarred profile. His finger strokes my cheek and continues down the right side of my body. I feel a sense of relief that at least one side might please him. And alongside the relief, resentment bubbles in my gut at his inability to enjoy all of me. Although, why would the scars be attractive to him, when even I'm repulsed by them? Tingling sensations through my body from his caresses finally shut down my mind.

I glance down and see Tom's magnificent erection. I don't want any more foreplay, I want him inside me. Deep inside me. I push my half-empty coffee mug onto the bedside table and reach for him. He rolls over to lie on top of me. When he braces his elbows on each side of my body, his eyes can't miss the panorama of my red, tangled scars which coil like vines from my face, down my neck and along my arm.

"Damn!" he says and rolls back to his side.

His penis curls in his groin like an abandoned slug. His look of mortification in no way equals my sense of failure and the grief washing through my body. I'm so ugly and distasteful, his body recoils from me.

"Shit. What the hell's wrong with me?" he blusters. "I thought this sort of stuff only happens when you get old."

"Or when you have to make love to a gargoyle," I whisper, the tears dripping down my cheeks and into my ears.

"Don't do this, Layla. It's all in your mind. This has nothing to do with you. Come on, let's get up and go for a walk."

"Why?" I sob. "You'd have to be seen in public with me." Although this pathetic statement would shame a twelve-year-old, my pity party is on a roll.

He doesn't answer, instead slides off the bed and pulls on his shorts. "Are we going for a walk or do you want me to leave? It's your call."

The finality of his words constrict my chest, making breathing difficult. Light-headedness muddles my mind and I can't think straight. Even though the humiliation swamps me, I don't want him to walk out. Not when it's been so long since we've spent quality time together.

Breathe in, hold, breathe out. Breathe in, hold, breathe out. "Don't go," *pant, pant.*

Sympathy flickers across his eyes. "You get dressed, and I'll wait in the lounge room for you."

The anxiety finally passes, and I shower quickly. It's impossible to find something in my wardrobe that says *bring back the sparkle of love in your boyfriend's eyes,* so I throw on my cargoes and a black T-shirt, brush my hair, push on a cap, and swipe on some mulberry lip gloss, without looking in the mirror. To walk from the bedroom out to the lounge room I have to imagine a firm hand pushing into the middle of my back, forcing me forward. Like a sulking child, I shuffle into the room. Tom turns from the window and flashes me a forced smile.

He claps his hands as if I am that sulking child. "Okay, we're going to forget the last hour happened, take Bennie for a walk," the dog spins in circles with excitement at hearing his favourite word, "and get some breakfast on the Corso. What do you say?"

Hooray was the word that comes to mind. He isn't leaving; maybe we can salvage the day after all. Upbeat is how I'm going to act. I cram the despair into my back pocket.

Although the sky was clear when I awoke, dirty, yellow nimbus clouds now smudge the blue, and a determined breeze stirs the branches of the Norfolk Island pines which line the seafront. My dad used to tell me if I could see enough blue sky to make a pair of sailor's pants, then it wouldn't rain. As we walk the sandy path above the sea wall, I squint through the pine needles at the sky. Just enough for a pair of pants—the rain should stay away at least until we get back home.

"This is the one you like, isn't it?" asks Tom, as he steers me towards the Bean There. I nod, pleased he remembers. The staff are used to my face and it will only be the customers who stare.

"Perfect."

With false gaiety, I tug my cap low over my face, tuck my arm through his, and head for an outside table. While Tom buys our coffees and orders a smoked salmon omelette for me and eggs Benedict for himself, I decide this morning is going to be about two lovers enjoying an outing. No mention of therapy, not seeing enough of each other, or failed sex.

"Won't be long, they're not too busy," says Tom, as he drags out the chair next to mine and tucks his long legs under the table.

I gaze at him and a wave of lust shafts through me. Reaching under the table, I curl my hand around the warmth of his firm, upper thigh. He raises his eyebrows, then lowers his hand to pat mine.

"Now let's talk about this idea of yours to go to New York for more surgery."

"I'd rather not, today."

"You know, your therapist has always counselled you to work through the denials and avoidance of issues that challenge you."

Why does he do this? We were going to have a normal meal and chat about inanities.

"How can you suggest I'm avoiding challenges after I met with Brian, faced the workplace, and set a firm date to start work again?" I ask.

He holds up his hand as if I'm a child in need of placation. "Alright. I'll pay that one. But if you want my honest opinion about this doctor, I think you'll set your progress back if you pin hope on yet another unachievable goal. Remember the woman who said she could laser off all the scars and how you believed implicitly it would change your appearance? You were inconsolable for weeks after when it didn't work."

Obviously there's no avoiding this discussion. "I've done some research on the doctor and he's had amazing results. Why can't you support me with something that has the real potential to restore my looks and my life?"

"Of course I'll support you, but it seems like a shocking amount of money to spend for a start, and it's forcing you back to work when I'm not sure you're ready."

"You don't think I'm ready to go back to work? Does Brian think that too? And Kelly?"

Tom shifts in his chair. "Brian is a bit concerned. After all, we deal with some fairly major clients and he knows you're still having those panic attacks. You must understand I'm only thinking of you and how it might be for you."

He stops, as the waiter places our breakfast in front of us. My appetite has vanished.

Tom picks up his knife and fork and slices into the bright yellow yolk, letting it run across the toasted sourdough and ham, and scoops it up with the creamy Hollandaise sauce. He sneaks a piece of toast to Bennie and gestures with his fork at my omelette. It's easier to comply than explain the loss of appetite, so I force a mouthful in and move it around my mouth. It's actually quite delicious, but a wedge of anger in my throat makes it hard to swallow. I push in another mouthful, pick up my latte, and wash the egg down with a swallow. My mother would cringe at this breach of table etiquette.

"Maybe you are thinking of me, Tom. And maybe you're right in everything you say. But if the day comes that I have to give up and accept this is the way I'm going to look for the rest of my life, I have to know I tried every avenue."

A sharp beep on Tom's phone diverts his attention. He scrolls down to check who's messaged, then responds to me without lifting his eyes from the phone.

"And I'll try to be there every gruelling step of the way, because you'll have your perfect life back the way it used to be."

His fingers dance over the keyboard as he makes this patronising statement. I want to rip the phone out of his hand and smash it on the concrete. Instead, I scrub violently behind Bennie's ear until he yelps and gives my finger a warning nip.

Tom doesn't seem to notice my agitation but gives me a pathetic half-grin of apology. "I know this conversation is important to you, babe, but Brian needs some info from me which is at home so I'd better make tracks. We can pick up where we left off later."

"No need. I heard what you had to say. Let's go."

Tom smiles, unaware of my sarcasm, his mind already on the work issue.

We leave the coffee shop and walk home, me in front with Bennie, and Tom a few steps behind, still poking at his phone.

&

As a diversion from the misery of his departure, I open my laptop to check emails. There's a new message. Nerves churn my stomach. It's from the Mt. Sinai Burns Unit. A response to my enquiry. They want a photo of my scars, my medical reports, my psychologist's reports and what my dog had for breakfast—well, maybe not the last one. They explain they can't be specific about the cost of any operation as everyone is different. They'd need to consider my particular case. However, the costs of staying at his private clinic are very clear. Frighteningly clear. I have no choice but to go back to work, full-time. Not only that, I will need to travel for the big paying clients. Regularly. It's hard enough on the Manly ferry, how will I manage overseas travel, let alone the embarrassment of meets and greets? I drop my head onto the table, defeat creeping in again. *Dammit!* I slam my fist onto the table.

"I want my life back!"

As if on cue there is a ping on the laptop. I raise my eyes to read the email:

Darling, your father and I have had endless discussions about your going to New York for more operations. I understand this decision to go back to work is tied up with the money you will need to undertake this option. I know I was not encouraging the other night, but our children are the most important people in the world to us. If there is even the slightest chance this doctor might make a difference then go for it. We are willing to take out a mortgage on the house to pay for it. We are very excited at this new glimmer of hope for you. The money means nothing to us—you do! Love you.

They can't be serious. Mortgage the house at their age? My God. Tears drip down my cheeks, leaving wet splotches on my black T-shirt. If my wonderful parents are willing to take such a huge risk, then I can toughen up and be positive about a return to work. I rip two tissues out of the box in front of me, blow my nose, scrunch them up, and toss them into the wastepaper basket. Then I respond to the most loving, generous note I've ever received.

CHAPTER 7

THE PERSISTENT BUZZ OF THE alarm wakes me and for a few precious seconds I think it's a normal day. But the clock only says six thirty and I never get up before at least seven.

Anxiety flutters my chest. Today is my first day back at work. I pull the sheet over my head and the fluttering turns into a deep crawling sensation of dread. Any second it will turn into another anxiety attack, so I take control, leap out of bed, and jump under a hot shower. And chant a mantra—*So Hum*. With the constant repetition of these words, my thinking mind has no room to produce a story of dramatic proportion about a day that hasn't even started yet.

When I push back the shower curtain, Bennie is sitting on the bath mat, his head tipped to the side, confused at this unusually early start. It's probably best to walk him before I dress for work. In leggings and a T-shirt, hair dripping onto my shoulders, we dash down the road, circle the block and come back. Bennie looks at me as if to say, 'Is that it? Where's my long romp on the beach?'

I hadn't thought of the consequences for my little friend. He's never known me to go to work, leaving him at home on his own all day. I slide down the wall to the floor and pull him onto my lap, hoping he'll forgive me for this drastic change in our routine. At least Mr. Bacik is going to keep an eye on him.

Tom texts to wish me luck, and I text back asking him not to meet me in the lobby as this is something I need to do for myself. Besides, the tension is still there between us.

The coat hangers clang as I pull out the light jacket of my dove grey pants suit. Not a random choice. Colour psychology is an important element in a workplace such as ours. Before the fire, if I had a client meeting, I would aim to establish trust and credibility with blue or blue-green colours. However, a more neutral shade diverts attention from the appearance and allows focus on the personality. So, neutral dove grey it is. I slip the jacket over a soft sheer-sleeved shirt. It's still cool enough for long sleeves, but that won't last much longer. As usual, I blow-dry my hair to hug my face and pull on a new, pale grey cotton head wrap with ties that drape down the left side of my neck. My collection of headwear grows each day. Online shops are perfect for people like me. I twirl in front of the mirror and decide there's nothing more I can do. The silver hoop earrings would have been perfect if only I had an earlobe on my left ear. But the fire melted my ear into a scarred blob, which hasn't been given priority with the plastic surgeries I've had to date.

☾

The elevator, loaded with workers who avert their eyes, skims up to the sixth floor. My self-protective mechanism clicks in and I sense the disconnection take place. I glide out of my disfigured body and float above their heads. It's a trick I learnt in hospital when the pain made me long to escape. A Buddhist friend sat by my bed and quietly spoke about transcending the pain and seeing the body as not really me, but as a vehicle in which to navigate this incarnation. Not sure if I agreed or even understood what she meant at the time. But one day, following her instructions, I found myself looking down on my suffering form, swaddled in bandages and splayed on the bed. The shock threw me back into my body, but I was so fascinated with the experience, I spent those long days of gradual healing perfecting this separation.

That may not have been what my Buddhist friend was on about, but it worked for me. At times I would hover in the hospital room, watching my family, with brittle smiles on their faces, attempt to hide their anxiety behind muttered platitudes.

An unexpected side effect is that during the body separation, I don't experience grief, loss, anger, or even irritation at my situation. Only a warm sense of love. It's when I'm back in my body all these emotions clamour for attention.

The lift stops at my floor and I merge into my body. With my insecurities and paranoia intact, I make the slow walk down the corridor. A deep breath, and I push open the door into the huge work area, or *the desk*—short for the trading desk—peppered with over sixty workstations. A dissonant buzz of voices—talking on phones, yelling across the floor to each other, exploding in frustration at market action—greets my entrance, and generates a warm ooze of familiarity. Until I'm noticed and the buzz dies to a hum. A number of heads turn, register surprise, fascination, or embarrassment on their faces, and quickly turn back to their computers.

"Layla! I didn't think you'd consider coming back. After, you know…" My gaze locks onto Clarissa. She is a senior executive assistant and senior purveyor of gossip in the workplace. I also recall she had a thing for Tom. She points at my head. "What a lovely turban thing."

There are a few raised eyebrows at her comment and a muffled snicker or two. I imagine a laser beam shooting from my eyes exploding her up-turned nose across her face.

I smile and reach up to touch my head wrap. "Gosh, Clarissa, so nice of you to notice it. Of course I was coming back. You'll see me here every day. And I have quite a hair cover collection for you to admire. In fact you should try them; it could save you hours in front of the mirror." A childish retort, I know.

The downward flicker of her eyelashes and pink flush in her cheeks tell me my laser beam has hit its mark. Glancing over her shoulder, I see a young Asian man raise his hand to me with two fingers spread in a victory sign.

Until this moment I hadn't known how I wanted to deal with my re-entry into the workplace, but now an old British saying comes to mind—*start as you mean to go on*. What I do next, I'm sure, will determine the colour of my future here.

I change direction and head away from *the desk* towards Brian's office. His door is open and he looks up as I approach.

"Come in, Layla. Glad you came in to say hello. Anything I can do to help you settle back in?"

"There is, Brian." I explain what I want and when he argues, I insist.

Weaving around long rows of desks, I locate my workstation, which is against the wall on the far left side of the work area. The two client files Brian and Kelly have decided I'm to start with are already on my desk. There is also a calendar of upcoming conference events.

A cold chill tugs at my spine as I recall the requirement to trawl conferences for the purpose of identifying new clients. My record for snagging a potential client's attention used to be unbeatable, especially if they were male. My investment strategies then maintained this initial interest. The new horror mask will certainly get attention.

Until Brian is ready, I flip open the top file and glance at the contents. Before, I was keen and mean; nothing stood in the way of my reeling in a new client. Now I'm digging deep for the required enthusiasm to even read the preliminary information.

The first file involves a company in Brazil. The second, a potential client in Korea.

Looks and charisma are high on the list of criteria for Brazilians and, coincidentally, also Koreans.

Some years ago I attended an international business conference in Singapore where I met a Korean securities broker. She was extremely beautiful, but had western shaped eyes and a pointed, rather than rounded, chin. I commented, asking if one of her parents was European. She shook her head, stating she'd had plastic surgery to stay on top of the game. That this was expected. Interesting, that Kelly gave me these two files. If I didn't know better, I would think she's setting me up to fail. Come to think of it, I don't know better.

Clarissa pokes her head over my low partition. "Brian is ready, Layla." I raise my eyes and notice the large room is almost empty.

She leads me down the corridor towards the largest of our boardrooms. Before pushing open the huge, silky oak doors, I stop, take a breath, focus my mind, and then enter. Over sixty faces turn and I attempt to make eye contact with as many as I can before they have a chance to turn away. I need them to have a good look, react in whatever way they need to and get it over with. Brian waves me up to the front of the room.

Before he can speak, I put my hand on his arm, letting him know this has to be my show. Brian nods and steps aside.

"Good morning, everyone. I won't keep you more than a couple of minutes. My name is Layla Danforth and although I know a number of you already, there are also many I've not met. I'm under no illusion as to the effect of my scarring on people who've not seen me before or, for that matter, people who have." I smile, trying to put them at ease. "I know exactly how you feel, because the first time I saw my reflection after the face stocking was removed, I was in total disbelief. Shocked. Appalled and devastated. And I'm still not used to it."

I scan the room, finally locating Tom at the back, his attention focused on the floor. Is he ashamed of me? I have a room full of people waiting to hear what I'm going to say. I'll worry about Tom later.

"Let me explain. I was in a house fire and have been in hospital and rehabilitation for over eighteen months. As far as I know, this is as good as it will get, so I want you to feel free to look at me openly without fear of offence and I also want to ask you to let me do my job without this," I gesture at my face, "always being the elephant in the room."

Some faces register surprise, others admiration, others disbelief but most keep eye contact. Except Tom, who is now looking out the window. Did he think my scars would go unnoticed if I said nothing? Despite asking him to let me find my own way today, I wish he'd come up the front in a gesture of solidarity.

"Would anyone like to ask me a question?"

There are smiles and head shakes, but no questions. I look at Brian, who indicates to everyone that we are done and people start milling towards the door.

Two women approach Tom; one pats his arm, the other touches his chest as they murmur something in his ear. I can't hear what they're saying, but it almost looks like they're commending his perseverance in staying with the freak girlfriend. The caring, long-suffering boyfriend. Crap, I need to get a hold of myself.

"That was a smart move, Layla. You haven't lost the spark that always put you ahead of the pack," says Brian, as he moves past me and leaves the room.

Kelly pastes a fake smile on her face as she walks up to me. "Feel free to check with me if there are any questions about the two files I've given you, won't you?" Then she follows the others out.

Be buggered if I'll ask her anything.

A tap on my arm diverts my attention to a young woman, who I don't know.

"I want to say how much I admire what you did this morning. Anything you ever want, come and find me. My name is Penny and I'm in admin."

Penny is followed by a number of other people, who shake my hand and thank me for making it easier for them. Then I look up to see Tom about to exit the boardroom. He holds up one finger, his sign to indicate he's available for lunch at one o'clock. I nod and he leaves. It seems my gamble paid off. Now to do my job.

☙

Lunch with Tom is a corner table in a nearby café where, shrouded in tension, we speak in staccato sentences about inanities. He studiously avoids the subject of the staff meeting. Halfway through my Caesar salad, I can't stand it anymore, so I plunge in.

"Were you embarrassed when I spoke to everyone in the boardroom?"

He glares, annoyed at my question. "I wasn't sure you needed to draw such attention to yourself, especially on your first day back."

"The alternative would have been to slink around in the vain hope no-one noticed my face and then deal with the horrified expressions when they caught a glimpse." He shrugged. "Tom, this isn't the Middle Ages where they lock freaks away as if they were subhuman. I did this for me as well."

He throws down his fork. "For God's sake, will you stop referring to yourself as a freak? That's what upset me. The fact that you thought you had to display what had happened as if you were a sideshow in a circus."

I'm stunned by his comment. "That wasn't it at all. No wonder you were unhappy if that's how you saw it."

"Look, let's drop it and enjoy lunch. It's done now. Brian was impressed."

What does he mean by that? Is he inferring I did it to get into

Brian's good books?

By this time the salad has lost its appeal and my small bubble of elation now sits like lead in my stomach. To preserve our relationship, I end the conversation. But when I think about his perception of what I did, my stomach clenches and I feel nauseous.

(

When I get back to my desk, there is a note from Kelly: *Thought I'd let you know, Layla, we are having a video linkup with our Korean prospects tomorrow. Dress to impress!*

(

Mr. Bacik, bent over his garden bed sprinkling fertiliser, pushes his hand into the small of his back, and straightens up when I open the gate to our block of flats.

"Hello, *kochana*, how was this first day back at work?"

"As awful as I imagined. But it's done now and I'm guessing each day will get better."

I tell him about confronting the staff when I arrived.

"Ah, such a wise, brave girl you are. I am very proud as if I was your tata. No," he chuckles, "more like your dziadzia, how you say, grandfather."

"Any girl would be happy for you to be their father or grandfather, Mr. Bacik. And thank you for the vote of confidence." A sudden wave of grief ripples his features. "What is it? Is something wrong?"

He waves my question away. "No, no, no. Nothing for you to worry about. Just a small memory of a little girl who was not so proud for me to be her tata."

What secrets did this dear old man have locked inside? Three sharp barks and scratching at the door tells me Bennie has heard my voice and his patience has run out. I grab the tanned, blue veined hand that rests on a small digging fork.

"Wait, I'll grab Bennie. I don't want to go inside yet; do you mind if we chat for a bit?"

He puts his other hand on top of mine. "If that is what you need, *kochana*."

No sooner have I unlocked the door than a cannonball of white fur hurtles into my arms, wet tongue slurping at my face. Then Bennie, finished with me, leaps to the ground and runs to Mr. Bacik, giving him similar treatment. We both watch the dog circle the small yard, lifting his leg with such rapidity, he topples over. Done with marking his territory, he settles on the ground, between myself and the old man.

By this time I've removed my jacket and am perched on the second step and Mr. Bacik has turned his attention back to his garden. His flowerbeds boast daffodils, sweet peas, and the most beautiful orange coloured tulips, interspersed with basil, dill, and parsley. An uplifting splash of colour against the dull red-dish-brown walls of the block of flats.

"Your children, Mr. Bacik, are they in Australia?"

He looks at me in surprise. "Why do you ask that?"

"You mentioned a little girl."

Suspicion clouds his eyes. "You are trying to open doors that are better left closed, my young friend."

"You know, Mr. Bacik, you make me feel so safe that I've often shared with you the secrets I can't speak about to many others. And when I speak about them, some of the pain is eased. It would be nice for once to be the listener."

He smiles at me, a smile that doesn't quite reach his eyes. "You are too clever with your words for me but maybe I can share a little with you. As long as Mrs. Bacik does not come out as she will not have this topic discussed."

The old man puts down his digging fork and eases himself onto the step next to me. Bennie, sensing some serious conversation is about to take place, perches his fluffy backside on the bottom step and puts his front paws up onto my knees. When I scratch behind his ears, he drops down and lowers his head onto his paws. Instead of looking up at me, his eyes are focused on Mr. Bacik.

"I am telling you quick version of something long and painful. Too much to tell it all." I nod as he shifts his position and looks into the distance. "You see when the Germans, they invade Poland, my parents, who are Jews, give me to Gentile neighbour who pretends I am their nephew. My parents are captured and I never see them again. I grow up knowing I am a Jew but pretending I am not."

He pauses, the pain of this duplicity dragging down the corners of his mouth. "My wife, also a Jew, also pretending she is not, and I, we had two beautiful daughters. My little Sofia is born with a sick heart and she died when she is three years old." He swallows and I reach over to place my hand on his. He waves my sympathy away. "Our second daughter, Anka, she is so beautiful." He looks at me, his eyes shining. "And so smart. Top of the class. Better than all the others. She is now a doctor with her husband doctor and two children." He draws in a deep breath and slowly releases it. "Two children I have only seen twice. Well, not so much children anymore. Her boy is sixteen years old and her girl is eighteen. "

"Oh, that's awful for you. Why do you not see them?"

He looks up as if to heaven. "God has twisted sense of humour, *kochana*. My Anka, she does not know about her Jewish heritage because we are so caught in the shame, we don't tell her. She falls in love with a Jewish boy but his family, they are against this relationship because she is not a Jew. This poor boy is worried not to cause a rift in his family and Anka, she comes to me so distressed, asking for my advice. Excited, I tell her this is not a problem. There is something you should know. We are Jews after all, I say, and there is no reason not to marry your young man."

He smacks the heel of his hand against his forehead. "I am stupid, stupid! Not to see this box of Pandora I open. She is so angry with her mother and me for our shame and our pretence, she does not speak to us for years. Her husband and her rabbi tell her we are to be despised, that we are no better than those involved in the Holocaust."

I'm disgusted with such harsh judgement of these people by their own daughter but keep it to myself.

"Have you seen her again?"

"She invites us to the boy's bar mitzvah and the girl's bat mitzvah. Only our grandchildren speak to us. Not like we are their grandparents, but only strangers." He shrugs. "To them we are strangers. My wife will not allow this humiliation again." Tears drip down the crevices of the old man's weathered face and catch at the edge of his mouth, causing him to swallow and swipe at his face.

I throw my arms around him and rock his sinewy body. "Stop now, Mr. Bacik. Don't tell me any more. I am sorry to have asked and caused you this grief."

"Grief is not caused by you, *kochana*, is caused by this denial of truth about myself and from depriving my child of right to be proud of her heritage. And now I must pay for this."

Bennie looks from me to Mr. Bacik, his head tilted to one side, and as I reach into my bag for a tissue, he leaps onto Mr. Bacik's knee and licks at the tears running down his chin.

"Ah, thank you, my little friend, no need for tissues with such a good tongue." He nudges the dog down. "But enough fussing around this silly old man."

"Maybe she'll change her mind. People do. Especially as they get older or the people they love get older," I insist, still gripping his trembling hand.

He starts to shake his head when a door slams. "Oh God, protect us, she is coming."

"Jozef, Jozef! What are you still doing out here?" To me, "Hello, *kochana*. How are you?"

She's feisty but still called me 'dear' so I'm not in trouble. I go to answer, but Mrs. Bacik has already turned back to her husband.

"I am waiting for you inside and…what is this? You are crying? What are you telling this poor girl? I am weeding around the herbs, you tell me, one hour ago. What has made you cry?" Her eyes have narrowed in suspicion and I swallow the sour taste of responsibility.

"I had a bad first day back at work, Mrs. Bacik and your husband is such a softie, he got upset." He pats my hand in gratitude.

His wife's stern expression softens and the earlier fear in her eyes is now a glow of love. She puts an arm around him and kisses his leathery cheek. "You silly old man. Come and I make you cup of tea. You come too, *kochana*."

"That's very kind of you, Mrs. Bacik, but I've had a big day and I need to walk Bennie and then do a bit of work."

Besides, both Mr. Bacik and I need time to deal with what he has revealed to me: internal scars no less horrendous than the ones I wear on the outside.

❦

Half an hour later, while I watch Bennie leap into the water at Shelly Beach to retrieve a stick, I contemplate how many of us carry grief of some sort. I have a twinge of guilt that mine is about my appearance—it seems so shallow in comparison. Mr. Bacik and his wife may appear normal, but inside they carry the worst type of grief: the grief of losing their children. Worse even than that, they have lost a child who is too ashamed of them to make contact. How does a parent survive that?

And yet they have. *Crap! When did I become so philosophical?*

Or is my rambling mind trying to avoid thoughts of the video linkup tomorrow morning? I toss the stick back into the water.

At least Kelly's note didn't say 'wear your best hat.'

CHAPTER 8

THE NEXT MORNING, I CORNER Kelly in the tearoom.
"I'm wondering if it's really necessary for us both to partic-
ipate in the video conference today."

She glances up at the white turban on my head and rakes her
eyes over the rest of my outfit. Pantsuit again, but white today.

"You must know from past experience, Layla, how important it
is for a client to trust their asset manager. After all, we ask them
to hand over control of huge amounts of money."

Is this woman telling me how to suck eggs? I take a deep breath
and bite my tongue to avoid a sarcastic response.

"Are you saying they won't feel comfortable enough to trust
me?" I ask.

"My presence might alleviate any initial difficulties, but I'm
sure once they get to know you, a rapport will be established."

She's given me two messages. One: at first view of my face,
they will want another investment organisation. Two: if her face
is also there, we might hook them in. I don't care if she's right, I
want to strangle her.

Oblivious to my murderous thoughts, she continues. "We tell
them we're a team and that will solve any discomfort."

"We are? I didn't realise. I thought those two files were for me
to manage."

Kelly lifts one perfectly plucked eyebrow. "It's up to you, Layla.
I'm happy to step back if you'd like to do this alone."

Why do I get the feeling I am being set up? I dismiss the alarm
bells.

"Maybe I will, Kelly. And if I need to I can seek your assistance."

She doesn't look the least bit put out, which tells me I have made a drastic tactical error. Too late now.

❦

At noon our time I sit in the boardroom with copious notes from late-night research. The Korean potentials haven't yet asked for an RFP—a document which details our investment products and funds management capability—but my role today is to interest them sufficiently to make that request.

The thing is, I need to first establish a rapport. In the past, I've been known to use my looks and sex appeal and when the client is hooked, my intellect. No wonder Brian expressed some anxiety to Tom, and Kelly is circling like a shark sensing blood. Today, success hangs on a startling presentation which smacks them in the face and leaves them no choice but to sign with our organisation.

Brian rushes into the room with a half-finished mug of coffee, runs his fingers through his hair, straightens his tie, and takes a breath. His role is to introduce me to Mr. Su and Mr. Kim, the President and Vice President of Geong Steel—straight to the big boys.

The large computer screen on the wall flickers to life and we face two Asian men dressed in shiny grey suits and colourful ties. One wears glasses, one doesn't. Neither one smiles. Brian nudges the camera so they can only see him while he makes the introductions.

"*An-nyong-ha-se-yo*, Mr. President, Mr. Vice-President?" He bows his head towards each man.

There is a lip twitch from Mr. President. "Good morning to you too, Mr. Townsend. We look forward to hearing your proposal so we can give consideration to working with your company." Brian's outstretched fingers press into the desk, his only response to the deliberate non-commitment evident in the man's words. "Your email indicated you have chosen your best person for this job. We look forward to meeting him."

Along with my irritation at his sexist assumption that I would be male, was a warm buzz at Brian describing me as the best person for the job.

"Mr. President, Mr. Vice President, I would like to introduce you to Miss Layla Danforth. Miss Danforth has many years of experience in asset management and has already put together a draft proposal for you."

Brian rolls his chair closer to mine and turns the camera to capture both of us. Mr. Vice President nudges his glasses up the bridge of his nose, probably to ensure his eyes do not deceive him. Mr. President visibly stiffens, narrowing his gaze.

"Good morning, Miss Danforth, it is our pleasure to meet you."

Icy politeness from the two men, and Brian's face is now two shades paler. A brick hits the pit of my stomach, but I won't give in.

"Good morning, Mr. President, Mr. Vice President." I change my mind about toadying up to them with a clever Korean greeting, even though I have one in front of me. "I'm very honoured to be working with you and would like to show you what I have prepared for your consideration."

Mr. President clears his throat. Mr. Vice President is still trying to peer myopically at the apparition on his screen. Perversely, I pull the camera closer to my face and prepare to launch into my scintillating spiel. Mr. President holds up a hand to interrupt.

"Am I to understand, Mr. Townsend, that Miss Danforth will be our investment advisor and represent our company in financial matters?"

Brian's breathing accelerates. "That was my intention. But of course, you, as the client, may have a suggestion to help us meet your needs more appropriately."

Traitor! I retain eye contact with the client but burn to look straight at Brian after his disloyal statement; to watch him squirm. Out of the corner of my eye I note, with satisfaction, the red flush creep from beneath the neck of his collar. He should know me better. I don't give up easily. I desperately want to ask these men what their problem is with me, but then they'd lose face and I would most certainly lose my job.

I smile at the camera. "Now what I propose is—"

As if I haven't spoken, Mr. President turns and exchanges a few muttered words with Mr. Vice President. They both nod at each other and turn back to the camera.

"Mr. Kim has reminded me of a meeting I must attend in ten minutes. This is most unfortunate. I offer my apologies for this oversight. Perhaps I will speak with you, Mr. Townsend, about further arrangements later today. He then makes eye contact with me and bows his head. "Goodbye, Miss Danforth."

I do the nodding thing back, positive this will be the last time I see their judgemental faces.

The screen goes blank, and Brian kicks his chair back from the table. We both remain silent. Brian studies his hands, clenched on his lap, while I swallow the bile rising like acid into my throat.

The silence gets too much for me. "Well, that went well."

Brian scrubs at his face with his open hands before he looks up. "I should never have put you through that. I'm so sorry, Layla." Despite the disaster of the last ten minutes, I feel a small wisp of pleasure that he is more upset for me than angry at possibly losing the contact. "You do know what this means though, don't you?"

Yes, unfortunately I do, but I let him go through the agony of spelling it out.

"I'm going to have to rethink your handling of this contact."

I slam the file shut and slide it across in front of him. "There you go. Do what you want with it. I'm not going to pretend I'm not angry at their biased behaviour, but I'm also realistic enough to know they don't have to have a reason to use another company. Being good at your job is obviously not as important as looking good while you do it."

"Biased behaviour?" he asks, with a wry grin.

I give an impatient wave of my hand. "Yes, they're making a decision about our products based on my appearance."

Brian fiddles with the edge of the file. "You know how much respect I have for your ability, Layla. Don't ever doubt that. But I have to do what's best for the organisation. Would you be willing to work alongside Kelly and have her as the face-to-face contact?"

"You mean I can be the brains and she can be the beauty? Let me think about that."

My last quip was meant to be sarcastic until I remember why I've come back to work. I need the money. And now my motivation has grown exponentially. I don't want to see that look of horror in another client's eyes. It's time to eat humble pie, and

I know it's going to taste like castor oil; and probably have the same effect.

"I apologise. That was a generous offer under the circumstances. But the client needs a front person with a solid support team. They need to know who's holding the reins. You're suggestion intimates I become part of Kelly's support team; that she holds the reins." Brian jiggles his knee. A sure sign he's uncomfortable. "We both know my track record, and the position I held before the accident, gives me the right to go in as the front person."

"Everything you say is true. But this is an unusual situation and I want you and Kelly to work as a team." He puts a hand on my arm. "This is the best I can do, Layla."

I slump in the chair. "I appreciate what you're saying. I'm just not sure how well Kelly and I will work together."

"Let me suggest that you and Kelly put aside whatever personal differences you may have and find a way." He pushes himself up from his chair, slides the file back to me, and walks to the door. "I'll be saying the same thing to Kelly, so find some time today to sit with her and decide how you'll do this."

He grasps the door handle, gives a tug, uses his foot to kick it further open, and is gone.

My bravado slides in a mucky pile to the floor and I lower my head to the table. Was I really so deluded as to think I could waltz back in wearing a horror mask for a face and have staff and clients eating out of my hand because I'm good at my job? My lungs constrict as a heavy blanket of anxiety drops over my face. I can't breathe, my head spins.

Suddenly, I'm trapped in a dark, swirling void. No escape. I flail for balance, falling into the deep emptiness. Flashes of light arc into my eyeballs and the fear intensifies. *Clear the mind. Breathe in, hold, breathe out. Breathe in, hold, breathe out.*

Finally, my airways relax and my breathing normalises. Objects in the room sharpen as I re-focus, but the sense of being trapped still vibrates the cells of my body. I can't stay in this office a minute longer. A glance at the clock on the wall tells me it's past my lunch hour. I know where I'm going.

As usual it takes a few seconds for my eyes to adjust to the dim lighting after the bright sunshine outside. It makes me wonder how many people topple down these stairs.

Gavin is in his usual spot at the bottom of the stairway and releases a slow wolf whistle as I descend. The effect is instant. As if I've fallen through the rabbit hole to a world where I'm no different from anyone else. Panic, grief, anger, indignation, all slip away.

"Ya know what, Layla? My mother used to tell me the story about the magical Lady of the Lake. She was dressed in white from head to toe and had an ethereal shimmer as she hovered above the water. She was the champion of every brave warrior, including King Arthur. It was my favourite story, but I haven't thought about it since I was a kid. Until you walked down the stairs."

For once my smart mouth has no answer. An embarrassed smile works its way across my face as I reach the last step. Still in Wonderland, I walk over to Gavin, bend down, and kiss him on the cheek.

"Thank you."

"Well, stone the bloody crows. Am I seeing things or is a white goddess kissing the cheek of a cruddy old toad?"

Gavin turns to face Clyde. "You just spoiled a beautiful moment, you fat bastard. I was about to ask her to marry me."

"She'd do better to marry a hopeless old codger like me than throw in her lot with you, Gavin, my boy," says the professor, from his shadowed alcove.

I wave my arm. "Hello, person being talked about is in the room."

"We know, darling. You've managed to claim all the attention while the rest of us are neglected," came a throaty voice from the bar. It's the woman who was there the first day I met Clyde. Lavender, that's her name. "You might glide in here like royalty, but be assured there's only room for one queen in this bar."

I'm not sure what she means, but it's clear I'm now one of the gang, so I make my way around the scattered metal tables and chairs and hold out my hand to her.

"We haven't properly met. I'm Layla. You're Lavender, aren't you?"

"Oh, a regular posh little miss, aren't we? It seems the others like you, so I'll take my chances." She holds out a large hand tipped with scarlet talons. "So love the turban, darling, but what's with *The Phantom of the Opera* face?"

I'm not sure whether to be flattered or offended. I wait for someone to jump up and admonish her for such an inappropriate reference to my scars. No one moves. In fact no one even seems to notice we're having anything other than a run-of-the-mill conversation. It's so refreshing, I smile. It seems whenever I come here, my spirits lift. And as candour seems to be the order of the day, I oblige.

"A house fire. All down my left side, including my arm and leg. Not a pretty sight is it?"

Lavender leans forward. "Darling, I'm a showgirl and anything interesting takes my fancy. Look at you. One side of you is an exotic, mysterious, dark beauty and the other side is a beast. Beauty and the beast in one neat package. Darling, I'm envious. I think I'm going to give you another name. Hmm, let me think." She taps one lethal nail against her cheek. "Ooh, I know, *Le Sourcil*: it means 'the eyebrow' as you only have one. Isn't it perfect?"

"You speak French?"

"Mais non, darling. I had a dear little French boyfriend back a bit and he taught me the names of all my appendages in French."

"The eyebrow? "

"Yes, yes, I know. He taught me things on the face as well."

Why is every conversation I have in this place like being at the Mad Hatters tea party? Why do I keep expecting the March Hare to lean over and refill my oversized teacup?

"You're a showgirl? What do you do, dance and sing?"

"I do all that, darling, and lots of naughty things too." One talon lifts my chin. "You should come one night. It would be an education for you."

She peers up at me through fluttering false eyelashes the size of outstretched birds' wings, spins on her stool, and crosses one well-muscled leg over the other. The tattoo I caught a glimpse of last time is a sapphire-blue triffid, which snakes up her lower leg. It gives me the opportunity for a quick change of subject.

"You've read John Wyndham?" She frowns at my question, so I point at her tattoo. "He wrote *The Day of the Triffids*. You know, like your tattoo."

"What's she talking about, darling?" She swings to face Clyde, her eyes narrowed.

Maybe I've insulted her by sounding like an intellectual.

Clyde places a drink in front of Lavender and lifts an eyebrow in question to me. I shake my head when he points at the white wine, and redirect his finger towards a bottle of mineral water. He zips off the top, half fills the glass, and turns his attention back to Lavender.

"The tattoo on your leg is out of a science fiction book called *The Day of the Triffids*, written by John Wyndham. I could get you a copy of the book if you like? Or the movie?"

"Well, how about that. I chose this because I liked it, but it actually has a story. Yes, darling, do get me the movie."

"Very good, Clyde, dear," trills a new voice behind me. I turn to see a middle-aged, roller-haired, sensibly-shod woman in a floral frock. The word dress doesn't cut it as a description. She could pass as a schoolteacher. She bobs her coiffed head at me.

"Hello, dear, I'm Mrs. Crompton." She then turns back to Lavender to continue the discussion. "Wonderful book. Mandatory for my Year Tens at the time." Good God, she *was* a schoolteacher. What on earth is she doing in here? "It's a post-apocalyptic novel, Lavender, dear, about a plague of blindness that afflicts the entire world, allowing the rise of an aggressive species of plant called triffids. I'll have my usual coffee, thank you, Clyde. How are you today, Professor?" she calls across the room.

The old man waves a hand in greeting, and Mrs. Crompton follows Clyde to a table where he places a large mug of coffee on a paper coaster. She picks it up and the look of pure ecstasy as she swallows a large mouthful seems exaggerated even for a coffee connoisseur. Clyde then gestures for me to follow him to the same table where we sat the other day.

I pull out a chair and sit, holding my mineral water. He remains standing, leaning his hands on the back of the chair next to me.

"You really do look lovely, today. White suits your olive complexion and dark hair."

"Are you channelling Alex Perry?" I snort. "Sorry, I never took you for a fashionista. And thanks for the compliment."

"There's a lot you don't know about our lad, *Sourcil*. Did you know he can sing like a choir boy?" calls out Lavender, listening unashamedly to our conversation.

"You sing? Have I stumbled into an enclave of entertainers who lurk all day at The Black Hole and come out at night like all-singing, all-dancing vampires?"

Lavender guffaws and holds up her glass. "*Sourcil*, you can be the *comédienne* of The Black Hole troupe. As long as your comedy loses its virginal flavour and heads down raunchy street."

The screech of a metal chair being scraped backward precedes Mrs. Crompton's input.

"I must insist you cease your attempt to corrupt this nice young woman, Lavender, dear. Just because your lovely young man allows you to flaunt yourself scantily-clad at that Silk Purse Club, doesn't mean Clyde will allow the same behaviours from his woman—what did you say your name was, dear?"

I open my mouth to call out my name, but she's already gone back to her coffee, or whatever is really in the mug. Lavender cackles happily.

Clyde's face is four shades of pink and I'm sure I match him shade for shade at the assumption I am *his woman*.

"Sorry, if she embarrassed you, Layla, but it's easier not to get into a conversation with Mrs. Crompton over the issue as she'll already have forgotten she said anything. Anyway, I imagine you came in for some of my barcological therapy rather than the enjoyment of our company."

He grins before turning to check no-one needs him at the bar, then straddles the chair, leaning his arms on the upright.

I'm not sure why I came in, but therapy of a sort is what I get every time I set foot in this weird place.

"You're probably right. I had a tricky day at work and couldn't think of anyone else I could tell about it."

He looks at me. "Oh? No boyfriend, family member?"

I can't meet his clear, honest eyes. "I suppose there is a boy-friend."

"You suppose?" He does his head tilt, shoulder shrug thing.

"God, I don't know why I said that. Yes, there is a boyfriend. Tom. Actually I work with him but so much has changed since the...this." I gesture at my face. Clyde waits for me to continue. "I feel disloyal even saying that. He's been wonderful, standing by me even though I'm now so different people stare and point. Poor Tom has to endure it as much as I do."

I can't believe I blurted all that out. I wanted to talk about work and end up whining about what has happened between me and Tom.

"So, Tom is finding it hard to cope with a girlfriend who was totally gorgeous to look at when the relationship started and is now a little blemished?"

I stare at him, about to berate him for such a simplification of everything Tom must be going through. Thing is, he's pretty close to the mark.

"I guess," is all I can manage. "But can we leave that for another time?"

"Definitely, especially as I now know there will be another time. So, tell me what happened at work."

When I finish the story, Clyde's pudgy knuckles are white from gripping the back of the chair.

"Those hypocritical bastards," he sputters. "You can't put yourself through that every day. There must be another job you can do; you must be highly qualified to be doing that work in the first place. For God's sake, Layla, you're too good for them."

He's right, and my parents would have backed him up without hesitation. But I must get the money for the operations and I don't have any faith that someone else will hire me looking like I do. There's no choice at the moment. Later, maybe.

"I think I might mosey up to this office of yours and stick a stiletto up their tight little arses, darling. And I'll bet a little background check on your Mr. President might uncover some unsavoury behaviours we could use to shut his narrow, judgemental little mouth."

Again, Lavender makes no bones about having listened to the entire conversation.

Instead of feeling indignant at such a breach of privacy, I am chuffed at her concern. A coil of warmth radiates from my chest at her willingness to spearhead an act of revenge against Mr. Su.

"As much as that suggestion sends the adrenaline rushing through my body, Lavender, I don't think it would do much for my professional reputation in the future. But it was a nice little visual for a moment there."

She slides off her stool and sashays over to where I'm sitting with Clyde.

"If you're not up for a delicious little act of revenge, then how about some fun?"

"Oh, I-I'm not sure. I don't think so. What do you mean anyway?" I stutter, confused and not a little dismayed at what she may consider as fun.

Clyde puts his hand on her arm. "Leave her alone, Lavender. I don't think she's like that. Your world and hers are different planets." He looks back at me. "Lavender's idea of fun would shock the socks off you."

She narrows her eyes, peers at my feet, and runs her gaze up to the top of my white turban. "Hmm, yes, darling, you might be right. I'd say *petit Sourcil's* life would have been very sheltered."

Now I feel indignant.

With a deep breath, I straighten my spine and look up at her— she is an extremely tall woman. "Is that what you think? For your information, I know how to have fun and have, in fact, engaged in quite risky behaviours in the past."

Squeals of raucous laughter burst from dark corners of the room. Lavender nearly chokes as tears pour down her cheeks and mascara streaks black lines to the corners of her mouth, like a clown. Gavin slaps his thigh in delight.

Even the professor's face has become animated and Mrs. Crompton calls, "Hush, hush, inside voices please."

I look to Clyde, positive he'll be on my side, but he's almost fallen off his chair, hooting with glee.

Lavender tries to speak and goes into hysterics again, grabs a serviette off the table, wipes her black tears, and tries again. "Risky behaviour it is then. Friday night at The Silk Purse. You're coming to watch my show, darling." She points at the professor. "I want to see you there too, darling. A nice shower and clean clothes from St. Vinnie's. Clyde will organise it—you're not on this Friday night, are you, darling?"

"Not anymore," yells Gavin across the room. "Am I invited too? I'll bring Mrs. Crompton. Although I'd rather bring Layla." He ambles over to the school teacher and gives her a quick hug.

"No offence, of course, Mrs. Crompton."

"None taken, dear. I'd love to come. My sister is such an old bore, and I don't mind watching Lavender dance and sing with those other nice girls. Although I do wish you'd wear more clothes, Lavender, dear."

I haven't been able to get a word in. My head swings back and forth as if I'm at a tennis match. Surprisingly, I feel a kick of excitement in my stomach at talk of Lavender's show. I haven't wanted to socialise since the fire, but this is different. This weird family of misfits has accepted me and to my surprise, I want to belong.

"What do you think, Layla? Will you come? Lavender's act is fantastic," says Clyde.

"I guess I can. I don't think I'm doing anything else."

I glance up at the clock on the wall and am shocked to see I've been here for two hours. I should have been back at work an hour ago. I tell Clyde I'll text him so he has my number, wave goodbye to the others, run up the stairs, and step back into the real world.

No sooner has the door slammed behind me than Godfather Guitar strums melodiously from my purse. A knot of panic forms in my stomach. It has to be someone from work. I stroke the screen and Tom's photo appears.

"Hi, Tom. On my way back now."

"Just like that? Calm as can be."

"What do you mean? I know I'm late but—"

"Late? Brian tells me about the abortive videoconference; you don't report back to Kelly. Then you disappear for nearly two and a half hours and no one has heard anything. Kelly even suggested you might have thrown yourself off the bridge. I was about to ring your therapist to see if he'd heard from you."

Report back to Kelly? I want to throw my phone against the nearest building and watch it splatter into a million pieces with Tom still blathering on about therapists and jumping off bridges. And I thought the characters in The Black Hole were weird!

"Well, you can relax, I went somewhere to sit and talk to a friend until I felt up to coming back to work."

"Who? Is it someone I know?"

A tiny spark of hope flickers in my chest. "Why? Are you jealous?"

Tom releases a long sigh. No, definitely not jealousy.

"It's obviously a male by that inane statement. Look, you talk to whoever you want to, but I'm only concerned about your welfare, and you could have at least let me know you were all right. I'll let Brian and Kelly know you're on your way back."

Now I'm really pissed off at him. "How about you let me do that? I'm a big girl, Tom. You worry about your job and I'll worry about mine. Thanks for the call, I'll talk to you later."

I press End Call before he responds. Or maybe he hung up before me and had no intention of responding.

The small bubbles of excitement and the relaxed, humorous sense of camaraderie, present only minutes before, evaporate into the yellow smog which hugs the tops of the buildings. But I'm not a quitter, so, pleased I didn't destroy my phone against a wall, I dial Brian's number and make a suggestion. He trusts me and agrees.

I turn in the opposite direction and head for Circular Quay. Even though it means I will need to put in a couple of hours work this evening, I don't have to go back with my tail between my legs and face big tits Kelly.

Or Tom.

CHAPTER 9

IT'S LATE AFTERNOON AND I'VE treated myself to a few hours on the beach with Bennie, a coffee on the Corso, and there's a vegetable stack in the oven, bathed in rich tomato sauce and drizzled with creamed corn. Time to pull out the laptop to review more ideas for Geong Steel's superannuation fund. My battery's low so I plug in and fire up the computer.

An electronic ping indicates emails. I scan the list and stop.

The work can wait, there's another email from Dr. Gassner's clinic in New York. I had sent photographs, taken when I was in hospital, of the damage on my face and body at different stages of healing. Then a recent one of only my face—a selfie I snapped with my eyes closed, so I didn't have to see it being taken. Yes, I think I just said that.

It wasn't from the famous doctor, but from an assistant who confirms receipt of the photos. He says Dr. Gassner has seen them, but states he can't properly assess either the damage to my skin tissue, or his ability to make a difference, without seeing me in person. Despite the reams of notes I scanned and sent to them, they would also like to speak with the team who operated on me previously. More delays, more red tape.

More time looking like this.

I reply, indicating I'll access the requested information and also set up communication between the clinic and the burns unit at Concord Hospital. How much easier it would be if I could jump on a plane and stand in front of them. And stay until they've remade my face. If I let my parents mortgage their house I could do exactly that.

Not something I'm prepared to do.

Enough moaning. My immediate goal is to find a way to res-urrect our reputation with Geong Steel and endear Stein and Laverick to Aquino Manufacturing in Brazil.

In my phone call with Brian, after I left The Black Hole, I agreed to co-operate with Kelly. If Miss Big-tits can re-ignite Geong's interest enough to request a proposal, I'll ensure she can offer Mr. Shit-faced Su something that will have him begging for our services.

Self-growth is good, right? This will be about working for the good of the team. The company will profit, the client will be happy, and I will have done my best. So why do I still have the manic urge to tip a bucket of iced water over Kelly's perfectly groomed blonde locks?

At eleven-thirty I close the laptop and crawl, exhausted, into bed. Tom hasn't called, but I'm too tired to even care. Sleep creeps blissfully over my body, relaxing all the tired muscles and I sink deeper into my soft bed...when the guitar chords of my phone strum me awake with a start.

"Hello?"

"Layla. It's me, Ruby. I need your help." I'm wide awake, my imagination leaping from disaster to disaster.

"What's happened, Rubes? Are you all right?"

"I sort of am, but Mum's going to kill me. I need you to come and pick me up so I can come back to your house and we can tell Mum I stayed there."

"What the hell are you talking about? It's a school night, why aren't you at home? Safe in bed. And why doesn't our mother know where you are?"

"Chill out, Layla. You sound parental." There is a pause. "Stop it, Levi, stop it," whispers Ruby but not softly enough.

"Who is Levi? And what are you doing with him at nearly midnight on Tuesday night?" I yell at the blameless phone.

"Settle, petal." Giggles, more whispering, and in the back-ground the deep, throbbing bass-vibration of head-banging music.

I'm tempted to tell her to phone Dad and deal with the con-sequences, but know I can't leave her in danger. She's definitely intoxicated, but from what, I don't know. As these thoughts spin in my head, I'm already pulling on jeans and a T-shirt and have grabbed my car keys.

"Address, Ruby."

"What's the address of this place?" she yells over the noise. There are unnatural giggles at the question. "What the fuck is the address?" Ruby demands. Someone must tell her because the next words are directed at me. "Dee Why, twenty-three Mason Place. We'll be waiting outside."

I'm in the car, backing out of the garage. "Correction, Rubes. There's no *we*. I'm picking *you* up, no one else. I'll be ten minutes." I hang up on her curses.

Luckily there's hardly any traffic and it's not long before I turn into Pittwater Road to head up the coast. My heart races with all the possible horrors that could befall my sweet fifteen-year-old sister before I get there.

A memory of Corinne expressing concern over some of the people Ruby hangs out with escalates my anxiety. Ruby's appearance the other night at dinner should have been a dead giveaway, but Mum had us all convinced it was merely teenage attention-seeking. Why wouldn't we believe her? She is after all the expert. And maybe there isn't too much to worry about.

I'll soon know.

Parked across the road from number twenty-three, I scan the scattered huddles of young people—some leaning against the fence, others lining the three concrete steps going up to the house and four stretched out on the lawn, giggling hysterically at the sky. But I can't see Ruby! I'm annoyed she's not waiting outside and push my hand on the horn. The only response I get for that is a number of middle fingers brandished menacingly towards the car.

I throw open the car door, thrust one leg out and stop. What am I subjecting myself to? It's no longer a matter of stalking in to find my sister. My entrance will be accompanied by drunken comments about my face. *Crap! This time I don't care.* Ruby's safety outweighs my sensitivities. As I reach the other side of the road I turn and hit the lock button on my keys. This is followed by raucous laughter at the implication I don't trust this bunch of space cadets.

Loud music shakes the small block house and my initial request for assistance is ignored. On the top step is a young teenager with hair gelled into spikes so sharp they could draw blood. I grab his arm and yell into his ear, "Where's Ruby?"

He peers at me through bloodshot eyes. "Who?"

I push past him. "Never mind."

Inside, the house writhes with a moving mass of sweating, tattooed, metal-pierced youths. The air is smoky and the strong, sweet taste of marijuana is thick on my tongue. Where the hell is Ruby?

Then I catch sight of her. She's wrapped around what can only be the love child of Tommy Lee and Lady Gaga. Even in the dim lights, metal piercings glint off his eyebrow and bottom lip. Both ears are adorned with black hatchet earrings which appear to slice through the ear—I'm hoping that's an optical illusion—and the upper half of one arm is heavily tattooed. I raise my astonished gaze to his hair—he looks like a startled cockatoo with a red crest. I shudder to think about the parts I can't see.

"Ruby!" I lurch across prone bodies and scattered furniture to rescue her from the dangerous punk.

"Whoa! Freakay, man," squeaks the redheaded cockatoo, pointing at my face. "Nightmare on Elm Street, man. What the fuck happened to you?"

"You think I look freaky? Have you looked in the mirror lately?" I clench my fist to stop myself smacking the little smart mouth.

"Shut up, Levi," snaps Ruby.

I grab my sister and drag her towards the front door. The cockatoo hops after us.

"Wait up, Ruby. The party's still shaking," he yells over the music.

We cross the road, and I throw open the passenger door, pushing Ruby in. She giggles and slaps at my hands. The boy follows and opens the back door.

"Out! You're not getting into my car."

I wrestle the door handle from him and push him back from the car. At the sight of our struggling, the kids milling on the lawn start to chant, "Fight. Fight. Fight." This sends Ruby into another fit of giggles.

"C'mon, Layla, don't be a spoilsport. Levi won't take up much room."

"No, you're right he won't, because he's not coming."

I manage to push Levi hard enough that he stumbles away from the car, giving me time to jump in, press the door locks and accelerate down the street. I'll find another way back to Pittwater Road without turning around in case Levi tries to wave us down and I'm unable to resist driving straight at him.

Ruby grumbles about abandoning 'poor Levi'. Too angry to respond, I switch on Ellie Goulding's "Burn" and, despite the irony of the song, sing at the top my voice. This not only drowns out Ruby, but keeps me from collapsing at the wheel from fatigue. My late-night resilience has diminished since the accident.

When we get home, Bennie throws himself at Ruby, excited at all the action this late at night. I send a message to Mum, which she'll see when she wakes, saying Ruby is fine, is spending the night with me, and I will get her to school in the morning. My sister has finally stopped her complaints and is now sulking. That's fine by me, as long as she goes to bed. I toss Ruby a pillow and bedding and direct her towards the spare room.

"Bed. Now. There'll be a discussion about this in the morning. And if you dare move from that room, I'll tell Mum everything."

She pouts. "You wouldn't."

I flash her a cynical grin. "Just try me, Rubes."

She raises her hands in surrender. "Fine. I got it."

I bury my head in my hands. Heaven preserve me from teenagers. For all my overt anger at Ruby, the relief at having her home and safe sucks the strength from my legs and I slide down the wall. Out of her sight.

Although I'm her sister, the age difference and her timid character—well, it used to be timid—have always given me a protective, even maternal instinct. Since she was born, I've felt a certain responsibility for her welfare. Matt was off with his mates, Corinne not interested, and Mum a bit too devoted to her professional principles of independent thinking and behaviour. Dad, well, he's a softie and we could all wrap him around our little fingers.

After forty minutes of tossing in bed, jumpy with anxiety because I need sleep to be able to perform at work tomorrow—or is it today, I glance at the digital clock. Clock watching is something I avoid once the light's out. I have this belief that if I don't look at the clock it won't be any later than when I looked at it last. One forty-five.

I punch my pillow as if a build-up of down on one side is all that's keeping me awake. That doesn't work. I lie on my left side, watching a perfect slice of moon reflect through the clouds, squashing the dark into corners and making comical shapes on the walls. My roaming gaze stops at a scrunched piece of paper on my bedside table. It's Clyde's phone number, tossed there when I emptied my pockets recently.

An insane idea teases at my mind. I clamp my eyes shut, counting passing cars. Twenty cars later, I open them and my hand snakes out to the piece of paper. Too bad I can't read it in this light and anyway, how rude would it be to phone a virtual stranger at this hour. But another voice counters that argument, saying he may have done a late shift at the bar and be happy to chat. The phone seems to have found its way into my other hand. I flick on the light, key in his number, and hit save into my contact list. Maybe a quick message.

Are you awake? It's Layla.

Within ten seconds a message comes back.

Sure. What's up?

Instead of messaging back, I dial his number.

"Hey, Layla. Nice surprise. Was about to listen to some jazz to slough off the bar vibes but talking to you is even better." I release the breath I was holding.

"I feel a bit embarrassed phoning you out of the blue and at such a shocking hour of the night, but I've been lying here trying to get to sleep and couldn't think of anyone else who might be awake."

"Something on your mind or was the thought of talking to me too much to resist?"

Before I can respond, the emotional build-up of my exhaustion, on top of finding my little sister in some sort of drug den, gurgles up my throat and turns into a sob.

"I-I'm s-s-sorry," I sniff, "I-I feel l-like an i-idiot." The sobs keep erupting and he waits quietly.

"Thanks, Layla," he finally says.

"Wh-why," I hiccough.

"I don't know. Crying on my shoulder, I suppose. It took some courage. What's happened?"

Clyde never ceases to amaze me. He doesn't suggest I stop crying or murmur platitudes about how everything will all be all right, he simply lets me be where I need to be. He'll regret it by the time I finish my sorry tale.

I tell him about all the work I've done to salvage the account and then the harrowing experience of extracting my innocent sister from punk city.

"At least she's safe and asleep in the other room," I whisper to him at the end of my litany.

"Do you think she was using more than dope?"

"I'm not sure. I don't think so. But others were; there was certainly heavier stuff being passed around. It's only a matter of time if that's the crowd she's hanging out with. I don't want to tell Mum. She's had enough heartache with me, but I can't let it go either."

"I know someone who may be able to help. It might give her a different perspective on the drug scene. What do you think?" he asks.

I sit up. "Really? Yes. Yes, definitely. Who is it and what can they do?"

"A friend of mine works with adolescents in a drug rehab centre. I'll have a chat with him. I'm sure he'll know what to do."

Tension seeps out of me. Of course there would be a solution, a way to keep my little sister safe. "When can we do it?"

"Well, we're all going to Lavender's show on Friday night, so not Saturday. Maybe Sunday if he's available. Unless that's too soon."

"Sunday's brilliant. The sooner the better. Each day between now and then I'll be worrying about what she's doing and with whom."

"Are we taking the redheaded cockatoo as well?"

"God, not if I can help it." I giggle. "But who knows?" We both pause. "Thanks, Clyde. I feel much better but still not at all sleepy. Can't imagine how I'll face tomorrow."

"Have you heard of Scheherezade and the 1001 Arabian Nights?" I nod, but of course he can't see that. He chuckles. "I can hear you nodding. Well, you get comfortable and I'm going to be your Scheherezade. I'm not much of a story-teller, but hopefully it'll bore you to sleep. When you feel yourself dropping off, turn off your phone and sleep."

"You'd do that for me?"

"Of course I would. Besides, I love the sound of my own voice."

Before I can respond, he starts on the tale of Ali Baba and the Forty Thieves. I snuggle down under the bedcovers, warm from the knowledge I have a new friend. The first person I've reached out to since my best friend from school days, Tegan, bent to her husband's demands to cut me loose. He said my face would give his precious offspring nightmares and Tegan should not have to bear the weight of my 'ill humour'.

☾

The next thing I know Ruby is shaking my leg. "Wake up! It's really late. Might be best if I skip school today."

I sit up, confused, trying to work out why Ruby is in my bedroom and why I feel like a truck has run over me. Then it all comes back.

I leap out of bed, entangling my foot in the sheets, and flounder on one leg, careening towards the wall. I slam my palms against the wall and turn as Ruby, grinning at my circus act, grabs my waist from behind and hugs tight.

"I love you, sis. You came out in the middle of the night waving your sword, fending off the bad teenagers. Thank you."

Clever move, Rubes. How can I carry out the planned parental dressing down when she's made me feel like marshmallow? Once my foot is disentangled and I'm upright again, I pull her into an embrace, stroking her still-soft hair. The bits not shaved and criss-crossed, that is.

"I'll always try to save you from bad teenagers, Rubes. And then when you get older, from bad men." I pull back from her and make eye contact. "But I think the bad teenagers are only part of the problem. It's the drug culture I'm wanting to slash at with my sword."

She lowers her eyes. "You're making a big deal out of nothing. It's all about experimenting and discovering who you are. Mum said so."

Desperate for a strong, black coffee, I grab her wrist and pull her along with me towards the kitchen.

"Well that makes it easier. If you're sure this is what Mum meant, we can tell her all about it and she can help you get to these parties. Easier than calling me in the middle of the night."

The coffee maker spits and splutters and I shove my cup under the spout.

Ruby's mouth hangs open and I can almost hear the cogs in her brain click into place.

"Mum might not have meant exactly that. You know, I might have misunderstood something. It would probably be better if we didn't tell Mum."

I widen my eyes in feigned innocence. "Oh, are you saying that maybe there's something not okay about this, Rubes?"

She kicks at the cupboard door, averting her eyes. "Sometimes you're really cool, Layla, and sometimes you suck. Anyway, I didn't do anything that bad."

The intoxicating aroma of my Vittoria organic blend soothes my fractured state and before responding to her ridiculous statement, I lower myself onto a stool. With both hands, I raise the mug of steaming coffee to my lips and close my eyes in reverence as the caffeine pumps through my system.

While I imbibe my drug of choice, she helps herself to cereal, fruit, and yoghurt and shovels impossibly large spoonfuls into her mouth. After three regenerative gulps of coffee, I place the mug onto the bench and face Ruby.

"I've got to tell you, Rubes, I don't even know you anymore. It's like this alien has inhabited your body." She swipes a blob of yoghurt off her top lip and licks it from her hand. "I want to know what you were using at this party."

"Will you be telling Mum?"

"I don't want to and I only will if I think you're in trouble."

"Is that the best you can do?"

"Right now I want to slap you. Then I want to scrub you clean, rip out the piercings and lock you in your bedroom until you're twenty-five. But I'll settle for hearing the truth and for you agreeing to some education so your future 'experimenting' is done intelligently."

"Sheesh, okay, but I can't guarantee the intelligent part." Her sense of humour always gets me and I have to turn away before she sees my grin. "It's just mainly smoking dope and I've used a bong a few times—Levi made it out of a plastic soft drink bottle." I try to keep my face blank. "I think Levi has taken acid or maybe ecstasy, but I'm not sure." The little shithead. I knew he was trouble. "And last night he said someone told him they would get him coke if we wanted to try that."

The coffee catches in my throat; I cough and splutter gasping for breath. When Ruby smacks on my back, I shove her hand away, and indicate for her to continue.

She hesitates as if she's going to add something and then shoves a spoonful of cereal into her mouth. Last night my mind had conjured up every worst-case scenario, and although she's only tried marijuana, Levi has dragged her into a dangerous environment where anything is on offer.

"My God, Rubes," I sputter, as soon as I can speak. "This is serious stuff. I'm stunned and I don't know what to say."

She takes her bowl to the sink and comes over, draping her arm around my shoulder and nuzzling into my neck like she used to do when she was small.

"I didn't really like it all that much. The joint didn't do anything at first and then I got a really mellow, happy feel. School's got harder too. I don't seem to be able to concentrate as much anymore and I want to get a good pass. Levi did speed one night when we were out together. I told him I didn't want to try it and he never pressures me. But he was really weird, hyperactive and couldn't sleep or eat, even after he'd been up all night." She pulled back from my neck, dragged a stool over and sat, facing me. "The thing is, I love Levi and this is what he does. If I don't do it too, I'm worried he won't want to be with me."

I take a breath and before I can say anything, she puts her finger against my lips. "Don't say it, Layla. You're going to tell me if he really cared about me, he wouldn't expect me to do this stuff. My friends have said it, but that's all logic, and right now I don't seem to be listening to my head, only to what I feel when I'm with him."

What do I say to that? Such a mature insight, but one that gives her permission to put herself in danger. It scares me, and also tells me, in the end, she'll do what's right. I'm just not sure what 'the end' will look like. Meanwhile, my mission is to change her mind about the drugs and that includes Levi. Looks like the cockatoo will be coming with us on Sunday.

"Rubes, I want you to meet a friend of mine. His name is Clyde and we're going on an outing on Sunday which will include you and Levi, if you want him there. It's to do with drug education and I need you to agree to do this."

She shrugs. "I suppose. I'll ask Levi. Not sure if he'll want to come." Then she does her puppy dog look at me. "And please can I not go to school today? I'm feeling sick."

"You know what, Rubes? I am too. Sick from worry about you; sick from no sleep, and sick from what I have to face each day when I go into work. But I've still got to go to work today and because you want to be a grown up as well, you have to go to school. I'll phone the school and tell them you'll miss the first two periods and you're going to get on a bus in fifteen minutes' time, go home, get into your uniform, and go to school. I'll be letting Mum know you're on your way."

Indignation at this perceived injustice, followed by resignation, flicker across her face. She sighs and heads to the bathroom. After retrieving my phone from the bedroom, I phone Mum, the school, and then my workplace to ask Kelly if we can bump a planned discussion back, as I'll be in a bit later this morning.

When I check appointments on my phone, I discover I have a session with Jarrod later this afternoon to work on my memory of the fire again. Even the thought of this on top of work issues and my fears for Ruby, sends a tingling sensation, like tiny stabbing knives, through my face and head. I drop onto the couch and take deep, slow breaths to stave off the dizziness and heart palpitations.

CHAPTER 10

IF I DON'T RUN I'M going to be late for my session. *Twang*. A message from Tom, who suggests dinner tonight. At my place. I answer with one word.

Okay.

At least I got through another day at work without a disaster like the one last week. The Korean clients were treated to a full visual of Kelly and agreed to forgive Brian for suggesting a face like mine could represent their organisation. That's my cynical version of events. The white-washed, official version states Brian and Kelly together, using my proposal, engaged the client's interest sufficiently to agree to the next step. Doubtless, the whole debacle gave Kelly a great deal of pleasure.

I clench my fists in anger at having to endure this demeaning situation, but remind myself to keep my eye on the prize. Banking is all I know and this is where my skills lie. The high salary I earn will take me to New York and the plastic surgeon, who will give me back my face and my life. Then I will mow Kelly down like a D9 bulldozer.

God, when did I get so nasty?

That's easy: the day half my face was burnt off!

❦

Jarrod hands me a glass of cold water with a slice of lemon. When I take a mouthful, the cold hits my sinuses. I press the palm of my hand on my forehead to ease the pain. With a sympathetic grimace, he reaches for the glass and places it on a table, out of my reach. Where I'm going, I won't need the water for a while.

"Make yourself comfortable, Layla." I grip the arms of the recliner and push back. "I know we've tried to look at the day of the fire a number of times already, without success. But we got so close last time, I have a feeling you might be ready today." I swallow back the rising fear, and take deep breaths as his voice overrides my internal chatter. "Now close your eyes and relax every muscle in your body," he says.

Frightened at where he is taking me, I try to resist the hypnosis, but he's too skilled and before long I'm floating, disembodied on a glass-surfaced lake, while snow-white birds coast above me on a warm up-current, and soft, fluffy clouds chase each other playfully across the sky. His voice is carried on the soft breeze as he guides me back to the night before the fire.

I had been out on an unintended bender with my best friend, Tegan, for her twenty-fifth birthday. I was supposed to stay sober to keep an eye on her while she let loose, so intended to stick to three glasses of wine. But someone pushed a cocktail into my hand and four cocktails later, I didn't know what I was drinking. I struggled home at about five o'clock and dropped, fully clothed, onto my bed.

The smooth timbre of Jarrod's voice suggests I focus on the events which followed, on that morning of January sixteenth. His words are seductive and I want to comply. But the fear is deeply embedded and the peace of floating above the lake appeals more than the terrifying events of that day.

"Take me with you, Layla. Tell me what you see."

I shake my head. He urges me again to relax and let go, coaxing me deep into trance until an image appears: again I'm standing in a corridor of doors. This time I will open it. The one at the end. Hands curled into fists, teeth clenched, I take a deep breath, and approach. Uncurl my hand and reach for the door handle. It morphs into a brick wall.

"What is it Layla?"

"Door's gone. Can't get through." Angry...beating my fists against the wall...not budging. Another entrance. Where? I run down the corridor. Not there. Panning the area, like a video camera. Then suddenly, engulfed by a black fog rising from the ground. I spin, out of control and drop to my knees.

"You're resisting, Layla. The memory is there. It's waiting for you. It wants you to access it. You can do it," says Jarrod.

Every fibre of my being wants to do as he bids. There is nothing I want more. Then suddenly, I am sucked away from the long corridor and into my old bedroom in Balmain. I can feel the hot sun beating through my window onto the bed, and when I try to move I'm caught in a tangle of sweat, last night's dress, and my cotton sheet.

A heatwave had been forecast for that day. Over forty degrees was expected; it must be already over thirty degrees. I untangle myself and stumble into the bathroom, my head whirling like I'm on a Ferris wheel, and suck water straight from the faucet. A glance in the mirror reflects dark indents under both eyes and two parallel lines down one side of my face from the fancy pattern on my pillow case. Black eyeliner and mascara streak my cheeks like a sad, painted doll and when I stick out my tongue, it reminds me of scum in a sink of dirty water. A pungent smell of alcohol is on my breath, mingling with remnants of cedar wood oil left on my skin from last night's shower. Then I am violently ill in the sink.

After rinsing my mouth, I clasp my stomach, my hands rasping against the rough lamé weave of my very small silver-grey cocktail dress. Squirming free of the clinging garment, I step into the cool porcelain bathtub and blast myself with a cold shower. A shrill bark penetrates my dull brain and I mumble unintelligible commands at my dog, Danger, to treat me with care.

To stay upright, I press one hand against the back wall of the shower, but as the room spins, nausea causes me to clamber back out of the bath. I fumble for a towel and, still dripping wet, slump to the floor with my head in the toilet bowl, retching until my stomach is squeezed dry. Draped over the bowl, I lose track of time. Finally my legs agree to hold my weight and I zigzag back to the bedroom, falling into the soft mattress.

As my eyelids drop over my eyes, something jerks a string in the back of my mind, but the tug is not strong enough to overcome the after-effects of the alcohol and I pass out.

An intense thirst draws me from sleep. Waving my hand in the general direction of my small bedside table in search of the water bottle, I register pulsing waves of heat. The mercury must be climbing through the roof, I've never known the room to be so hot. I crack my eyes open and am blinded by a glaring finger of sunlight spearing through the curtained window, unsympathetic to my self-inflicted state. My eyelids slam shut. Still flailing for the water, my arm knocks the bottle to the floor. The heat has sapped my energy and it's too much trouble to reach down and pick it up. Instead, I try to gather enough saliva in my mouth to swallow and relieve the thirst but my throat is so parched, it's like scraping the sides of a rusty old can. A deep breath leaves me coughing, my mouth filled with the taste of smoke. *Smoke?*

My eyes spring open again, but nothing is clear; a mist thickens the air. Not a soft, cooling mist, but hot, like a furnace, and I blink to ease the sting. I try to breathe. Heat sears the back of my throat. *Oh God!* Flames devour the curtains and feed off the end of my timber bed. Fear paralyses me and a scream wedges in my throat, stoppered by the thick smoke. I leap out of bed but the floor burns my feet and I hop from one foot to the other, before jumping back onto the bed. *Shut the bedroom door!* Must isolate myself from the fire. No, that's madness. The flames are here; licking around the bed towards me. I'm going to die and it's going to be the most horrific death imaginable.

Got to get out. I glance at the door, but the blistering paint cracks and pops as a wall of flames licks the wood. The glass doors onto the terrace. If I can get through them and call for help, I'll be safe.

I roll off the bed to the other side, but the doors are locked and my mind is too fuddled to work the lock. I'm losing strength. I pound against the glass. Can't someone hear me?

At this thought a violent jolt of shock shakes my body, but I don't know why. Is it something I see? Or hear? Oh, God, I can't bear the heat and my throat burns like the bed. A shrieking siren sounds outside. Help is coming. Then the flames rear up from my bed sheets and there is a shocking smell. The smell of flesh burning. I can finally scream and no amount of smoke can stop the bestial noises erupting from my throat.

The excruciating, unrelenting pain. I fall to the floor, rolling to extinguish the flames, and roll into my water bottle. In desperation, I rip off the lid and tip it over my head, but instead of cool relief, I am stabbed with a thousand knives. *I want to die. I want to die. I want to die.*

A cold finger on my forehead brings me back to the room, to Jarrod's concerned face looming over me, his lips pursed in a shushing sound as he calms my screams.

"Hush, Layla. You're safe. It's over. It's over."

He shifts the hair from my perspiring face, and hands me the glass of cold water. Between sobs, I gulp it as if I'm still burning and can't get enough water to stave off the heat. I shake and shiver, sloshing water onto the chair, and his hand circles mine to take the glass.

Relaxation music, played to calm me when the session began, still seeps from small speakers on the wall. The woody, slightly spicy aroma of frankincense oil, which weaves its way from an oil burner to my nose and taste buds, replaces the smell and taste of burning flesh.

Gradually, the shaking lessens and my heart rate and breathing normalise. Jarrod pats my hand and murmurs more soft assurances that I am safe. I have an urge to roar my despair and beat at him for putting me through something so horrific a second time. No-one should have to live it once, let alone twice. But at the same time I accept the logic of releasing the horror and fear. Besides, I wanted to know how the fire started. I asked him to do this.

"I am sorry you had to go through that again, Layla. Did it help? Were you able to see how the fire started?"

"There was something, but my memory won't bring it forward. A sound or…it's just out of reach…something gave me a shock; I was calling for help…no, it's too deeply suppressed." I thump my hands on the armrests in frustration, tears threatening again. "Damn. I went through it for nothing. I still can't remember!"

"I know you want to know what happened, but perhaps this is too traumatic after all and we would be better to find a way to move forward."

"No. I didn't cause the fire. They all think I did, by accident, but I didn't do this to myself. I didn't." I can't let go of this. For God's sake, I'm the victim here, not the cause of this horror.

"Alright, Layla. We'll continue, for now." He waits for my breathing to slow, handing me the water again before speaking.

"You remembered far more than you have before. And by opening yourself up to the whole event, you may have loosened more of that memory and another small trigger may bring it forward for you." He walks over to his desk and picks up a file. My file. "I received an email from Dr. Gassner in New York yesterday. He has looked over your pictures and read the notes and wanted my opinion on your mental state."

"And what did you tell him?" I ask, with forced calm.

"I said you might not be ready to hear a negative response from him."

I take a deep, slow breath. "Is his response negative?"

He closes the file. "Not at this point in time. Although, as he will tell you and your other doctors, he cannot be sure until he sees you in person." He locks his gaze with mine. "Can you go there, knowing he may not be able to help?"

My composure dissolves. "No! I won't give up hope of changing this." I gesture at my face. "I have to believe he can help. Don't tell me I have to learn to live with looking like a monster. I won't!" I sniff. "I can't." I jump from his mind-probing chair.

Non-reactive, as usual, he nods sagely. "I think we've had enough for today, don't you? All I am saying is you must be prepared for any outcome, or all the good work we have done will be for nothing." He walks me to the door. "The strength which made you the person you are will carry you through this. Our physical appearance is merely a shell, a vehicle to carry the true self—"

"Oh, no, doc, not the 'she might be ugly but she has a great personality' speech."

He tips his head to the side, his face inscrutable. "Let me explain." I stop, with one hand on the door knob. "Your internal self is the realm of your private thoughts and values; your capacity to love, and your deeper sense of purpose. The only success anyone needs in life is on the inside. The rest is about what others think of you based on their inadequacies, false beliefs, and negative experiences. Would you really want to live a life measured by the latter?"

I sigh. "Noble sentiments, Jarrod, and I'll give them some thought. But somehow I don't think I'm quite there yet."

He smiles and guides me through the door.

ⓒ

Hiding in a corner of the Manly ferry, I send a message to Tom. *Not sure if I can do tonight. Session harrowing.*
As we're docking he responds.
Only night I can do this week. Company might be good. Should I speak with your doctor?
I breathe back the annoyance from his patronising comment and shove the phone back into my bag, without a response. In the past his reply to such an invitation would have been: *Can't wait, coming now. Get naked.*
But I guess it's hard for him to manage too and I need to cut him some slack. I pull the phone out and message back.
Okay, come tonight. I'll cook vegie lasagne.
His response: *I'll come anyway.*
At least he still has his sense of humour.

ⓒ

"That wasn't bad for vegetarian."
Tom scrapes his plate for the last pieces of lasagne and leans back in his chair. I'd refused to discuss the session with the psychologist until we'd eaten and spent time discussing trivia like a normal couple. But are we a couple? Or am I his project: one that gives him karmic merit for later.
"So, how did the session go?" He refills my wine glass with the fruity Cabernet Merlot he brought, and I watch the deep garnet liquid swirl up the side of the glass, while I search for words to describe what I relived this afternoon.
"Horrible. Vivid. Real." I sip the wine to give me a moment to calm the shudder which jolts my upper body. "This time I was there. The fire was burning. It was hideous."
Tom reaches over and places his hand over mine. "No wonder you didn't feel like company tonight." He shakes his head. "How ghastly. Poor Layla, having to go through it again." Somehow

his response doesn't match the pain I endured this afternoon. I'm not sure what I expect from him. "Any indication of the cause?" he asks.

I slip my hand away to pick at a crust of herb bread.

"No. That's where it got hazy again. But I know there was something not right. I just got a hint of it."

Tom looks down at his plate. "Do you think you might be trying to find something sinister when it's not there?"

A slap across my face might have been kinder. How can I answer a comment that minimises something so critical?

I'm saved by the twanging rhythms of Godfather Guitar and I lean over to the sideboard to grab the phone.

"Hi Mum. I'm just finishing dinner with Tom." I glance back at him.

"I won't keep you, darling. Was wondering how you went with the psychologist today."

"Traumatic and not something I want to talk about on the phone." Especially not now. "Can I drop over later in the week?"

"How about Friday night for dinner? And I wouldn't mind your thoughts about Ruby, too. Not sure what is going on there, but I can't talk to her anymore."

This could get tricky. I don't want to betray Ruby's trust and certainly don't want to lie to Mum. But Friday is out anyway—I'm going to watch Lavender strut her stuff. God help me.

"Actually, I can't make it Friday. I'm going out after work."

"Oh? With Tom?"

I glance over at Tom, who, although searching the iPod for music, has one ear tuned to the conversation.

"Er...no, just some other friends."

I don't know how to explain the gang from The Black Hole. Not to Mum and certainly not to Tom. Luckily, Mum gets the hint.

"Obviously you don't want to tell me with Tom there, so I won't ask more questions now, but you can bet I'll ask them later," she says. "How about Sunday?"

"Mmm, not Sunday either. I'm doing something with Rubes."

"Oh? She never mentioned that to me. I'll ask her about it tonight."

I groan. How did I ever think I could keep any of this from my mother? "I'd rather you didn't ask her, Mum. It's a sister thing. I thought she needed some big sister time, so we're having the day together. Can we leave it at that?"

"All sounds very mysterious, but with her current attitude I think that's a great idea. Let me know when you have time to visit. Anyway, I'll see you when you pick Ruby up for your sister time. Love you, darling."

"Yes, you will. Love you, too."

I place the phone back on the bench. Tom's frowning concentration on the words of John Legend's "Redemption Song" tells me he's pretending not to be interested in where I'm going Friday night. Probably due to the fact I never go out. Not with him, or girlfriends, or family. I stay in or go to my parent's home. He looks up as I scrape back the chair to sit down.

"That was Mum," I say, not elaborating on the Friday night comment. In my new world of powerlessness, I pathetically take power where I can.

"I gathered as much. How is she?"

"She's good. A bit worried about Ruby, though."

"I couldn't help overhearing you're spending the day with your sister on Sunday. Just the two of you?" My heart does a twirl with delight at his curiosity about my activities.

"Not sure yet. Maybe one of her friends as well."

I'm surprised at my reticence to tell him anything about Ruby's activities. Perhaps I don't want him to judge her by his high standards. Or don't I trust him with this information? While I'm silently debating this in my mind, Tom picks up both our plates and takes them out to the kitchen. When he returns, he passes close by the back of my chair, flicks the end of my ponytail, and sinks down into the stuffed armchair. Like a husband after a hard day's work. I wish.

The lilting tones of Katie Melua singing "Piece by Piece" drift from the surround sound and I have a desperate longing to dance in Tom's arms. It was something we often did after dinner, when he still enjoyed pressing up against my face and body. The longing is almost a physical ache and I can't resist standing and holding out my hand.

He fidgets like a young boy and a hot flush creeps up my neck and cheek. *Crap.* He's going to refuse my request. Then, as if he's changed his mind, he heaves himself out of the chair, grasps my hand, and swirls me around him, pulling me into his arms as I complete the turn. I feel like a real woman again—desirable, delicate, and feminine. A moment like this has been my fantasy for more than a year; it is unbearably exquisite.

Instinctively, I press my cheek against his and freeze. Too late. It's the scarred side of my face. Maybe he won't care. He shifts imperceptibly and runs his hand down my shoulder…oh God, that's the scarred arm. His hand lifts and skims above the skin until it reaches my hand and he twirls me out and away from him, then back, briefly, and away again. The moment of intimacy has passed—if it ever existed. Perhaps it was all in my mind.

To put him out of his misery, I pull my hand away and flop onto the couch as if I've had enough. Difficult as it is, I even manage a smile, so he doesn't feel uncomfortable about his inability to see past the scars.

"Are you staying tonight?" I ask, unable to resist a small payback.

He averts his gaze, picking at the piping around the armchair. "I'd love to, but I've got a breakfast meeting and don't want to disturb you early. I could come Friday night."

Is he kidding? It's clear he's not comfortable staying, but at the same time he needs to know what I'm doing on Friday night. My immediate urge is to retain the mystery, but then reject this. If I don't explain it becomes a game of subterfuge.

"I'm sorry, but I'm going out with a couple of friends I've met from one of my support groups on Friday night."

Only a slight deviation from the truth. Especially since I hate support groups.

"You probably won't be late. I could come over after."

I'm trying to keep my expression neutral. My mother always said my face gives me away when I lie.

"I might be late. One of the others is organising where we're going, and I'm not sure what that will entail yet. I'd rather not watch the clock worrying about you being here on your own."

I'm about to suggest he come Saturday night when I remember I'm meeting Clyde Sunday morning with Ruby and Levi, the cockatoo.

"Do you think these friends are healthy acquaintances, Layla?

It mightn't help if all they do is remind you of your accident."

I flutter my eyelashes at him. "Are you sure you're not jealous?"

His eyes flick to the ridged scarring on my face. Choked with humiliation at his unspoken response, I rush from the room, down the hall into my bedroom, slam the door, and lock it behind me. Only then do the tears flow.

Within seconds Tom knocks on the door. "Let me in, Layla. You've misunderstood something again. I can't explain myself if I don't know what I've done."

I walk to the door and lean my forehead against the cool timber. "Tell me, Tom, when you look at me, what do you see?"

"What are you going on about? I'm not going to answer that."

"Please, humour me."

I hear a sigh of frustration from the other side of the door. "I don't know what you want me to say, but...alright, I see a person who's been badly injured and gone through a lot of pain. Someone who is angry and sad, even irrational at times but a nice, generous—"

"Please go home, Tom. I didn't misunderstand anything," I respond, my throat clogged with emotion.

Even now I hope he'll say he loves me and doesn't want to leave. That my appearance makes no difference to him. But all I hear is another sigh of frustration, followed by his retreating footsteps and a soft thud as the front door closes behind him.

CHAPTER 11

IT'S FRIDAY AFTERNOON. I'VE SPENT the week hiding in my corner, studying current and prospective client files, and responding to Requests for Proposal. In collaboration with big tits Kelly, of course.

And I've made a decision. On Monday I'll tell Brian I want to be the front person with clients of my choosing, not Kelly's. Brian will question the decision. For God's sake, even I'm questioning the decision. But I have to show I'm capable of doing the job. The whole job, and not as Kelly's unseen shadow. This neat slot which hides me from prejudice and censure doesn't fit, even under my present circumstances.

It's an inherent characteristic. I was raised to believe I can do anything, and despite all my fears, it seems I have to prove to myself I can do this. And maybe I have to prove something to Brian and to the people who stood in the conference room that first day, congratulating me on my courage.

Tom and I have been cordial with each other, and he's tried to apologise. However, the attempt was preceded by the words 'I don't know what I've done but...' We even had lunch yesterday but could find nothing to talk about except work, my next appointment with the psychologist, and the weather. We both steered clear of my social engagements for the weekend. How sad that we've been reduced to this.

❦

Tonight is Lavender's show. I'm having second thoughts. These people are practically strangers, and I've agreed to traipse after them to an unknown venue to watch a mystery stage show. The words 'raunchy' and 'risky' have been thrown around. How raunchy? How risky? It might be terrible. Or worse, I might be subjected to jeers and insults from strangers in the club. On cue, my breathing catches and I open my mouth, gasping for air. *Breathe in, hold, breathe out.*

Clarissa, finished for the day, stops near my desk. "Are you all right, Layla? Can I get you something?"

I wave her away and she backs across the room, her eyes fixed on my face. The woman appears genuinely concerned. Not that I care at this moment. *Breathe in, hold, breathe out.*

This outing isn't going to work. It's a stupid idea. When I shut down my computer I'll head home. At least I've come to my senses before parading my paranoid, disfigured self out on the town, and making a complete fool of myself. Relieved, I reach for my bag, and as I loop it over my shoulder, it strums for attention. Do I want to answer the phone? A glance at the screen indicates it's Clyde.

"Hi. I was about to phone you," I say.

"Good timing then. We're all grabbing some dinner before going out. Lavender doesn't come on until after ten."

Crap. He sounds so happy about the outing.

"I was thinking I might not come after all."

Clyde doesn't miss a beat. "Do exactly as you like, Layla. I don't want you to feel pressured into coming. We'll miss you, though, especially Gavin. I think he was going to ply you with alcohol and propose again."

"Near miss then." The tension seeps out of my neck and shoulders.

"Well, in case you change your mind, we're meeting at the Dragon Palace, the Vietnamese restaurant in Oxford Street near the hotel; around seven-thirty. Gavin and I are buying for Mrs. Crompton and the professor."

"In that case, I hope the professor's had a bath."

Clyde snorts at the comment. "You can be sure Mrs. Crompton will let him know whether his personal hygiene meets her standards."

As usual I'm completely comfortable chatting to Clyde. What

if I regret my decision not to go? These people are the only friends…are they friends?…I have socialised with who didn't know me before. Which means I don't have to excuse or compensate for what I am.

"You know what? I think I will come after all."

I have a change of clothes with me but am debating what to do between five-thirty and seven-thirty. It's too far to go home; I could stay at work or sit in a park.

"If you're at work, Layla, we could have a drink before the others join us, so you don't have to hang around like a wet sock until seven-thirty. I've just finished my shift." Is this man magic? A leprechaun—a very big leprechaun? Or a mind-reader. "Do you know the Grapevine? It's not far from Oxford Square."

"Is it dark?"

Clyde chuckles. "So dark I'll need you to whistle the James Bond theme tune to identify yourself."

"Sounds dark enough. Meet you there in about forty minutes." A smile lingers on my lips as I end the call.

*

Oxford Street, venue of the annual Gay and Lesbian Mardi Gras, is alive with early evening shoppers, tourists promenading the famous nightlife strip, and office workers out for a few Friday night drinks. I'd loitered in Hyde Park for fifteen minutes, but still arrive earlier than anticipated. Outside The Grapevine, my heart rate escalates at the thought of stepping into a trendy bar on my own, even a dark one, then hanging until I can spot Clyde. I close my eyes and take three deep breaths.

"Hi Layla. Good timing. I just got here myself." He steps from the road onto the footpath.

Definitely a leprechaun.

We make our way into the bar and I experience a twinge of discomfort at being beside Clyde instead of Tom. But the discomfort has nothing to do with being out with someone else, it's about how Clyde looks. His belly bulges over the top of his trousers, battling to escape the confines of his button-up shirt. And his soft jowls threaten to engulf his shirt collar.

I swallow the acid taste of my hypocrisy, ashamed at this ironic and shallow inability to separate the person from their physical appearance. This man is my friend; he's shown me nothing but kindness.

I can't make eye contact.

He ushers me in and smiles down at me with unmistakable pride at having me on his arm. I have an urge to stick something sharp into my eyeballs—it's what I deserve.

"You look amazing, Layla," he says, appraising my figure-hugging black tunic top. It has red panels down each side, a high mandarin collar, and long sleeves—always long-sleeves. To cover the scars on my left leg, I wear black tights and knee-length soft, grey boots. My hair is capped with the obligatory headscarf: tonight's is black with silver beading on one side.

"Thanks, Clyde. Nice of you to say so."

Lame response, I know, but I've become so unused to compliments about my appearance, I can't think of anything else to say. With my head lowered, I seek out a table in a dark corner, while Clyde gets our drinks.

People stream into the bar, and I watch Clyde weave through the milling bodies trying to keep the drinks from spilling. A few patrons make derisive comments at how much room Clyde needs to get through the crowd, and I'm surprised to see him laugh, unaffected by their rudeness.

He puts my white wine on the table, and flops onto his chair.

"You know, Clyde, I heard some of the remarks from people when you were coming back from the bar, and was surprised at how you reacted." He raises his eyebrows, obviously unaware of his own reactions. "Well, you didn't get upset or angry at their rudeness. I think I would have."

Clyde sucks the foam off his ale and leans back in his chair. "Oh, that. Why would I get upset? I never take that stuff personally. Probably had a bad day and I'm a good-sized target."

Part of me admires the nonchalant way he deflects aspersions on his size, and part of me is annoyed that he appears to do nothing to change himself.

"You have a fierce look in your eyes, Layla. Let me guess. You don't understand why I wouldn't simply lose weight to stop the teasing." My hot flush of embarrassment must be visible even in the dark room. "Looks like I hit the target," he says with a grin.

Damn it, he could do exactly that, though. Lose weight to stop the hecklers.

"You can't blame me. Here I am sentenced to a life time of being subjected to taunts, judgement, and rejection through no fault of my own, and I would do anything it takes to change it. All you have to do is go on a diet, and you don't do it. You seem to prefer how you are." I clap my hand to my mouth. What have I said? "God, Clyde, I'm so sorry. That was incredibly insensitive and not something anyone should say to a good friend."

He frowns, regarding me in silence. I hold my breath, waiting for his customary acceptance, which has so far allowed me to retain the prejudice I have about his weight. Talk about people in glass houses.

"I am what I am, Layla. If the time comes that I choose to change that, I'll do it for myself, not because society or my friends are offended by how I look."

Unable to respond, I bury my face in my glass of wine, wishing I was at home with Bennie, who allows me to air all my prejudices about myself, and others, without a word of admonishment. Still sipping my wine, I feel Clyde's warm hand grasp mine and squeeze it. When I look up he has a wide grin on his face and the knot in my stomach relaxes.

"The thing about friends is they can say what they think, so when you said I was a good friend, I knew I could kick back and let it rip," he said.

"Bastard," I mutter.

The air is clear again, but his words stay with me. How I wish I had his strength. It's my shout, so I hand him some money and let him run the gauntlet once more. He can handle the embarrassment better than I can.

When Clyde returns with the second round of drinks, I ask him more about the strange group we're having dinner with. To my surprise, I learn the professor was one of his lecturers at university, and Clyde is well acquainted with the old man's family, who no longer acknowledge the professor.

"I didn't know you went to university. What did you study?"

"Law."

I must have misheard, it's so noisy in this bar. "I'm sorry, did you say law?" He nods and takes a mouthful of his beer. "But you're working in a bar. Shouldn't you be sitting in a nice office billing people every time you fart?"

"Hmm… Exact question my mother asked. Without the fart reference. When I didn't immediately go into a commercial legal practice, she was distraught, telling me I was throwing away the opportunity to be wealthy and respected. She actually said I'd never get a decent job."

I can't resist the obvious response. "And how wrong she was— look where you work." He chuckles. "Anyway, back to the professor."

"A great man and a great teacher. He'd been a closet alcoholic for many years. Finally his wife couldn't take it anymore. She left him and that removed the one element of stability he had. He ended up being fired by the university, drank himself deeper into ruin until his two daughters became so ashamed of him, they disowned him as well. I think after that he didn't care and the drinking became a suicide mission."

"You must have been close to him when he was your lecturer?"

"He was incredibly wise and I loved him like a father. I'd never had one, so I wasn't really sure what they were supposed to be like. We lost touch when he left and I hadn't seen him for years until he wobbled into The Black Hole one day. I guess I now see it as my mission to look after him."

"I like him," I say. "He might guzzle the grog like a mindless siphon, but his wisdom and mental acuity snap from his eyes. When they're not too bloodshot." Clyde chuckles. "What did he say when he saw what you'd done with your studies?" I give him a playful poke in the ribs, so he knows I'm not serious.

"He looked shocked at first and then he laughed until the tears ran down his face. When he could finally speak again, he said, 'So glad you decided not to take life too seriously, my boy.'"

"I like him even more," I say.

Twisting my wrist to check the time, I discover I'm still clasp-ing Clyde's hand. It feels natural.

We arrive at the restaurant only minutes before Gavin walks in with the professor and Mrs. Crompton.

The professor sits next to me at the table, looking vulnerable in his second-hand suit and his washed hair, plastered flat on his head. Without thinking, I lean over and kiss his forehead. The dear old man's neck and cheeks flush and although his lips move, he's unable to form a coherent response. Which makes me want to kiss him again, but I refrain; I don't want to embarrass him further. A hovering waiter relieves the tense, silent moment and we give him our orders.

Clyde is deep in conversation with Gavin and Mrs. Crompton, so I edge my chair closer to the professor.

"Clyde tells me you were his lecturer at university."

His hand flutters in his lap. "Oh, dear me, that was a lifetime ago. He was one of my favourite students, you know."

I reach for his hand and place my other hand over his to soothe him. "Are you disappointed he isn't doing anything with his studies?"

The professor looks at me with surprise. "Oh, but he is. Well, he didn't at first. Wasn't interested in joining a law firm. But then he spent a few years in a community legal centre. And of course he's doing the PhD." *What?* "On the efficacy of alternative dispute resolution with young offenders. I think he works in the bar almost as a hobby." He notes the shock on my face and his eyes reflect concern. "Oh dear, I hope I haven't spoken out of turn. He hasn't told you, has he?"

"No, he hasn't. He has happily let me believe he's not tried to make anything of his life." I draw in a breath and huff it out angrily.

The professor extracts his hand and places it on top of mine as if he is now the soother.

"Even if he wasn't studying, he's made a wonderful success of his life. He's a good man who has helped so many people." He grins. "I'm one of his projects, you know."

I nod. "I know he regards you very highly, Professor, and I apologise for my stupid comment. I seem to have a bad case of foot in mouth disease tonight. I think I might be one of his projects too," I add, with a wink.

Before I can delve further into Clyde's life, two waiters appear brandishing plates of steaming food. The sweet and salty, yin-yang fragrances of cilantro, mint, fish sauce, star-anise, garlic, and eye-watering chilli bring a halt to the conversation as we stare, like predators, at the delicious fare. In hungry silence, we reach across each other piling our plates from the hot, aromatic selection.

The old man scoops up a forkful of beef noodle salad, closing his eyes in ecstasy as he chews. Once he swallows, he continues our conversation. "If you're not one of his projects, he certainly cares about you. Clyde is a good friend to have."

"Yes, I'm learning that."

I dip a spring roll in chilli sauce and continue eating while the professor attacks a bowl of pickled bamboo and chargrilled carp. The spicy, sweet smells of the food form a comfortable fug around us as we talk.

"Professor, can I ask you something about Clyde's family?" His mouth is full so he nods. "A few times he's alluded to the fact his mother doesn't particularly care for him. I just wondered what he meant."

While he tries to swallow so he can answer, sauce dribbles from his mouth down his chin. I reach over and dab at it with a paper serviette. He smiles his thanks and it seems our relationship shifts with this random act.

"It's probably not my story to tell and I don't want to gossip," he says.

Of course, he's right, and I wave away any further response. But he leans over with a mischievous glint in his eyes.

"However, I don't want you to think he's…what do you young people call it? A loser?" He nods, satisfied with the word. "Yes, a loser. He's definitely not that."

I open my mouth to say that's not what I think—knowing that's exactly what I had thought before tonight—when he speaks again.

"His father didn't want the responsibility of children and walked out on the family when Clyde was very young. I think his brother, Tyler, is the definite favourite." I nod in agreement, my mouth stuffed with pickled bamboo." Unfortunately, the few times I've met his mother, she couldn't let an opportunity to criticise Clyde pass. The fact he's as genial and as balanced as he is attests to his incredible strength of character." He leans closer to my ear. "I'd make a good guess, that's the reason for the weight. Protection against his mother's criticism." He glances over at Clyde with an unmistakable look of affection. "Somehow, though, he wouldn't be Clyde without it. And we all like him exactly as he is."

I dip my head to hide a guilty flush of shame. I don't deserve to be included in the *we* he refers to.

My judgement about his weight makes me no better than his mother.

CHAPTER 12

CLYDE PUSHES OPEN THE DOOR of The Silk Purse, and I blink to adjust my vision to the mist of orange and yellow light painting the walls and floor. Rainbow banners and pennants flutter from the walls and ceiling, where coloured balls dangle at different heights. Gaudily dressed women and scantily dressed men gather in clusters, screeching with laughter, their arms draped around each other. The atmosphere is technicolour, edgy, and loud.

I sidle up to Clyde. "Is this a gay bar?"

"All that and more, my friend."

I swallow the nervous flutter in my chest and glance at Mrs. Crompton, who stifles a yawn. It's past her bedtime.

Gavin waves us towards an empty table while he goes to the bar. Before he can hack his way through the crowd, a harassed young man grasps Clyde and the professor by their shirt sleeves. With dramatic hand gestures, he insists we all follow him to the dressing rooms, babbling about an emergency and Lavender being 'in a terrible state.'

"She said I couldn't miss you," he says. "She said to look out for a big, fat bastard, a dark haired woman with a scarred face, a seventies throwback, a smelly old man, and someone who looks like my second grade teacher." He waggles his hands in agitation. "I thought you'd never get here."

We look at each other, not sure how offended to be by the callously accurate descriptions. Curiosity wins out and we all traipse after him.

He opens a door and we walk into a scene of unmitigated chaos. Amazonic women balancing high, plumed headdresses are running to and fro in tight skirts or tiny, lamé shorts, waving feather boas, and screeching indignantly at anyone who steps in their path. But the loudest screeches, or wails, come from the far corner where Lavender stands in all her glory, stamping her feet like an angry child. Next to her a large man in a sequined costume with purple glitter eye-shadow, bird-wing eyelashes, and a wide, very red mouth tells her to 'shut the fuck up!' The man then pulls on a long, curly red wig and suddenly I'm looking at a woman. I spin my gaze around the room and, as if I've squinted to view an optical illusion, I realise I'm not in a room full of tall, muscled women, but a room full of men dressed as women. Clyde and Gavin look at my gaping mouth and roar with laughter.

"You didn't know?" asks Gavin. I shake my head. "I can't believe she didn't know," he says to the others. Even tight Mrs. Crompton isn't surprised to find herself in a dressing room with a gaggle of drag queens.

"Will you stop entertaining yourselves when my whole life is in peril," screams Lavender, as she slumps into a chair. "Focus, you miserable cretins."

How did I miss her bobbing Adam's apple?

"What a lot of noise you're making, Lavender," tuts Mrs. Crompton. "What has happened?"

Lavender leaps to her feet, knocking the chair backwards against the kneecaps of a passing queen, who curses, punches Lavender in the arm, kicks the chair out of her— or is it his, way—and keeps walking.

"Stupid bitch," hisses Lavender. She turns to face us. "My whole act is ruined. It all depended on singing backup from three morons who haven't shown up. I'm ruined. I'll be a laughing stock." She throws her arms around Clyde's neck and howls.

He grimaces at us over her shoulder and pats her back. "Well, change the act. You have an extensive repertoire. There must be something different you can do." She howls louder. "What can we do to help?" He grins and adds, "Mrs. Crompton might know a bawdy tune or two."

Lavender stops howling and pushes away from Clyde. "That's it! You'll all have to help me." A shiver runs down my spine and the professor's eyes widen in terror.

"Clyde, you'll have to sing and you," her crimson talon points directly at me, "you'll be perfect. Can you dance?" I shake my head vehemently. "It doesn't matter. They'll be looking at me anyway. Don't move any of you."

She rushes over to a large walk-in cupboard filled with costumes, while I check out the exits for a quick getaway. Before I can sneak out, she's back and has me by the arm.

"Here, put this on." She thrusts a black and white domino-style costume at me. "And put this on your face." She holds up a *Phantom of the Opera* mask and again demands I get changed and stop 'fucking around' or she'll dress me herself.

I push the clothes back at her. "I'm sorry, but I can't go out there. Not in front of all those people. I'd like to help, but not this."

I back away thinking it's over when Lavender, a wild look in her eye, leans into me, almost spraying me with her saliva as she gives me a sharp slice of her opinion.

"So, you want to keep leading that sorry excuse for a life you've clung to since this," she sweeps her arm to encompass my face and body, "…this accident? Where's your backbone, girl? Where's your *joie de vivre*, your *grab life by the balls*, your *fuck the system*?" Her voice is rising with each word. "Will you lie on your deathbed and whimper, 'I wish I'd been even more ashamed of myself? Will you—"

"Oh, for God's sake, give me the fucking clothes."

I snatch them back and march to a screen. I need privacy. As I turn to throw Lavender a malevolent glare, a sly smile creases her powder-packed face. Damn. She played me, manipulated me to react exactly as planned.

Before I disappear behind the screen, I see her thrust a pair of black tights and a crimson velvet doublet with puffed sleeves at Clyde. The look of horror on his face sends the others into hysterics and I send a quick prayer of gratitude to the god of drag queens that I got the costume I did. Clyde refuses to budge and tells Lavender what she can do with her costume.

I call out, "If I have to do this, so do you."

He knows what a huge undertaking something like this is for me and, as if he's going to the execution block, he bows his head and moves to a secluded corner to change. I think Gavin might be in danger of wetting himself if he laughs any harder.

"Now you, Gavin, take the other two out the front and when

we come on, you cheer and applaud until you're hoarse."

The others trip over each other in their haste to leave, in case she changes her mind and decides to include them in the act as well.

It takes me some time to remove my boots and tunic top, as I continually check to ensure no-one is privy to my scars. But in this environment, no-one pays me the slightest bit of attention. I pull on the domino costume, leaving my head scarf on to cover the bald patch.

The costume is black on my good side with a thin, spaghetti strap and tight leg. The opposite side, which is white, is loose and flowing with a long sleeve and full pants, gathered at the ankle. It works to cover the scars on my body. I twist the half-face mask until it sits the right way, pull the elastic around the side of my head and tuck the top of the mask under my scarf. When I look in the mirror, I'm entranced.

The right side, the unscarred side, is the face I've seen in the mirror all my life: eyebrow intact, skin smooth and unblemished and hair thick and glossy. Now, hidden behind a mysterious, white, diamante-studded mask, the scars on the left side are invisible. There's nothing to indicate the shocking ravages which lie beneath the mask. As long as you don't glance at my neck, that is. It's the best I've seen myself look since before the doctors unwrapped me from my cocoon of bandages. I'm still admiring myself in the mirror when Lavender charges over and grabs me by the arm.

"I need you to sing with me. Do you know "Dancing Queen"?"

Abba? She couldn't be so heartless.

"Everyone knows it. Unfortunately."

"What did you say?"

I shake my head in denial of having said anything against the immortal group.

"How does a rather large seventeenth century fop fit with "Dancing Queen"?" I ask, indicating Clyde, half hidden behind a rack of clothes. Lavender is decked out in a sleek, white cat-suit, a la Agnetha, with a cape and a long, blonde wig.

"Don't get picky, darling, it was the only costume big enough. Besides when he starts singing, they won't care what he's wearing."

On cue, poor Clyde walks out in his very tight tights and hip length doublet with a white wig balancing on his round head. His jaw is clenched tight and his hands are white-knuckled fists. Lavender hustles us to the wings of the stage, but I can't make eye contact with Clyde without collapsing into giggles. He looks so hilarious, I almost miss Lavender's introduction.

"Ladies and Gentlemen. Mesdames et Messieurs." The tall, thin emcee winks at the audience and adds, "Yes, we are multi-lin-gual here at The Silk Purse." He pauses for effect, draws a deep breath, and gestures to the side stage. "It is the time you have all been waiting for. She's the madam of plight, and the passion in the night. She's the exotic and the erotic; she's the softness in yin and the swelling of yang; she's the 'q' in mystique and the 'Oh' in a good bang. She's as sultry as the Tango, with the sweetness of mango; she arrives incognito and leaves with your libido. Ladies and Gentlemen, it's time for a little one hand clapping, as the other hand is going to be a little preoccupied. Please give a very warm welcome to Miss Lavender La-bia."

The audience is in a frenzy of expectation. And with a tap on my nose with her lethal fingernail, Lavender says, "Show Time," and sashays onto centre stage. She moves in time with the beat of "Dancing Queen", thrusting her white, lycra-clad hip to the left and right and shimmying the belt of silver bells dangling below her waist. Clyde and I exchange frazzled looks. We're about to prance about on a stage in front of over a hundred people who will either adore the act or draw blood, depending on their moods.

After lip-syncing the first verse and chorus of the Abba song, Lavender caresses the microphone while swinging her hips back and forth and whispers to the audience.

"Dahlings, I have a wonderful surprise for you tonight; two surprises in fact." She grinds her hips to the husky sound of Frida's voice and continues. "I have, waiting in the wings, a beautiful, but sad creature." I squirm at being called a sad creature and Clyde whispers that he can only imagine how she will introduce him. "It is the beauty of the beast; from the tragic to the magic." She winks at the emcee as she mimics his earlier introduction. "From the ashes to the lashes, from the highbrow to the eye-brow, from Madam Butterfly to the watery eye." There is loud laughter as her description becomes more ridiculous. "Give me a break," she growls into the mic. "From the fires of hell, I give you, *Mam'zelle Sourcil.*"

She gestures wildly for me to dance onto the stage. Clyde gives me a shove and there I am, moving to Abba, throwing my hips around and flicking my hair around my masked face.

Something strange happens to me. The costume and mask change me from Layla the freak to an exotic, masked showgirl, and despite the unthinkable act of performing in public, on stage, I'm not anxious. In fact, I have once more fallen down the rabbit hole and am in a magical place where nothing and no-one is as it seems.

As I twirl, Lavender reaches down and hoists me above her head. I squirm in fear, but she keeps a firm hold, so I lie back and point one black stockinged leg up to the ceiling, responding to the heady vigour of sheer improvisation. She lowers me to the ground and whispers again into the mic, "*Mam'zelle Sourcil.*"

A small, red-faced man in the front yells up to the stage. "Mamzel Sore Sal? What kind of a bloody name is that? What's she sore from?" He dissolves into raucous laughter at his joke.

Lavender glares at him, while I twirl around her.

"Not Sore Sal, you moron," she hisses, "*Sourcil*. It's French.

"Well what does it bloody mean?"

"It means one fucking eyebrow."

"Then give us a look at her face!"

My heart vaults in panic and the flight instinct surges through me like hot lightning. Before I can flee, Lavender's hand clamps onto my arm and while I struggle, she smiles smoothly at the audience.

"Ah, but I have not shown you my next surprise."

Someone tells the idiot in the front to shut up and the room grows quiet. She glares at me, with a wordless threat if I dare to leave. I nod in submission, shrugging free from her manic grip.

"Continuing our international line-up of perverse talent, I wish to introduce a man who's been around for a very long time. For centuries, in fact. Yes, for your listening pleasure I give you that Portuguese explorer and plunderer," she winks, "Mr. Vasco Da Gama, or as we know him, Fatso Da Drama."

The hilarity reaches a crescendo as Clyde strides onto the stage, and I can swear I hear Gavin's laugh above the others.

Lavender gestures at Clyde. "He is the original Portuguese Man-of-war." She slides a lascivious gaze down to his very visible crotch. "Ooh, there are no prizes for guessing where he's got his torpedo hidden." She smacks Clyde on the bum. "Bloody hell, Vasco, is that a weapon of mass destruction you've got down there?" Clyde plays along, grasping his crotch and mincing across the stage.

When the noise finally subsides, Clyde reaches for the mic and to my shock, launches into Adele's "Set Fire to the Rain". His voice is mesmerizing. I'd expected a parody of a song to add to the comedy. A rough yank from Lavender reminds me we are part of the show. Another mic is shoved in front of the two of us and we sing back-up to the spine-tingling sound coming from the fat man in tights.

The song is done, but the audience remains silent, mouths agape at the Vegas-worthy quality of his song. A roar of approval erupts from Gavin; the professor claps so hard and loud his face turns red, and Mrs. Crompton actually whistles. One by one people rise to their feet and the club explodes with their applause. Lavender leaps between Clyde and myself and holding both our hands, bestows magnificent bows on the cheering patrons of The Silk Purse. She is the star of the night for delivering such a wonderful show and when we try to scuttle off-stage, the clapping, yelling, and stamping feet insist we come back for another bow.

Breathless from exhilaration, I chase after Clyde as he heads out the back, obviously eager to get rid of the tights. "Hey, Vasco," I yell.

He stops and looks at me. "You called, Sore Sal?"

I scrunch my face in disgust. "Enough of the Sore Sal." He shrugs and grins at me.

"You know, you look beautiful in your costume." My breath catches. Twice in one night, after not hearing a compliment in a very long time.

"Thanks. I didn't know you could sing like that."

Lavender, after taking more bows, appears behind us and slaps Clyde again on the backside. "I told you he has the voice of an angel. You two saved my butt tonight. Not only that, but I will be the toast of the town after this. You'll have to make regular appearances."

We both look at her in disbelief and in unison snap, "Never!"

She sighs. "Oh well, I can dine out on tonight for a while. Thank you, darlings." She kisses us both full on the mouth, roars with laughter, and prances ahead into the dressing room.

I flop onto a chair like a puppet whose strings have been dropped. Clyde dashes behind a screen and I see the tights fly over the top followed by a loud sigh of relief. A smile creeps across my face at the memory of his large form squashed into the very graphic tights.

Time for Alice to leave Wonderland. I haul myself up and remove my costume, leaving the mask until the very last. But my hand seems unable to shift it. Like Jim Carey in the movie, *Mask*, it won't come off. Well, I don't want it to come off, ever. The voices of Gavin, the professor, and Mrs. Crompton force my hand, so to speak. I reach up and expose the red puckered scars that make up the left side of my face.

The others are waiting when I reappear.

"Lavender's gone on to The Graveyard— a nightclub down the road—and wants us to join her," says Gavin. "The professor and Mrs. Crompton are piking out, they've had enough excitement. What about you, Layla?"

"Home to bed for me, Gavin. What a night!" I move to stand beside Clyde, who places a hand on my shoulder.

"Me, too," says Clyde. "You go with Lavender, Gav, we'll be right."

"You sure?" We all insist and Gavin scoots out the door, ready for an all-nighter.

The professor tries to tell me how proud he is of my performance, but it's late and his brain is jumbled from the alcohol he's consumed. I put an arm around his narrow, slumped shoulders and usher him out the back door.

Clyde hails a cab and the four of us pile in. Mrs. Crompton lives with her sister at Woolloomooloo, so she's our first drop-off. The Quay is my destination. My car's parked near the ferry terminal in Manly, so I won't be walking the streets at night. The professor gives no destination. Of course, it's too late for him to get a bed in one of the shelters. That's a problem I can't solve, so I squeeze his hand. It's the best I can do.

The cab pulls up at the Quay and before I exit, I place a kiss on the professor's cheek. Clyde points at his cheek, so I lean into the front and kiss him as well.

"Thank you for one of the best nights I can remember," I say.

Before either of them can respond, I run across the road to the bus stop where the late night bus will take me to Manly. I've missed the last ferry.

As the cab pulls away, I look back and touch my face, wishing for the hard plastic comfort of the mask again.

CHAPTER 13

A ROUGH, WET TONGUE ON MY arm, followed by a des-perate whimper, drags me from the fog of deep sleep. By the stream of sunlight on my wall, I know I've slept late and poor Bennie must be desperate to go outside.

"All right, darling boy. I'm sorry to neglect you." He needs a walk, but I think he needs a pee first.

I'm wearing satin boxers and a singlet top which, of course, means both my scarred arm and leg are visible. If I crack open the door and let him run out to pee on a bush, no-one will see me. He scampers down the hall, pawing the floor near the door. I pull it open and he darts down the stairs, lifting his leg on the closest bush, with a look of embarrassed relief.

"Hey, you bad dog. You not do your business on my plant."

Bugger. Mr. Bacik is outside and we've both been busted. Bennie drops to his belly and drags himself submissively towards the old man. I don't think I can get away with that. I duck into the laundry, wrap my sarong around my boxers and step out the door.

"I'm sorry, Mr. Bacik. It's my fault, I overslept and he couldn't hold on any longer."

His eyes light up with interest. "You overslept, huh? Does this mean you go out and enjoy yourself last night?"

Pleasure ripples through my body at the memory. "You could say that. I had a wonderful evening."

"So, your Tom, he finally take you for a good time?"

He heaves himself up, obviously deeming the conversation worthy of leaving his gardening for a bit. He walks over to the step, sits down, and pats the space beside him. I look around to ensure there's no one about, then join him.

"Actually I didn't go out with Tom." He raises his eyebrows, but says nothing. "I went out with Clyde and some of his friends. You know, the man you met when we were at the coffee shop a while back."

He nods slowly. "Yes, yes I remember. Very nice man. Bennie liked him. A bit, you know..." He puffs up his cheeks and holds his hands out around his belly to indicate a wide girth.

"That's the one. You know he has an amazing singing voice. He sang last night. And I danced. On a stage. In front of people."

He claps his hands and hugs me. "Oh, my Layla. So brave. This Clyde makes you live again, I think."

"I suppose he does. I hadn't thought of it like that. He's become a good friend."

His eyes look away into the distance, and a small smile moves his lips. "My Anka, she could sing and dance. A voice like an angel's harp. Her music teacher say she can sing like a professional." He sighed.

The last thing I meant to do was stir up memories of the daughter he'd lost. It isn't right this dear old man should lose contact with his child because of a well-intentioned mistake. There must be a way they could reunite. Children have such power to punish a parent.

I grasp his hand and hold it for a moment before standing. "It was lovely to chat with you, Mr. Bacik, and now I'd better get dressed and take this patient little fellow for a walk."

Bennie's head jerks up and his ears twitch forward. He always knows when I'm talking about him.

The old man waves me back into the building but remains on the step, lost in his thoughts.

❦

An hour later, with a mushroom omelette on my mind, I push open my door and jog into the kitchen. Bennie, exhausted, gulps water from his bowl and then collapses on the floor. I crack two eggs into a bowl, add chopped shallots, mushrooms, and parsley, then fry garlic, beat the egg mix, and add crushed pepper. My mouth watering, I lift the bowl to tip it into the sizzling frying pan when my phone strums insistently from the kitchen bench. I check the caller ID. Tom.

"Hey, Tom. How are you?"

"Good. A bit tired. I went out with some of the people from work last night." Interesting, he didn't mention that yesterday.

"Oh? Who was there?" I bite my tongue, but too late.

He hesitates. "Just some of the guys. And a couple of the women."

"Did Kelly go?"

"I think she might have been there." Dead giveaway. As if you wouldn't be completely aware of whether Kelly was in a room or not. "How did your night go? Enjoy yourself?" he asks.

The words tangle themselves at the back of my throat as I try to rearrange the possible explanations in my mind. *I spent the evening on the stage of a drag club singing Abba with a female impersonator and Vasco Da Gama in front of over a hundred people. Or, I spent the evening with a cast of weirdos, from a place called The Black Hole, where we all drink each afternoon, but who I've never mentioned to you.* Tom would be on the phone to my psychologist before I had finished the story. A lie it had to be.

"Quite nice. We had a few drinks and some dinner at a Vietnamese restaurant and then I came home."

"Yeah, sounds a bit like my night. Pretty ordinary." Now I know he's lying! I don't miss the irony of the fact I am also lying, but I can justify my lies based on the unbelievability of the truth. Whereas there is nothing unbelievable about Tom and Kelly ending the night together. An insistent worm coils tighter and tighter in my stomach at the image of them wrapped in each other's arms having hot, insatiable sex. And I will bet there were no limp appendages when he caressed Kelly's face. Now I'm angry.

"Right. Ordinary. What a shame for you. Anyway, gotta go. Got things to do." My finger is on the 'Off' button.

"Wait, Layla. I wanted to check about tonight."

"We made no plans for tonight, so nothing to check." There, that will show him I'm not waiting around for him.

"Oh, good. Because I can't make it anyway. Something's come up."

"Something?"

"Yeah, boring family stuff, but I told Mum I'd drop over and talk tonight."

All I can see through my angry hurt is "LOSER" flashing in neon lights across my forehead. As if he's going to his mother's. I mumble goodbye and hang up.

Life comes to a halt. Traffic noise has dimmed, the music on my iPod is indiscernible, and Bennie's sympathetic whimpering sounds a long distance away; even my heart seems to have stopped beating. The bowl of egg mix comes into focus, and with it my utter desolation at Tom's increasing disconnection from me.

A burst of rage erupts through me and I hurl the bowl against the wall. Splatters of egg, parsley, and mushroom stick to the ceiling, the cupboards and the stove top, then slowly trickle down towards the kitchen bench. Bennie barks and covers his head with both paws.

Instead of rushing to clean up the egg, I snatch my phone from the bench, wipe egg splatters off it, and march out to the front room, away from the scene of the crime. Not giving myself time to think about the consequences of my next action, I dial Kelly's mobile phone.

I give her time to say no more than "Hello..." before taking control of the conversation.

"Hi, Kelly. It's Layla. Tom tells me he's seeing you tonight and I wanted to ask if you would mind discussing some product research referred to in the proposal I gave you yesterday. This is his area of expertise, after all."

I can hear her drawing a deep breath. "So, Tom said he's seeing me tonight?"

"Yes." I force my voice to be upbeat and chatty. "He explained it was to talk work as you'd run out of time on Friday. I think it's a great idea and would really help me if you could both nut out that clause for me."

"You must have misunderstood him, Layla. I have no plans to meet Tom tonight. And he certainly didn't say anything to me last night when we were out with the others."

Ha! So she was there last night. But now I've made a fool of myself by my jealous suspicions about tonight.

"Oh. How could I have got that mixed up? Early dementia, ha ha. Right, then. Talk to you later. Enjoy your weekend," I babble at the cool, disinterested woman at the other end.

She waits until I've garbled myself into a corner before responding. "I hope you sort this out, Layla. I'll see you Monday." I smack myself on the forehead over and over until Bennie snaps at my arm.

What an idiot! I have no doubt our friends and work colleagues already wonder why Tom is with such an ugly, damaged, paranoid woman when he could have his pick of perfect women. Kelly for one. I don't know whether he's sought intimacy with anyone else since the fire, but my paranoid and irrational behaviours are sure to drive him there. Once Kelly tells him about this conversation, I'll have probably succeeded. Suddenly, I have a need for my father's company. The one man I can depend on.

Because now I not only have egg on the ceiling and wall, but also on my face.

&

Turning my little blue Getz into the driveway, I notice Corinne's car. I open my door and hesitate. That's a person I don't need to deal with today. If no one has seen me arrive, maybe I can pull my door shut and sneak out again. Too late. Bennie shoots out of the car and up the front steps, in search of Ruby.

A squeal from the back of the house, followed by the dull thump and splash of a body hitting water, tells me Ruby's in the pool. When I step onto the back patio, Mum is there with her feet up and a glass of something cold in her hand. Corinne is next to her, and Ruby's in the pool with two friends. Neither friend is Levi, the cockatoo. A strange puppy is running from one end of the pool to the other, chasing the girls as they swim up and down. Bennie nearly wets himself with excitement.

I wave my hand, collecting everyone in the gesture. "Hi Mum, Corinne." A bit louder, "Hi Ruby and Ruby's friends." A chorus of hellos follow. Corinne taps the table, vexed at my sudden appearance. She manages a thin smile.

Mum holds out one arm. "What a lovely surprise, Layla. Come and give me a hug." I lean over and kiss the top of her head, and still holding her hand, pull out a chair and sit.

"If it's okay with you, I thought I'd pick Rubes up now and she can stay the night."

"Sounds lovely, darling. You two work it out together."

I jerk my head in the direction of the puppy. "Did you finally buy Ruby a dog, Mum? Every kid needs an animal."

My mother purses her lips. "No, that's Kandy's puppy." I frown, having no idea who Kandy is. "Her friend, the one at the far end of the pool."

I squint back at the girls. Ruby is half out of the pool on her belly, cuddling the puppy. "Why hasn't she ever had a dog, Mum? She loves them."

Corinne looks away as if she wants nothing to do with the conversation between myself and my mother.

"Whenever I suggest it, she's been adamant she doesn't want one. She hasn't wanted any sort of pet. Not since that dreadful accident with the kitten."

I shudder at the memory of five-year-old Ruby discovering her beloved white kitten drowned in her blow-up kiddie pool. If I recall correctly, her nightmares started around then. Or was it before that? Too grizzly to think about.

"Dad not here?"

"No, darling, he's playing golf. He always plays golf on a Saturday afternoon."

She's right. He's done it for as long as I can remember. I'm not sure why I forgot today. Obviously too upset about my calls with Tom and then Kelly.

Because I've been such a little bitch with Tom, I decide to make retribution by being nice to my sister.

"How's work going, Corinne?"

"Pretty much the same. I sell books. People buy books. Not exciting like your job, Layla."

I bite back my customary sarcastic response. "My job's been a bit more disaster than excitement lately, I'm afraid." I decide to give her an opportunity to engage in conversation by asking what might have been disastrous.

"That's a shame. Any more juice, Mum?" She's already out of her chair, heading for the kitchen.

"Why don't you get Layla a drink while you're there, Corinne?"

I catch Mum's eye. We both know how Corinne will feel about that. Nonetheless, she comes back with a glass of juice and puts it in front of me.

"Mum tells me you're having the day with Ruby tomorrow. Hopefully you can drag something out of her about the company she's been keeping and what she's been getting up to," says Corinne. "She certainly won't tell me anything."

I want to object to her comment, but it's true. Ruby would never confide in Corinne. In fact, none of us would, or ever did, when we were kids. Corinne always believed she was the odd one out, so she had us believing it too. Although Ruby is much younger, she shuns Corinne as much as the rest of us. I truly wish it wasn't like this. I get no pleasure from seeing Corinne alienated, but she does nothing to change how we see her. I try again to engage with her.

"I'm really enjoying the wonderful painting you bought me, Corinne." She looks up but doesn't respond. "Every time I look at it, it reminds me of your kindness; how you gave me something beautiful after I lost everything in the fire." To my surprise, she looks away as if she doesn't want acknowledgement for the gift. A sign of humility. I keep misjudging her.

"That's good," she mumbles and walks over to the pool to speak to one of Ruby's friends.

"Has anything more happened with the American doctor?" asks Mum.

"I sent all the photos and medical records, and he's also spoken to Jarrod, but Dr. Gassner seems to think it's too hard to say for certain if he can help until he sees me in person."

"Are you thinking of flying over?"

I sigh. "I don't know. Yes, I suppose I'll have to. I can't yet, though. There's the money and then there's also the fact of my recent return to work. I can't ask for time off straight away. My position there is shaky enough as it is."

"You know your dad and I meant it when we offered to help." Mum reaches for my hand and with her other hand strokes my scarred face.

"Mum, you've done so much already. I really was hoping to do this myself. I had an idea that maybe I could go over once I've saved some money, let him look at my face, and stay for the operations. Get it all done in one go."

"Your dad and I were wondering if it might be worth someone else having a look at the evidence found at the fire. If there was any liability on the landlord's part, you could sue him. That would give you the money you need." She stops to have a drink and waves to the girls in the pool. "I also get a sense you can't move forward until you know it wasn't your fault. Am I right?"

She's more right than she realises. It sounds crazy, but I have this belief that if it was my fault; if I did cause it somehow, then I don't deserve to have my old life back. That I don't deserve expensive surgery.

"Worth thinking about," I say. Then I remember the session with Jarrod. "I told you didn't I, that something hovered at the edge of my memory during my session the other day?"

"No, you told me there was something, but you didn't want to discuss it on the phone. You sounded so distraught I wanted to wait until you felt like talking to me about it."

"I saw the fire, Mum. I saw the flames, I felt the unbearable heat, the pain, the terror..."

Her arms are around me, stroking the back of my hair; she murmurs soothing noises. "Oh, darling. No wonder you couldn't speak of it. How terrible for you."

My mother's compassion gives me permission to crumble, and I burst into choking sobs. She gestures for me to follow her to the privacy of her bedroom.

"I thought I saw something," I say. "The memory was too elusive, but my body recognised it and went into a shock response. If only I could have seen it clearly. I'm not even sure if it was something or someone. What if it was someone?"

"No, darling. Don't take your mind there. That's too horrible to even contemplate. It had to be something out of place or ... I don't know."

With my head buried in her warm, rose-scented neck, I nod, sobs still hiccoughing in my throat. She's told me exactly what I need to hear. That something bad happened, but it was not deliberate and I was nobody's target. Mum rocks me in silence, for once not asking for details of my session. Thank goodness.

There is a sharp rap on the door and Corinne pokes her head into the room. "I thought I might as well go as I seem to have been excluded again."

I don't respond to her petty comment, but my mother releases me, reaches for the box of tissues, then pats the bed next to her in invitation to Corinne.

"I'm sorry, dear, but Layla was telling me some of her memories of the fire have returned, and it quite upset her."

Corinne's eyes widen. "What... What have you remembered? Do you know what happened?"

Her reaction causes me a twinge of shame at my ungenerous thoughts about her. She really does care. "Nothing about what caused the fire. Just memories of the fire itself."

"Oh. So you still don't know if it was an accident or not?"

I blow my nose into a bunch of tissues and shake my head. "No. It's so frustrating."

Corinne edges over to the bed. "I think it's better to leave the past in the past and get on with your life. I can't see what good it does you to keep trying to drag this up."

My social worker mother responds to this. "How can she let it all go if she can't bring it forward first and heal from the knowledge? Nobody heals from trauma by sweeping it under the carpet." She rips out another tissue and dabs at my face. In a flash of blue, Corinne spins and is gone.

Mum looks from me to the empty doorway, pats my leg, and leaves in pursuit of Corinne. I'm self-centred enough to think I need her attention more than Corinne and feel a little abandoned; especially as I had begun sharing with her the horror of my last session with Jarrod Leighton.

Corinne's odd, self-deprecating behaviour has always had the power to grab Mum's attention. Matt, Ruby, and I demanded our share of parental attention in the normal way: with loud, humorous behaviour; sporting, artistic and academic achievements, and overt sibling rivalry. Like the story of the prodigal son, it seems parents break their necks to love a lame duck child and let the others snatch what love and attention they can.

When I walk back outside, Mum and Corinne are nowhere to be seen. Ruby and her two friends have climbed out of the pool and are sprawled on deck chairs. At the sound of car wheels crunching in the driveway, the girls jump up, yell goodbye, and run down the side of the house, puppy in pursuit, to meet whichever parent it happens to be.

Ruby sees me and hurries over. "Hey, Layla. I'll get my stuff and we can go. I'm staying the night, aren't I?"

"Yes, I hope so. Then we don't have to answer lots of questions about what we're doing in the morning. I'll wait here. Can you be quick? I'd like to go as soon as I can."

She runs into the house, as eager to get going as I now am. I notice leaves have fallen into the pool from the blue gums in the backyard, so I grab the long handled scooper and make myself useful while I wait.

Childhood memories flash through my mind as I circle the pool. Memories of Matt and me playing in a rubber ring, tipping each other into the water to take control of the ring like pirates taking command of a ship. Corinne would sit on the edge of the pool watching, her face sullen; but she'd turn away if we gestured for her to join us. In the insensitive way of children, we would then tease her, chanting, 'cow-face Corinne, can't win a thing,' and erupt into giggles.

A strange urge overtakes me to return to that time when we were children and instead of teasing Corinne, to take her hand and bring her into our sibling fraternity. If we had been more loving and inclusive, despite her unlovable behaviour, would I have a sister I could love and share with now?

"Come on, sis. I'm ready," calls Ruby from the sliding back door.

"Have you told Mum you're going?"

"I poked my head into her study, but she and Corinne are having a D and M, so I waved, held up my bag, and left."

"Good enough. Let's get out of here." I scribble a quick good-bye to Mum on a scrap of paper, put it under a mug on the kitchen bench, and follow Ruby out to the car.

❦

When Bennie and I walk through the door Sunday morning, sticky from the sea and covered in sand, Ruby is at my small dining table, shovelling Weet-Bix into her mouth. Her hair is mussed and she has one pyjama-clad leg on the chair, her knee almost under her chin.

"You should have woken me, I would have come with you," she says, wide-eyed with indignation.

I'm halfway to the bathroom to shower myself and Bennie, and yell back, "I tried. It was like trying to wake up a boulder."

Her response is muffled, but I can imagine what she said, probably accompanied by eye rolling. I step into the shower, gripping a reluctant Bennie by the collar. Once I start lathering him with my sandalwood and geranium shampoo, he zones out. Revelling in the feel of my hands scrubbing his head, tummy and back. I rinse the shampoo off the dog and poke my head around the shower screen.

"Hey, Rubes, can you grab a doggie towel, come and get Bennie, and dry him off, please?"

When she comes in, I slide back the shower screen to hand her the dog. Her eyes snag on my scarred body and she gasps. I thrust Bennie into her arms and shut the screen.

"Sorry, Rubes, I forgot."

"Shit, Layla, I'm sorry I reacted like that. It's just that I didn't expect it. I really am sorry, it's not that bad you know."

"Stop while you're ahead, Rubes." My voice sounds harsh as I try to manage my emotions from Ruby's reaction. She's not to blame, though, and I don't want her feeling guilty. "It's okay, sweetheart. I didn't mean to snap at you. Wait until I'm out and I can give you a hug."

"That'll be nice," she murmurs, and pulls the door closed.

I look down my left leg, at the puckered and rope-like scars, still red and angry. I force my eyes away and launch into Leonard Cohen's "Hallelujah". As I sing the words at the top of my voice, everything else is pushed from my mind, and by the time I step out of the shower, I'm cleansed in more ways than one.

CHAPTER 14

CLYDE HASN'T TOLD ME WHAT he intends for today—I'm not even sure if he's remembered. While Ruby dresses, I dial his number.

"Hi, Layla. Still on for today?"

"That's what I was checking with you. You haven't told me where we're going, when we're going, or what we're doing."

"What about I meet you at the Quay at eleven. Are you bringing Levi?"

Crap, I'd forgotten about him.

"I suppose we'll have to if we're brainwashing Ruby about drugs. If we don't do him too, he might undo the good work."

"Okay, well I'll leave that to you. Get him to meet us there as well." I disconnect. Now to tell Ruby the good news that she can bring the cockatoo with her today.

"Hey, Rubes. Would you like to bring your friend, Levi, with us today?"

She's brought out my hairdryer and is brushing Bennie as she blow-dries his fur. She doesn't look up to answer.

"Already asked him. He's waiting to hear what time."

"Oh. Well, tell him to meet us at the Quay at eleven. By the way, where does he live?"

"North Shore. He can get a train there."

North Shore? Does the little punk come from a wealthy family? I'm now keen to know more about him. Funny how we make assumptions about people based on how they look. The irony of this thought causes me to chuckle. Ruby, with Bennie locked under one leg while she phones Levi, shakes her head as if I'm a lost cause.

"He's good to go. He was supposed to go to some bar mitz-thingy, but he's convinced his mother to let him come with us instead."

"Do you mean a bar mitzvah? He's Jewish?"

She shrugs, brushing the hair around Bennie's ears. "I don't know. But his parents are weird."

"Have you met them?"

"Not really." I fix her with a glare. "All right. No, I haven't because he's not supposed to have a girlfriend who isn't Jewish."

"Oh, Ruby. So he keeps you secret from them? That's not good."

"Well, if they weren't so racist, he could tell them."

"So I'm helping you to deceive his parents? I'm not sure if I can do this, Rubes."

She drops Bennie and throws her arms around me. "Please, please, please, Layla. I only told you because I trust you. We really want to spend time together. Don't go all parental on me. You're my sister, you're meant to help me with stuff like this."

I hug her back—after all, I owed her one. A hug, that is.

"Okay, let's see how today goes and then we'll talk more about it. Maybe his parents won't be so bad if they meet you."

She plants a wet kiss on my face. "Thank you, darling sister. This is a noble thing you do," she parodied, "helping two star-crossed lovers."

"Lovers?" I snap.

She kisses my shoulder. "Just a figure of speech."

God, I hope so. I try to remember how old I was when I lost my virginity. Sixteen, I recall. Not much older than Ruby. *Bugger!*

☾

The ferry bumps against the wharf, disgorging its Sunday cargo of city wanderers. I always wonder where people are going as I watch them disembark. Some will probably make their way to The Rocks. A quaint cobblestoned village from convict times which has become home to art houses, eateries, and an eclectic weekend market. Or perhaps to the movies, although there are so many suburban theatres now, people don't tend to bother coming to the city anymore.

Ruby jolts me out of my musings with a hard jab to my ribs. "Look, there he is." I glance around for Clyde's bulky shape but can't see him. "Over there. Levi!"

Oh, she means the cockatoo. I forget that she doesn't even know Clyde.

Levi slopes towards us with his cap on backwards and his hands squashed into the pockets of his baggy, low-slung jeans. His face lights up as he sees Ruby and when he smiles I have to admit he doesn't look too bad. Especially as the cap covers his ridiculous red coxcomb.

He's finding it hard to make eye contact with me. I won't make it easier for him, not after what he said the night I picked Ruby up from the party. He scuffs his sneaker at the pavement.

"Um, I wanted to say sorry for that other night, Layla. You know, what I said about your face and calling you freaky. I'd been drinking and taking…some stuff… and it took me by surprise." I remain silent and he clears his throat. "Your face, it's not that bad, really—".

Ruby gives me one of her glares. "It's okay, Levi. She gets that you're sorry, don't you, Layla? Besides *she* called you a cockatoo because of your hair."

"Really?" he asks, with a pained expression on his face.

God save me from precious teenage boys.

"All right, I accept your apology. Let's leave it alone now," I say.

Levi smiles and does that thing where they waggle their closed fist with the thumb, forefinger and pinky poking out. "Hey, Layla. Caps rule, man!"

Caps rule? Of course, he's looking at my cap, pulled low over my face, trying to make a connection. Not going to happen.

I half-smile, half-grimace at him. "I'm glad you could join us today, Levi. Ruby tells me you were supposed to go to a bar mitzvah."

"Yeah, man. One of my cousins. Dead boring, though. I told my mum the parents of one of my friends was taking us on an ed-u-cat-ion-al out-ing," he says, with hand and body rap moves. I raise one eyebrow and he stops the posturing. "That's what Ruby said, but I wasn't really sure." Levi looks down at his feet. "The thing is, my mum wants you to call her and tell her what we're doing and introduce yourself."

I stare at him. "What? I'm not a parent and what am I to tell her about Ruby? Apparently you're not supposed to have a girlfriend who's not Jewish." Ruby glares at me. Levi glares at Ruby. I throw up my arms. "For God's sake, I'm not going to lie to your parents, Levi."

He drops Ruby's hand, which he's gripped since arriving. "No, you're right. I'll head on back home and tell them it was cancelled. No sweat."

Out of the corner of my eye, I see Clyde walk over to where we're standing—his broad shoulders hunched as if to lessen his bulk. Ruby's eyes widen as she realises this is the friend we're meeting. Funny, it's starting to surprise me when I see people's reactions to Clyde's size; although they were my reactions as well when I first saw him. Now he's become just Clyde to me. When I look at his face, I don't so much see the fat, pudgy cheeks, but more the twinkling eyes and generous smile; someone who makes me laugh.

I turn to include Clyde in our group. "Hi, Clyde. This is my sister, Ruby, and her friend, Levi."

Everyone says hello and Levi and Clyde do a man shake where they smack hands, punch fists, and wiggle fingers.

Clyde glances from Ruby to Levi. "Why such serious faces? We're not going to an execution. It's a drug rehab centre."

"A what?" say Ruby and Levi together.

"We're going to chat to people who thought drugs were cool and then found they weren't. I know one of the counsellors there and he's organised for a few of the kids to spend some time with us."

"Sounds boring, man," says Levi. "And anyway, someone needs to call my mum and I don't think that's going to happen."

"Well, if Levi's not going, I'm not going either," says Ruby, stepping back and grasping Levi's hand again.

I look at Ruby and raise my eyebrows. She knows exactly what I'm not saying. That if she doesn't come, Mum will be hearing about her recreational activities. She pouts and lowers her eyes. I need to win this one if I'm going to save my little sister from the greedy, gaping maw of the drug scene.

I pull my phone out, then think better of it, not wanting the

Jewish parents to have my number. "Levi, call your mother and then give me the phone. Oh, and what's your last name?"

Ruby lifts her head and gives me a hopeful smile.

"Newman," he says, already dialling.

He tells his mother that it will be his friend's older sister she will speak to, not the mother, then hands the phone to me. I explain to Mrs. Newman how aware I am of the temptations of recreational drugs to teenagers nowadays; that my mother is a social worker and our connections have allowed us to have access to an educational session on drugs and we would like to offer this opportunity to Levi as well as to my sister to prepare them for potential temptation. Levi's mother is impressed with our sensible, preventative actions and asks me to tell Levi she and his father will be interested in hearing about his excursion when he gets home. When he takes back the phone, I can't help but feel a smidgen of admiration for the respect evident in his voice when he speaks to his mother. If he would only do something about the hairstyle and metal.

Clyde gestures towards his car. "So, we ready to go?"

I certainly am. I'm feeling almost jubilant. Clyde has proposed a perfect solution, and I can feel I'm at least doing something to help Ruby navigate this minefield she's blundered into.

❦

A high fence circles the Centre. Other than that and the double metal gate, it looks like a large house surrounded by trees, with wooden tables and bench seats scattered throughout the yard. Clyde's friend, Stephen, meets us in the reception area. He's an Aboriginal man with dark, intense eyes and a wide, welcoming smile. Ruby and Levi are immediately drawn to him and it's easy to imagine young people opening up to this man in the group sessions Clyde told us about.

Stephen takes us into one of the rooms where the walls are covered in pastel, pen and ink, and acrylic artworks. No one speaks as our eyes follow the dark despair depicted by the pictures pinned haphazardly around the wall. It's as if I'm in a gallery surrounded by variations of Edvard Munch and Hieronymus Bosch nightmare paintings, except the dark anguish in most of these pictures makes Munch's *The Scream* look like a Sunday school picnic.

"Most of these are painted by clients who tell us they don't have a drug or alcohol problem. So we give them their choice of art equipment, play music designed to unlock their carefully stored perceptions of themselves and the world they live in, and these are some of the results." He gestures at the walls.

"They're awful," says Ruby. "These people must have terrible parents and dreadful lives, not like mine or Levi's."

"I think you'd be quite surprised at some of the backgrounds, Ruby. And in many instances, this despair is as a result of the drugs, not their background. Once the drugs are in charge, their backgrounds, family and upbringing cease to exist. Addiction is a great leveller."

Ruby and Levi exchange glances but don't comment on this.

"And have you tried drugs, Ruby? Levi?" he asks.

Levi is obviously waiting for Ruby to answer this one. She rolls her eyes as if Stephen is on the wrong track.

"Are you for real? You think we have a problem?"

Stephen shrugs. "I wouldn't know. Do you think you have a problem?"

"Of course not," says Ruby; Levi nods in agreement. "We've only tried a couple of things at parties."

"Yeah? What things?" asks Stephen.

Another look is exchanged as they consider how much to divulge, or so it seems to me.

"Bit of dope. Dropped acid a couple of times. Took "E" a couple of times. No big deal," answers Levi.

My eyes bulge and I can feel my tongue warming up to explode at this choice piece of information. Silly me, even though I knew there were harder drugs at the party I rescued Ruby from, I still believed she would only have smoked dope. Clyde places his hand on my arm to warn me to stay calm.

"Pretty normal stuff, then?" says Stephen.

Normal stuff? I swing my head towards Clyde, sputtering in protest. He grips my shoulder, manoeuvres me towards the door and before I can get the words out, has steered me into the hallway.

I flap my hands around pushing his arm away. "Did you hear that? He's telling them it's normal to do that stuff. Let me go back in."

"He's just gaining their trust by listening and matching their responses. He knows how to do this, Layla. He's good at his job. Let's follow his lead."

He's right, of course. But it's shocking to hear something like that from my baby sister, who I still think of as being five years old.

If I lean back I can still see into the room where Stephen, Ruby, and Levi sit in deep conversation.

"More than anything I want to go back in," I whisper to Clyde, "but you obviously think we should let him have some time with them."

"Might be a good idea." He gestures across the hallway to a room which looks like a kitchen with a big dining table in the middle. "Coffee wouldn't go astray. They'll find us when they're ready."

We wander in and see a middle-aged woman sitting at one end of the table with a coffee and an open magazine. The pale green bench tops are worn but scrubbed clean and an urn simmers next to the sink.

The woman looks up, her eyes widen a fraction at my face, and then she smiles to cover her surprise. "Hello, I'm Patricia." Clyde introduces us both.

"Are you here visiting someone?" she asks.

I give a half wave of my hand. "Not really. Well, we're visiting Stephen. That is, my sister is…"

She cuts off my bumbling explanation. "Stephen's great. He's so good with the kids. Your sister will be fine." She gestures at the urn. "Have a coffee and relax."

Crap! She's got me all wrong. She thinks my sister's an addict.

"No, no, I didn't mean that there's anything wrong. She's just talking to Stephen. It's more her boyfriend, really."

Shut up Layla! Both Clyde and Patricia watch me as nonsense spurts from my mouth.

Clyde turns to the cupboards above the sink, pulls out two mugs, and unscrews a jar of instant coffee.

"Coffee it is then. Milk, Layla?"

I nod and decide to stop my unwanted defence of Ruby. Patricia has returned to her magazine. I grimace at Clyde and dart my eyes in Patricia's direction. He grins and shrugs, clearly finding me amusing.

Within minutes, Clyde places a mug of coffee on the table and we both sit. The woman drains her coffee, closes the magazine, and pushes back her chair.

"Back to work. Hope everything works well for your sister."

"No, she's fine. No problems at all."

The patronising, half smile she bestows on me at the door tells me she's heard this before. I quell the frustration with a deep breath and wonder why it matters what she thinks. When I glance back at Clyde, he's watching me, a small frown creasing his forehead. His gaze holds for a second too long and I notice the mix of gentleness and intensity in his clear hazel-coloured eyes. At such close proximity, I'm not influenced by the bulky shape of his body, and again can see a masculine beauty in the straight line of his nose and the strong bone structure of his jawline, cleverly disguised by layers of fat. I'm overcome by a sudden urge to beg him to lose weight, but stop myself in time. He's never once asked me to be anything other than I am, and as a friend I owe him the same respect.

The shuffle of feet sound in the hallway and I half stand.

"Here you are," says Stephen from the doorway.

Behind him are Levi, Ruby, and two other young people. Stephen gestures towards the two strangers.

"This is Anna and Colin. Guys, this is Layla, Ruby's sister, and Clyde, Layla's friend, and also a good friend of mine."

The girl, Anna, has a haunted, ethereal look about her. Her skin is pale and her body is rail-thin. Anna glances at Clyde and then her eyes move to me, taking in the scars. She mouths a silent curse and then smiles as if in recognition. Perhaps she thinks our suffering connects us. Colin is of average height but looks more robust than the young woman. He thrusts out his hand to shake Clyde's. He's unable to look directly at me and nods with his eyes averted.

"Anna and Colin are nearly at the end of their stay here and have been mentoring some of the others. They've offered to chat with Ruby and Levi, sharing their own experiences with drugs.

Are you okay with that, Layla?"

I glance over at Ruby, who nods at my unspoken question. "I guess. That would be good. Thank you both."

Ruby sidles past the group gathered in the doorway and reaches for my hand. "Levi's going to speak with Colin alone, and Anna and I will go and sit and talk. Do you want to come with us, Layla?"

A rush of warmth flows through me at her offer. She must know how much I want to be a part of what she's going through. Underneath the questing teenager, my beautiful sister still exists. The chair topples backward, I jump up so quickly from the table.

"Clyde and I will stay and have another cup of this dreadful coffee," says Stephen, grabbing a mug from the cupboard.

Colin and Levi walk off, deep in conversation about motorbikes. Anna turns and leads the way down the hall and out into the garden. Ruby and I follow behind like two faithful dogs.

"Do you mind if we walk a bit?" Anna asks, in her soft voice. I go to answer and stop myself, realising this is Ruby's show and I'm just along for the ride.

Ruby moves up beside her. "Sounds good to me. Nice garden. How long have you been here, Anna?

"This time? Or over all?"

Ruby's step falters but with a quick glance over her shoulder at me, she falls back into step with Anna.

"I'm not sure. I suppose, over all."

"Well, my family first brought me here five years ago." She looks up at a thin branch of an acacia tree, its leaves dancing seductively in the slight breeze. "Was it five years? Yes, that would be about right. It was the crystal meth that got me. I was here for six months the first time and this is my third and last time."

Something about this statement sends a shiver up my spine.

Anna looks directly at Ruby. "You haven't gone there yet, have you?" Before Ruby can answer, she answers for her. "No, I can tell you haven't. Have they offered it to you yet?"

I'm about to answer in the negative to this ridiculous question, as I know Ruby would not have been involved in something as dangerous as crystal meth, when Ruby raises her head and nods.

I gasp, but in time slam my hand against my mouth. Ruby and Anna are trusting each other with total honesty, and I don't want to remind them of my presence.

"Levi and I were out at Narrabeen Beach one day and the brother of someone he knew from school sat down and offered us a free trial. He called it crank—I didn't know at the time it was crystal meth. He told us how good it would make us feel, that it's like sitting on a rainbow with happy juice pumping through every cell of the body. I didn't know too much about it and stupidly..." Thank God, she used the word, stupidly. "... thought it might be fun, seeing it was free. Levi stopped me and told the guy, maybe another day."

Where is Levi? I want to hug him till he screams for release.

"So you're here because of the crystal meth?" asks Ruby. Anna nods. "What made you take it the very first time?"

Anna doesn't answer at first. She rubs her hands together over and over and then, noticing what she's doing, reaches up to a tree and strips off a handful of leaves. Like a keeper releasing doves, she throws her arm up and opens her hand to let the leaves catch in the breeze and spin to the ground.

"My twin brother died from encephalitis when I was fourteen. I was depressed and put on a heap of weight. My friends weren't coming around as much—I didn't really want to see anyone. One night I was at a party where this bloke handed me a glass pipe. He was clever, he must have been checking me out, because when I hesitated, he told me it would make me feel alive again and I would forget all my pain. As a bonus, he added, it was great for weight loss. Magic! Just what I needed. So I sucked on that pipe."

She spins and grips Ruby's shoulders. "It was sensational. It was like a great air hose blew out all the dark, negative bits and I felt golden and powerful, special, and desirable. I could dance like Beyoncé, argue like a lawyer, and was convinced there was nothing I couldn't achieve."

"That doesn't sound too awful," mutters Ruby.

"Oh, Rubes," I sigh. They ignore me.

"It wasn't awful at all. But when it wore off I was back where I'd started and I couldn't bear it. Not after tasting such splendour, such...brilliance, such...magnificence."

I can't see Ruby's face but her stillness tells me she is riveted by the story.

"Levi's friend said you could be a social meth user, like, just at a party or something. Why didn't you do that?"

"'Try me once and I might let you go, but try me twice and I own your soul.' That's from a poem supposedly written by a girl found dead with the needle still in her arm," says Anna.

I want to be sick but swallow convulsively, straining to hear her next words.

"Well, I couldn't resist after that first time, so I did try it twice, and a third time, and now…it owns my soul," she says.

"What else did the girl say in her poem?" whispers Ruby.

Anna stops walking and when she turns to face Ruby, I can see her face. Her eyes are glazed, lifeless, and her features are blank as she recites: "'The nightmares I'll give you while lying in bed, the voices you'll hear, from inside your head. The sweats, the shakes, the visions you'll see, I want you to know, these are gifts from me. But then it's too late, and you'll know in your heart, that you are mine, and we shall not part. You'll regret that you tried me, they always do, but you came to me, not I to you.'" She stops and looks over Ruby's head. "There's more, but you don't need to hear it."

The tears leave a wet salty taste in my mouth as they wash my cheeks, and although Ruby hasn't taken her gaze from Anna, tears splash her T-shirt. My sweet sister reaches out to clasp Anna's hand.

"But you're here, you've been helped, so it's all going to be all right again, isn't it? You'll soon be home with your parents."

Anna's eyes clear and her focus penetrates Ruby's stare. "I will do and say whatever it takes to get out of here. Do you know why?" Ruby and I take simultaneous deep breaths and Ruby shakes her head. "Because the only parents, the only friend, and the only lover I have is crystal meth. Even though I know it will kill me, I don't care. The day they let me out, I will go willingly to the first dealer I can find and lose myself in the euphoria of this thing which is my saviour and my destroyer."

For some reason she's trusted us with this information which I'm sure Stephen doesn't know. Otherwise he would not consider her rehabilitation complete. My head spins with the weight of her disclosure.

Anna turns to me and once more her eyes appraise my face. "It doesn't matter whether you tell them or not, I have no choice."

She turns back to Ruby. "I hope I've been able to help you. At least then I'd know I've done something good."

The wraithlike creature turns and, as if floating on air, moves through the garden, the breeze blowing her thin cotton dress against her bony hips and lifting strands of her pale blonde hair. We watch until she disappears around the corner of the building.

The sudden caw of a magpie seems magnified in the empty space left by Anna's departure. Her words hang between Ruby and myself, claiming the air we would need to speak. The fatalistic pronouncement is almost beautiful in its definitive simplicity and for a few moments I am empty. Then my mind breaks through the emptiness and a hard fist of grief punches me, reminding me of the utter futility in the impending loss of this young life.

Anger takes the place of the grief. Anger that these scumbags trawl the streets and crash teenage parties, luring innocent young people, with a truckload of potential, into their sick, cruel nets; destroying their lives for a fistful of dollars.

Somehow, I must save Ruby from this. I grasp her shoulders ready to yell my fears at her; force her to say 'no' to these insidious mind and body killers, when she falls against my chest and sobs; great, gulping hiccoughs of despair.

Stroking her soft auburn hair, I murmur soothing words.

"She's going to die. She's so beautiful and so young and she's going to die. I didn't know. It was fun and everyone was doing it." She lifts her wet face and looks up at me. "I don't want to do that stuff anymore, Layla."

A wave of relief at this declaration mingles with sadness over her loss of innocence. I pull out a tissue from my bag and mop my sister's face. She moves my hand down to her nose and gives a loud blast into the tissue. We both giggle.

Ruby steps back from me, pushing the soggy tissue into her pocket, then reaches up and bumps her finger along the ridges of my face.

"You're much luckier than her, Layla. Your scars are on the outside, but hers are on the inside. She's already pressed the self-destruct button, hasn't she?"

I look in wonder at my fifteen-year-old sister and nod. Her words lodge in my brain and I feel small and petty in comparison with Anna.

"When did you get so wise?" I ask.

Ruby's fingers lock with mine and together we walk back to the house. When we reach the kitchen, we linger at the doorway, not ready to plunge back into the quotidian hum of normality. Levi stands by the window staring out, as if he has the weight of the world on his shoulders. Clyde calls Levi's name and without speaking, we make our way down the hall and out the front door.

Stephen is nowhere in sight and I shrug off a slight discomfort at not thanking him, or at least saying goodbye.

"Stephen had an emergency and asked me to say goodbye. I thanked him for you," says Clyde.

I'm still not ready to speak, so I nod my gratitude and trail Clyde to the car.

☾

After some time, I notice we've turned towards the coast, but consumed by my thoughts, I have no idea where we are. Clyde swings into a car park, pulls into a space and with the motor still running, opens his door. The smell of sea, fish, and vinegar smacks me in the face as I look over the wide, sandy expanse of Bondi Beach.

"Cool. The beach." Levi pushes his door open and steps out.

Ruby scoots across the seat and jumps out behind him. With her arms outstretched, she twirls around and around, rips off her sandals and jumps down onto the sand. He follows and chases her, squealing, towards the water.

I twist in my seat to face Clyde. "Not bad. I couldn't have thought of a better place myself. And if you don't mind, I need to do exactly what Ruby just did.

"I suppose you want me to chase you, too."

I slip off my shoes and jump out of the car. "You'll never catch me," I call, as I leap down to the sand and start running.

For a big man, he's fast. All I hear is the squeak of the sand as he closes in on me and before I reach the shallows, Clyde grasps me around the waist and spins me in the air. I reach back to grab him around the neck and he loses balance, toppling to the sand with me sitting squarely on his belly. The undulations of his stomach as he laughs throw me onto the ground where I lie, panting for breath.

The sound of Ruby's squeals float in the air as Levi splashes her. And as I lie gazing up at the streaky clouds chasing each other across the sky, Clyde's hand closes over mine. It doesn't feel awkward or presumptuous, just comforting.

"Can you see the greyhound stretched out as she streaks across the sky?" I ask.

"No, only a terrified rabbit, trying to escape the jaws of your greyhound," he answers.

A dark shadow blocks the sun as Ruby leans over me, shaking droplets of water from her hands onto my face.

"I'm starving. We haven't had lunch, remember? Can we get some fish and chips?"

Pushing myself up onto my elbows, I squint at her. "Great idea, Rubes. Get some money out of my bag in the car and get drinks too."

Clyde releases my hand, reaches into his pocket, and tosses the keys into the air. Levi deftly catches them and the two shadows disappear. Clyde reclaims my hand.

"She isn't cured, you know. Stephen should know that. You have to tell him," I say, without preamble.

He turns his head slightly, pushing his cheek into the sand. "I take it you're not talking about Ruby." I shake my head, coating my hair in more sand. "He knows," says Clyde. "He told me she'll seek it out—the crystal meth—the minute she walks out the gate. And if she resists, it'll find her."

"Can't he do something? That's his job. That's why she's there."

"He spoke to her parents and told them the truth. They don't want her institutionalised indefinitely. They've decided to sell their home and move somewhere else in the hope it will save her."

"Does Stephen think it will?"

"He can't say for sure, but he agrees with the parents that it would be good for her to go home and have what time they can with their daughter. Who knows? Miracles happen."

We remain silent and I experience a surge of emotion towards Clyde which I can't identify, and squeeze his hand. I glance sideways at him and catch his grin.

"Did Levi speak to you about his conversation with Colin?" I ask.

"Enough for me to know it had an impact. At least whatever Ruby and Levi do in the future, they'll be armed with information." He holds my gaze. "They're good kids, Layla. Even Levi."

"I hate to say it, but you might be right. About Levi, I mean." Clyde snorts as he gazes up at the sky again.

"I've started an exercise program," he says.

This sudden shift in subject matter startles me.

"What? Why?"

"It's time. I've got a personal trainer and I've decided to get healthy. Even eat better. Not until after the fish and chips, though."

A tremor runs through me at his words. "Your mother will be pleased."

"I'm not doing it for her."

I suck in a breath, not sure if I want to hear that he's doing it for me. Those sorts of statements come with obligations.

"I'm not doing it for you, either. So don't get excited."

How ridiculous. As if.

"Oh, well, that's good," I mumble.

He chuckles, releases my hand, and pushes himself into a sitting position, brushing the sand from his hair.

"Here come the fish and chips."

I sit up and see Levi and Ruby stuffing chips into their mouths as they prance across the hot sand towards us.

C

My mouth is half full with a juicy piece of white grilled fish when I catch Levi close his eyes in ecstasy and toss a curl of calamari into his mouth. Time to find out more about this lad. I push the remaining fish aside.

"So, Levi, have you got much family in Sydney?"

He swallows the calamari before answering.

"Two aunts, an uncle, five cousins, and grandparents on my dad's side. No one much on my mum's side. Except her parents but she doesn't see much of them."

"You've never met the grandparents on your mother's side?"

"I might have when I was young, but no memory of them."

"Maybe you will see them again one day. Where do you go to school, Levi?"

Ruby grabs a chip from the bag on my lap. "You sound like the KGB, Layla. Levi goes to Dalton College and is the person I've chosen to be my friend. He's also been through as much as you and I have today, so why don't we leave off the interrogation."

Clyde clears his throat and turns away to hide the grin on his face. Well, that put me in my place. I shove another piece of fish into my mouth.

☾

We stay at the beach until the sun is a red ball behind us, turning the streaky clouds pale pink, orange, and golden yellow. No-one wants to leave. The emotionally turbulent events of the day have linked us into an unbroken circle; a club of exclusive members. Breaking the circle to scatter and go home feels like a betrayal or diminution of what we've shared.

A short rap tune heralding a message on Levi's phone forces our decision to go. His mother wants to know when he'll be home.

Instead of dropping Levi, Ruby, and I at Circular Quay, Clyde insists on delivering each of us to our respective doors. When we pull up at Levi's address in Turramurra, I'm surprised to see a huge federation style home sprawled across sloping lawns and accessed by a long, pine tree-lined driveway. I wonder what his father does for a living, but decide not to risk another interrogation.

We stop at the gate and Levi's hand is on the door handle when I reach over from the front seat and grab the sleeve of his T-shirt.

"Levi, if you ever give my sister alcohol or drugs again I will take it up with your mother and father. Remember, I now know where you live."

He looks at me as if considering his words. "I've never forced Ruby, it's always been her choice." I'm about to snap at his insinuations when he continues. "But after today, I think we'll both make different choices. And, thank you for that."

Levi steps out, leans back in to give Ruby a kiss on the cheek, salutes Clyde, nods at me, and swaggers off down the driveway.

When we pull into my parent's home and Corinne's car is in the driveway again, I push Ruby out, tell her to say I was in a hurry, and urge Clyde to back out as quickly as he can, preferably without the motor making a noise.

"Don't you want them to meet me?" he asks.

"What? No, it's not that. It's my sister, Corinne. I don't think I can deal with her today. We don't get along and yesterday was enough for me." I smack my hand against his leg. "They'd love you. And I think you'd like them."

I realise this is true. Mum would be fascinated with Clyde, and Dad, well, Dad would be happy that I have such a good friend.

"Okay," he says, backing out.

I thought for a minute this was going to get awkward, but Clyde, in his usual way, doesn't seem to mind what happens. Unlike Tom, who would have badgered the point until he exposed an underlying agenda.

Did I really just compare them?

Clyde drops me at my car, which is parked near the ferry again. When I lean over to kiss his cheek, he touches my shoulder as if to hold me there a moment longer. For the first time I wonder what it would be like to kiss him.

And I don't mean on the cheek.

CHAPTER 15

ONE OF THE BIGGEST CHALLENGES of my work day is choosing something to wear that says intelligent, capable woman you can trust. Not freaky, scarred, scary woman. My open wardrobe gapes at me, taunting me with the task of transformation based on limited choices. I flick through, rejecting possibilities until…yes, the plum pantsuit. I even have a black, plum- trimmed turban to wear with it.

Since the accident, I've poked, pulled, and cajoled my hair into a slew of styles. Some passable, some ridiculous. For a while there was a heavy, almost blinding fringe. It covered only a fraction of the scarring, but put me in constant danger of tripping, walking in front of cars, or eating the dog food instead of cereal for break-fast. Then there was a strip of hair pulled from the centre which dangled uselessly across my left eye. Similar risks as the fringe. Another perkier style involved short bits trained to brush forward from the turban or headscarf over the left side of my face. Oh, and the hair above the bald patch teased and fluffed to confuse the observer into thinking there was a bundle of hair where there was none. Ruby shrieked when she saw that one, saying I looked like I'd stuck my finger into a power socket. In the end I had to admit, nothing stopped the stares. Now, as my hair grows, I blow-dry it towards my face, or let it fall straight down on both sides, under whatever paraphernalia I happen to have covering my head that day.

❦

Despite the time spent in front of the mirror, I'm not protected from the malice of insensitive teenagers. Still smarting from a cruel taunt as I'd stepped off the ferry, I force myself through the glass doors of Stein and Laverick, and duck into the staff kitchen. I grab a double shot coffee, while avoiding eye contact with the early morning gossip groups gathered around the table.

Last week Brian agreed to let me front my own clients. I'd reasoned if I couldn't sell him that proposal, then I had no place doing this job. Since then, I've had three face-to-face meetings with clients. One had already considered our proposal and was keen to go further. The other two were coffee and portfolio chats with follow-ups scheduled. A little awkward, but I still felt confident I was back on my game.

Today's client representative is an art buff. I've done my research on the company and on this rep. I close my hand over the two tickets I wangled for a preliminary viewing of the Archibald Prize finalists at the Art Gallery of New South Wales. Once I've dazzled the client with my brilliant proposal, these tickets will seal the deal. I'd almost forgotten that rush of adrenaline when you have a client drooling with gratitude at, not only your product, but your attention to their personal interests.

Product management have provided me with a list of investment strategies to work with and I've got fall-back positions if my first options aren't suitable. My proposal is solid and I'm confident will meet the client needs. Nothing to worry about. I'm in my stride. The accident has not diminished my capacity to bring in the big bucks for Stein and Laverick.

The computer screen displays an outline of the strategies my team and I have put together. Time for a final skim.

Crap. I have the luck of the Irish. Kelly appears out of nowhere and props her intrusive arse on the edge of my desk.

"Morning, Layla," she says, from her perch. "I hope you haven't had any more little domestic misunderstandings with Tom." *Crap again.* I'd forgotten about that. But I can only blame myself for that unfortunate phone call, so I have to suck it up. I decide to feign nonchalance.

"Oh that? I'd completely forgotten about it. Totally sorted."

She raises one eyebrow and shrugs.

"Prep all done for your meeting this morning? Would you like me to cast an eye over the strategies?"

I have a manic urge to push her off the edge of the desk and watch her stiletto-clad feet flail in the air in full view of all our work colleagues. I quell the urge.

"No thanks, Kelly. I doubt you can add anything to what we've put together."

She slides off the desk, moves behind me, and glances over my shoulder at the computer. Like a ten-year-old, I want to cover the screen with my hand.

"I'm pretty busy, so I'll get back to it, if you don't mind," I say, minimising the screen.

As she strides away from my work area, she glances back over her shoulder and to my surprise there is a glint of admiration in her eyes. In different circumstances I may even have liked her.

When I look up again, Tom is approaching my desk. I try for a sparkling smile, too late remembering the scars on the left side of my face don't allow a full smile. I thrust my hand up to hide what must look like a grimace.

"Hi, Tom. Did you have a nice weekend? No more family issues?"

His eyebrows lock in a slight frown as if trying to work out what I mean, then his face clears. "No. All good on the family front. Quiet weekend, really. You?"

At first, I'm not sure what to tell him but decide I have nothing to hide. "A friend took me, Ruby, and her new boyfriend for some drug education. Remember how concerned we were about Ruby that night at Mum's place? It was confronting but exactly what they both needed to hear."

Tom nods, rolls a chair up to my desk, and sits. "That's good. She certainly looked a bit feral that night."

A surge of protectiveness rushes through me and my fists clench at his words. I no longer feel he has the right to comment on my sister. How sad. Before the fire he was family and I would never have given a comment like that a second thought.

"So, who's this friend who took you?" he asks, oblivious to my burst of annoyance.

I shuffle some papers into a pile. "Clyde. He was one of the people in the group on Friday night. Coincidentally, he has a friend who's a drug counsellor, so he organised the outing."

"And he wouldn't happen to be the friend you ran to after our little disagreement at work, would he?"

"I'm not sure, he might have been. Yes, I think we did have a coffee and a chat that day," I babble. Glancing up I see a wry look cross Tom's face and in that moment I want to deny Clyde. "There's nothing in it, Tom. If you saw the size of him you'd understand."

I stop speaking, aghast at what I've said. Clyde is a kind and loyal friend and I pay him back by trashing him in a pathetic effort to regain Tom's waning affection.

"Bit of an ugly bugger, is he? Overweight?" He snorts.

Self-loathing snakes through my gut at this betrayal. How could I have goaded Tom into scoffing at Clyde? I don't like this side of myself. I wonder if it's new, or if I just haven't recognised it before.

"Forget I said that. It was unkind, and I'm the last person to comment on someone's looks. He's been a good friend to me."

Tom doesn't refute the reference to my scarred face and the unsaid words dangle in the air between us. Thankfully, the awkward silence is interrupted by Clarissa strutting towards my desk with documents in her hand. Although she's heading to me, her eyes are fixed on Tom. She places the documents in my outstretched hand and then touches Tom's arm.

"Is there anything you'd like, Tom?"

What is this woman doing?

He shifts in his chair. "No. No thanks, Clarissa. All good, thanks."

She blinks slowly, pivots, and walks back down the corridor as if I'm not in the room. A few steps away she slows and turns back as Tom raises his head to watch her retreat. The look they exchange makes me want to rush to the Ladies and throw up. I now know where he was Saturday night.

"Are you serious?" I ask, my face hot with the shock of this revelation.

I jump up, grab a stack of documents, and try to escape; but the toe of my shoe clips the desk leg, lurching me forward. Tom reaches to steady me and I slap his hand away.

"Layla. Wait. You've misunderstood."

I ignore him and half run down the corridor towards the boardroom. He doesn't try to follow me.

Kelly or Clarissa? Kelly and Clarissa?

&

With my back against the closed door, I take three deep breaths and turn to the window. If I watch the street activity, it might erase the last few minutes from my mind. After all, I'm good at losing memories. Besides, I have to focus on this meeting.

After a few minutes, I place my paper pile on the table. I have graphs, short and long-term projections, and a history of the products I'm suggesting. All I need now is the client. A sharp rap on the open door announces Susan Pearson, Executive Assistant to the CEO of the client company. I thank the receptionist, and hold my hand out.

"How nice to meet you, Miss Pearson. Would you like tea, or coffee?"

The woman is tall, quite heavily built, with short, straight black hair. I feel the muscles in my shoulders and neck relax, thinking another woman who is not a fashion model herself is going to appreciate my skills and expertise over my appearance.

She misses a beat, then thrusts out her hand, her eyes flickering over my scars, before scanning the room.

"And you, Miss Danforth. Call me Susan, and I would love a coffee."

"Please, Susan, have a seat, and I'm Layla."

I pour the coffees and take a seat opposite her. I'm about to start my presentation when she interrupts me.

"I hope you don't mind me asking, but is that a burn scar?"

"Yes, it is." I reach for the computer to start the PowerPoint presentation.

"It looks to be quite recent. Is it?"

I tamp down the urge to grab the nosey bitch by the throat and tell her to mind her own business and instead manage a tight smile.

"Over eighteen months. But I'd prefer not to discuss it; let's talk about some investment strategies.

"You seem angry about discussing this, Layla."

Now she's really stepping over the line.

"Not angry, Susan. I don't see the relevance to our meeting today and would like to concentrate on our business."

"In a situation like this one can't separate the person from the business. Wouldn't you agree?"

I clench my jaw and take a slow breath through my nose. "The person and the person's appearance are not quite the same thing. Wouldn't *you* agree?"

The woman raises an eyebrow and gestures for me to begin.

She examines and questions every detail of the proposal, but has to admit my proposal will enhance their current portfolio. However, her gaze constantly flicks away from the proposal back to my face, as if the scars irresistibly claim her attention. And even after two hours of close contact, no warmth emanates from her towards me. In the past, it only took minutes of conversation with clients to establish the strong rapport and trust necessary for a good working relationship.

At least I still have the art preview tickets as a sweetener. That should work.

At the end of our discussion, I hand her the two tickets to the art show. When she sees what they're for, a flash of excitement ripples her features.

"I thought you might like to join me for this preview…"

The shadow of hesitation on her face brings me to a halt. Without responding, her fingers close over both tickets and she slides them into her handbag. No gallery preview for me, then.

I escort her to the door, thanking her for her time.

Instead of heading down the corridor towards the lifts, she asks the way to Brian's office, explaining she wants to say a quick hello and brief him on the meeting. Something about her explanation doesn't feel right and with a sense of dread, I close the boardroom door and lower myself onto a chair. Within seconds panic grips my chest, my head whirls, nausea washes through my body, and my throat closes. *Deep breath in, hold, release the breath. Deep breath in, hold, release the breath.*

I lose track of time as I focus on winning the battle with this anxiety attack. When my heart-rate finally decreases and the dizziness clears, I glance at the clock and note I've been alone in the room for nearly twenty minutes. A sudden rap on the door shocks me into conscious awareness and when the door begins to open, I pick up my pen and scribble rubbish on a pad, like a kid caught out at school.

"Layla. Thought you might still be in here when I didn't see you at your desk."

It's Brian Townsend. Fresh from his *tête a tête* with Miss Susan Pearson.

"Just making some notes from the meeting. What can I do for you, Brian?"

Brian pulls out a chair, but instead of sitting, he stands behind it, then walks over and pours himself a coffee, walks back, jiggles the cup on the saucer, takes a sip, places it on the table and finally sits. To avoid a repeat of the previous twenty minutes, I concentrate on keeping my mind clear of assumptions and sit, motionless, with my hands in my lap, waiting for Brian to speak.

Finally he clears his throat. "How do you think the meeting went?"

As patient and polite as I'm trying to be, I can't play these games.

"Why don't you tell me, Brian? I'm aware Miss Pearson scuttled straight to your office after leaving me. Obviously my opinion of how the meeting went is not why you're here."

A bead of sweat trickles over the ridge of his frown.

"You don't make it easy for me do you, Layla? But then that's why I've always admired you. You're a straight shooter." He rakes his fingers through his thinning hair.

He's right, I won't make this easy. I wait for him to continue.

"First of all, Susan Pearson asked me to give these back to you." He holds out the two tickets for the art gallery.

My chest tightens, squeezing the breath out of me. Brian waits for me to take the tickets. I can't bring myself to touch them or to speak. This isn't how it was meant to work.

He places them on the table and holds my gaze. "She thinks you may not have dealt psychologically with the effects of your injuries—"

I leap to my feet, sending the chair wheeling backwards into the wall. "How dare she? How dare she analyse my mental state after one short meeting." I round the table and eyeball Brian. He presses himself back against the chair. "She had the audacity to question me about my scars and when I wanted to move onto the proposal, she accused me of having a problem with discussing my injuries."

Brian stands, obviously not comfortable with me looming over him, and grasps my shoulders. "Layla, you don't need to be upset about this—"

"Not upset!" I exclaim. "I presented a brilliant proposal which, I might add, she admitted met all their requirements." My voice hits a hysterical note. "And now you come in here like a circus dog, prancing around in response to this woman's crazy assumptions." I bite back the words. Too late.

Brian's hand smacks the board table. "Enough, Layla. Perhaps she's right. I've never heard you lose your temper like this before. It would be very unfortunate if that happened with a client and I can't risk it."

I sit down, an icy calm seeping up my spine. "I guess you'd better say what you came to say, Brian. Are you firing me?"

He slumps onto the chair. "Of course not. You're too valuable to lose." I raise an eyebrow at the contradiction between this and his last statement. "I want to offer you something different." He holds his hand up to halt my response. "And don't think I made this decision in the last ten minutes. Susan Pearson is the fourth client to express discomfort when dealing with you."

The fourth client? I've only had three others. So, every client, regardless of the quality of my proposals, has complained about working with me. I feel like I'm drowning. My arms, limp at my sides, are unable and unwilling to drag me back to the surface. The blood pounds in my eardrums and a wet film over my eyes blurs Brian's outline. I swallow, and swallow again.

He gives me a moment before continuing.

"Similar to our initial agreement, I want to offer you a position where you don't have client contact. Someone else would be the front person and they would brief you on the client's needs. You could co-ordinate research on both the prospective client and relevant products and make suggestions as to investment strategies."

I stare at him. "Let me clarify. You're offering me a job in a back room where no one can see me, doing the hard graft for people who will then be praised for their expertise. Have I got that right?"

Brian sighs. "Layla, you're making it sound far worse than it is. I think you'll feel more comfortable in the long run, not having to worry how clients might react to you." He places his hands on the desk and pushes himself up. "You have a think about my offer. Don't make your decision straightaway."

His words leave me feeling like a paper cut-out of myself: flat, bloodless, and devoid of emotion. Still seated, I make direct eye contact with Brian and when I respond my voice is a cold monotone.

"Fuck the job. And fuck you, Brian."

I stand and leave the room.

When I reach my desk, the implications of what I've done chill my body. No work, no pay, no operation, no life. My gaze darts to the window. A quick leap would end the misery. And condemn my family to more grief from such a self-indulgent act.

I gather a few meagre possessions from my desk and, without a word to anyone, I leave the building.

❧

How I make it to Macquarie Street and down that alleyway, I will never know. My eyes are blinded by tears and for once, I don't care who stares because I can't see them. The cold metal railing guides me down the steps into the familiar fug of sweat and hops.

"MacArthur Park" spills from the speakers and without checking to see who's there, I sneak into a dark booth and slump against the wall. The lyrics of the song bring forth a fresh flow of tears as I accept the loss of my livelihood and everything this represents, including hope of re-igniting my relationship with Tom.

A gust of air disturbs the stale odours as the door at the top of the stairs opens and closes. I look up from my dark corner and see Mrs. Crompton, small square handbag dangling from her arm, make her way down the steps and over to the bar.

"My usual coffee, thank you, Frankie," she says, which is code for, 'a good slug of brandy in a coffee mug, thank you, Frankie.'

I don't know Frankie, but he obviously knows Mrs. Crompton. She doesn't notice me and I shrink back against the shadow of the wall, not wanting to speak to anyone. Except Clyde, and he's not here.

I'm not sure how long I've been curled up, with my knees tucked under my chin silently weeping, when I feel a hesitant tap on my shoulder. A hand with dirty fingernails holds out a paper serviette like a flag of truce. Without looking up, I grasp the serviette, dab at my eyes, and blow my nose. He slides into the seat opposite and waits for my attention.

"Th-thank you, Professor," I sniff. "I hope I didn't disturb you."

"Of course not. You probably require a hug more than a serviette, but I'm not the most agreeable person to hug. Would you like to tell me what has you so distressed?" When I don't respond straight away, he looks down at his threadbare trousers. "I see that was very presumptuous of me. Please forgive me. Of course you don't want to talk about your private woes to someone like me."

Still clutching the sodden serviette, I grasp his hand, dirty fingernails and all. "No. That's not it at all. I…don't know where to start."

He reaches over with his other hand and pats mine. "Let's start at the beginning, shall we? As you can imagine, I have no pressing engagements. I'm all yours as long as you need me."

I hesitate, searching his face for signs of inebriation. I can't bare my soul to someone too drunk to comprehend what I'm saying. But his eyes express empathy and interest and his attention seems focused on me.

At the end of my sorry tale, a tear drops from the professor's eye, tracking down his unshaven face to join the other stains on his tweed jacket. He slides another serviette out of the stainless steel holder and dabs at his face.

"Now I'm an old man with a pickled brain, so let me make sense of what you've told me." I wait for him to continue. "Bear in mind, I will just be stating facts, so forgive me if it sounds a bit cold."

"We'd be here all day if you were going to describe all the crazy emotions I've felt over the last eighteen months."

"Very good. So, you need your job to have this operation, which might or might not fix the scars on your face. And you need to fix the scars on your face because your life was perfect before and unbearable now." He looks at me for confirmation and I nod. "Right. And now you've lost your job, and therefore the ability to earn the money for this operation. Oh, and your boyfriend is cheating on you. But even before you knew that, you knew he was unable to be intimate with you looking as you now do." A warm flush creeps up my neck at this last statement, but the professor doesn't seem in the least embarrassed. "Do you think that covers it?"

"When I hear it put like that, it sounds so trivial. So many people face life and death situations daily and I'm worried about some scars on my face and body."

And hearing his summary about the Tom situation makes me wonder, perhaps not for the first time, why I would want someone who seems incapable of loving more than my exterior; and who can't see I'm still the same person I was before the fire. Although, I don't want to be overly harsh with Tom.

Damn it, yes I do. He's cheated on me!

"And your family, are they supportive?" asks the professor.

"Extremely. We are very close. Except for my older sister."

"Ah, I must admit to being a little envious of a loving family."

I grasp his hand again. "Of course. I'm so sorry, Professor, how selfish of me to whinge on about my problems like this."

He leans forward, his puffy eyes focused on mine. "Unlike yourself, every problem I have is entirely of my own making. Nothing *happened* to me. I wrote, directed, and acted in my own tragic play. And not only did I knowingly destroy my own life but also the lives of my family. I hope I am able to do a little better next time." He gazes silently down at his glass for a few moments as if the impact of his own words make it too hard to continue. Then he throws back the dregs of his drink, catches the attention of the barman, and turns back to me. "Now we have looked at all the events worthy of despair, let's look at those which might balance your situation even a little."

"Don't go all Pollyanna on me, Professor. I don't think I'm in the mood to count my blessings today."

His hand has a slight tremor as he takes the glass of vodka and orange juice from the barman and lifts it to his cracked lips. After three large mouthfuls, he exhales with a look of pure ecstasy on his face. I don't think I ever realised how essential booze is to an alcoholic.

Like Anna at the rehab centre, he believes life offers him no other choices than to keep using. I have a sudden urge to fix him. Or at the least to re-unite him with his children.

Who am I kidding? I can't even fix myself.

Although it had bothered me before, that people like Clyde and Gavin would feed the old man's alcoholism, I think I now have a glimmer of understanding. If they didn't give him a safe place to drink and supply him with reasonable quality alcohol, he could be on the street drinking methylated spirits or even ethanol. And I wouldn't be sitting across from him today.

"Humour an old man, my dear. Would you like to hear all the wonderful things I can see in your life?"

I shake my head, throwing my hands up in surrender. "Knock yourself out, professor."

"An interesting saying. I'll assume it doesn't mean you'd like to see me unconscious." He chuckles at his joke and a grin creeps across my wet face. "As we've already acknowledged, you have a loving, supportive family. You now have a very different and interesting group of friends…" we both glance over to the bar, "…who feel honoured to have met you. Admittedly, some of us are a little different and some, like myself, are society's rejects, but we are here for you, Layla. And I hope our friendship will give you the courage, in time, to seek out other new friendships with more socially adept individuals."

Again, I feel some shame that the descriptions he has used are exactly the ones I used when I first came into The Black Hole. If I'm truthful with myself, might probably still use, although now with a touch of sentimentality.

"It's true you haven't got a job, but you have an excellent set of skills and qualifications with which to find yourself another position and, I'm guessing here, you probably have some small savings to keep you going for a while." I nod. "That leaves us with the problem which seems to be distressing you the most, which is your capacity to have this plastic surgery on your face. Would you mind explaining to me what this will mean for you?"

Where to start? "Do you have any idea what it's like to be ridiculed, reviled, and pointed at every time you set foot outside of your home?"

The professor opens wide his arms and indicates his dirty beanie, stained jacket, and battered duffel bag. "Of course I do. I'm a dirty, smelly, useless old alcoholic. If I'm sitting in a park, people pull their children close to their sides and detour around me. Teenagers tease me, play tag with my belongings, and sometimes I get beaten up for a night's entertainment—solely because people believe I am a non-human, of no value. The biggest mistake I've made is to agree with them."

He seems to mull this self-revelation over for a moment, staring into his glass. Then he raises his head and again locks me in his gaze. "Is that what you do, Layla? Do you believe what others tell you about yourself?"

This question takes me by surprise. "I don't have to believe what others say, I can see it in the mirror. It's real. And that's what tears me apart."

"So, when you see this reflection in the mirror and are repulsed by it, do you attack it?"

I scrunch up my nose, wondering if he's a little insane. "If I did that, I'd probably be locked away. That sounds ridiculous. "

"Yet you are attacking yourself from inside. What is the difference?"

I'm about to point out these two behaviours in no way resemble each other, when it strikes me he may be right. Whatever job the outside hecklers may do on me, I can do better myself. How many times have I stated aloud how much I hate myself? How ugly I am, how useless, how undesirable? And that's not counting the internal verbal abuse. I shudder at the messages I've been pounding into every cell of my body since I first held a mirror in front of my scarred face. It's a wonder this body still carries me around. My throat clogs and I can feel the tears welling in my eyes.

"I don't know how to stop it," I whisper, swiping at my nose with another serviette.

"Let the people who love you show you who you are, not the ones who don't. And you need to be one of those."

The truth of these words is like a punch in the gut. Images run through my mind of those who've treated me no differently since the fire and those who are repelled by my scars. To my surprise, as predicted by the professor, they fit neatly into two categories: those who love me and those who don't.

This time when he lowers his eyes to caress the glass, he doesn't look up again. I watch him without discomfort, aware he's retreated back into his alcohol-infused haze. This man must have been a wonderful professor in the prime of his life, when he was sober. Clyde was lucky to have him as a mentor and it's now easy for me to see why he feels he owes the old man so much.

It's clear our conversation is over and with a renewed sense of peace and a whole lot to think about, I place a kiss on the top of the professor's beanie, climb the stairs and step back into the real world. I still have no solutions to any of the problems I brought in with me, but I've made one decision. I'll stop beating up that woman I see in the mirror every day. It's the best I can do for now.

Despite the last half an hour, I have to confess, I still can't let go of my unquenchable desire to have the surgery.

CHAPTER 16

WITH THE PROFESSOR'S WORDS WHIRLING around my head, I turn towards Circular Quay. As I pass a Starbuck's café, a middle-aged woman bursts through the door, bringing with her the deep, rich aroma of coffee beans. She apologises, holds the door open for me, and smiles. Like iron filings to a magnet, my body leans towards the door. I've had nothing to eat or drink since my rushed cup of coffee first thing this morning. I'll get the next ferry.

After ordering a soy latte and a croissant with ham and Swiss cheese, I move to a small table, ignoring the stares and whispered comments. While I wait for my order, my mind goes back over all the professor said to me. It seemed so logical and clear when we were hiding alone in The Black Hole. But the startled looks and barely concealed comments once again pierce me like a thousand tiny daggers. Perhaps one day in the future I may, like the professor, be more philosophical about it.

A young girl, with a Spanish accent and a nose piercing, puts my coffee and croissant in front of me and tells me to enjoy it. As I lift the latte glass, I notice a narrow-faced man with droopy bloodhound eyes, and a moustache which hangs in sympathy with his eyes. He studies me with more than a passing interest, his brow furrowed as if he's arguing with himself over a decision. To discourage his attention, I reach for a magazine, left on the table, and make a pretence of reading. Still staring at the magazine, I take a bite of my warm, cheesy croissant. Before I can place it back on the plate, the chair on the other side of my small table screeches as it's dragged backwards. I look up.

"May I join you?" he asks.

Swallowing my mouthful, I shake my head. "I'd rather be alone, if you don't mind."

He leans forward. "I have something that might interest you. Give me a moment of your time and then I'll leave, I promise."

"I don't even know you, so I doubt whether anything you say will interest me."

He doesn't move but his head drops like a chastised puppy. "I understand you'd not want me to join you. You don't know me, you're eating and you might want privacy—"

The interaction has drawn the attention of several people and although I suspect this dejected, self-deprecating behaviour is a clever ploy on his part, I take the path of least resistance.

"Oh, for goodness sake, sit down and get it over with."

He plonks himself on the chair, his moustache giving a pleased twitch, and pulls a card from his shirt pocket.

"Schuster and Beasley – Lawyers. I'm Jason Crane, I work for Mr. Beasley. At the risk of offending you, I couldn't help but notice that you have an injury. An accident?"

"You're soliciting business for your firm?" It's so ridiculous, I want to laugh. "You have a nerve, Mr. Whoever-You-Are, imposing yourself on a complete stranger. I wonder how the owner of this establishment would feel if he knew."

A flash of alarm flickers across his face and he pulls out a large blue handkerchief to dab at the sweat darkening the tight collar of his shirt.

"No. Don't be concerned. You deserve to be compensated for whatever happened." He gestures at my face. "You've heard of No Win, No Pay, I presume? Our firm has a high rate of success. Why don't I leave you my card in case you change your mind?"

Before I can formulate a suitably cutting response, or call the manager, he pushes back his chair and escapes. Can this day get any weirder?

Rattled by this strange encounter, I leave my croissant unfinished, gulp the last few mouthfuls of coffee and walk down to the wharf. Thrusting my hand into my bag to search for the ferry ticket, I realise I'm clutching a rectangular piece of cardboard—the sleazy lawyer's business card. I release it into the depths of my handbag as if it's a hot coal, content in the assumption it will never emerge again.

C

Whenever I trudge up the hill to Hula Nights, I chant another mantra, learnt at a Buddhist retreat a friend and I attended some years ago: *Om Mani Padme Hum*. It keeps me focused on the walking and I don't notice the time. However, today the mantra that inserts itself into my head is different: *I'm unemployed again*. Same rhythm, but with the opposite effect of my usual chant. By the time I reach my building, I'm in a deep funk again.

In the half-light of dusk, Mr. Bacik is bent over the garden, communing with his vegetables. Next to him, with four legs splayed outward and head resting between his forelegs, is Bennie. Halting at the gate, I watch the peaceful scene for a moment, grateful once again to my old neighbour for looking after my furry friend. Although, I suspect he gets as much out of it as the dog. Then Bennie's head jerks up, his nose sniffing the air. With a yelp of delight, he streaks through the open gate and leaps into my arms. I bury my face in the soft fur on the top of his head, and the professor's words flash through my mind. Bennie definitely fits on the list of those who love me and don't care about my appearance.

"Layla. Hello. You are not so late from work tonight? This makes Bennie very happy." Mr. Bacik pushes himself up from the ground, places the palm of his hand against his back and stretches, groaning. He beckons me over. "Come, come. Tell me about your day. In fact, tell me about your weekend. We don't talk for so long."

Still holding Bennie, I take my place on the step and Mr. Bacik joins me.

"Well, I'll be home most days now as I've lost my job." Damn, the stupid tears start to drip down my face.

"Ah, this is good news for Bennie but bad news for you, I think." He pulls out a clean handkerchief and dabs at my face, not flinching at touching the scars. "What will you do?"

I manage a watery smile in response, grateful he hasn't asked for details, and instead focusses on the future.

"I'm not sure. Unless I can find a job where I hide in a dark room and pass clever suggestions through a slot in the door. Then no one's sensibilities have to be offended by the sight of me."

This small foray into self-pity brings with it a fresh flow of tears, which Bennie tries to lick from my neck as they slide in a trail down to my shirt. He whimpers, buries his head in my chest, and puts one paw over his face. It's pathetic and funny.

Mr. Bacik shakes his head, a deep frown furrowing his forehead. "No. No. No! I will not sit and hear such talk. You are so beautiful, sometimes it takes my breath away." I lift my gaze, wondering when he lost his marbles. "I can see from your face, you don't believe me. Even with this small scar you look like an angel. Mrs. Bacik said just this thing to me last week."

Small scar? Angel? He must be losing his eyesight as well as his marbles.

With Bennie squashed between us, I fling my arms around his neck, my eyes and nose both dripping onto the collar of his shirt.

"You are the sweetest, kindest man I know. I know it's not true, but I love you for saying it. I only wish the people I work with could borrow your rose-coloured glasses."

His rough, work hardened hand pats my back. "People only see their own shame and fear. Maybe you remind them of their vulnerabilities, so they must put you away from them. How many times do I see this happen to the Jews. The Nazis had to get rid of us because we remind them of their own cruelty and their own fear. Your situation, it might be different but is also the same."

Neither of us speaks except to chuckle when Bennie wriggles frantically to escape. He lands unsteadily, loses his balance, shakes himself all over and slumps to the ground with a sigh. I loosen my hold on the old man and lean back against the step, my mind leaping to the loss of his grandchildren. Such a tragedy for him and even more for them to not know the love and wisdom of their grandfather.

"You know, Ruby's new boyfriend is Jewish."

Mr. Bacik raises his eyebrows. "This is true? A Jewish boy. I must tell Mrs. Bacik."

"He looks a bit weird though," I say. "This boy has red dyed hair sticking straight up on top of his head, a piercing through his eyebrow, and another one through his lip. Is that normal for a Jewish boy?"

Mr. Bacik roars with laughter, which elicits a yell from inside his flat. Mrs. Bacik wants to know why he's making crazy noises. He yells back that it's nothing and turns to me, still grinning.

"I wouldn't know anymore, *kochana*." He holds his hand against his heart. "But I think my Anka would not allow her boy to look like this. She is very strict, I think. Although, of course, I am not so sure any more and the boy is fifteen years old now."

"Maybe you could be a surrogate grandfather for Levi. I'm sure his parents wouldn't mind."

"A boy like that. He would not want an old man like me to tell him about life. But if he comes to your house, I am very happy to meet him and to say hello to your Ruby again."

I kiss the top of his head as I stand. "I'll do that. Bring him in to see you. It might not hurt so much, not seeing your grandson, if you can make a difference with this one."

He shrugs and turns back to his garden.

Leaning against the door to the foyer, I let Bennie scarper in, and then we climb the flight of stairs to our flat on the first floor. It's probably incredibly presumptuous of me to even think Levi would give the time of day to Mr. Bacik, but it might be a good thing for both of them—worth a try. And for a few minutes it takes my mind away from my own sorry situation.

The room is already dark, so I switch on the lamp in the front room and fling my bag onto the table. It lands on its side and the contents spill across the surface.

I'll fix it later. First, I need to change out of the plum suit of shame, into curl-up-and-sulk clothes. When I return from my bedroom, I shovel all the paraphernalia back into the bag, pushing aside old cash register dockets and used tissues to throw in the bin. Caught in the mess is a business card.

I push it over with the used tissues, then snatch it up and thrust it into my pocket.

CHAPTER 17

A SOFT WASH OF PEACH BLEEDS from vivid cayenne as nature paints a masterpiece across the dawn sky. I stare until my eyes water, searching for the answer to my burning question. Is it too much to ask for it to be written in black across the fiery crimson surface of the sun?

No. Still not there.

Picking up a handful of soft, white sand, I regard my furry companion.

"What do you think, Bennie? I'm at the desperate end of the barrel. How will I get the money to go to New York?" He tilts his head and whimpers. "Yes, I know it's sad and pathetic. But you need to answer my question."

Bennie sneezes, spraying my hand with sandy saliva. *Yuck.* I wipe it down the leg of my pants and feel the cardboard outline of the rogue business card, shoved into my pocket last night. I pull it out.

Schuster and Beasley – Lawyers. Shyster and Sleazy more like. I can't believe I'm even looking at this again. But I must find a way to see Dr. Gassner in New York. I seem to have run out of options, unless I allow my parents to re-mortgage their house. No. I won't do that. I gaze back out at the ocean, where the sun is still low enough on the horizon to light a diamond studded path across the water to the beach.

Bennie's ears prick up at the delighted bark of another dog, splashing in the shallows, and he runs to join in the fun. I look back down at the card. A phone call can't hurt, surely. Then I can make up my mind armed with more information.

I haven't mentioned this to any members of my family, or Tom, but interestingly, I discussed it with Clyde last night.

(

He'd phoned not long after I arrived home from The Black Hole. The professor having told Clyde I'd been at the bar earlier.

"Sorry I wasn't in when you came today," he said. "The professor told me he was sober enough to chat with you. You probably couldn't have had a better shoulder to cry on."

"He was so sweet, Clyde, and everything he said to me was comforting and thought-provoking at the same time. He must have been an amazing teacher when you first met him."

"He was. Still is, in fact, only his audience has changed."

"Sure has."

"So, by the sound of it, you've had a shocker of a day. How would you feel about having dinner with a fat bastard sometime this week to take your mind off it?"

"Both the fat bastard and the dinner would have to be pretty special to do that."

"Challenge accepted. Dinner won't be a problem, but I'll have to do some work on the fat bastard."

"I think dinner would be nice. What about Wednesday, are you working that night?"

"No, I'm not...Shit."

"What?"

"It's Wretched Wednesday. The night I have dinner with my mother."

An insane idea had occurred to me. "I could come."

"God Almighty, Layla, I wouldn't put my worst enemy through that...but, hang on, what's going on here? Have you had a personality transplant? The Layla I know would hardly subject herself to a room full of strangers, let alone a close encounter with the Mother From Hell."

I grinned at the image. "Well, it would certainly take my mind off losing my job, and we can play tag at being the least socially acceptable person in the room."

As I said this, I pinched my arm to make sure I hadn't done that leave-your-body caper again. Because he was right; normally I would rather have my toenails extracted with a pair of pliers than do what I've just suggested. When I lost my job I must also have lost my mind. Or perhaps I wanted to give something back to Clyde, and if playing buffer between him and his mother even once was helpful, then I'd do it. And then again, maybe I was worried Clyde might think we're going on a romantic date if it was only the two of us having dinner.

"Even Tyler's wife doesn't come."

"Tyler. The brother with the good name. Your mother likes him, right?"

"Yep, that's the one. How about a compromise. If the reaction is even semi-positive when I make the suggestion to my mother, I'll tell her we're only calling in for a drink and nibbles, then we're going out to dinner. That way I cover my butt with her and we still get to go out to dinner."

"What if she's put out that you're not staying? I don't want to cause trouble."

"If it gets sticky, we'll gobble down dinner and go out for coffee and dessert. Tyler has begged off many times. Which reminds me, I'd better check he's coming this week. She won't mind me leaving if he's there."

"Now that's settled, there was something I wanted to bounce off you, if that's okay?"

"Sure, I'm very bouncy," he chuckled.

I didn't comment on that, in case I incriminated myself. Instead, I described my encounter with the man from Shyster and Sleazy and the card I didn't throw away.

"When he ran his spiel, it seemed ridiculous, but the more I think about it, the more I wonder if it could be the answer to my financial issues."

"Do you have a case? I understood the original arson investigators found no evidence of negligence or foul-play."

"That's what they said, but there may have been a fault with something in the house—heating…or wiring. And he'd have insurance for those eventualities, so it would be worth finding out and going for compensation, wouldn't you think?"

"It won't hurt to check it out. And if you don't like these lawyers, there's plenty of others like them. I imagine it'll be a bit like selling your soul to the devil, though. Are you ready for that?"

"Not sure about that one."

"I'd better go. I-er, thanks for asking my opinion. You know whatever you do I'll support you. I'll give you a call tomorrow after I've spoken to my mother."

"Thanks, Clyde. You're a good friend."

I heard a grunt as he ended the call. It occurred to me he'd listened but hadn't influenced me one way or the other with regards to the lawyers. Clever. I'm still not sure why, but it seemed important to have his approval. That's normal with a friend you respect, isn't it?

☙

My musings are interrupted by a sharp yelp from Bennie, as he romps back from playing 'who can choke on more salt water' with his canine buddy. He launches his two wet, sandy front paws at my chest and I roll back to escape him, but it's all a game as he licks my face, pulls my hair, and growls with excitement. I push him off, spit sand from my mouth, and brush my clothes down.

"Okay, funny boy, let's go home."

My phone gives two twangs as we pass the ocean baths. A message. From Tom.

Everything okay after yesterday?

He's kidding. I lost my job, found out he's been cheating, and he asks if everything is okay.

Sure. Everything okay with you? I perch on a concrete step and wait while he works out how to respond.

Two twangs: *Fair go, Layla. I'm concerned about how u r feeling.*

I want to respond in capitals. Capitals with exclamation marks because that's how you yell in a text. I hit the first few letters on the keyboard. What if I am ending the only good thing left in my life? But as the thought flashes through my mind, it seems to have a question mark at the end of it. How long is it since anything has been good with Tom? Or have I been living in a time-warp fantasy?

Hard to believe, Tom. Let's make it easy. You don't have to play solicitous boyfriend anymore.

A much longer pause this time. I return a wave to one of Mr. Bacik's swimming mates, who has emerged from the pool in his very revealing budgie-smugglers. I try to keep my eyes above his waist, but like a car wreck, I can't look away. To make the sight even more unappealing, he has a large belly under which the miniscule nylon swimming costume clings precariously, clearly outlining the tiny slug nestled beneath his belly.

Two twangs: *We need to talk.*

Yes, he likes talking as long as he doesn't have to touch me. Despite my last text, I keep my options open.

Perhaps. But not yet. Must work through yesterday—both events.

Two twangs: *OK. Remember ur decision. I wanted to talk.*

Scumbag. I can't help but think he's covering his butt, so he comes out smelling like a rose. I shove the phone back into my pocket and we climb the steps up to Hula Nights.

❦

"Good morning, Schuster and Beasley. Can I help you?"

I take a deep breath. I can't back out now.

"Yes I would like to speak to…" *Crap.* I can't remember the name of the dishevelled pimp who gave me the card.

"Hello. I didn't get the name of the person you'd like to speak to."

"I'm terribly sorry, but I actually don't recall the gentleman's name. He gave me your company's card in a restaurant."

She gives an impatient sigh. "Perhaps if you describe him, I might know who you mean." I try to describe the man as kindly as possible. "I think you might mean Mr. Beasley's assistant, Jason Crane. Let me put you through."

Mr. Crane admits it was he who interrupted my lunch yesterday and is very keen for me to come in and meet with Mr. Beasley. It can't hurt to speak to them, so I agree to a meeting first thing Thursday morning. I have to go into the city anyway for my next appointment with Jarrod.

❦

Godfather Guitar strums as I step from the shower, so I grab a towel and run, dripping, to the kitchen where I've left the phone. I'm breathing hard by the time I pick up.

"Hello."

"Ooh, heavy breathing. Must be my lucky day."

"Hi, Clyde, I've run from the shower. I feel like a drowned rat and I'm dripping water all over the kitchen floor."

"Now I'm really feeling lucky. Just got the visual of you naked, body glistening with water. Don't speak, let me sit with that for a minute."

"I will not. Wipe that image immediately." He laughs. "I've put on a pair of plumber's overalls and an Akubra hat. Replace it with that visual. Now tell me why you've phoned."

"You're a hard woman, Layla, but I'm about to pay you back. For some unfathomable reason, my mother was ecstatic about me bringing a friend to dinner and already had the menu planned by the end of the conversation. I've told her we must be gone by eight thirty as we're meeting friends for coffee and dessert. So make sure our stories match when she interrogates."

"Crap! Now I can't pull out even if I want to. The menu's been planned."

"Exactly. If you give me your address, I'll pick you up at six thirty so we can be there by seven." I give him the address, including the name of the block of flats. "Hula Nights? That's hilarious. Great position though."

"I'm quite proud of that name. Not many people can boast such a kitsch name. And you're right, the views are stunning. I'll show you when you get here. Come a bit earlier."

"Love to. See you between six and quarter past. And dress to kill. Literally. Because by the end of the night you'll probably want to do just that."

I hold my breath, not sure what I'm getting myself into.

"That was a joke, Layla. See you tomorrow." I hear him chuckling as he cuts off the call.

Now I have three things to dread. Dinner with Clyde's mother, a meeting with Shyster and Sleazy, and my next session with Jarrod. A visit to my parent's home might distract me, and besides, I need to check how Ruby's doing. Mum finishes work early on a Tuesday, so I'll head off after lunch.

❦

We chat about trivia while Mum makes tea. I have a mouthful of ginger nut biscuit when the questions start.

"Alright, enough small talk. Why are you really here, darling? I can tell there's something you want to talk about. What is it?"

Mothers-to-be must be sent to Super Sleuth School before they're allowed to give birth, I'm convinced of it.

"I've got an appointment with some lawyers. Depending on what they say, I'm thinking of going ahead with a lawsuit against the landlord."

She takes a sip of her tea, lowers her arm, and then brings the cup back up to her lips, biding her time.

"I have a feeling that's not the whole story. What else has happened?"

My mother did Advanced Sleuth Studies.

I follow her actions and take a mouthful of tea before answering. "I don't have a job anymore." My eyes tear up as I make the admission. She waits, knowing there's more. "Four clients refused to work with me. The last one said it was because I was unstable, was carrying too many unresolved issues from the accident, and they didn't think I would be up to the job. That's the official version, anyway."

Mum gasps at my words and pulls me into her arms. "Oh, darling, how unjust and untrue. People are so stupid and cruel. I can't believe Brian would fire you for that. In fact, he can't."

I pull back, eyes lowered, looking at a pink rose splashed across her skirt.

"He didn't exactly fire me. He offered me a job hiding in a back room and I told him what I thought of it and walked out."

I glance up as she raises her eyebrows, a small grin tugging at her lips.

"Well, I raised you to be clear about what you think you deserve, so I can't argue your response, darling."

"I know," I wail, eight years old again. "But now I have no job and therefore no income which all equate to no Dr. Gassner. So,

I have no choice but to sue for the money."

With one arm around me, Mum dunks the hard ginger nut biscuit into her tea and quickly dangles it over her mouth before it drops.

"In hospital, I recall you saying the fire alarm didn't wake you. At the time, I assumed you were too deeply asleep, but what if it wasn't working? Then you'd have a reason to sue the landlord, wouldn't you?" I nod, my mouth full of biscuit.

"Mmm…but," I swallow the ginger nut, "not sure why I said that. I can't remember anything that would indicate there was a problem. There are so many blanks in my memory."

"As always, we'll support whatever route you take. Perhaps, in time, you'll remember something that will be of use."

The front door closes and I hear footsteps down the hall.

"Hi, Mum".

It's my sister, Corinne. She's like a bloodhound, sniffing me out whenever I appear at the house, ensuring I don't get a larger slice of the parental attention pie.

"I didn't know you were coming over this afternoon, Layla."

"Spur of the moment decision, Corinne. Should I have asked your permission first?" I snap, annoyed she's interrupted the discussion I'm having with my mother.

Mum rolls her eyes, releases me, and reaches up to give Corinne a hug. "I don't think you two realise how much you miss out on by waging this continuous battle against each other. Sisters can be such a comfort to each other."

My sarcastic response halts at the flash of pain in my mother's eyes. She hates watching two of her children in constant conflict. I'll make an effort, for her.

"Sorry about that comment, Corinne. I came over here to tell Mum I'm going to look at filing a lawsuit against the landlord."

Her jaw drops at my statement. "Really? You want to blame someone else, when it was probably your fault?"

"Hang on, I'm the victim here, Corinne."

"You're right about that. It must feel better that way, hey?"

I recoil, stung by her insensitivity.

"Corinne, that was uncalled for," says my mother.

Her face pales at Mum's admonishment and with her eyes averted, says, "Sorry, that was a bit mean, Layla. I'd actually like to help with your lawsuit. You know, with support and research and all that."

I'm speechless at this bogus flag of truce. Well, that's my cynical opinion. But Mum's eyes shine at the apology and the possibility we might do something sisterly after all these years, so I swallow the words jostling to leap from my tongue.

"Er-that's very kind of you, Corinne. That might be helpful. I could call you after my meeting with the lawyers on Thursday."

"Would you like me to get some time off work and come with you to the meeting?" she asks.

Now I have an urge to lift up her shirt and see if there is a metal casing with different buttons: Nice Corinne/Nasty Corinne. I only know how to respond to Nasty Corinne. This will take a bit of getting used to.

"No, that's all right. Besides I have a session with the psychologist straight after."

A look of concern flashes across her face. "I hope he's not going to try and force your memory again. Do you think it might be better to tell him you want to let it go?"

Mum's gaze flicks from me to Corinne and back, not willing to miss a word of this unusual exchange.

"I'm pretty sure I've remembered all I'm going to. But you never know."

My mother jumps up and brushes down her skirt. "Right. So you two are going to collaborate on this lawsuit and Layla will phone you after she's spoken to the lawyers to work out how you can help, Corinne." Like a good social worker, she's summarised the salient points of the conversation. Or else she wants to confirm the moment before it is denied by one of us. We both nod in agreement. "Why don't I open a bottle of wine? I'm sure it's late enough." Mum rushes into the kitchen and leaves us on our own.

"How are you going at work?" asks Corinne.

I cringe at the question. "That's the other thing. I've lost my job. The clients weren't comfortable dealing with someone who looks like a freak."

It's obviously harder to accept Nice Corinne than Nasty Corinne, because I could swear her eyes registered a flash of satisfaction at my news. But I convince myself it's my imagination.

"That's terrible, Layla. People can be so cruel. I can see why it's so important for you to give this lawsuit a go." And there is Nice Corinne again.

The front door opens and slams shut, followed by the loud thud of Ruby's bag, full of school books, hitting the floor.

"What's everyone doing here?" she calls, coming up behind my chair and throwing her arms around my neck from the back. I hang onto her arm and spread kisses from her elbow down to her hand as she squeals and pulls away.

By this time Corinne's lips have tightened into a thin line and I try to send telepathic messages to Ruby to include her in the greeting. To my great relief, she walks over and gives Corinne a one-armed hug. Then Mum comes in with the wine and the awkward moment passes.

It's not until Dad arrives, providing a distraction, that I can get Ruby alone in her room to see how she's been since Sunday. I think I'd fantasised a makeover or a reversion back to the old Ruby after her encounter with the ephemeral Anna. But her hair is still shaved on one side and although the piercings have to be removed for school, they are being re-inserted as I watch. So, no change there.

Ruby jumps onto the bed, curling her legs under her. "Am I going crazy or were you and Corinne being nice to each other out there?"

"I know. She started being nice to me, so I figured I should be nice back. We might even get to like each other." Ruby rolls her eyes. "But I want to know how you're feeling after your experience with Stephen and Anna on Sunday."

She doesn't answer straight away. Unlike her usual spontaneous behaviour, she seems reflective.

"I can't get her out of my mind. Anna, I mean. Almost like she wasn't a real person, just a wispy ghostlike message to make me stop and think about the things I was doing." I'd been standing, but now I lower myself to the bed next to her and take her hand. "That stuff Levi and I thought was so clever and such fun, has taken her over, eaten her up. It's like her body has already died and all that's left is this shell that makes human noises and does human stuff." She looks up at me, gripping my hand. "It gave me a shock, Layla. And the shock didn't come until that night and the next day. I didn't like that you took me to that place, but it worked. I can't guarantee I won't share a joint ever again but there's no way anything else will pass these lips," she straightens her arm and points at the crease where her arm bends, "or these veins."

My sigh of relief is audible. "And Levi?"

"I don't think his experience was as heavy as mine, but we talked about it and some of the things Colin said shook him up. We've both agreed we don't want to end up like that. Levi said it would be hard because of the group he hangs out with, but I'm hoping he might dump some of his deadbeat friends."

I push back her hair, like I used to when she was small. "One day at a time, hey?" She smiles and nods.

"I guess you know about that one, Layla." She glances over at a photo of herself and Levi making weird faces on a beach. "Do you like Levi a bit better now?"

"He's growing on me, Rubes. Do you want to hang out next weekend?"

"Don't get carried away, sis. I'll see what Levi's doing first."

I grab Ruby and tickle her. "Dreadful child. Come on, let's get back to the others."

As we push through the doorway together like children, Ruby says, "I s'pose now you aren't working, your week will be a bit slow."

"Oh God, Rubes, I wish that was the case."

CHAPTER 18

WHEN CLYDE KNOCKS ON MY door soon after six fifteen, I've already changed five times. I stop only because he's there and I'm too embarrassed to rush back in and change while he waits. I mean, what do I wear when visiting the Mother From Hell'? And who am I kidding? She'll take one look at my face and it won't matter whether I'm wearing an evening gown or a hessian sack.

"You look gorgeous, Layla," says Clyde, handing me a bunch of wildflowers. I bury my face in the flowers to hide the heat flushing my face. Flowers move the dinner into the date stratosphere, surely, and that's not what I want.

"It doesn't mean it's a date, it means I wanted to buy you some flowers," he says. *Crap.* He's read my mind again. Clyde moves past me, drawn towards the living room windows. "Wow. What a view. And the beach is only minutes away. I love it."

"Thanks, I was lucky to get it. And thanks for the flowers. They're beautiful."

He turns back from the window and his gaze moves from my purple headscarf to the purple button up shirt with sheer sleeves and silky, fitted black trousers. He smiles without saying anything more.

After the short house tour and an inspection of the chipped concrete steps leading down to the beach, we leave for the dreaded dinner.

Clyde chats about the tottering trio—Lavender, the professor, and Mrs. Crompton—telling me Lavender harangues him about us doing an encore at The Silk Purse. An image of the diamante mask covering the left side of my face almost has me agreeing.

Almost.

I'd forgotten to ask where his mother lives, but after we cross the bridge, we take the Wentworth Avenue exit and head south towards Maroubra.

"You have an amazing singing voice, Clyde. Why don't you sing more?"

"I sing at a club a couple of nights a week if I'm not rostered at The Black Hole," he says.

Again I've assumed I know something about his life.

"Oh. On your own?"

"Celia sings with me sometimes."

What was that twist in my gut? Not jealousy, surely. "Um-Celia? Is that a friend, girlfriend?" I know I'm prying, but now I'm very curious.

He glances sideways at me and grins. I notice he has a dimple indented into his left cheek and his hazel eyes crinkle at the corners when he smiles. "She's a friend I've known since uni. We started singing together about five years ago." He concentrates on the road for a minute. "She has a boyfriend, Ron. He's a friend as well." I'm about to change the subject when he puts on his indicator, turns into Anzac Parade. "Why?"

Thank goodness he can't see my face. "N-no reason. Silly question. Just curious. What's the club?"

"The Grunge Factory in Pyrmont."

"I've been there. Back when I was still at uni, a few of us went. You weren't singing, though. A lot of jazz and blues, isn't it?"

"Pretty much."

He turns off Malabar Road and pulls up behind a navy blue Audi, outside a block of red brick flats. The Audi's rear lights switch off as we stop.

"Shit. There's the perfect brother. Another night of listening to his achievements."

This is it. And I will not have a panic attack, I tell myself, as I feel my heart rate rise. Clyde looks over when I place one hand on my chest and take short, panting breaths.

He puts his warm hand over mine. "I'll distract Tyler'; you stay there until you feel okay."

A thinner, sharper-featured version of Clyde, with dark, well-groomed hair, leaps out of the Audi and gives Clyde's shoulder a playful thump.

"Hey, Bro. Good to see you."

Tyler has obviously been primed about his brother bringing a guest and is trying to peer over Clyde's shoulder into the car.

"Hi, Tyler, how's the family?"

"Good. Good. We managed to get Olivia into Lady Hurst Kindergarten, and Penny is now a partner in her firm. How about you?"

"Oh. You know. Humming along."

By this time I've managed to head off the panic attack and step out of the car. Clyde walks back to his car and grasps my hand. Before he can introduce me to Tyler, a woman, I presume is his mother, throws open the front door and rushes down the path. Behind Clyde's bulk, I glimpse a slim figure, with lips that may once have resembled her son's but are now thin and tight with candy-pink lipstick leaching into the small lines which surround her mouth. Her hair is dyed blond with a curled fringe, and seems too long and girly for her age. The smile she radiates at her oldest son shows teeth slightly stained from nicotine.

"Tyler, sweetie. Come and give your mother a hug." Tyler lifts her off the ground and she squeals her delight before demanding he puts her down. "Clyde Norbert." She trails her gaze up his body. "I see you haven't started that diet yet."

He wasn't kidding, she must do this every time she sees him.

"All the more for you to hug, Mum." He winks at me, drawing me forward. "I want you to meet Layla, one of my closest friends."

A warm feeling stirs in my stomach at his words, but I'm also watching their faces. I've assumed he has prepped them about my scars, and I'm interested to see how they avoid either looking at, or mentioning my face.

"Layla, this is my mother, Sonia, and my brother, Tyler."

I thrust out my hand to his mother. She flinches and smacks her hand across her mouth.

"Oh my lord, what happened to your face?"

Tyler groans at his mother's insensitivity, but Clyde just raises his eyebrows and moves closer. Me, I want to throw my arms around Clyde and hug him till he screams for mercy. This must be the first time someone hasn't thought it necessary to prepare another for my scars before they introduce me. It's great.

"I was burnt in a fire. I also have scars on my arm and leg," I say, in the spirit of spontaneity.

She shakes her head, clucking her tongue. "Such a shame." Then she points to the right side of my face. "And look how beautiful she is on the other side."

I must be mad, because I think I actually like Sonia Campbell. At least I like that she doesn't tip-toe around my disfigurement. Clyde puts an arm around his mother, but she wriggles free, turning back to Tyler to link her arm through his.

Maybe like is too strong a word.

"I hear Penny got her promotion. I'll be sharing that with the girls at water aerobics on Saturday. Are you still working at that horrible bar, Clyde? Come on in, Layla, I've got horsey doovers, Pimms, and some nice bubbly." *What's Pimms?* I think I've worked out what horsey doovers are. I hear an almost inaudible groan again from Tyler and a snort from Clyde.

"The gang at The Black Hole all said to say hi, Mum."

His mother shudders. "Don't be ridiculous. They don't even know me and I certainly don't want to know the types you'd have in that place."

It's clear Clyde's best protection against her criticism over the years is his humour. I swallow a giggle at a vision of her facing off against Lavender. Might be an even match.

We traipse behind Sonia into a poky lounge room, decorated as if it is five times the size. There are two lamp tables, two sofas, and a recliner rocker chair. A bookcase climbs one wall with photographs crowding for prominence along the top. Most are of Tyler with his exceptionally attractive wife and daughter, and one of Clyde dressed in a cap and gown—a shoulder and head-shot, not full body. A three-panelled Chinese screen, with Ming vases painted on each panel, hunches in one corner and in deference to the revival of wallpaper, one wall features stiff, parallel lines of green bamboo on a beige background. This woman's taste in interior design is so terrible, it's almost fashionable.

Sonia Campbell gestures to one of the sofas. "Sit down, Layla. I'll go and get some drinks. Would you like a Pimms? Tyler, can I get you a Pimms too?"

Clyde is left to get his own drink. I drop down onto the couch and sink about thirty centimetres into the cushion, my knees nearly touching my chin. I hate to think how low to the ground Clyde will end up if he sits next to me. I weigh fifty-five kilos.

"Pimms would be lovely, thank you, Sonia. I've never had one," I respond.

Clyde pauses at the doorway to the kitchen. "That's because it became extinct in the early eighties. Wait till you see what she puts in it."

Now I really want one.

Tyler reaches into a bag he has in his hand and pulls out a frosted bottle of Seresin Sauvignon Blanc. "We'll share this with dinner, Layla, so don't worry that you'll have to have a second Pimms."

His eyes have not yet met mine and I can see that under his polite exterior, he finds the sight of me repulsive. I don't blame him, though, even though it pisses me off. It seems his mother has raised him to believe he deserves everything in his life to be perfect and aesthetically pleasing. Like his wife, his daughter, his car, and by the sound of it, his job.

"Sounds good, Tyler."

Clyde walks into the living room with a beer in his hand and a plate of Jatz crackers with squares of cheese on top. I wish they'd told me this was an eighties theme night, I could have dressed appropriately. I wonder why Clyde's grinning, until I see his mother appear holding two parfait-shaped glasses containing a light brown liquid, with a slice of cucumber, a wedge of orange, and a sprig of mint, all bobbing against the side of the glass.

With a flourish, she hands me a glass and plonks down next to me. "I hope you don't think I'm rude, but I can't take my eyes off those dreadful scars. How is it when you go out in public? I can't imagine how embarrassing it must be for you."

Clyde rolls his eyes and clenches his jaw. She obviously still presses his buttons. Tyler looks over the top of our heads at the bamboo wallpaper.

"Why don't you get to know Layla, Mum, instead of getting to know the scars? There's a lot more to her, surprisingly enough."

That sounded very much like my parting shot at Clyde the first day I met him at The Black Hole. I glance over and catch his wry grin. *Cheeky bugger.*

I give him a scary frown and turn back to his mother. "You don't stand on ceremony, do you, Sonia? Brutal honesty."

She chokes on a mouthful of Pimms, and busies herself searching for a tissue.

"I suppose you're saying what most people think, and don't like to say." I turn to Tyler. "In fact, I would bet Tyler is only seeing the scars as well."

Tyler flushes hot red up his neck and into his face. "Really, Layla, I don't think that's necessary…," he mumbles, annoyed at being caught out.

"You can't blame us for wondering about something so…well, so…there," adds Sonia.

Her lips draw into a hard line, protective instincts rearing up at Tyler's discomfort, not to mention her own. I've done a good job tonight. Now, I have to fix it, for Clyde's sake.

"I'm good to go, if you are, Layla," says Clyde.

I shake my head. I won't run tonight. "Sorry about that, Sonia. I didn't mean to make you uncomfortable. I came because Clyde is a very good friend and I wanted to meet his family. This is probably as difficult for me as for you. I don't often subject myself to the close scrutiny of strangers. Go ahead, ask me whatever questions you want."

Clyde groans. "Cripes, what have you done?"

Sonia's eyes widen and she leans forward as if the conversation is just between the two of us. "Yes, well, I'm only trying to understand. So, do you work? Was it hard to get a job looking like you do? Do you have many friends, a boyfriend?"

Well, I asked for this.

While I formulate answers to her questions, Clyde moves over and perches on the arm of the chair next to me. "You don't have to answer, Layla". His arm, stretched along the back of the sofa, touches my neck. It gives me the courage to continue.

"No, I don't work. Not anymore. My scars were too confronting for clients. I had friends; I had a boyfriend; but some of the friends and the boyfriend couldn't cope with my new look. As you might imagine, all this has made me a bit prickly, so forgive me if I react harshly in any way."

"Oh dear, how unpleasant life must be for you," she says.

"Well, that would be quite an accurate assessment. Since the accident, there hasn't been much to get excited about, but I want you to know one of the best things that's happened is meeting Clyde."

Sonia's glance flicks up to Clyde and surprise registers on her face. I can't see Clyde's response to my disclosure.

"He's one of the only people who hasn't been prejudiced by the way I look." I decide to add my pièce de résistance. "You must be very proud at having raised such a kind, insightful human being."

Clyde leans over and whispers, 'touché' in my ear.

Sonia is still looking a little dazed, but pulls herself together. "Yes. Yes, he's always been such a wonderful boy." She glances over at Tyler, whose mouth is hanging open. "They both are. I'm such a lucky woman."

She reaches up to Clyde's arm on the back of the sofa and pats his hand. Probably the warmest touch he's had from her in years. She lifts her glass and takes another long pull of her Pimms, holding the cucumber away from her nose, then pats my leg.

"You know what, Layla? Despite how you look, I think we might get along all right. And at least Clyde's weight isn't as noticeable when he's next to you."

There is a moment of black silence and then I feel irrepressible laughter gurgle up from my gut. My body shakes until I can't hold it in, laughing until tears flow down my face. Within seconds of my outburst, Clyde explodes with laughter and Sonia Campbell, unaware we are laughing at her, joins in. Tyler sits, speechless, gripping his glass of Sav Blanc.

☾

It's not until we are in the car and Sonia Campbell's front door has slammed shut, capturing Tyler inside, probably for a final post-mortem on Clyde's ugly, disfigured friend, that Clyde drops his mask of good humour. He slams his fist against the steering wheel.

"Damn her. Damn her. I keep thinking maybe she is not as bad as I imagine and each time I see her again she proves me wrong." He turns to face me. "I'm so sorry Layla. Sonia behaved ignorantly and Tyler was no better."

His face is red with anger, or maybe embarrassment, I'm not sure. I touch his arm. "That was nothing to some of the situations I've endured. Honestly. In fact, I found her quite refreshing." He raises a suspicious eyebrow. "No, really. I hope you don't think I'm rude but she was so over the top, she was like a caricature and I just found the whole night incredibly funny."

A grin twitches the corners of his mouth. I poke him in the ribs. "Come on, I want your two best moments of tonight."

He starts the car and pulls out from the curb, his mouth pursed while he thinks. "Okay, here's one. For the first time in my life, Tyler was not the centre of attention. Not only that, he was so dazed by your speech, he was stuck for words. Another first. And what Sonia said about my weight not being so bad next to you. Horrible, but disturbingly funny."

We both dissolve into hysterics again and decide we will have her statement, about my scars making Clyde's weight less noticeable, laminated and use it as our motto. *Our motto?*

We cross the Spit Bridge, heading for Manly. In Sonia's mind, dinner had gone well. She even gave me a hug when we left and invited me back again. Not to be outdone, Tyler said he might bring his wife, Penny, to the next family dinner. This of course elicited an outburst of pathetic gratitude from Sonia, but like children with a shared secret, Clyde and I poked each other, giggling with the knowledge Tyler's wife will probably skin him alive when she finds out.

Instead of driving to my house, Clyde drives down to the beach. He pulls into a parking space, tells me to wait, and runs across the road, returning with two cappuccinos and two slices of mango cheesecake. We never did have our coffee and dessert. He balances the coffee and cake on the roof of the car and opens my door, telling me to leave my shoes in the car, while he removes his shoes and peels off his socks.

"Come on, coffee and dessert on the beach. Here, take this," he says, handing me a towel from the back seat.

I sling the towel over my shoulder and grab one of the coffees while he takes the other and the cheesecake.

"And by the way, this is Weight Watchers cheesecake."

We run down the steps to the beach. "Sure it is," I say.

Even with the towel turned sideways, our bodies are touching when we both sit, legs stretched out, balancing our cake and coffee. The sky is heavy with clouds, but as I lift the latté to my lips, they part as if a cosmic finger has stretched the loose weave of a tapestry. Lasers of moonlight from the now-visible chunk of moon turn the sea into liquid pewter and glint off the waves like curved scales. We both absorb the beauty in silence.

Mango cheesecake is one of my favourites, but unable to shift my gaze from the ocean, I multi-task: stare at the sparkle of moonlight over the water, shovel the delicious dessert into my mouth, and savour the amazing blend of sweetness and acidity. Follow with a mouthful of frothy coffee, and I'm in heaven.

I sneak a look at Clyde's profile as he watches the nocturnal play. The shadowed light allows me glimpses of a strong jawline and straight nose. The extra flesh on his face and neck is shaded, and I sense a strange sensation curling in my stomach at an undeniable attraction. Aware of my attention, he turns to face me and reaches over to wipe a dollop of cheesecake from the corner of my mouth with his finger. When he then licks the cheesecake off his finger, a rush of lust shoots through me, and I know he is going to kiss me. I want him to kiss me. It's dark, the time when my face looks its best. This is the time for him to kiss me.

His eyes probe mine, and I can almost hear his yearning. Then he blinks and turns back to stare at the ocean.

That's not how it was meant to go.

"You know I had your back tonight. It might have looked like I left you alone in the lion's den, but I wanted to let you handle it your way. I thought you'd want that," he says quietly, out into the night. I nod, letting him know he was right. "I would have snotted Tyler if he'd said anything to upset you."

I giggle at the thought of Tyler with his perfect nose in a crumple.

"I wouldn't mind being a fly on the wall when Tyler gets home tonight and tells Penny she has to come to the next dinner. Anyway, he was all right. Especially considering he's the Chosen One. What's the story with you two and your mother?"

Clyde groans and twists his coffee cup into the sand for stability. "You don't want to hear the lament of my childhood, surely?"

"Sure I do. I want to know more about you, so give me the gossip."

He raises his eyebrows and, reaching for my hand, places it on his outstretched leg, then interlocks his fingers with mine.

"The short version is my father never wanted to commit to my mother, so she got herself pregnant with Tyler. He was furious, but she convinced him to stay. Apparently she had a healthy, attractive pregnancy and Tyler entered the world the epitome of baby perfection."

"Looks like nothing's changed there," I say.

"No." He pauses for so long, I wonder if he's decided not to tell me more.

"And?"

"My father, or should I say, the man who impregnated my mother, told her not to try that caper on him again, saying it was only because Tyler was such a good baby, he'd decided to stay. Then she got pregnant with me—by mistake, she likes to say." He turns to look at me. "These are basically her words, the ones I heard a thousand times as a child."

My stupid question is about to open a Pandora's box and now I wish I hadn't asked it. I seem to make a habit of this. "Don't tell me anymore. I didn't mean to rake over old wounds."

I reach up to put my finger against his lips, but he pushes my hand down and shakes his head.

"It's okay. I subjected you to my family, so it's only fair to furnish you with the dynamics." I shrug and he continues. "With me she bloated, she was sick, hormonally scratchy, and when I was born, all I did was scream. I think he lasted three weeks until he packed up and told her he would have stayed if not for me." Clyde unlocks his fingers from mine and begins rubbing my hand rhythmically, almost as if he's planing wood. "She spent the rest of my life, until I left home, letting me know I was the cause of her loneliness, the reason Tyler had no father, and why she'd spent the best years of her life struggling to put food on the table for two children, on her own."

I'm so glad he didn't tell me this before we went to dinner. My fist would have involuntarily leapt at Sonia Campbell's face the minute I saw her.

"I'm amazed at how good your relationship is with her, considering such emotional abuse."

At last he stops rubbing my hand. "It took years and a lot of help from the professor until I could see she was doing the best she could, and being the only person she knew how to be. I'm sure she loves me in her own funny way, and she lives in such a narrow world of misery that I haven't got it in me to add to that anymore."

Not as generous as him, I can't let it go. "Why does she torture you about your weight constantly? After all, she's the reason you needed the padding."

Clyde smiles. "At the risk of you telling me I'm a frustrated psychologist, I suspect she blames herself for my weight and believes that if I could only get rid of it, she wouldn't have to keep feeling guilty."

"We are a sorry lot, we humans. I guess I should feel sad that she's never had someone to love. A partner, I mean."

"Atta girl, Layla! You've joined the Let's Find Something To Like About Sonia Campbell Club. Welcome to the family."

Extracting my hand from his, I push myself up and brush off the sand.

"On that tragic note, we probably should go home."

Clyde makes a show of struggling to stand, then takes off across the sand.

"Race you back to the car. Loser has to go to the next Wretched Wednesday."

Shrieking in dismay, I try to cover the ground between myself and Clyde but, like I said before, for a big man he moves incredibly fast. I throw the towel at him, hoping it will tangle in his legs but he jumps over it and keeps running, up the stairs to the car.

"No. No. No! Not another Wretched Wednesday."

I collapse against the door of the car. Clyde pushes it open from inside and I fall onto the seat.

By the time he stops outside my flats, my stomach hurts from laughter and too much cheesecake. I feel happily light-hearted, despite his weird mother and sad childhood.

Clyde comes around to my door and opens it.

"Anything on tomorrow?"

I'm about to say no, when I remember my meeting at Shyster and Sleazy.

CHAPTER 19

AFTER WEAVING IN AND OUT of the back streets of Willoughby for fifteen minutes, I find the address. The building is narrow, with a modern façade painted a purple-grey. But when I push open the door, it seems that's where the modernisation ends.

A sign on the brick wall inside the door indicates the solicitors are up a dark, dank-smelling stairway. On the ground floor to my right is a dog grooming parlour. High pitched yapping, howling, and the lower timbre of big-dog barking, pounds my eardrums, as a dog parent opens the door, looks back and waves at her dog and, thankfully, closes the door on the cacophony again. What am I doing here?

The crumpled business card in my hand reminds me the name is Schuster and Beasley. I chant the name in my head in case I slip up and call them Shyster and Sleazy.

The plain glass door at the top of the stairs is emblazoned with a surprisingly impressive metal nameplate. I reach over to grasp the door handle and stop. I'm not sure if I want to tell my horror story again. Especially to a mob of gangsters (their office space has my imagination soaring). Before I can release my grip, the door flies open and I lurch into the poky reception room.

The black-clad, black-lipsticked young woman, who has facilitated my entry slaps her hand over her mouth in shock. Then she calls out, "She's here, Mr. Beasley."

Good heavens, are they so desperate for clients that the whole office was on high alert waiting for me? I spin around, but the gothic receptionist has her back against the door, as if to head off an escape.

For a moment, I wonder how they knew it was me, unless Mr.

Crane, the office pimp, described me—described the scars, anyway. A small, hairless man appears from the hallway and, with a pudgy hand outstretched, takes short footsteps towards me.

"Nice to meet you, Miss Danforth. I'm Randy."

Oh my God, did he really say he's randy? How am I to keep a straight face? Mr. Crane, his eyes drooping, hovers behind him and I notice he's still sweating into the collar of his shirt. This sight dampens the humour.

I insert my hand into Mr. Beasley's small, soft one and attempt a smile.

"Good to meet you too, Mr. Beasley. I should be clear straight away that I'm just coming to have a chat. I've made no decision about what I want to do."

"Of course, of course. But I'm sure you'll be champing at the bit by the time we finish our discussion. And please, I'm Randy."

Oh God, he's said it again. Thank goodness Clyde's not here with me. We would both be giggling like silly kids at this man all but telling me he's horny, every time he opens his mouth.

An hour later, I'm seeing little Randy in a different light. He's very convincing and is positive we can sue for at least a couple of million dollars. I already envisage my new face and maybe Tom back by my side. Maybe.

Randy wants to contact the detective in charge of the initial investigation and also wants to inspect the site of the fire. I guess it can't hurt and I don't have to pay him anything until we win the case.

Goth Girl, her black lips stretched in a forced grin, gives me a friendly wave as I leave. I'm probably her ticket to a salary increase.

There's still a few hours until I have to be at Jarrod's rooms, so I drive down to Cremorne Point to get the ferry to the city from there. As I'd hoped, the boat is nearly empty at this time of day and on the outside deck, with my cap pulled low, I'm reasonably inconspicuous. Purple-grey clouds scud across the sky, playing hide and seek with the watery sun. I lower my gaze to the coastline, where the vaulted roof shells of the Opera House reflect the mucky grey of the clouds. The building's usual white brilliance is dimmed, almost blending with the battleship-coloured sea.

With a thrill of pride, I realise how much I've progressed over the past few months. From being safe and cocooned in my family home, I now live on my own, have braved the workplace, had the self-respect and courage to resign, have instigated a legal process, met new friends, and even exposed myself to Clyde's family. It seems I've been slaying small dragons without recognising it.

A sudden impulse strikes me as I step off the ferry.

Instead of heading for a coffee shop near Macquarie Street, I take a sharp turn towards Stand C from where the Balmain buses leave. Up until now I've not had the desire or the courage to go near the burnt-out shell of my Balmain terrace. Now, I think I'm ready. And if Randy and Jason Crane intend to traipse over the site to get a feel for the case—not that it makes any sense to me, it's basically a vacant lot—I know I have to go there first.

With my cap and oversized sunglasses shielding a good portion of my face, I step onto the blue and white bus, pay my fare, and clutching the backs of the seats, move to the rear. It's always a toss-up for me whether I attract more attention sitting at the front, instantly on display to newcomers, or at the back, which means I have to pass every passenger to step out. Sometimes a kind bus driver opens the rear door, but not often.

Several streets away from my stop, the panic sets in. Luckily there's no one beside me, so I turn to face the window, taking deep breaths. *Breathe in, hold. Breathe out. Breathe in, hold.* By the time I stand to press the red button, the dizziness has faded and I'm able to make my way down the bus and step out onto the footpath.

The bus pulls away and I'm four houses from where it all began.

This is the street I trod daily, flushed with Tom's love and the dazzling success of my career. Where I carried armfuls of bright flowers from the corner shop; where I jogged and cycled—one of the beautiful people—with my thick hair swishing from side to side while I enjoyed the glances of admiration and the open smiles from passers-by.

The memory scours the open wound in my heart.

Lifting my leaden feet, I trudge past the houses until I stand in front of number twenty-four. The neighbouring terraces, both damaged by the fire that swept through mine, have been restored to their former state. I stare at the vacant lot, and see it now as devoid of menace, a benign emptiness. Empty except for a portion of the brick fireplace and a small garden shed—surprisingly untouched by the fire. It's hard to imagine this is the place my dreams mutated into the nightmare that is now my life. The place I ceased to be the person I thought I was and became a stranger. A tragic, pitiful stranger.

Some months ago Tom told me the landlord, who has a temporary overseas posting, had decided not to rebuild until he came back to Australia. This means no-one will care if I venture onto the land. The low, blue wrought-iron fence separates me from the small strip of land. With my eyes closed, I reach for the latch and push the gate open.

One step, another step, and I'm there; standing on my small front terrace in front of the lead light and timber door, flanked by three arched windows. I imagine myself turning the brass doorknob and pushing open the door into the lemon-yellow living area. Straight ahead is the red carpeted staircase leading to the upper level. A chill scuttles up my spine—that's where my bedroom was. I'm a master of suppression and force my mind away from the stairs to the narrow galley kitchen beyond, and step through the red painted back door before opening my eyes again. There in front of me is the green garden shed where I kept my body board, gardening tools, and my pushbike. I'm pretty sure everything would have been removed, but decide to check anyway.

As I kick the bent aluminium door open, stale, mouldy air catches in my throat. Against the back wall is a rake, a small shovel, a sun hat, and the bent wheel of an old bike. And there, balancing on a narrow shelf is my fluorescent-green body board. A poignant reminder of a time when I wore skimpy bikinis; of summer days lying outstretched on a warm beach; of running into the cold waves of the ocean and swimming until my arms ached, laughing at Tom being dumped by a dirty wave.

I reach out to stroke the smooth, fibreglass surface of the board and my eyes snag on the ridged scars along my arm. The moment is shattered. These ugly deformations mean I no longer wear a swimming costume in public. Nor do I swim, when it means removing my hat to display the bald patch on the side of my head. And that's without the damaging effect of strong sunlight on my skin. No, now I sit and watch others dive through the waves, emerging speckled with diamond drops of cool, salty water, smiles on their faces at the sheer joy of the sea.

A sudden rustle and something scurries across my foot. It was just a lizard, I'm sure of it. As my heart moves back down from my throat, there is a creak and a tinny snap of the door blowing shut. In a panic, I spin around and a spider's web wraps itself around my face and when I flail in the dark, trying to find the door, something lands on my hand and runs up my arm. I squeal, wrench open the door, and trip over the small metal lip, landing face down in the dirt.

Spitting soil and grit from my mouth, I raise myself onto my haunches. Inches away from my face, a flash of red catches my eye. Half buried in the dirt is a piece of shiny, red paper.

Something about it trips a memory which slithers around my mind, slipping out of sight each time I try to pin it down. The paper itself isn't important, but its sudden appearance near my face triggers a flashback. Not of an image, but a visceral reaction in my gut—fear, panic, and shock which I breathe through until it calms.

I shake the dirt from the scrap of paper and I'm about to drop it back on the ground, when I change my mind and shove it into my shoulder bag. After pushing myself up, I brush the dirt from my clothes and hair. I glance back into the shed, but decide to leave the board behind. It was part of a life that no longer exists.

Back on the footpath I edge close to the blue gum tree. Its leafy branches used to shade my small concrete patio, framed with delicate cast iron lacework. The rough bark is comforting under my hand and the tree's steady presence is a reminder that life goes on. For the first time, I feel no resistance to this fact. Perhaps I've vanquished another demon.

Time for my appointment with Jarrod.

&

"Have you had a fall, Layla?"

I follow the direction of Jarrod's eyes and see a hole in the knee of my tights and dried blood clogging the weave of the fabric. I feel a surge of warmth up my neck in embarrassment at my disreputable state.

"Oh. Yes, I did trip over. I'm sorry, I didn't notice what I'd done." I might as well tell him as he seems to dig out my secrets with his fancy hypnosis anyway. "I went back to the house in Balmain. Well, where the house used to be. It was my first time. Do you think that was a good idea?"

He raises his eyebrows and nods. "If it means you've taken one more step forward from your past into your future, then it was a very good idea. If you think it has further traumatised you, then we may have to work with that."

I chew on my bottom lip for a moment, considering his words. "I think I can say it was definitely the former. It certainly stirred up emotions being there, but I also laid some fears to rest as well."

"Are these emotions you wish to explore further, now?" he asks.

I shake my head. "Not really. They were nothing new. Loss of the old life and all that."

He smiles and indicates for me to sit back on the recliner chair and relax. "We can work with whatever comes up for you." He walks over to the small table which holds a jug of water and glasses, pours water for us both and brings it over. "In case you are concerned that we're going back to the fire again, I'll put your mind at ease. What I'd like to do, if it's all right with you, is to look at the days after the fire which I know were also traumatic. If you can talk me through them, it may serve to unlock more memories."

I nod my agreement and close my eyes as his mesmerising voice stills my mind and guides me back through my memory files.

"It's a week after the fire. January twenty-second. You have been brought out of a drug induced coma. Take me through this waking up and anything else you can remember from that early time. I don't want you to dissociate from your body if you become fearful, I want you to stay connected while we explore this, Layla."

I struggle to focus. I'm swimming through mud. Faint voices in the distance…I must get to the surface, to the voices, or I will die. Black fog smothers me…the voices urge me to fight it, to come back. An explosive burst of fear forces me to drag myself through the thick murky ooze. I need air; but must break through the muck to reach it. Now the voices are right in my ear, no longer distant. My eyes flutter open. I'm momentarily blinded by the light over my head. The faces nod and smile. Not sure who they smile at. This place of semi-consciousness has no anchor; it is a detached bewilderment of alien surroundings and forms.

"She's coming back. Layla. Can you hear us? Do you know where you are?"

The lights are too bright and I close my eyes, but the voices pester me to tell them who I am. They said, Layla. I know Layla. But like a pillow pressed to my face, the black smothers me.

The voices urge me back again. I want to sleep. They repeatedly ask me if I know who I am. I'm Layla, and I've got a hangover. Who are these people in my bedroom?

Through the slits of my eyes I see white-clad figures leaning over me and my face feels tight as if a stocking is pulled over it, covering all but my eyes, nostrils, and mouth. Nothing is familiar. A spiral of fear darts through my stomach and I try to speak. But my throat feels as if someone has scraped off the skin with a potato peeler and all I can manage is a low moan.

Then a face I recognise leans over me. It is my mother. Tears flow down her cheeks. Not sure why she's crying, I try to lift my arm, to reach for her. A hundred knives simultaneously stab into my arm, and my screams bring the uniformed strangers back to the bed, pushing my mother away. Someone says "morphine." And the pain recedes. It is then I realise I am wrapped like a mummy. Not just my face, but most of my body.

It is my father, with a doctor beside him, who explains what happened. I think it's my father. This man with my father's voice seems much older with unfamiliar deep lines dragging at his face. My siblings are in the room and although I want to see them, every time one of them comes near me, they burst forth with loud sobs. I think Tom is there as well and I want him to hold me, but he doesn't. No one holds me. Not even my parents. It seems I am brittle glass, ready to break into a thousand pieces if touched.

My father tells me I have been burnt in a fire. Since the day I was rushed through the doors of Emergency, he says, they have filled me with fluids and kept the air from the burns. And placed me in an induced coma for over a week.

Today, the day they have woken me, I am told, I must be taken to the bath. My family step away from the bed, confident the medical staff will do what is best for me. After the brakes are released on my bed, I'm wheeled into another room where a tub filled with ominous purple water awaits. The action of rolling me onto the stretcher is synonymous with being rolled across a bed of nails with the points fiercely sharpened. Then a hoist lifts me off the bed and lowers me into the bath. They don't explain in detail what they will do and I discover why.

After the bandages are soaked, the nurses begin removing them. The pain I had experienced before was like a squirt of lemon in the eye in comparison. As there is no skin, the bandages are stuck to raw, bleeding flesh and any calming words from the nurses as they rip them off are drowned by my primal screams. The process of debriding my body, neck, and face takes over an hour, and is followed by the application of anti-bacterial ointment and re-bandaging. By this time I am a shaking, sobbing mess.

Two hours later, when the agonising pain reduces to a hot burn, they tell me they must do this every day.

This is when I begin to wish I had died in the fire.

Soft encouragement from Jarrod floats me back to the hospital room. My family once again surround the bed and I notice my sister, Corinne, in the room, but separate from the gathering. I note my mother does not respond to my sister's distance with compensatory attention as she usually does. Corinne's gaze is planted on the patterned vinyl floor, her face is pasty, in shock. Or is she jealous my mother has both eyes on me. No. Surely she's not so needy. As the others clamour around the bed, Corinne slips out the door, and I want to call her back, make her part of the circle. I don't remember when I next see her.

Like a slide clicking through a projector, the memory vault releases another image. I am still in hospital and a doctor stands over the bed examining my scarred leg. The debriding baths have finally stopped and the operations have commenced. Apparently there is swelling in my leg and the doctor informs me he will need to drain it.

"Don't look so worried, Layla. You won't even need anaesthetic as most of the nerve endings have been destroyed. You won't feel too much. We'll do it here in your bed."

What does he mean? Even a little bit is too much. Before I can protest, a rather large nurse with a scowl on her face rolls in a small table containing Betadine, sealed plastic packages—which she proceeds to rip open—and an arsenal of scalpels. While the doctor explains they have to cut the flesh to reduce the pressure and drain the fluid, they both snap on gloves. The large nurse holds me down on one side and another nurse materialises to hold the other side. The doctor now wears a mask, but he smiles and his eyes crinkle at the edges—at least I think it's a smile, maybe it's a smirk at such a gullible patient.

My masochistic gaze follows his hand as he reaches for the scalpel and positions himself above my scarred and swollen leg. All I feel is the pressure as he slices down through the dead nerves. It's creepy but it doesn't hurt.

Oh Christ Almighty! To everyone's surprise, especially mine, there *are* live nerves and he's sliced into them. I scream for him to stop, but he says, "Nearly there, Layla." Another slice. Another bloodcurdling scream. "Nearly there, Layla."

"Fucking stop, right now!" The doctor doesn't even acknowledge me. "Tell him to stop. He has to stop. I can't do this," I plead with the scowling nurse.

Her grip tightens. "Doctor knows what he's doing. I'm sure it's not that bad."

"If it's not that bad let him cut you, you fucking bitch!" I scream. I want to scratch her eyes out and wish I knew more gutter language, but I've exhausted my repertoire.

"There you go. Told you it wouldn't take long," says smug Dr. Liar, packing up his tools of torture. If only he wasn't on my left side, I would aim a kick with my right foot in his face or somewhere lower.

The hospital slide show ends and I float, exhausted, in a milky vapour, until a cool touch in the middle of my forehead brings me back to the room. As usual, Jarrod passes me the glass of water. Still trembling from the traumatic journey I have taken yet again, I reach with both hands, closing them around the chilled glass, and watch the beads of condensation swell and gather at the base before dripping onto my lap.

"Take your time and don't get up until you feel strong enough."

I lift the glass to my lips and drink, watching the level drop with each swallow.

"This has been a very cathartic session, Layla. A lot of anger was released and we still have much more to go. I'm sorry to take you through such painful events, but I'm hoping as we break through the layers of your memories, those buried underneath will emerge and we might finally discover the whole truth of what happened." I close my eyes. Painful doesn't even begin to describe it. "You're in the process of re-defining yourself and that's only possible if you can deal with each event that changed your life and move through to the other side."

As much as I hate this process, I have to believe it will heal the emotional trauma, if not the physical. And I now know, I need as many memories as I can uncover to win my case for compensation.

I rock the recliner forward, and he wraps his long fingers around the glass to take it out of my hand.

"There appears to be some unresolved issues with your mother and your sister." I draw back in surprise, ready to argue. He shakes his head. "It's all right, that's not our priority at the moment."

I watch as he strides across the room, an elegant man in his sixties with a shock of thick, white hair and grey-blue eyes. I hate where he takes me in these sessions, but I trust him.

I place my hands on the soft velour arms of the chair and push myself up, finally able to speak.

"I can't thank you for the session, but I'm sure, like you've said, it was useful."

He smiles, hands me my cap, and opens the door for me.

"I'll see you next time, Layla."

CHAPTER 20

A HOT WIND RIPS AROUND THE building as I step out onto the footpath, and I slap my hand onto my cap to hold it in place. Today is one of those weird, hot days that get dropped into the middle of spring to warn you summer's coming; keep you on your toes. At least I don't have to wander aimlessly through the city in a post-therapeutic haze; I've told Clyde I'll drop by for a drink, so I have a purpose and a destination.

Unlike previous forays to the bar, I don't dread an altercation with Lavender. In fact, I'm hoping she'll be there. I recently discovered a different side to her—this woman…man…person— when we bumped into each other at a café soon after my debut into musical theatre.

On this particular day, Lavender had been the last person on my mind. It had been a normal day of dodging Kelly, ignoring Tom, and pleasing Brian. By lunchtime, I desperately needed a change of scenery, so had wandered up George Street to The Rocks. Lining the narrow streets were a plethora of pubs, funky cafes and sleek restaurants, but my favourite spot was on the Kendall laneway: a little café that serves Sydney's best all day breakfasts. I was famished.

The yeasty smell of home-made bread and seriously strong Campos coffee hit my olfactory senses when I pushed open the glass doors. Before scanning the room for a private table, I'd taken a moment to close my eyes and breathe in the mix of aromas, settling the internal chaos from the morning at work. When I focussed on the room again, I saw, out of the corner of my eye, a flash of bright red hair. A squeal of excitement confirmed it was Lavender—a glorious startle of emerald green and silver—

squashed against the wall in a far corner. So much for privacy and anonymity. She flailed an arm over her head, calling for me to join her, and a surprising rush of pleasure surged through me at the notion.

After a plate of peppery poached eggs doused in truffle oil, and homemade baked beans spiced with chilli and paprika, my digestive system was wide awake and ready to take on the world. Which was a good thing as I had an urge to pry into Lavender's life as a cross-dresser. She'd always been brazenly up-front with me, so I came straight to the point.

"Have you always wanted to dress as a female?" I asked.

She grinned at me and ran a finger down the scar on my neck. As if letting me know I had a right to ask such a question only because of my own weird situation.

"As long as I can remember. I used to put my mother's clothes and jewellery on when I was small and she'd chuckle at how cute I looked. When I was still doing it at fourteen she no longer saw the humour." Lavender gestures to a waitress to refill our coffee cups. "My father came home early from work one afternoon when I was fifteen and found me in full makeup, in a dress and heels I'd bought from the local charity shop."

"Oh, no. What did he do?"

She fingered the handle of my cup. "He ripped the clothes off me until I was standing in my underpants—unfortunately they were lacy knickers." A grin rippled her grim features. "Then he beat me, cut up the clothes, and locked me in my room until my mother came home. He told her I had to be out of the house by the end of the week. I haven't seen either of them since."

"I—I don't know what to say. Only fifteen and on your own. God, Lavender, I'm so sorry."

I leaned over and threw my arms around her neck, as if this loving gesture could make the fifteen-year-old feel better.

She kissed my cheek and patted my headscarf. "Water under the bridge, or shit down the sewer, darling. I'm a happy little queen now, with friends who like me however I dress. And my Lancie, who thinks I'm fabulous. Silly fellow."

She probed about my accident and my love life, and I found myself divulging the miserable story of Tom's inability to make love to me as a result of the scars. I had to convince her not to hunt him down to avenge my damaged sensibilities. By the time I had to scoot back to work, I felt I had found a good friend.

Until I returned to my normal life, anyway.

(

I bring my thoughts back from Lavender and focus on giving the weathered black door a hard push.

Unlike before, I no longer creep into The Black Hole like a cat entering a dog kennel. I clatter down the stairs, one of the regulars. Gavin is in his sentry position at the bottom, eyes closed and swaying in time with the soulful sound of Gladys Knight singing "Midnight Train to Georgia". The speakers would probably self-destruct if music from any era other than the seventies leaked through.

Despite my noisy entrance, Gavin doesn't hear me, so I stop behind him and place a kiss on the top of his head. Before I can move, he grasps me around the waist and drags me onto his lap where he kisses me full on the lips. I'm shocked at his audacity. To cover my reaction, I push playfully at his chest and we both nearly topple off the chair.

Giggling, I regain my balance and glance over to the professor's booth, but it's empty. My shoulder's slump in disappointment. I've missed the old man.

"It's *Le Sourcil*," calls a familiar, rasping voice from the bar. Jumping up from Gavin's knee, I hurry over and, emboldened by Gavin's warm greeting, embrace Lavender and air-kiss both cheeks. She's wearing a peacock-blue sheath dress with shoes and eye-shadow to match. It's like someone's thrown three blobs of vivid blue paint against the bland landscape of The Black Hole.

"Great to see you, Lavender. I was hoping you might be here." I indicate her dress. "Fabulous blue."

Lavender slides off the stool and, with her hands on her hips, does a twirl.

"I know, darling, I saw myself in the mirror before I left home. Don't you love this colour?" Her eyes light on the rip in my tights. "What on earth have you been up to, *Sourcil*? Have you been brawling?" Before I can answer, she tilts my chin. "And look at you, darling. White as a sheet on washing day. Tell Auntie Lavender all about it. "

"No. I haven't been brawling. I fell over on my way here and scraped my knee."

She frowns and makes a murmur of sympathy. I'm not sure whether it's because I fell, or that I'm out in public wearing ripped tights. I indicate neither is a problem.

"And as for looking pale, I've just come from therapy. It was all a bit dramatic. I think I'm a bit drained."

I can't believe how good it feels to speak so openly about these things. Usually I would never mention a therapy session to anyone but family—and even then only under pressure.

She studies me for a moment, then grabs me around the waist, lifts me into the air as if I'm a doll, and plonks me onto a bar stool.

"If you're drained then we need to fill you up. Clyde!"

Clyde does a *Dirty Dancing* slide along the floor, a suave action in the movie, but not so much with someone his size. Good for a laugh, though. He then leans over the bar and gives me a chaste kiss on the lips—my second in minutes. More random lip action than I've had in months.

"You want therapy? We have therapy in a hundred different bottles. We have vodka, bourbon, whiskey, wine," he chants, like a snake oil salesmen.

I was going to have wine, but I think I need something more medicinal after my rugged session. "Make it a whiskey and soda."

"Into the hard stuff today? Hope we don't have to get the bouncer to chuck you out."

We all glance over at Gavin, who's playing air guitar along with the opening high-pitched guitar riff from Creedence Clear Water Revival's "Up Around the Bend". The suggestion is so ridiculous we all roar with laughter. Gavin stops playing and glances over, his eyes narrowed, suspicious he's the joke. But the pull of Creedence is too much and he lifts the air guitar high in the air, working his fingers and face into such a convolution of frenzy he appears to be in mid-seizure.

"Oi! Joe Cocker! Get up here and do something useful," yells an unfamiliar voice from the top of the stairs.

I glance up to see a bloke in his mid-thirties hovering the large front wheels of his wheelchair over the lip of the top step.

"Jeezus, man, take it easy," yells Gavin, his air guitar forgotten as he races up the steps two at a time. Clyde lifts the hinged door on the top of the bar and follows Gavin up the stairs.

"Who's that?" I ask Lavender.

She rolls her eyes. "That's Wild Willy. Used to be some important athlete—football I think—until he was tackled in a game and snapped his spine. He's a miserable mongrel. Don't let him get to you."

I take it from that she means he will try to get to me. I'm not in the mood for someone else's crap. Maybe I should go.

Lavender swings her head back to glare at me. "Don't you edge off your seat as if you're about to make a run for it, Missy."

I flash her a fake grin and swallow. Caught out.

We both swivel around to watch Gavin and Clyde carry the wheelchair and its passenger down the stairs. Wild Willy's face could probably be described as handsome if it wasn't for the bitter twist to his mouth and the flat, suspicious look in his eyes. He wheels himself over to the bar and stops in front of Lavender.

"That'd be right. A bloke comes out looking for a bit of action and the only fucking tart in the place has a fucking dick."

The tightening of Lavender's jaw and the flare of her nostrils tell me he's pinched a sensitive nerve.

"You're a miserable piece of shit, Willie. No way you'll ever get any action if you just squat in that wheelchair moaning about being a cripple all day."

Satisfied to see Lavender snap at his bait, his lips curl in a sneer and as he pivots the right wheel away from her, his eyes light on me. I instinctively turn my left side away from him.

"What have we here? What's a little honey like you doing in a place like this?"

When I don't answer straight away, he drives the wheelchair into my stool, causing me to grip the edge of the bar to keep my balance. This action makes me decide the little arsehole deserves the full effect, so I spin around to face him.

"Holy crap! And I thought I had problems." He guffaws.

Lavender steps off the stool and with her peacock blue shoe pushes at the chair while he grips the top of the wheels to stop the movement.

"Fuck off, laughing boy."

Despite the rude, insulting remarks, I have a sliver of empathy for this man. In one moment his life changed forever—from an elite athlete to a paraplegic. Instead of hiding away like I have, he punches life in the face; angry at the cruel circumstances that have reduced him to a nobody in a wheelchair.

Sliding off the stool, I stretch out my arm. "I'm Layla. Regardless of whether you put shit on me or not, you're still going to be in that wheelchair and I'm still going to be covered in ugly scars. So why don't you just get on with it and stop insulting nice people. You never know you might find life's not that bad."

A flicker of embarrassment crosses his face and is quickly covered with a sneer. He then begins to clap slowly. By this time Clyde has returned from taking an order of drinks to a group in one of the booths on the other side of the room. He grips the handles at the back of the chair, and while Willy's hands are occupied clapping, wheels him away from us. Meanwhile, once again, the irony of my own words is not lost on me.

Lavender squeezes a smile around her pursed lips. "Well, well. I'm a proud little queen today. My *petit Sourcil* has shut that big-mouthed moron up when no one's been able to before."

I suck my whiskey through the straw. "I sort of saw myself in him. That lashing out at everything and everyone when there's nothing tangible to blame."

"Hmm, I see. A wee bit of sympathy for the offensive bugger," she says.

I chew on my straw. "Probably more than a wee bit," I say, releasing a sigh.

Clyde returns again and before going back to the other side of the bar, he gives me a one armed hug and pulls me into the side of his chest.

"Sorry about that, Layla. Willy's big mouth knows no bounds. The stupid bugger is a cesspool of anger. I think we're the only bar in town that still lets him in. I told him if he insults patrons again, he'll be banned from here too."

I snuggle into the space under Clyde's arm. It's strange, but down here I almost feel like I have a claim on him. Outside, in public, we're only friends and, of course, he doesn't fit the boyfriend image I cling to.

Did I really just think that? I glance over at the mirror and shudder at the distasteful person I see reflected back at me. I turn away from her.

"I'm fine. I felt a bit sorry for him."

No-one speaks and I wave my hand to let them know it's not what they think; I'm not seeing a disability as an excuse for bad behaviour. I switch the subject to the professor's absence.

"It's unusual not to see the professor. Is he all right?" I ask Clyde.

"He'll come rushing down those stairs any minute now. I talked him into offering some literacy aid to street kids at a boy's shelter. This is his third week and it means four hours without a drink. I can set my clock by how long it takes him to get here." He looks at his watch. "He's about five minutes away."

"That's wonderful. Do you think it might get him back into his teaching again?"

Lavender lifts her beer in a salute. "You're so precious, darling. And so naive. Explain to her what it means to be an alcoholic, Clyde darling."

I'm certainly not naive and feel quite indignant at her remark. "You underestimate me, Lavender. Of course I know what an alcoholic is. But that doesn't mean he can't be rehabilitated." She snorts at my comment. "Imagine how it would be for him to be sober and to reunite with his family."

She swings her body around to face me and brandishes a hot-pink fingernail. "Darling, that little bunch of snobs wouldn't give him the time of day, sober or not. And if they deigned to give him their precious time, it would be loaded with conditions and judgements." She waggles her finger from side to side. "No. They'd drive him back to drink. We're his family now, including you—so remember that."

She swings back to face the mirrored bar. Her words send a jolt of hot awareness into my gut. She called me family. What if the doctor in New York gives me back my face? Would these people, my fellow freaks, fit into my life then? I've always imagined I would slip back into my old life after the surgery. Or is that person gone? I am confused and filled with shame at even thinking this about the only people who have accepted me, scars and all.

I glance up and meet Lavender's eyes in the mirror. Her head tilts to the side as if I'm a specimen she's studying. She knows what I'm thinking, I'm sure of it.

Clyde's warm hand taps my shoulder. I break my connection with Lavender and look up.

"I'm on a break for half an hour; got time for a chat?"

"Sure. That's why I came." I stand up to follow him.

"Excuse us for a bit, Lavender," he says, as we walk off.

"Not a problem, darling. You might as well spend time with her while you can."

She knows, but I want to tell her she's wrong. I don't.

As Clyde and I slip into the vinyl bench seats in one of the booths, I hear the front door slam shut and Lavender calling out to the professor. Glancing around the corner, I watch him doddle down the stairs, closely followed by Mrs. Crompton, who must have arrived at the same time.

Clyde taps his watch. "Told you. Right on time."

We both lean our bodies out so he can see us, and wave. He gives a cursory wave, but his attention is focused on the glass being handed to him by Gavin. Mrs. Crompton smiles and waves, but her eyes flash back to the coffee mug receiving a generous splash of brandy from the bottle Gavin has upended after serving the professor.

Clyde's voice brings my attention back to our corner.

"So, tell me how today went. The lawyer and the psych."

I take a deep breath, which catches in my throat from the overwhelming gratitude I feel at having someone else, other than my parents, with whom I can share the events of my day. My instinct is to make physical contact with Clyde, an intimacy to acknowledge this odd heart expansion. But Lavender's words have me confused, so I lock my fingers together and hold them in my lap while I tell Clyde about my decision to start legal proceedings against the landlord.

After I describe the cast of characters at Shyster & Sleazy, I wait for him to tell me they sound too dodgy to trust. He gazes into his coffee mug, every now and then swirling the muddy contents.

"It sounds like you made the right decision. He mightn't look an appetising prospect, but he may surprise you. And it doesn't matter what he's like if he achieves the outcome you want, does it?"

I unlock my fingers and grasp his arm. "No. You're right. And thanks for the vote of confidence. It means a lot."

He lifts his cup, swallows a mouthful of coffee, and places it back on the table. "How did you go with your therapy session?"

I hesitate, not sure how much I want to share with anyone. But Clyde is the person I feel the safest with at the moment, so I give him a brief rundown, leaving out a lot of the drama. He doesn't speak for a while.

"I knew it must have been terrible, but I guess there was no way to really imagine the horror of it. You're amazing, considering what you've been through." I give him a thin smile and pick at a soggy corner of my cardboard drinks' coaster. "I think I understand why it's so important to find some reason for all this. Why you need to follow through with the court case. If there's anything I can do, you only need to ask."

By this time, I've shredded the coaster. "I went back to the house as well." He frowns, not sure what I mean. "To Balmain. The house where the fire was."

He stares at me. "God. But that must be the first time. I'm sure you said you hadn't been back." I nod. "That's huge, Layla. What made you go?"

"I'm not sure. It was after I came out of the lawyer's office. They told me they'd need to send someone over to get a feel for the scene and have a look around, and I knew I wanted to be there first." Clyde nods at my reasoning. "It was weird. Just a vacant block of land really, but I could see all the rooms in the house, walk through them like it was still there." I notice his coffee has gone cold, with scum forming on the top as he listens. "The shed out the back was still intact and I went in. Some of my stuff was in there."

"Did you take it? Your stuff, I mean."

I run my tongue over my dry lips. "No. I ran." His hand closes over mine. "It was part of a life I no longer have. And there wasn't much—a body board, a few other things."

Clyde slides his cold coffee off to the side. "A body board, huh?" A small grin plays at the edge of his mouth. "I reckon one day you'll proudly wear a swimsuit and ride a body board and when that day comes, I make you a promise that I will ride a board alongside you." He blows out his cheeks and puffs out his chest to make himself look bigger than he already is. "You and I, we'll own the waves on that day."

"Only because there'll be a mass exodus from the water when they see us coming," I say.

He lifts his hands in surrender. "Whatever it takes."

And once again the weight of my day lifts from my shoulders and I feel lighter. It's not that Clyde thinks everything is funny, it's more that he seems to have an ability to recognise the existence of the duality in all things—as if nothing is ever exactly as it seems.

Two strums from my phone—a message from Mr. Sleazy: *Have already filed application for proceedings against landlord and spoken to investigator. Landlord back in town. Going to fast-track this. Can we meet again next week? Wednesday? Randy.*

Clyde watches me read the message and raises his eyebrows. I place the phone on the table and turn it to face him.

"It's happening. The wheel has begun to turn. I'm scared, Clyde."

He spins the phone back to me. "It's probably a good thing. No more wondering if... Besides you can jump off any time you want."

"I suppose you're right and mixed with the fear is a small sense of relief."

Clyde reaches over and spins the phone back to himself, tapping the screen.

"Randy? Really?"

CHAPTER 21

M Y BACK IS TO THE door. On one side of me is my lawyer, Randy Beasley, dressed in a blue suit and wearing a fat, red and blue polka dot tie. His small sausage shaped fingers rest in his lap giving a sense of mindless calm, as if he's in church. Next to him is Jason Crane in shirtsleeves with the perennial dark ring of sweat around the top of his collar and on my other side is my sister, Corinne. It's a Friday morning, only four weeks since my initial meeting with Randy and he's already engineered this mediated negotiation with the defendants and their lawyer. How he pulled this off in the time is a mystery, but I begin to suspect he has more skills than I gave him credit for.

We arrive early, on Randy's instruction, so we can manipulate the neutrality of the venue before the defendants and their legal representative arrive. The mediator—a young, enthusiastic lawyer with a big smile and guileless eyes—has played into my lawyer's strategy by allowing us into the room, rather than making us wait in the lobby for the defendants.

Randy notes her error with a smug grin at Jason Crane.

The heavy oak door opens, admitting the landlord, Peter Agostini, and two strangers, who he introduces as Harry Levett—representative of his insurance company, Fairwether Mutual—and Lawrence Groat, Fairwether's lawyer. The irritation evident in the lawyer's voice when he greets the mediator indicates he's noted our early arrival together with the rapport we've established with the mediator.

As I didn't turn around to greet them, none of the men have yet seen me. They walk around the table and when Randy introduces Corinne and then me, the look of shock on both their faces at my ravaged face and neck, is game, set, and match to us.

A slight tic in Randy's jaw and a narrowing of his eyes is all that gives away his self-satisfaction. Opposite, Peter Agostini, newly arrived from Singapore, can't make eye contact with me. Lawrence Groat—a sharp-faced man with a large nose and a thatch of mousey coloured hair—tries to re-establish his credibility to his clients by making a show of taking documents from his briefcase and tapping them on the table, before lining them up side by side. The insurance representative, a slim man with an army-precision haircut, sits in motionless, steely silence.

I glance sideways to make sure I'm not dreaming Corinne's presence. This is a new experience for me, having her as a support person. For nearly twenty-eight years her only acknowledgement of my existence has either been in the form of derision or indifference. I'm still not sure where this new version of my sister has come from and although it smacks of ingratitude, I can't help feeling a touch suspicious.

*

She'd phoned as I was finishing breakfast yesterday morning, and I immediately thought something had happened to Mum or Dad to prompt the phone call.

"Hi, Corinne. What's up? Is everyone all right?"

There was a pause before she responded. "Er... Mum told me you're having a meeting with the lawyer tomorrow morning and I thought I would offer to come with you." I know she offered to help a few weeks ago, but I never dreamt she actually meant it.

"Oh... Don't you have to work?"

"Obviously not, or I wouldn't be offering."

Ah, that sounded more like the Corinne I know. I decided to accept the olive branch.

"That would be good. To have someone with me. Thanks, Corinne."

I gave her the address, and we agreed to meet before the appointment. There was an awkward silence before she abruptly ended the call.

𝒞

"Would that work for you, Layla?" asks Randy. *Crap.* I was miles away and have no idea what they were saying.

The mediator, who invited us to call her Michelle, flashes me a sympathetic glance. She must think I have brain damage from the accident and decides to help out.

"Actually, before Miss Danforth answers, I might summarise a few points so we are all on the same page."

I love her.

"Mr. Groat has explained there is no evidence to suggest negligence on his client's behalf. Mr. Beasley has informed him that the Arson Squad has agreed to reinvestigate the matter. Due to the urgent requirement for Miss Danforth's medical attention, her lawyer is moving ahead immediately with the case. Mr. Agostini and Mr. Groat have also been informed that Mr. Beasley will be ready to share preliminary findings in as little as two weeks."

"That all seems in order," I say.

Corinne clears her throat and all eyes switch to her. "I'd like to say that a number of times I expressed concern about the wiring being faulty in that place in Balmain. We were quite worried about the fact it wasn't attended to."

What is she talking about? She hardly ever came to Balmain. I know she wants to help, but she can't make things up. And then her words unearth a memory of something I had a concern over some months before the fire. It wasn't the wiring but I can't think what it was…

"I never heard about this. Who did she tell? Was this in writing?" asks Peter Agostini.

I am trying to formulate an answer when Corinne jumps in again.

"They were phone calls. It's not our fault if your agent didn't record them."

Then I remember. I had burnt some toast one morning and cringed, in anticipation of the ear-splitting scream of the fire alarm. There had only been silence. I knew there was a safety issue which my scrambled brain couldn't recall, until now.

"Excuse me," I say. "My sister is right to say we lodged a complaint. It was actually the fire alarm, which didn't seem to be working. And I asked the agent to have it fixed."

Lawrence Groat puts up his hand to halt the discussion. "If I may?" he asks of Michelle, the mediator, who nods for him to continue. "There seems to be some confusion about the issue which makes me wonder whether this complaint, with no accompanying evidence, has been manufactured to put blame on my client."

Next to me I hear Corinne release a slow, irritated breath and when I glance sideways, her lips are pulled in a hard line.

"I'm sure I sent an email about the fire alarm to the estate agent's office," I tell him. "I can't remember if I sent it from home or from work and I lost my home laptop in the fire. I might be able to have someone check the records at my old workplace."

Lawrence Groat pastes a patronising smile across his face. "Why don't you do that, Miss Danforth." He directs his attention to Michelle. "My clients and I would like to leave it there for today."

The mediator looks to Randy, who agrees to end the session. She thanks all parties. Agostini, Groat, and Levett scrape back their chairs, nod to each of us and leave the room. The mediator, who now seems to remember the rules of neutrality, also leaves the room.

"I'm a bit confused. It feels like nothing was achieved," I say to Randy.

"On the contrary, even if not a word had been spoken, they know you'd immediately have the sympathy of a jury. You can be sure they're discussing an out-of-court settlement."

"Because of the way I look?"

"Unfortunately, yes. But we have to take the advantage where we can get it," he says.

"Don't we have to prove they were responsible?"

"Normally that would be the case, but I'm going to play it so they have to prove they weren't responsible."

"It sounds like you think we have a good chance of winning."

"I do. Especially once your sister threw in that little piece of information. Even though it wasn't quite correct." He gives her a wink and I see a smug smile play across her lips. "But the fire alarm malfunction is just as good. They'll be worried." I can't confront Corinne here about her spontaneous fabrication, but I certainly don't want her muddying the case with more lies. Even if she is trying to help.

The four of us go down in the lift together, but when the two men walk away, I'm in the awkward position of not knowing what to say to Corinne. She stands beside me, her face a blank.

"Well... thanks for coming with me." She shrugs in response. "I don't suppose you'd like to get a cup of coffee?" I ask.

Corinne shrugs again.

"Might as well," she finally answers.

Another surprise. This is going to be agony, but I need to make sure she doesn't lie again.

Across the road is a small coffee shop. I gesture at it and still without speaking, we cross over and choose a table out the front. I order a cappuccino and Corinne orders an iced chocolate with an extra scoop of ice cream. While we wait for our drinks, I try to formulate the right words to address her statements at the mediation.

"I was very grateful you came with me this morning."

"So you said." She wasn't going to make this easy.

"Yes, I did. I wanted to talk about that statement you made about us lodging a complaint with the agent about the wiring." Her head is lowered, lips puckered, sucking at the iced chocolate, and she raises only her eyes as I speak. "There was never a problem with the wiring and no such complaint was made. It's probably better not to make things up."

Her back stiffens and her teeth clamp down on the straw. "Even when I try to help, I'm not good enough for you. Am I, Layla?"

"It's not that. Like I said I'm really grateful, but we have to be able to prove things we say."

"That lawyer seemed to like what I said. And you brought up the fire alarm, so at least it jogged your memory. My guess is your lawyer won't care whether it's the truth or not as long as he wins the case."

I would have agreed with her before today, but now I'm not sure whether I misjudged Randy. She digs her parfait spoon into the ice cream and shovels it into her mouth.

"Besides you'll be rich if you win. Lucky Layla."

My anger flares; a match igniting in my chest. "Did you say, lucky Layla? Are you serious? I don't care about money, all I want is to feel like a normal person again. That money is for plastic surgery. I…" My indignation at her callous comment balls in my throat, blocking further speech.

"Some of us have never had the opportunity to be beautiful, at least you had it for a while. Be thankful for that."

My mouth is open and ready to snap back when I stop myself. This is more than a cruel statement—it's a deep, long-held jealousy. One I never saw. Not clearly. My anger simmers down to a bubbling pity. Despite everything, it's hard to watch her pain, as if I've caught her naked. I can't apologise for who I am—or was. But I can acknowledge her help.

"I'm sorry about what I said before. You're right, what you said did jog my memory of the fire alarm. In fact you've probably hit on one of the key ways to win this." Even as I say this, I feel a dissonant twist in my stomach at being a party to her deliberate dishonesty.

"I thought so." She sucks loudly at the bottom of her glass as if to irritate me and then, pushing the glass to the middle of the table, she gets to her feet. "I've got some things to do so I've got to go. Let me know when you need my help again."

I nod, barely able to raise a smile. As she disappears down the street, the waiter places the bill in front of me.

There's so much I don't understand about my sister. I've never known whether she loves me or hates me. I know she's always resented me. Naïvely, I don't think I realised how much. Although some of her behaviours when we were children should have tipped me off.

When I was small I wanted long hair like Rapunzel. It took me years, but by the time I was eight years old I was finally able to sit on my hair. One morning I woke up and my hair had been hacked off to above the ears while I slept. Corinne denied having done it, but had forgotten to get rid of the scissors under her pillow, which still had pieces of my hair stuck to them. When I had to go to school, Corinne led the jeers against me. I was inconsolable for months until enough hair had grown to be restyled. She was punished, of course, but nowhere near as much, or for as long, as I was.

I ponder my sister's sudden interest in my life. Not to mention her alarming ability to lie on my behalf. Even though she's my sister, we are complete strangers. I've never been able to dredge up true affection for her, just a perpetual sadness at her incongruity within the family. A shiver runs up my spine making the hairs on my arms stand on end as more childhood memories surface. Of other small acts of cruelty hidden from our parents, and somehow explained away by Corinne, when I ran to them for help. Perhaps I shouldn't encourage her involvement in this lawsuit. She's too much of a loose cannon. But I also don't want to reject the only gesture of sisterhood she's ever offered.

Two strums on my phone remind me I'm still sitting alone at the table. I check the message. It's from Clyde.

Remembered ur meeting the lawyers and know ur in the city. Need help urgently. Can u come to bar?

With some relief, I throw my thoughts of Corinne aside and respond.

On my way to bar. 10 mins away.

Grabbing my bag from the back of the chair, I take off towards Macquarie Street and suddenly remember I haven't paid. When I rush back to the café, the waiter is on the footpath looking for me and even my profuse apologies don't erase the suspicion from his face.

After all, who would trust someone who looks as rugged as me?

CHAPTER 22

HEAD DOWN, SUNGLASSES ON, I charge through the mid-morning stragglers. By the time I wrench open the door of The Black Hole, I'm panting for breath.

"She's here," yells Gavin, and before I've taken three steps down, Clyde throws his towel to Gavin, grabs what looks like a suit of clothing, and runs up the stairs to meet me. Surprisingly, he isn't in his normal faded jeans, but instead wears a long-sleeved navy shirt and black trousers.

"Turn around, I'll explain as we go."

Normally, I would refuse to budge until someone gives me the full story, but it's been a weird morning, so I let the weirdness continue, and follow Clyde without question.

"It's about the professor," he says as he hurries me along the street.

I gasp, sure something terrible has happened to him.

"He's okay. Well, something has happened, but not what you're thinking."

"For God's sake, get on with it."

"Sorry. Yes. His daughter's getting married today—"

"But how does he know? They don't speak to him, do they?"

By this time, Clyde has hauled me onto a bus and we both flop onto the ripped vinyl bench seat.

"This is his older daughter. She got a message to me because I'm their emergency contact for him. She said if he could stay sober for twenty-four hours and manage to dress properly, he could go to the church to watch her be married. However, she was clear her mother would not welcome him at the reception."

"Bitch," I mutter under my breath. "He should be walking her down the aisle, not skulking in the back pews."

"My sentiments too, but he was pathetically grateful for being told he could watch from the back, and agreed to the conditions." He scrapes back his thick hair. "I was his minder to make sure he didn't touch the drink. He kept to his promise yesterday, but by early this morning he had the shakes and this look of terror in his eyes at the thought of not having a drink for another seven hours. Gavin and I kept him talking and plied him with cups of coffee. He was doing really well. Then he disappeared."

"What, from your place or the bar?"

"He'd been at my place, then I brought him to work. Gavin had to duck out, so I was on my own. One minute he was sitting in the booth and the next minute he was gone."

"So have you found him? Is that where we're going?"

"One of the blokes who works at the City Mission found him gripping a bottle and babbling incoherently about daughters, weddings, and me. They phoned and now we have to get him sober enough to get to that bloody wedding."

"So why do you need me? What do you think I can do?"

"You're a woman and somehow I think you'll be able to convince him to go. He'll be so ashamed of letting me down, he won't hear what I'm saying."

"Well, I can try."

I'm doubtful I'll have any influence, but something about this old man tugs at my heart. Besides, I can't forget how much he helped me the day I lost my job.

Clyde jumps up and presses the stop button and we both hurry off the bus.

"First we have to get some supplies."

He leads me into a convenience store and fills a bag with high sugar fruits like figs, pears, bananas, and a packet of dates.

"Fruit? Is that for him? I thought greasy food was the best thing to soak up the alcohol."

"Yeah, well, so did I, but I recently read that high fructose sugars are really good for metabolising the alcohol. Don't know if it's true, but I'm willing to try anything." He jerks open the fridge and grabs a large bottle of Coke.

We cover one more block and then cross the road to the Mission. The door is open and various specimens of depleted humanity loiter on the front step and inside the door. Still follow-ing blindly in Clyde's wake, I squeeze past those in the doorway, walk through a large common room, down the hall to a small office. A formidable looking woman, with severely short hair and wearing a shirt and trousers, stands up from a desk when she sees Clyde in the doorway.

"He's down here, Clyde. Won't talk to anybody though. Told me he's worth less than dog shit on the bottom of a shoe. Not in a good place, if you know what I mean."

She notices me, blinks twice when she sees my face, and holds out her hand. "Mim Crawford, how do you do?" I shake her hand, introducing myself as she leads us back down the hallway to another room. "He's in there. I'll leave you to it." She disap-pears, back to her office.

In the room is a single day bed, a small square table with three chairs, and an old, faded armchair next to the day bed. The lone figure of the professor huddles in one of the chairs at the table, his head in his hands. This small ragged bundle of misery twists at my heart.

Clyde crosses the room and places his hand on the old man's shoulder. "Professor, it's me, Clyde. We can fix this."

The professor jerks as if he's been touched with a hot poker and pushes his hand up to halt any further interaction. Without speaking, he wraps his arms around himself, rocking from side to side, moaning like a wounded animal. Clyde tries to hold him, glancing back at me with a look that tells me this time he's really frightened for his friend. At every approach from Clyde, the professor twists away from him. It seems Clyde was right, the old man is too ashamed of his behaviour to let Clyde help him.

I'm so far out of my comfort zone, I want to turn around and run from this place. I have no idea how I can help the professor and am terrified I'll make things worse. But I've been in his place: ashamed at who I've become and racked with self-pity. So I have to try. I gesture for Clyde to come away and leave the professor alone for a few minutes. We hover near the doorway until the old man's agitation decreases. When he stops rocking and the moaning has become almost inaudible, I take the bag of fruit, cross to the table, and pull out a chair.

After a few minutes he registers my presence.

"It's Layla, Professor."

He whimpers. "Have you come to witness my shame?"

I don't answer him and eventually he looks up, his face tight with anger and guilt.

"Well?"

I still don't speak, but instead reach for his hand and hold it in mine. Half expecting him to snatch it away, I tighten my grip, but at the same time gently stroke the top of his hand with my other, scarred hand. His eyes watch the movement and his face softens. The rigidity seeps from his shoulders and he takes in a deep breath, releasing it in short puffs.

"Have you got a minute? I wanted to tell you how I went with the lawyers today."

He frowns, seeming confused that I've steered the conversation to myself.

"Maybe I didn't tell you, but I made a decision to hire a lawyer and sue the landlord. We had our first meeting today with the defendants."

As I speak, I pull a fig out of the bag, break it in half and offer it to him. He shakes his head, but I insist he tries it and take a bite from my half. Taking my lead, Clyde disappears down the corridor and a minute later comes back with a glass which he fills with Coke and puts in front of the professor, before moving away again.

"If it ends up in court, it will mean I have to go through everything that's happened to me all over again, so I'm not sure if I've made the right decision."

His hand reaches for the glass of Coke and he drinks thirstily. He places the glass on the table and directs his attention to me, speaking hesitantly.

"It seems to me...it doesn't matter what the outcome of this action is...you've discovered enough...self-respect to take action. I think whatever happens, you'll know...what's right or not."

"Thank you, Professor. But how can you talk to me about self-respect when you're not showing any for yourself?" I ask, my hand resting on his.

He pulls his hand free. "I wondered...when this conversation would pivot back...to me. I do not deserve...to see my daughter married. I destroyed that possibility this morning...and I will not discuss it further with you… or anyone else."

I'm about to admit defeat, when I remember some of the things he said to me not so long ago.

"Professor, remember the day I lost my job and you helped me through it?" He shrugs as if he doesn't want to encourage me further. "You said two things to me that I haven't forgotten. The first was that when people treated you as a nonhuman, of no value, the biggest mistake you made was to believe them. It looks to me like you're still believing them. And, in fact, like me, you're doing more damage to yourself than all of them put together."

"Oh for goodness sakes, Layla," he says, all hesitation in his speech vanished. "This is ridiculous."

I put up my hand to let him know I haven't finished.

"And the second thing you said which had even more impact, was to let the people who love you show you who you are, not the ones who don't. Right now there are two people in this room who love you, and are trying to show you who you are. So, unless everything you said to me was a crock of shit, then you need to get your arse out of that chair, shower, and do everything you can to sober up enough to go to this wedding."

His eyes are closed and he sits motionless, not moving or speaking.

"Oh, and the other thing is, I'm coming with you as your date."

God. Where did that come from? I glance up at Clyde whose cute, fat cheeks dimple from the huge smile on his face.

Finally, the professor opens his eyes and reaches for the bag of fruit. "I'm guessing this is part of the treatment?"

The relief washes through me, and I slump back into the chair. "Yes. Clyde insists it will help, but I'm not sure I believe him."

He reaches for a pear and bites into it.

With pear juice dribbling down his chin, he regards me intently. "And you say you're my date?" I nod, not game to say anything more in case he changes his mind. "A trophy girlfriend. That should get their tongues wagging."

A self-demeaning comment trips to the end of my tongue and dangles on the edge, threatening to contradict my argument. I swallow it back, pleased with my self-control.

Clyde pushes away from the door jamb, walks over to the table and leans over the old man. "She might have agreed to be your date but she won't be bathing you. That's my job, so get your arse into that bathroom."

He blinks innocently. "Are you sure, Layla? It might be a deal breaker."

"Completely sure, Professor."

He pushes out of his chair, falters, and with Clyde holding him by the elbow, they head down to the bathroom.

There's no time for me to go home and change, but luckily I dressed up for the lawyers' meeting in my grey suit and grey turban, which will do to sit at the back of the church. However, I'm wondering if I'll make things worse for the professor by escorting him to the church. Will his family see him with a freaky looking woman and judge him on the company he's keeping? At least Clyde will be there and they know him.

(o

After a long shower, clean clothes, rehydration, and twenty laps of the corridor, the professor is as good as he's going to get. Clyde hails a taxi and we pile into the back seat to a round of applause from staff and clients of the Mission.

The taxi driver is a sharp-featured Indian with a fat moustache. He has a spring-loaded statue of the Hindu god, Ganesh dancing on the dashboard, and the thick, spicy aromas from a tiffin box filled with curry and rice, cling to the interior of the cab. He beams at our entrance, thrilled to be cruising into the traffic amidst cheers, believing we must be celebrities of some sort.

"Where is it I am taking such important persons?" he asks.

Clyde pulls a note from his pocket. "St Thomas's Anglican Church, North Sydney."

I'm wedged between the two men on the back seat and try to shift discreetly so my thigh is not pressed so hard against Clyde's.

He bends his head to my ear and whispers, "If you want more room I could get into the front with the bobbing Ganesh."

I giggle and shake my head. Then he taps the tip of his nose and screws up his face, gesturing at the professor. I know what he means, there is an overwhelming smell of aftershave clogging my nostrils.

"You smell very nice, Professor. What's the name of your cologne?"

He turns from the window to face me and I see the man he must have once been. With his hair washed and combed, his face shaved, and dressed in a suit and tie, he is quite handsome; there is even a hint of sophistication—remnants of his old life.

"My cologne? I believe it's called Scent of Sexagenarian. Do you like it? I found it in the bathroom cabinet."

"It clashes with the curry, but you smell better than you did before," says Clyde.

The professor may sound relaxed and even glib, but his arms are pressed tight against his sides and the tendons in his neck stand out, pulsing with tension.

"Are you scared about seeing your family again, Professor?"

"Never been more terrified of anything in my entire life, my dear. In fact, if you were smart, you would have me handcuffed to you to ensure I don't bolt the minute this car stops."

Lost for words, I reach over and clasp his hand. When we pull up outside the church, I don't let go. Instead, I slide across the seat after him and we find ourselves in the midst of staring strangers, still holding hands.

Clyde pays the driver and steps out, saying he could wait in the park nearby until the ceremony is over, rather than us descending *en masse*. With my death grip still on the professor's hand, I grasp his sleeve, and hiss at him to stay. He agrees, but decides to first have a look around.

When Clyde walks away, it's as if a protective wall has disappeared and I feel cold and exposed. Although, I imagine, not nearly as exposed as the professor feels. No one has approached us, thank goodness. Then I feel the professor stiffen beside me and I follow his gaze. An attractive older woman, with sleek silver hair and dressed in an emerald-green sheath dress and jacket, her hand linked through the arm of a pretty, fair haired young woman, is effusively greeting new arrivals.

They've seen him. The older woman's mouth purses as if she's sucked a lemon. Then her eyes move to my face and her jaw drops in shock. To my relief, Clyde returns and follows the line of our vision. The woman nudges her daughter, whose face softens and then hardens at the sight of me holding her father's hand. Perhaps I have made things worse for him by coming. I release his hand and try to move away, but he pulls me into his side and puts his mouth to my ear.

"If you move, I'll run."

Other eyes are now upon us and a number of people have recognised the professor. His ex-wife and daughter make their way towards us.

"Could you have made yourself any more obvious?" hisses the ex-wife. "Hello, Clyde," she adds. He nods in response.

The professor ignores her remark, releases my hand, and holds his two hands out to his daughter. "Tracey. What a beautiful young woman you have become. I can't tell you what it means to see you again."

She glances around, as if to make sure no one is watching, ignores his outstretched hands, places a stiff hand on his shoulder, and pecks his cheek before stepping back out of reach.

"Father, good to see you again."

I want to smack the spoilt little bitch's face, but I haven't been introduced yet. Then I'll do it.

"I'd like you to meet my good friend, Layla. Layla, this is my daughter, Tracey, and her mother, Barbara."

Tracey nods, then excuses herself to greet some friends. Missed my chance. Her father's eyes, filled with longing, follow her retreat.

Perversely, I hold out my scarred hand and the ex-wife smothers a small squeak, before an admirable retaliation.

"And how do you know Tracey's father? Are you one of his alcoholic friends?"

At first I'm speechless at her intimation, as well as the insult to both the professor and myself. But the professor's answer gives me the courage not to take her shit.

"Basically, we just use each other for sex," he says, pinching my bottom.

I don't speak until she's caught her breath and the unattractive red flush has dissipated.

"Actually we met when our two groups had a social night."

Composed again, she lifts one perfectly plucked eyebrow.

"Your two groups?"

"Yes. Alcoholics Anonymous and Penitent Pyromaniacs."

I gesture at my face to illustrate the point. At this Clyde nearly chokes and the professor squeezes my hand, his face still impassive.

She pulls out a lace crocheted handkerchief and mops at her neck. "Sarah should never have invited you. This is worse than I'd imagined.

The professor sighs, lowering his eyes. "Relax, Barbara, I'm not going to spoil my daughter's wedding. You go back to your guests, and we'll stay as invisible as we can."

She turns away, mumbling, "As if that's possible."

We stand there like naughty children, still holding hands.

"She seemed happy to see us," I say.

The professor chuckles. "It went better than I expected, actually. Barbara acted true to form and at least Tracey came over and greeted me. She swore she'd never speak to me again when I left home."

He tugs at my hand, guiding me away from the front entrance of the blonde brick cathedral to a patch of grass near the small, arched side entrance.

"Tracey has grown into a beautiful young woman, hasn't she?"

I can't say what I really think: that she is an unpleasant spoiled brat. "Very beautiful. You must be proud, Professor."

He nods, glancing over my head as if he might be rewarded with another brief view of his daughter. Then his grip tightens and he takes a deep breath. Following his gaze, I see the wedding cars have arrived. The passenger door opens and out steps a tall, slim man with a thick head of greying hair and a smug grin. This is the man who is giving the professor's daughter away. He bends over, reaches in, and hands out the bride. To save the professor any indignity, I take only a side-glance at his face, but it is enough to see the tears pooling in his eyes. With my gaze now averted, I rummage through my bag and hand him a tissue. Then Clyde and I hurry him through the side door, towards the back pews, and force him to take a seat next to the aisle where she will pass.

A rustle of tulle and satin is the only contact he gets as his daughter, Sarah, follows her three bridesmaids down the aisle to the front of the church. With a veil over her face, I'm unable to make out her features, but her escort, who I presume is her mother's partner, still wears his smug smile.

By the time the ceremony and the signing are over, we've been sitting on the hard wooden pews for nearly an hour. Then the priest announces the married couple and they turn to face their friends and family for the long walk down the red-carpeted aisle.

Now I see this daughter is darker, like the professor. She has a mass of brown curls caught on the top of her head. Her eyes sparkle with happiness and I note that both she and her new husband are not the required super slim shape of rich, North Shore socialites. I like her more than the professor's younger daughter.

As she approaches the back of the church, the professor starts to tremble. Sarah is his oldest child and the one he spent the most time with before leaving the home. I don't usually pray, but I'm in a church so I formulate an apologetic request—apologetic because I only pray as a last resort—that she will at least smile at the professor.

She is two bench rows away when her gaze rests on her father. At first she frowns in confusion and then recognition dawns on her face, followed by a joyful smile. I hear a short sob catch in the professor's throat at her initial response. But now she releases her husband's arm, veers towards her father, and with her arms outstretched, gathers him in an embrace. She kisses his cheek and I overhear her whispered words.

"I love you, Daddy. Thank you for coming."

The groom reaches across his wife and shakes the professor's hand, before they move to the doorway and are mobbed by the other guests.

Unwilling to disturb the moment, I wait silently beside the professor, trying not to sniff too loudly as the tears run down my face. Finally, Clyde gestures to the side door and we make our way out onto the small sandstone path.

"Would you like to go around to the front and speak with her?" I ask.

He shakes his head. "No. That moment in the church is the memory I want to keep. Let's go."

Naïvely, I imagine that special moment in the church will be a catalyst for the professor to give up drinking, reunite with his children, and live happily ever after. But that's not how it works for an alcoholic. By the time we're in the taxi heading back, his shaking has magnified tenfold. Clyde reaches into his backpack and pulls out what looks like a bottle of orange juice and hands it to the professor. His greedy guzzle and the slowing of his tremors tell me the truth.

So, no happily ever after.

Just a continuous downward spiral made bearable by the memory of that one moment.

CHAPTER 23

THE PHONE AND I ARE in a stand-off. I refuse to pick up the message. Finally, the screen fades to black. This is the first contact Tom's made since the day I told him I didn't want to talk. The phone is on the coffee table and Bennie puts his front paws on the table, barks once and using his snout, pushes the phone towards me.

"All right," I say, and picking it up I press 'Messages.'

It was only one night. We're friends, aren't we? Call me.

Only one night. And now I'm wondering how many other *one nights* there have been. At least he's admitted it. Before I can think twice about it, I respond.

Coffee at Bean There this afternoon?

It's ten minutes before he responds.

That will work. 3.30?

Not exactly the enthusiasm I hoped for. I can match that level of enthusiasm, no problems.

OK.

I don't know why, but I miss him. More specifically, I miss the Tom he was before the fire. I don't miss the weird dynamics that emerged after I came out of hospital. I can excuse his lack of intimacy and awkwardness in the hospital. I put it down to the limits of such an environment. But as much as it physically pains me to admit, the last six months with him have consisted of a string of excuses to cover the truth that whatever we had no longer exists.

After pressing send, I lean out the window, distracting myself by watching board riders in the surf; small dots rising up and down with the swell. A cloud of seagulls wheels and dives over the sea, their rancorous cries signalling a fish sighting as their wingtips skim the surface of the water.

It's Saturday morning and I can hear Mr. Bacik's voice over the bird calls as he shouts to his wife. There is still an idea bubbling away in my head about encouraging a relationship between Levi and the old man. He and Ruby are catching the bus over tomorrow to visit me and to go to the beach. At least I can introduce him to the old man and then it's up to them where they take it.

Ruby and I made the arrangements last night when I rang Mum to tell her how the meeting with the lawyers had gone. I kept Corinne's behaviour to myself. Mum would probably only see it as part of the ongoing friction between us.

☾

The wind has risen since lunchtime and I have to hold my cap down to stop it blowing away, as Bennie and I head towards the coffee shop to meet Tom. Pine needles, blown from the trees, are strewn on the concrete walkway which borders the beach, and as I scrunch over them, they release a sharp, clean scent. The wind skitters over the ocean, sucking spray into the air and coating my face and clothes with damp saltiness. Bennie presses close to me, using my leg as a buttress against the wind as we cross over to the Corso. Tom is already there and I release Bennie's lead so he can dash at Tom's legs, whimpering a greeting, his body quivering with excitement.

Rather than this reunion between Tom and my dog giving me a warm, secure feeling, it revives my old yearning for Tom, and the lost potential of our future together. Swallowing the tide of grief at what we have lost, I paste a bright smile on my face, and offer my right cheek to be kissed, before taking a seat. There is an awkward moment when neither of us is sure why we're here or what to say.

"It's good to see—"

"How are you—?" I gesture at him to go first and wonder if this will be half an hour of uncomfortable small talk.

"I was a bit hurt you didn't want to speak to me. It's been weeks, Layla."

At first I can't respond. He's talking about being hurt? Not a mention of the reason I couldn't speak to him. Was he always this self-focused and I didn't see it? I decide I'm going to be mature, detached, and rational.

"You lied to me about sleeping with someone else, Tom. We were going to get married. My whole future has gone down the toilet. I've lost my job. I look like a freak." So much for mature and detached, let alone rational. Tears drip down my face.

"And I loved you," I sob.

He stares down at his hands, draws in a deep breath and shifts in his chair.

"It's been so hard, Layla. I didn't ask for any of this, either. I really wanted to be there for you, be the dedicated boyfriend. I suppose I haven't done a very good job of it."

My indignation whooshes out like a balloon deflating. He's right. We're merely two victims of a shocking event, both doing the best we can.

"No, you haven't done such a good job but then neither have I. I couldn't accept this." I gesture at my face and body. "I wanted it to be different. I still do and will take whatever action I can to improve it. But you know what, Tom? I'm going to release you from any commitment you might feel you still have to me. I'm letting you go." My chest caves and my heart feels like it's being squeezed dry. I want to suck back the words and swallow them, but it's as if someone has wound me up and the key is still turning. "Now it's official and you can sleep with whoever you want without guilt or lies."

He still can't meet my eyes, and ignores my last barb. "It's hard to imagine life without you, Layla. But if this is what you want—" He shrugs as if defeated.

A spark of anger flares around my dried out heart. He could have at least fought to keep me. But then I spit on the spark, determined not to keep living in some fairy-tale illusion.

"Will you be all right?" he asks.

"Without you? I think so. I've actually got some very nice friends who've been a great support." He raises his eyebrows in question. "No-one you know."

"You mean that fat bloke? Are you sleeping with him?"

I swallow, hating myself for the 'fat' comment about Clyde.

"Under the circumstances, that's really none of your business. I might pass on the coffee, there's probably nothing more we need to say."

He raises his head and looks at me, his face a mix of relief, tinged with disappointment. I know why he's relieved but am puzzled for a moment by the other. Until I realise he will no longer be admired for being the long-suffering boyfriend. Shockingly, my treacherous body sways towards him, a flicker of desire still burning. I pull back. I've humiliated myself enough and need to pick my crumpled pride up and shake it out. Pushing back my chair I stand, lean over and kiss his cheek. Then turn and walk away. Bennie looks from me to Tom, gives Tom's hand a last lick and scampers behind me. I don't look back, and I don't stop crying the entire way home.

Slumped on my sofa three hours later, I count the bridges I have burnt (an unfortunate use of language) since becoming 'Layla after the fire'. My job, my boyfriend, my old friends—even my best friend, Tegan. She stopped calling for fear her two small children would cry in terror at the sight of me. Not that my anger made me good company for anyone. Now my friends consist of an obese barman, a transvestite and two alcoholics. Oh, and a long-haired bouncer who thinks it's still the seventies.

☾

I struggle out of bed, and check the clock. Ruby and Levi are due any minute. A throbbing headache, brought on by the emotional distress of the Tom farewell yesterday afternoon, has eased, thanks to two Panadols, and a reasonable night's sleep. But I look terrible from the crying. What a ridiculous thought. I look terrible even without the crying.

Manic scratching at the door tells me Bennie can hear Ruby's voice. They're earlier than I expect, so must have had good bus connections. I gulp down the last spoonful of cereal and open the door. With Bennie weaving between our legs, Ruby and I stumble out to the living room, Levi trudging behind.

Unlike yesterday, it's a warm, sunny day with no wind, so I'm not surprised when, only minutes after they arrive, Ruby sidles up to me and rubs my arm.

"Is it okay if we take Bennie down to the beach?"

At the word 'beach', the terrier squirms with such excitement he, as usual, loses his balance.

"You've certainly got Bennie's permission. Yeah, go now and come back for lunch." As they turn to leave, I touch Ruby's arm. "Remember my neighbour, the old Polish man? He would love to see you again, Rubes, and I told him about you too, Levi. He's got a grandson who he never sees and I thought it might be nice for him to meet you. Do you think you can bear chatting to an old man for a while?"

Before Ruby can answer, Levi responds. "Sure. Old people are cool. My dad's parents come and stay a couple of times a year and we hang out a bit. Don't much see my mum's parents. Remember, I told you about that? The couple of times I've seen them they creeped me out a bit because they wouldn't stop hugging and touching me."

"I don't think you'll have that trouble with my neighbour."

He shrugs and nods his assent. The three of them scramble out the door, and I can hear laughter as they run down the rough, concrete steps towards the beach. I would have gone with them, but remember what it was like to be fifteen, trying to snatch any opportunity to be alone with my boyfriend.

Through the window, I see them walk the path towards Shelly Beach. Ruby squints up and waves. Skipping ahead with Bennie, she's my little sister again. From here I can't see the shaved head or the startling eye make-up, and Levi, shuffling behind, is devoid of his normal teenage bravado. She turns back to him and calls out; he runs towards her, clasping her hand and pressing a kiss to her cheek. Then they continue hand in hand. I'm definitely softening towards this boy. If only I could have a word with his hairdresser.

Levi has promised Ruby he won't use drugs until both their exams are over. He seemed surprised at how much clearer his mind was and how his retention of school work had improved. His father also commented on the improvement in his marks.

As for Ruby, she's done a complete turnaround. Not interested in using illicit drugs. She surprised me by saying she now corresponds with Anna, the girl at the rehab centre. When I asked why, she told me she couldn't bear the thought Anna might die, and having another friend might give her more to live for. I'm proud of Ruby, but I know how devastated she'll be if Anna chooses the drugs over friends and family. A probable choice.

When they've disappeared from sight, I move away from the window, open my laptop and spend some time researching drug deaths statistics. Too depressing, so I check my emails. There's another one from Dr. Gassner's private clinic saying he's had a cancellation for an appointment in four weeks' time. His secretary indicates it can often take six to eight months for an initial appointment. She ends her sentence with an exclamation mark, as if she's given me extremely exciting news. When in fact her news elicits a somersault of panic in my stomach. Legal proceedings are in the early stages and I haven't the money to go. I can't tell her I'll come, but I can't bring myself to refuse the offer, yet. Instead, I click to the next email.

It's no good. I can't concentrate on anything else. Not with Dr. Gassner's email ticking like a time bomb, waiting for my answer.

Mum would lend me the airfare for the trip. Probably Matthew would as well. God, even Corinne, in her current magnanimous state, might buy my ticket.

Before I can explore my options further, Ruby and Levi burst through the front door. They're both gripping the lead of a wet, sandy Bennie, to stop him from hurtling through the apartment.

"Outside," I yell. "Hose him down first." I swing open the door of my small linen cupboard and toss her a towel. Bennie yaps at me, miffed at not being groomed under a hot shower.

Giggling, Ruby and Levi trip over each other as they drag Bennie out the door, down the stairs, and around the side to the tap. In their scramble to get out, they drop the towel on the step, so I follow them out, tossing it to Levi. Ruby hoses the salt and sand off Bennie's squirming body and as she reaches for the towel, the dog shakes like the spin dryer in a washing machine. Ruby's squeals of indignant mirth have Levi and I double over with laughter. In retaliation, she darts the hose from Levi to me and back again, causing us to run, screaming for cover with Bennie, now loose, barking behind us.

The squealing, laughing, barking, and splats of water on their kitchen window, bring Mr. and Mrs. Bacik to their door to see what's happening. The other tenants either don't care or are out.

"Ruby, *kochana*! You sound like someone is murdering you," exclaims Mrs. Bacik.

Gasping for breath, Levi looks up at her. "Not her, us," he pants. "She's using water torture."

"Ah, so this is Ruby's Levi." She steps into the yard and grips Levi's face between her hands. "A strong face you have, my boy."

The old lady looks over at her husband and shakes her head. His head drops slightly and he closes his eyes. This confuses me for a moment and then I understand. Like me, they must have entertained the fantasy that this could be their grandson, their Levi, and I want to snap my fingers and make it so.

Mrs. Bacik pastes a smile on her face and touches his hair. "But this hair? So crazy and red." Her eyes track down his face and see the metal protruding from his lip. "Ho, ho. What is this?" She turns to Ruby. "You like this?"

Ruby moves next to Levi and takes his hand. "Of course. I like everything about Levi."

Mr. Bacik shuffles over and shakes Levi's hand. "Welcome, Levi. For Ruby, we are going to like this metal business, too."

There is an awkward silence. The Baciks unsure of their place, Levi embarrassed by the yearning in their eyes and Ruby looking from one to the other, frowning.

"You know what? You guys remind me a bit of my grandparents. The ones I never see." He looks over at Ruby. "I mean my Mum's parents."

Mrs. Bacik throws her arms around the boy and squeezes him. "Such a lovely boy." She pulls away and gestures to her flat. "Come, come. I make some tea and we all eat fresh *paczki*. Like donut," she says to Ruby and I.

This weird boy has unwittingly given the best compliment these two old people could hear. I want to run over and squeeze him, too. I don't, though. It might be just enough to make him turn and run.

Ruby flashes Levi a look of alarm, but the little I know about Mrs. Bacik tells me she needs to feed Levi to fulfil a deep maternal urge, long suppressed by her daughter's rejection. So, I drag my reluctant sister towards their door.

Not only do we enjoy the best donuts I've ever tasted, but the pleasure on the old people's faces moves Levi to promise another visit very soon. At this, Mrs. Bacik's eyes glisten with tears and she nods at her husband.

Mr. Bacik clears his throat and addresses Levi. "My wife and I, we have a request to make." Mouth full, Levi nods. "We wish to be these grandparents you don't have. Not take their place, you understand, just to treat you like a grandson. What do you say?"

Levi swallows and licks his lips. "That would be really cool. Yeah, man, I'd like that." He reaches across the table and stuffs a third pastry into his mouth. "And these are the best *paczki* I've had, Mrs. Bacik."

"What you mean, Mrs. Bacik? You call me *Babcia* and this is *Dziadzia*." She indicates Mr. Bacik.

Levi runs his hand through his red crest. "Can do, Grandma. I mean *Babcia*, and *Dziadzia*." He holds up his hand and to my surprise, the old man doesn't hesitate to do a perfect high five. "No probs, man."

Mrs. Bacik pushes another *paczki* at Levi and watches as he eats. Then reaches for her husband's hand.

"Look, Jozef. We have a grandson."

&

I turn out the light, but instead of giving in to the exhaustion of a crazy day, I wonder what Clyde's doing. Not only do I wonder about him, I need to hear his voice before giving in to sleep. *Did I say need?* Besides, I want to share another bizarre day with him. There is enough moonlight flowing through my window to see the phone. He answers on the third ring.

"Hey, Layla. Do you need a bedtime story?"

A shiver of excitement jags through me and a ridiculous image of Clyde next to me in bed, telling me a bedtime story, blocks the section of my frontal lobe responsible for speech.

"Layla?"

"S-sorry," I mumble. "How was your day?"

"Would have been better if you were there." I giggle like a nervous teenager. "Are you alright?" he asks.

I pull myself together and attempt to sound sensible.

"You'll never guess what happened today. Remember my

inspired idea to introduce Levi to Mr. Bacik so the old man could play grandfather?"

Clyde grunts. "You mean your evil surrogacy plan?"

"That's the one. Well, it worked. Mr. Bacik actually suggested it and Levi was all for it. I was so proud of that boy."

"I don't know Mrs. Bacik but I liked the old man. I can't imagine going through the horrors they've been through and then being shunned by their only child. Sounds like our Levi might fill that void for now."

"I hope so. When I think about my impressions of that boy the first night I met him, it's hard to believe how attached I'm becoming to him."

"Cockatoo crest and all?"

"Unfortunately, yes."

"Layla?"

"Yes?"

"You've phoned me again. I think I must be growing on you a bit."

I am about to make a joke but instead admit it. "Well, maybe a bit."

He's silent for a few seconds as if enjoying my capitulation. "Want to come to Luna Park?"

"What?" I had curled up under my blanket, ready to hear his warm voice ask me out somewhere nice. "Did you say Luna Park?"

His deep chuckle makes me smile. "It's Lavender's fortieth birthday, and she's organised a private party at Luna Park. She told me I must invite you. Although I would have anyway."

Clyde?" He grunts again. "Have you noticed, we've never been anywhere together that hasn't been tragic, bizarre, or incredibly funny?"

"Don't be ridiculous. What about dinner at my mother's house?" I snort. "Okay," he says, "you might be right."

Although I was joking, my life has blazed with colour since meeting Clyde, despite my best efforts to remain shrouded in an innocuous, grey underworld. And most surprising of all, I find I like it.

"What do you say?"

"About Luna Park? Well, I could ask: why are you dragging me on another bizarre outing?"

I know he's grinning.

Until I met Clyde, the word 'no' would have been uttered before an invitation to go anywhere was completed. But this time, I accept the invitation without even thinking about it.

"When?"

"Her birthday is on Saturday, but she's working, so the party's on Friday night. Did you phone because you need me to be Scheherazade again?"

The image of Clyde dressed as a Persian princess is too much. "No, thanks. I'm good."

Then I remember why I phoned.

"Can I ask you something?"

"Sure."

"I had an email from the clinic in New York, saying they've had a cancellation and could I come over for a personal consultation in four weeks' time."

"And despite this being your concerted goal, you're scared shitless, you're in the middle of a legal battle, and it's all too soon," he says.

"How do you do that? Are you psychic? God, I hope not. My mind is not a place for the faint-hearted."

"Sorry, bad habit: pre-empting what you're going to say."

"It would be annoying if you weren't always so bloody accurate." He chuckles and apologises again. "As it happens, you're right on all counts. They gave me twenty-four hours to accept the appointment or it will be given to someone else. I don't know what to do."

"Regardless of the above restrictions, do you have the money to go? If you haven't, then it's all academic until the outcome of the legal process."

"I have and I haven't. I have some savings, but that's what I'm living on and it would mean a big chunk out of that just for the trip. But I'm sure Mum or another family member would lend me at least the airfare if I really wanted to go."

"I'm thinking we should look at the scared shitless reason," he says. "Want to talk about that?"

I scramble for a rational explanation. "I'm not sure. I suppose I've set in place a sequence of events. You know, if they say the operation can be done, then I need the money from the legal action, and therefore I need the legal action. Besides, I've got my mind focused on seeing this litigation through now that I've started. I think I need the comfort of doing things in sequence."

Clyde is silent for so long, I wonder if our line has disconnected.

"Hmm. So, back to the scared shitless reason. Which I might add you cleverly dodged." Not so cleverly, it would seem. "Have you thought about the possibility of going over and being told they can't fix your face?"

It's like he has a probe that plunges straight into the heart of a matter through a hole so narrow, there is no room for excuses, denials, or lame logistics.

"I don't think I'm ready to hear that yet," I whisper.

"Then I guess that's your answer. You deserve to do it in your own time. It sounds like it's not time."

"Do you think I'm a coward?"

"There's nothing cowardly about you, my sweet Layla. You're braver than I could ever be. Anyway, you've got twenty-four hours. You might change your mind tomorrow but if not, then stay on your current track."

"I emailed back this evening, asking for more time and they agreed to give me until five p.m. Friday afternoon, New York time. That's early Saturday morning for me."

"Right. Three circuits of the Wild Mouse Ride on Friday night and you'll have made the decision to catch the next flight to New York."

"Do I dare ask you to remind me what the Wild Mouse ride is?"

"One pulse-pounding, nerve-shredding minute of dips and dives where you scream out over the harbour and are then flung back at shocking speed to where I'll be standing on solid ground waiting for you."

"Such a wuss. I need you there holding my hand."

"Oh God, not Sophie's Choice," he says. "And by the way, Lavender's birthday is a theme party."

I release a long, breathy groan. "No. I don't even want to ask." Clyde doesn't speak. "Go on, you might as well tell me."

"Wild West. You know, Cow-persons and Indians."

"It's official. You are no longer my friend," I say.

He chuckles. "You know you don't mean that. Goodnight, Layla. I'll see you Friday. I'll be the one on the bucking bronco."

CHAPTER 24

CLYDE IS AT MILSON'S POINT wharf when I step off the ferry. I spot him immediately in the crowd of people moving on and off the boat. He's already over six feet tall but the Stetson hat easily adds another few inches. As if his size and my disfigurement aren't enough to draw attention, we are now two costumed, walking sideshows.

"It's Pocahontas," he hoots across the crowd.

"Meeting John Wayne," I retort.

We halt two metres apart and I'm not sure who starts laughing first, but it's so infectious, there are soon smiles on even the dourest, after-work faces surrounding us.

He's right, I'm Pocahontas. I considered dressing as the Lone Ranger because of the mask, but the woman in the costume shop, once she could look me in the eye, talked me into the suede, fringed Pocahontas outfit. It even came with long, suede boots. To deal with the bald patch, I wrapped a large bandanna around my head and stuck a feather through it. My hair, I pulled into pigtails. Of course, I'm wearing my oversized sunglasses even though the sun has set.

Clyde raises one hand in salute. "How, Pocahontas."

Rolling my eyes, I groan at his clichéd greeting. "Sound like paleface stuck for words," I respond.

He hooks his thumbs into his empty gun belt, and I'm conscious of his gaze roving my body. My face heats with embarrassment, but the tiny flutter in my stomach tells me I'm flattered as well. Clyde never seems to see my scars. This is his greatest gift.

"Hard for an old cowboy to be clever in the company of such a purty li'l lady." He tugs at the red handkerchief tied around his neck. "Would you do me the honour, ma'am, of allowin' me to escort you through the wild environs of this here Luna Park? I done hear there's danger at every turn."

When I incline my head in assent, he takes two long strides, clicks his plastic spurs together and crooks his arm. It's as if he draws the attention from me, allowing me to believe I'm an anonymous part of the crowd. Even if only with him by my side. Again, it's enough for me to relax and enjoy myself.

Beside the gaping mouth, which is the iconic art deco entrance to Luna Park, stands Mrs. Crompton. I recall watching an old cowboy film when I was a kid. The stars were Roy Rogers and Dale Evans. I swear it's Dale Evans, an older version, in front of us. From the fringed blue skirt to the white shirt and blue vest, the white hat, sitting at the back of her head to protect the grey coiffeur, and the risqué red lipstick. The only deviation from authenticity is her ever-present square handbag, held close to her body in the crook of her arm.

"Howdy, ma'am," says Clyde, his mouth twitching. "I already have the care of one purty lady, but I'm a big ole cowboy and can most probably take on another one." He holds out his arm and she links her arm through his, giggling like a girl.

She leans across Clyde, pats my arm in greeting. "You're looking very ethnic, dear," she says.

Smothering a grin, I nudge Clyde in the ribs. "Where are we meeting the others?"

"Lavender has hired the Big Dipper room. There's drinks and food there, and then we can all be let loose on the rides."

The last time I went to Luna Park was ten years ago when it first reopened. After a tragic fire on the ghost train which killed seven people, it had been shut down for years. Tegan and I were celebrating end of year exams and wanted to release our stress by screaming like kids on the rides. It's impossible to even walk into the mouth of the huge laughing face, without a smile.

"Here we are. It's in this building," says Clyde, as we walk through the entrance of the Big Top and into the party room. "As incredible as we think our costumes are," he winks at me, "we'll be insignificant daubs of grey against Lavender's friends."

"Insignificant works for me," I say.

Mrs. Crompton nods, tapping her handbag to ensure it's still on her arm. At first I assumed she was protective of any valuables in the handbag, but now I have my suspicions there may be a small flask of emergency brandy buried in the bag.

"Daahlings!"

Lavender's greeting jags across the room like an electric current. She waves both arms in the air to attract our attention. As if she needs to. I glance at Clyde; his mouth hangs open, like mine, at the sparkling apparition loping towards us. She's wearing black stockings with a lace suspender belt below a tiny black cowgirl skirt, edged with red fringes, which sways provocatively with each step. Her top is black with red lacings and covered in flashing diamantes, and her spike-heeled black boots are mid-calf with intricate stitching encircling the top. Her diamante studded hat is tilted on an angle and looped around her shoulder is a horse-whip.

"*Sourcil*, you look fabulous. You too, Mrs. Crompton. And Clyde you look...big, darling. Big and manly." She winks a birdwing eyelash at him and drags us across the room through shrieking groups of champagne-guzzling party-goers.

"Great costume, Lavender," I yell over the babbling throng. "Quite the sex kitten."

She stops abruptly and Mrs. Crompton smacks into her side, protecting her handbag from impact. "If you think I look yummy, darling, come and meet my Lance." This must be her partner. "Clyde thinks he's to die for. Don't you, darling?"

Clyde blinks, releasing a loud breath. "Wouldn't quite put it like that, but he's a good bloke."

Lavender giggles and launches at two men with their backs to us. "Lance, darling, you must meet my friend, *Sourcil*."

A dark-haired, olive-skinned man turns around and the breath catches in my throat at his beauty. The man should be on a billboard, in tight undies. Wearing low-slung suede cowboy chaps with an eye-catching leather codpiece, his top half is naked except for a small suede vest and a neckerchief. If I had a fan I would be waving it front of my face to cool down. This lad obviously spends a lot of time working out and he has guns in more places than his holster.

"Close your mouth, darling."

The heat flushes up my neck at being caught out staring. I

shove out my hand to cover my embarrassment. "Nice to meet you, Lance. Your costume is divine."

Lavender hoots with laughter as do the rest of the scantily clad cowboys clustered in the group. "That's Alonzo. This one is Lance." She points to a tall, lanky man in his late thirties with a receding hairline, and a trendy jaw stubble. He's wearing a similar outfit to Alonzo.

"Hello, sweetie." A light of recognition widens his eyes. "Oh, my gosh, you're *Sourcil*, the girl Lavender keeps talking about. With the scarred face. Not that she keeps talking about your scarred face, sweetie, only about you."

This gushes out in one breath and so guilelessly, that although I am now the subject of intense scrutiny by all in earshot, I find it hard to take offence.

"It's not that bad," he says. "Oh, who am I kidding," he flips his wrist towards me, his lips twitching, "it's terrible."

And then I too am laughing, because it is so liberating to hear the blatant truth rather than sympathetic consolations.

Lance looks over at Lavender and winks. "I like her."

And, ridiculously, I'm pleased he does. Another round of champagne and I'm one of the girls.

After countless plates of finger food, Lavender announces it's time to hit the rides. I insist we follow the others. They're so flamboyant and loud, I'll be less noticeable.

An hour later, Clyde and I step off the Wild Mouse ride, breathless from the lurching, breakneck speed and the wild fling over the harbour. He straightens my bandanna and pokes the feather back into place, pushing hair out of my eyes. When he's finished putting me back together, I return the favour. I've just finished patting down his hair and placing his Akubra back on his head, when I hear a familiar voice.

"Well, look who's here. The Indian princess herself."

I turn around and nearly step on Tom, he's so close. He stumbles back and Kelly, *yes, Kelly, not Clarissa*, grabs his arm to steady him. Who else has the lowlife been sleeping with? His eyes are bloodshot. He's drunk.

When the shock of seeing him subsides enough for me to speak, I first step closer to Clyde. "Tom. What a surprise. And Kelly." What more can I say?

"Didn't know you were into dress-ups, Layla," he slurs.

I ignore his comment and turn to Clyde. "Tom, this is my friend, Clyde. Clyde this is Tom and Kelly." Clyde greets them politely as they both scrutinise him.

Tom grins, a nasty upturn of his lips. "This must be the fat bloke you told me I had no reason to be jealous of. I can see what you mean."

I nearly choke with embarrassment, which shifts into a cold anger—not only at him but at myself for betraying Clyde. Clyde stiffens and without moving, distances himself from me. Kelly releases Tom's arm and moves over to a nearby shooting gallery.

"I'm going to let that go because you're drunk, Tom. Please excuse us."

I turn to go and see Lance, Lavender, and four of their friends have disembarked from the ride and are standing next to Clyde. Tom explodes with laughter at the colourful group and a healthy wave of loathing rushes through me. His arrogant snobbery and social intolerance tumble out of his well-groomed exterior exposing him as a common bigot. Uncertain of how to respond, I glance down to see Clyde's fists clenched. Next to him, I'm sure Lavender's talons have unsheathed, like a tiger.

Not sure what else to do, I call out to Kelly, telling her to take 'her boyfriend' away. She purses her lips, closes her eyes in a slow blink and strolls over, taking Tom's arm. But he pulls free and reaches over to touch the right side of my face.

"She was beautiful. Absolute perfection. But now..." he drops his hand. "How do you think it's been for me now that she's ruined?"

Clyde moves closer to Tom and grabs his shirt collar. "You're a shallow, blind moron and if you can't see her real beauty, then she's well rid of you. Now fuck off before my friends and I give you a hand out of the park."

"Christ, you two make me want to throw up," says Kelly, her eyes narrowed at Tom. "You need to get over your pathetic guilt at not wanting her anymore and you," she points at me, "need to start living in the real world. A world where you'll never be the little beauty queen again."

She flicks her gloss of hair over one shoulder and stalks away. Lavender's posse of cowboys flex their oiled biceps and move a step towards Tom, who mumbles a half-hearted curse and lurches after Kelly. I'm speechless, thoughts whirling through my head. It's the first time Tom has verbally admitted his repulsion of my disfigurement—all his early denials were lies. And Clyde, even though Tom blurted the awful comment I had made about him, still defended me. More than defended me. Tears of shame well in my eyes, which I keep averted. Lavender nudges my arm.

"Fix it, *Sourcil*. Or I'll boot you out with your bigoted ex-boy-friend."

God, if only there was a hole in the ground for me to sink into. I nod, raising my head and she winks at me.

"By the way, I like her." She gestures towards Kelly's retreating back, before spinning theatrically and summoning her entourage to follow.

Clyde hasn't made eye contact. "We might as well go back, apparently there's music." He turns to follow them.

"Wait," I say. He stops, but only half turns towards me. "I'm so sorry."

"For what, Layla? For Tom insulting me? Or for giving him the ammunition in the first place?" There's no trace of humour in his eyes, only a shadow of pity, which brings me undone.

"God. All of it. It's not how I feel and you must know that. He's a spoilt little boy, who can't bear it when life doesn't meet his expectations. I fed into that by steering him away from thinking you were a rival at first, and the minute the words were out of my mouth, I hated myself for them. And it was all a waste of time as he didn't want me anyway." I'm babbling but my mouth won't stop.

"Do you really think I'd get upset about someone calling me fat? Forget it, Layla. It's your business what you say to Tom, not mine. He's a jerk. I'm surprised you took so long to realise it."

I reach for his hand. "I need to know you forgive me. I know you don't need it, but I do. Please, Clyde, I care so much about you." I'm almost begging, all dignity gone.

"You're forgiven, but remember for next time, I don't normally bother with forgiveness, Layla. It's an arrogant behaviour because it means I blame you for something, which I don't. Let's forget hipster boy and go drink champagne and dance."

I think I feel better, but I need to work out what he actually said. Did he forgive me or didn't he?

❧

We've been back in the party room for an hour. The dance floor is a chaos of flailing, sweaty bodies, undulating to the DJ's music. To the casual observer, Clyde and I might appear comfortable and happy, but I can feel the distance and what I interpret as his disappointment: that he's made a mistake, and I'm not the person he thought I was. My old need to be perfect at everything and loved for it, is eating at my gut, churning up into my throat. I'm desperate for him to say something to remove my guilt and, at the same time, know how woeful that sounds. Surprisingly amongst all this turmoil I've hardly given Tom a thought, and now I wonder how long Kelly will put up with him.

A loud screech from the microphone draws cries of protest, as Lance taps to see if it's working. When all eyes are focused on his stubbled face, he cues the DJ and is joined by Alonzo and two other very camp cowboys.

With a fifty's doo wop, doo wah beat and synchronised hand and body action, they sing the Marilyn Monroe version of "Happy Birthday, Mr. President" but change it to "Happy Birthday, Queen Lavender". It's fabulous, hilarious, and is followed by a huge cake in the shape of a crown with all forty candles blazing. We sing the traditional "Happy Birthday" and as we chant 'hip hip hooray', a petite, round-faced woman, clad in black, and with a bright blue streak down the front of her short, jagged hair, rushes breathlessly up to Clyde.

She throws her arms around his neck and he lifts her off the ground in an intimate embrace.

"Sorry I'm late, babes. Got held up."

"Not late, right on time," he smiles, obviously happy to see her. "Oh, meet Layla. This is Celia. My good friend and music partner."

God, why is my stomach whirring like there's an eggbeater in there? And my smile. I can't see it from the inside, but it feels strained. I push my lips wider. Now I probably look like a creepy clown.

"Celia, so nice to meet you. Clyde's told me all about you. Well, not too much. He said you play at Pyrmont and you went to uni and..." I stop prattling as Clyde raises his eyebrows in amusement. "Er...are you singing tonight?" I look from one to the other.

"Sure. Didn't Clydesdale tell you?" Shit, a nickname. I hate her. Not a bad one, though. He is a bit like a heavily built, shaggy workhorse with soft, brown eyes. They're both waiting for me to respond to something.

"Sorry, what did you say?"

Her glance at Clyde says, 'this one's slow as well as disfigured.' Well, I'm pretty sure that's what it says.

"I said, Clyde and I offered to play a couple of sets for the party. You could come up too, and sing with us if you like." Bugger, she's either really nice or really mean.

I wave my hand. "No, I'd spoil the sound. I'd rather listen."

She turns to Clyde. "Let's go, babes. Nice to meet you, Layla. Chat later."

They start with a couple of R & B numbers until people yell requests. Clyde launches into Gotye's "Someone That I Used to Know" after which Lavender asks for disco music.

One of the cowboys grabs me and we fling ourselves around the dance floor. Part of me is having a great time and the other part is still crumpled from the insult Tom threw at Clyde. I watch him as I wiggle my booty against the cowboy's tight buckskin-covered arse. Clyde seems so comfortable with Celia up on stage—like a hand slipped into a soft, familiar glove.

It's official—I'm jealous. Not only of their easy relationship, but of her capacity to see the person she cares about, not his weight. To give myself credit, I hardly notice it anymore myself, but the hypocritical prejudice is still too deeply embedded for it not to hover just below the surface.

As I watch the swirl of bodies gyrate to the rhythm of the music, I decide it's time to go home. Decision made, I thank my dancing cowboy, and turn to leave the dance floor.

"Hey, beautiful people," says Celia. "Clyde has made a request. It's a really, really oldie, but a goodie. So grab someone you want to hold close and have a smooch to the Beatle's legendary, 'Hey Jude.'" Yeah...definitely my cue to leave.

I'm halfway across the floor, wondering why I can only hear Celia's voice when someone grabs my arm.

"Care to dance?"

Clyde smiles and holds up his arms, old-fashioned waltz style. Glancing at the stage, I catch Celia's eye and she winks at me. Once again I have misread a situation. In a burst of joy, I bypass his outstretched arms and curl my fingers around his neck, nuzzling into his shoulder. He hesitates for a beat and then wraps me in a safe embrace.

There was a moment where I almost expected him to break my grip from his neck and tell me I was overstepping the bounds of our relationship—especially after the Tom debacle. Ridiculous tears of relief spill onto his collar and I sniff loudly. He moves back from me and uses his thumb to wipe a tear from the corner of my mouth, then pulls me back into his chest.

The emotional message of "Hey Jude" weaves its magic through the room and when I glance around Clyde's shoulder, a rainbow mix of couples sway on the darkened dance floor. My heart beat thunders in my ear drums at the intimacy of our embrace and what it implies. I inhale his clean, soapy smell and wish the world outside this room didn't exist. A feather light brush across my ear sends tingles down my spine and my muscles turn to jelly as Clyde's mellow baritone harmonises softly with Celia's voice.

By silent, mutual agreement, we leave as the last threads of the song fade out. Clyde waves to Celia, who is placing her guitar in its case, and we seek out Lavender to thank her for another memorable evening. I glance around for Mrs. Crompton, but Clyde tells me one of Lavender's cowboys called her a taxi some time ago and walked her out.

Clyde takes my hand as we wander past the dark, hunched shapes of the now silent rides. Under the boggle-eyes and glaringly white teeth of the Luna Park mouth, Clyde stops. "Can I take you home?"

I bite back the panic and nod. I know what he's asking.

CHAPTER 25

WHILE BENNIE WHIMPERS ON THE other side of the door, I fumble the key. It flips out of my hand and lands two steps down. Clyde places his warm hand on the back of my neck and then retrieves the key. He slides it easily into the lock and Bennie leaps into Clyde's arms. Not mine.

"I don't have to stay, Layla," he says.

"I want you to."

I can't make eye contact so lean over to bury my face into Bennie's furry head before Clyde aims him at the open doorway and sets him free. I walk into the kitchen.

"Coffee?" I ask.

He's still wearing his Akubra hat. He pushes it back from his forehead with one finger and shakes his head. "No, thank ya, ma'am. Just you. In bed. Naked."

A flood of lust battles with the ever present fear he will be repulsed by my scars. It would be easier not to risk the same humiliation I had with Tom, but sneaking a look at Clyde's twinkling eyes and the slow smile of desire on his lips, I stamp on the fear.

"Well, cowboy, this little Indian squaw is about to oblige you."

In a heartbeat, he's inches away, holding my face between his large, warm hands. As his lips lower to mine, my flight response tries to kick in, but another, stronger urge takes over. Then he's crushing me to his chest and the urgent thrust of his tongue in my mouth hurls a lump of emotion into my throat and I can hardly breathe. I'm a woman. Someone wants me. And, God help me, I want him.

A sharp bark for attention tells me Bennie is back. Clyde kicks the front door shut, picks me up, and carries me to the bedroom as if I'm the weight of a doll. He drops me onto the bed and we both laugh as I bounce, sinking into the feathered quilt. He flicks on the bedside light and pulls my suede boots off, one at a time, tossing them across the room. His Akubra follows and I reach up to push his thick, shaggy hair out of his eyes. Together we struggle to lift my fringed Pocahontas top over my head, revealing the scar down my arm.

I focus on his face and, aware of my scrutiny, he kisses me again before shrugging off his vest, tugging at his neckerchief, and trying, unsuccessfully, to dislodge one boot with the toe of the other. When he sits back to pull them off, I am acutely aware of how exposed I am—my hair fallen away from my face and neck, and naked to the waist. I reach over and flick off the bed lamp.

To my surprise, Clyde flicks it back on. He unzips my skirt and yanks it down. By now he's unbuttoned his shirt and I can see his pale, flabby stomach. I lurch to the side of the bed and douse the light again.

He stills. "I'd like the light on."

Is he being heartless? "Well, I want it off. You know how self-conscious I am about the scars."

He takes a deep breath. "Whatever this is. You and me. I want it to start in complete honesty. I want to know all of you and I want you to know all of me. Otherwise it won't work."

"I can't. Not yet. It'll be easier if we can't see. We can build up to the other stuff."

I know he'll give in; he always does. And to be honest, I think I need time to get used to his naked body as well.

The bed creaks as he leans over to stroke my hair. "I don't know what Tom did, but I'm not him. To me, everything about you is beautiful and every time I touch you, I'm as randy as a bull in stud."

I warm at his words, the lust rising in me again, and feel my way to the open front of his shirt, move my fingers down his chest. But I'm used to Tom's firm, flat stomach and pull back my hand as my fingers fall into the pouchy dips and rolls. It's okay, I tell my hypocritical self, it will take time for us to get used to each other.

Clyde grabs my hand. "If you're not ready to have the light

on, then it's not time for us to do this yet. It's not only about me accepting you, is it? It's about you accepting me as well."

I feel my face tingle with shame at his prescience. Again, I wonder if he can read my mind.

He sits back from me and starts buttoning his shirt. *What have I done?* I really do want him. I'm sure I do.

"You're wrong. Clyde, I want you to stay. I'm so used to hating myself, I can't believe anyone else wouldn't feel the same. Please don't go."

But he's pulling his boots on, so I grab an old sleeping T-shirt from under my pillow and slip it over my naked breasts. I switch the light on.

Even through the pain etched on his face, he smiles. A sad smile. "I'm not making ultimatums and I'm not trying to punish you, Layla. Maybe we were better at being friends than trying to be lovers. It's my fault. I couldn't resist you."

Sobs catch in my throat and I can't speak. My mind is a cloud of turbulence, swirling between confusion and disbelief. Disbelief that someone could feel like this about me despite how I look, and confusion at these feelings I have for Clyde which bounce between who he is and how he looks. Is he right? Do I have to love myself as I am before I can love him?

Clyde rips a handful of tissues from the box on my bedside table, dabs at my tears, and hands me the tissues to blow my nose. After a good blast, I finally speak.

"Maybe I won't be able to ever do this with anyone if I can't with you. I want to. I really do. What can I do to fix this?"

He purses his lips, looking past me at the dark ocean through the window.

"Don't have the answer to that one. But I can't help thinking your first step is to get past those scars."

I know what he's not saying. That while ever my own looks matter, everyone else's will as well.

This time when Clyde stands up and moves to the bedroom door, I don't try to stop him. It seems I'm destined to listen to men walk down my hall and out of my life. I know that sounds pathetic, but it's how I'm feeling tonight.

For some reason the hole left by his departure seems greater than when Tom left.

❦

I'm exhausted. Not surprising after only three hours sleep. The Pocahontas costume huddles accusingly in the corner of my bedroom—a reminder of last night's disaster, and my admirable ability to drive off anyone who might validate this damaged version of myself.

I sink onto the bed, an internal battle raging in my head. On the one hand, Clyde and the gang at The Black Hole were never meant to be a long-term alternative to my usual circle of friends. They were fill-ins; fellow freaks to give me a small sense of belonging until I could go back to my old life. Perhaps this isn't such a disaster, losing Clyde. It just happened a bit sooner than I'd planned.

Who am I kidding? I've formed strong emotional attachments to them all. They love and accept me as I am, and Clyde not only accepts me, but desires me. And last night I felt the same. These people are my true friends and I want them in my life. Despite what happens next. The real question will be whether they will want me.

Anyway, I haven't time to keep flogging myself over last night. I've arranged to accompany Randy Beasley this morning to meet with a detective at Balmain Police Station. I'm surprised Randy is willing to do this on a Saturday, but the police officer who handled the initial investigation goes on four weeks holiday from Monday, so we had no choice.

I glance at the clock. The deadline for my response to New York has come and gone. So, by default I have chosen not to take the offered appointment. My first thought is to phone Clyde, but remember I can't do that anymore. Well, I can but it wouldn't be fair.

❦

After my shower, the mirror is coated with condensation. I

swipe it with my palm and clear a space. A dab of concealer under the eyes might help. I giggle, a desperate sound, as I consider the scars which cover most of the left side of my face. No, not enough concealer for that. I lower my arms, straighten my shoulders, and force myself to stare at the woman glaring back at me. You may have lost Clyde's love and friendship, I tell her, but you can't let yourself lose what he showed you about yourself. I rearrange my face and smile—more of a grimace—but it's enough to shift my mood.

The temperature is climbing as summer approaches, so I've had to hunt out a light cotton top, still with long sleeves, but cool enough for the twenty-seven degrees forecast today. The top is the colour of fresh, green grass and I pull out a headscarf patterned in greens, yellows, and oranges to tie around my hair. I slash on lipstick, a little brighter than normal.

The old *fake it till you make it* philosophy is on overdrive today.

I plaster another false smile on my face and swallow back the shame and grief which keeps gurgling up to my throat like a drain pipe blocked with garbage. I'm determined not to waste the gifts given to me over the past few months by Clyde and his enclave of weird and wonderfuls. So, I will take one more step forward and do the next thing, to the best of my ability.

☾

DS Constable Keenan, a heavily built man with white-blonde hair and pale white eyebrows, is waiting for us when we walk through the Roman porticos at Balmain Police Station. His expression is inscrutable when he glances at my face, but a double blink and an almost inaudible intake of breath gives him away. We've met before, but I was a mummified body on a hospital bed at the time. He leads us into a small, bare conference room with a rectangular table and four chairs. We decline coffee after he warns us it tastes like bitter dishwater, and take our seats across from him at the table. He has a manila folder and a box marked 'Exhibits' which he places on the table between us. I've probably been shown what's in the exhibits box, but it would have been soon after the accident and I'm not sure I remember, exactly.

He flips open the file and looks up at us. "Fire Examiner's report states cause of fire was a candle, left near the downstairs curtains, which ignited the curtains and then spread to the rest of the house."

Randy shakes his head. "As I'm sure your report shows, Miss Danforth does not recall having lit a candle or even having one in the area identified as the source of the fire."

"However," says Detective Keenan, "Miss Danforth has been diagnosed as suffering from traumatic amnesia." Before Randy can counter this inarguable statement, the detective continues. "I understand you're suing the landlord for negligence. Why now? Have you discovered something new?" He glances from Randy's face to mine.

Randy told me to let him do most of the talking, so I leave him to answer.

"My client, Miss Danforth, has, as you have stated, suffered from traumatic amnesia, but has begun retrieving some of her memories from around the time of the fire."

He asks what I've remembered, and Randy continues. "One crucial piece of information is the fact the fire alarm was faulty, and she had asked the estate agent to have it repaired some weeks before the fire. No alarm was heard at the time of the fire which would indicate it did not go off. That makes the landlord liable."

DSC Keenan turns to me. "I can see how that would give you a case, but it still doesn't explain the fire. Have you been able to remember anything else about that morning, Miss Danforth?"

Randy shakes his head on my behalf and I'm about to agree when I remember the red wrapper I thrust into my bag the morning I went back to Balmain.

"There was something..." I shake my head knowing how stupid it sounds to call a lolly wrapper evidence. "No, it doesn't matter."

"Sure it does." The detective smiles at me and I decide to tell him.

Randy shifts in his seat, uncomfortable that I am about to disclose information about which he knows nothing. I suppose I should have spoken to him about it first, but it's too late now.

"Well, not long ago I returned to my old house in Balmain. I mean, where the house used to be. I went into the shed and when

I came out, I tripped, falling face down on the ground. As I got up, I caught sight of a red lolly wrapper which triggered a sharp memory of something red that I'd seen on the day of the fire. I couldn't lock onto it in my mind, but I reacted with extreme fear and anxiety, as if the red colour meant something."

Randy twists in his chair to face me, his cheek twitching. "Why didn't you tell me about this?"

Keenan says nothing, but his eyes are watchful.

I include them both in my explanation. "It seemed ridiculous at the time. What was I going to tell you? That a red lolly paper had something to do with the fire? Besides, I put the emotional response down to the fact it was the first time I'd been back to the scene of the fire."

They both want to ask the same question, but Keenan gets in first.

"Why now?"

I look at the blank wall behind the detective and shake my head. "The red image keeps coming back to me and each time, I'm more convinced it could mean something. Not the lolly paper, but something red."

Keenan pushes the exhibits box towards me and tells me to remove the lid. He tosses me a pair of disposable gloves which I pull on before reaching inside. There are remnants of charred curtain, twisted metal from the kitchen and other miscellaneous and innocuous leavings. I pick up what looks like a blue hair clip; the shape vaguely resembling a butterfly with sparkly stones set around its wings.

"Why do you think this wasn't completely destroyed?" I ask.

"Sometimes the heat of the fire creates such a strong updraught something can be blown away before being completely destroyed, if it's light enough," answers Keenan. "Is it yours? I don't recall it meaning anything to you when we first asked."

I turn it over in my gloved hand. "I remember this. I gave it to Ruby on her sixth birthday. Not that I've seen her wear anything like this for a long time. I must ask her if she wore it at the Balmain house. Do you think it's important?"

Detective Keenan shrugs. "I wouldn't have thought so, but the fact it presents a mystery to you might mean it's important. In cases like this, the unexplainable is always important." I take a breath to speak and he pre-empts me. "Even if it is only a hair clip."

"Can I keep it? It'll be easier to show it to her, rather than trying to describe it."

He rubs his jaw. "Can't see why not. We'll photograph and record it." We wait while he takes the photo and has me sign and date a register which lists the exhibits. "You sure you want to do this? Rake up cold ashes, so to speak." He allows himself a slight grin at the joke.

I nod. "I have to. I need to get my life back."

The detective scrapes back his chair and stands. "Well, if you need anything, give me a call. Be glad to assist. When I'm back from holidays."

Randy thrusts out his hand to shake the officer's. "Thanks for your time and help."

As we walk down the steps from the station, I pull out the hair clip. "Wonder if I'm clutching at straws with this. I haven't seen Ruby wear it since she was about seven years old. Maybe some other little kid who had one the same, dropped it in the yard after the fire." I turn it over. "No, of course it's hers, some of the plastic has melted. Has to be from the fire."

Randy's stiff posture tells me he hasn't forgiven me for the lolly wrapper information, but he won't miss an opportunity to give his opinion.

"A clue is always worth following. They lead to the most unexpected places. And I can help with that. If I know about it, that is." He glares at me.

"Point taken. Won't happen again." He grunts in response. "What now?"

"Now I'm going back to plan an ambush for our landlord's insurance company. That old email your workplace found asking the estate agent to check the fire alarm is a gem. What can you give me to do with the faulty wiring issue your sister raised?"

I don't want to tell him Corinne lied. "Er, I think she made a mistake and was remembering the fire alarm."

He puffs out a breath. "I suspected her memory might have been a bit vague on that one. At least it jogged your memory. Tell her to check her facts next time. We need to maintain our credibility."

We've reached his car and he hits the unlock button on his keys.

"I'm trying to set up another mediation session in the next week or so. I've supplied Lawrence Groat with documentation from your doctor which emphasises the importance of your having this surgery as soon as possible. For the optimal results. It's clear the more this drags on, the more you'll be disadvantaged." He rubs his thumb and fingers together in a money gesture. "I've also submitted psychological reports which indicate it is becoming harder to cope with your injuries. I'm hoping they'll get the picture; that the compensation will need to be higher the longer it takes because your needs will grow. Hit them in the hip pocket."

"So, how much are we asking for?"

"Four million."

"What?"

He raises an eyebrow at my stunned look. "Probably won't get that much, but you always ask for more than you're willing to settle for." Climbing into the seat of his Honda Civic, he wriggles his short fingers in a girly wave. "I'll let you know as soon as we have a date for the meeting. You think on that red wrapper and show your sister the hair clip."

I wave back and my first urge as his car disappears down the street is to head to The Black Hole. But for the same reason I can't ring Clyde, I also can't go to the bar. It wouldn't be fair.

I fight the rising despair, and remind myself I am responsible for this disaster.

&

After a lonely Saturday night, Bennie and I head over to my parent's home for a Sunday barbecue. Eager to grab Ruby alone first, I corner her in her bedroom as soon as I arrive.

"Hey Rubes, how is everything going? You still good with Levi?"

She flashes me a goofy grin. 'He's extremely cool and…he told his mum about the Baciks."

"I'm glad he did that. Was she okay about them having a role in his life?"

"Yeah, they thought it was nice. Especially as they are Jewish. They want to meet them, though."

"And when are they going to meet you?"

She screws up her face. "Not sure. He's all for it, but I'm scared they'll stop him from seeing me and while they don't know, he's not disobeying them." I raise my eyebrows. "Well, not directly." She grabs a letter from her bedside table and opens it. "Look. I've been writing to Anna. You know, the girl from the rehab centre."

Nice change of subject. "Sure. You told me you were in touch with her. Is she all right?"

Ruby raises her eyes, alight with the hope this connection might save Anna.

"She sounds good. She's been home from the centre for a couple of weeks now and tells me she's trying to avoid her old contacts and keeping mostly to herself." Rubes looks back down at the letter. "Her parents have put their home on the market and Anna says she owes it to them to do her best, despite the urges. We've arranged to meet in a couple of weeks at a coffee shop in Chatswood. She's so clever, Layla, you should read the letters, they're beautiful. I know if she doesn't go back to those drugs, she'll do something really important with her life." Ruby hands the letter to me.

She's right; the letter is like reading poetry. When I hand it back, words catch in my throat and I have to swallow before speaking.

"Fingers crossed she can get back on track. She couldn't ask for a better friend and support than you, Rubes. I'm proud of you."

At the sound of Corinne's voice calling from the front door, Ruby shoves the letter back into her drawer and jumps up from the bed.

"Come on, I don't really want Corinne in here."

I'm about to berate her for such uncharitable thoughts about our sister and stop myself. It makes me sad that Corinne's unpleasant nature causes the rest of us to put up walls, but decide that talk can wait for another time.

"Hi, Corinne," I call out. Where are you?" Ruby gives me a quizzical look at my overly chummy greeting. I throw her a mock glare.

"I'm in the kitchen with Mum. What's it to you?"

Ruby flashes me a told-you-so grin, and I nudge her with my hip as we both head to the kitchen. When we walk in, Corinne is pouring herself a glass of juice, but doesn't offer one to Ruby or myself.

"I love that bag of yours, Mum," says Corinne, reaching out to finger the bright red cloth of the bag my mother has slung over the back of a chair. "It looks new."

She shrugs. "No. I just don't use it much."

My eyes are riveted to the bag, and I feel the tremors of a panic attack. What is it with red? This is crazy. First a lolly wrapper, then a bag. Am I going to spin out whenever I see the colour red? With my back half turned away from the others, I take deep, steady breaths, gripping the kitchen bench for support. I need to find out what this means, and soon.

Ruby bounces over and pours herself a juice. "I've gotta admit I even like that bag, Mum. If you ever want to get rid of it, you can give it to me."

"Sorry, Rubes, I have first dibs on that one," says Corinne.

I'm unable to add to the bag compliments. In fact, I wish someone would put it out of sight.

I turn and leave the room so I don't have to look at it anymore.

CHAPTER 26

THE AIR IN THE ROOM is chilled. Partly from the air-conditioning and partly from the icy looks being exchanged across
the table. It's the moment I have imagined for months: an offer to
settle out of court; my ticket to New York; my opportunity to go
back to the future.

Randy was barely able to contain his excitement when he
phoned to say the insurance company had all but acknowledged
partial liability for the faulty fire alarm, based on there being no
record of it being repaired following my written complaint.

This is our third meeting and again, like the last time, I lied to
Corinne when she wanted to come, telling her I was not allowed
to bring anyone but my lawyer. Is that a shameful way to treat
her? Probably.

My stomach churns with apprehension as I imagine all the
possible outcomes. I pray this will be clean and simple, not a
battle between boardroom gladiators, like the previous meeting.
I shudder as I remember that last mediation.

&

Randy had warned me before we went in to the second meeting
it might be bloody. He was going for the jugular, and Lawrence
Groat would be furious with the size of the payout he was requesting. Michelle, the bouncy young woman who had mediated the
first two meetings, had prattled her welcoming spiel and asked
for our proposal, smiling in anticipation of a smooth negotiation.

With a flourish, Randy made a show of requesting documents

from Jason Crane, placed them on the table and then slowly perused page after page, finally retrieving the page he wanted. Everyone knew it was part of the theatre, and I could see Lawrence Groat's knuckles whiten as they clenched his monogrammed pen.

Randy tapped the page in front of him. "This is the one we want." He glanced up at Michelle. "I wonder if you would write these figures on the whiteboard."

She stood, glanced at Groat, who shrugged, then she snapped the cap off a whiteboard marker.

"Before we look at the numbers," Randy continued, "I want to reiterate that our request for compensation is based on the fact that if the fire alarm had been functional, Miss Danforth would have woken in time to escape before incurring any injury."

"That is simply conjecture as no one can prove the alarm didn't work," retorts Groat. "Your client has no memory of anything on that day and it's ridiculous to say no-one heard it, therefore it didn't work."

Michelle admonished him to wait until the proposal had been put forward before objecting.

"Now, taking into account past and future medical expenses, income loss..." Randy eyeballed Agostini, Groat, and then the mediator. "And bear in mind, Miss Danforth's career earned her a considerable salary before the accident, together with the fact she still had approximately thirty-eight years of working life until retirement. From a career she can no longer pursue for reasons outlined in the report you have before you."

Randy quoted an amount, which was then written on the board.

"Apart from the medical expenses outlined above, Miss Danforth is considering specialist surgery in New York, so we have calculated approximate cost of surgery, post-operative care, airfares, accommodation, food and transport for a minimum of four months." He calls out a figure to the mediator. "And we must take into account my client's pain and suffering since her tragic accident, some of which will be ongoing." Randy allowed the amounts to be added and nodded to the mediator.

The colour drained from Lawrence Groat's face as the total appeared.

"Mr. Beasley requests a lump sum payment of four million dollars be paid to the plaintiff," said the mediator.

The landlord's mouth dropped open, and Lawrence Groat's Adam's apple bobbed as he swallowed. Randy sat back with a benign look on his face.

"Mr. Groat, would you like to respond?" asked the mediator.

"Damn right I'll respond!" This burst of indignation brought a flicker of a smile to Randy's lips and a raised hand from the mediator. "The only issue of liability you can dredge up is that the fire alarm may or may not have worked on the day of the fire. Then there is the small matter of the fire examiner having deemed the fire accidental due to a candle left burning by the plaintiff."

"Mr. Groat, do you have a counter offer?" asked the mediator.

"You've got nothing, Beasley. You know that and I know that."

Randy Beasley, unruffled by the heated response from his opponent, gestured to my face and arm, which he had asked me to leave uncovered today. I had worn a light jacket over a sleeveless top and removed the jacket when we entered the room.

"I'm happy to take this to a civil jury, Larry, and they may rule for a larger payment than the conservative amount we are requesting."

The landlord, Mr. Agostini, ran his gaze from my face, to my neck, and down my arm. He lowered his head, but not before I saw the distress in his eyes at somehow being responsible for my disfigurement. If I wasn't so fixated on this surgery, I might have had the courage to stand up and put an end to everyone's misery—everyone except Randy—by withdrawing my suit. But I sat there, a silent and willing party to this exorbitant claim.

"Conservative? You're living a fantasy, Beasley." Groat scraped back his chair and got to his feet. He looked to Michelle. "I need a coffee. Let's have a break."

She nodded and asked us all to be back in the room in half an hour.

Feeling uncomfortable with the obvious hostility between all parties, I slipped out to the toilet and sat in a stall for ten minutes, not wanting to have to face Mr. Agostini's shamed looks. When I walked back towards the conference room, I heard Randy and Lawrence Groat in the hallway, barking at each other. I stepped back out of sight, but stayed to listen. I knew what was happening, as Randy had warned me that most of the negotiations would be done in what he termed 'corridor discussions.'

"Your client is at fault for leaving a candle burning, Randy. You haven't a shred of evidence to prove negligence on the landlord's part. Your case is based on pure fiction."

Randy guffawed. "Are you telling me you're willing to risk her standing up in front of a jury, displaying those shocking injuries? Injuries which we attest she would never have incurred if your landlord had fixed the fire alarm."

"I'm sure we can come to an agreement here, Randy. Neither of us wants to take this to court. I've phoned my client and they're agreeable to paying what we'd have had to outlay in court costs. We're offering two hundred and fifty thousand dollars."

I couldn't see Lawrence Groat's face, but this response told me he felt as sickened as I did at the thought of going to court.

I had to strain to hear Randy's measured response. "You insult us, Larry. Are you going to go in there and tell that poor girl that all she's been through, and will suffer for the rest of her life, is worth a fucking two hundred and fifty thousand dollars? You're a bigger arsehole than I first thought. Four million or it goes to court."

Randy must have turned away from Groat because he called him back.

"Wait, Randy. Five hundred thousand and that's more than generous."

"Three and a half million and I can't go lower."

"Let me speak to my client to see if they'll go any higher than five."

I clutched my chest. For the first time, I believed there might be enough for me to have the surgery.

"You do that, Larry, and I'll see you back in the conference room."

I couldn't slip past as Groat was pacing the corridor, talking on the phone to his client, the insurance company. They hadn't considered my case important enough to even send a representative today.

❧

Slight pressure on my arm brings me back to the present meeting. Randy wants my full attention as Lawrence Groat makes his offer. The mediator had obviously summarised the outcome of the last meeting while I'd been reliving it in my head. Now she directs the defendant's lawyer to put their proposal on the table.

Despite the faulty fire alarm—or rather, no proof it had been repaired—until we handed Lawrence Groat the therapist's report outlining the devastating and ongoing psychological, physical, and financial trauma caused from the fire, they had tried to deny culpability. Randy believes the report changed the game. It probably should have been submitted in the beginning, but it seems it was one of his tactics to hold it back.

We're in Lawrence Groat's boardroom, a concession by Randy to appear as if he's giving the defendants a home advantage. However, the barely hidden gleam of satisfaction in Randy's eyes indicates he knows this is going to be his moment of triumph, regardless of the venue. My hands, clenched under the table, are clammy despite the chill, and I've already run to the toilet twice while we waited outside for the signal to enter the polished teak chamber.

In response to the mediator's direction, Groat confers in whispers with his client, the CEO of the insurance company. The size of our claim obviously shocked them out of their apathy enough to send, not only a representative, but the head honcho. I understand this man has the authority to make a financial decision on the spot. It bodes well for us.

Groat then stands, parading a string of presumptions and circumstances in an attempt to set a scene which will make their offer appear generous. Randy sits back, his face inscrutable, as usual, waiting for the offer.

"So, we acknowledge the extent of Miss Danforth's injuries, both physical and emotional, the probable need for her to make a change in her career path, which may lower her earning capacity, and her ongoing medical costs." His voice then rises in volume. "However, the plaintiff must acknowledge the absence of evidence to prove fault on the defendant's part as well as her own unfortunate state of inebriation which caused her to allow a candle to burn unattended. Further, intoxication could quite conceivably have dulled her senses with regards to hearing a fire alarm."

Randy leaps from his seat, jabbing a stubby finger at Lawrence Groat. Inscrutability gone. "How dare you, Groat. How dare you stand there in front of this woman who has endured the most horrific pain and emotional suffering, due to negligence on this man's part." He points at the guilty face of Mr. Agostini. "And arrogantly use the fact she had a drink of alcohol, in a desperate attempt to save this big bastard of a company from giving her what she deserves."

It may be naive of me, but I wonder, briefly, if Randy might actually care about me as a person. Not just about the impressive fee he will receive. I'm glad now that he's the man fighting for my future, despite any initial misgivings.

The mediator demands they both sit down, but neither pays her the slightest attention. She picks up a heavy book and slams it on the table, silencing the two lawyers.

"Sit!" she says, glaring from one to the other. Like naughty boys in a schoolroom, they both sink into their chairs. This woman has hidden depths.

Mr. Agostini, his bottom lip quivering, turns to Lawrence Groat. "For the love of God, pay the money to this woman. Her life is ruined. This is why I have insurance. I can't bear to hear this fighting over dollars—" Randy thumps his thigh in glee as the CEO grips Mr. Agostini's arm and half drags him from the room, before he can damage their case further.

"You were saying, Lawrence?" says Randy, no longer bothering to hide the grin on his face.

Groat rolls his chair back from the table. "I would like a moment to confer with my client privately."

The mediator nods her agreement, and Lawrence Groat hurries out of the room.

I am a veteran of difficult negotiations and I know Mr. Agostini has now turned their flimsy attempt to justify a meagre offer upside down. Instead of leaping with excitement at his ineptitude, I want to go out and give my old landlord a hug.

Within five minutes, Lawrence Groat and his client, minus Mr. Agostini, are back in the room. The mediator, Michelle, indicates he should continue.

"My client is willing to make an outstandingly generous offer which is not open to negotiation. I repeat, this is not open to negotiation." I can almost feel Randy trembling with excitement beside me. "Two million dollars and a signed agreement that your client will make no future claims."

Goosebumps dance across my skin. Two million dollars! I can see my future blossom before my eyes. A vision of my new face, followed by images of smooth arms and legs, parade before me. Imagine, no hiding in crowds, no more ducking from ridicule... It takes all my self-control not to jump onto the table screaming, *yes. Yes. We'll take it.*

"I'll give consideration to your offer and we'll get back to you within seven days. Although, I will say, it is far below what is fair and my gut tells me to advise my client to reject the offer and take the matter to court."

Groat glances at the man beside him, who barely moves his head in a nod. "The offer stands for seven days and will then be withdrawn."

Everyone is bluffing. This is the game of negotiation. Groat knows it, Randy knows it, and I know it. Despite this, I fear Randy still wants his day in court.

Not if I have a say in it.

Randy and Jason Crane make a show of indignation at the offer by slamming files together, being barely civil to the defendant and Groat, and offering only a curt handshake to the mediator. She also leaves the room, as her neutrality will be compromised if she stays alone with the other parties. No-one discusses the offer until we're all out of the building and the woman has headed down Pitt Street.

"Let's find a coffee shop. I need cake," says Jason Crane.

I smile, remembering where I first met him.

"As long as you aren't going to solicit while we're in there," I say.

He has the grace to look sheepish, but not Randy.

"My man's trawling picked up the best client I've had in a long time. Don't knock it." At least he grins after saying it.

"I'm trying not to see myself as simply dollar signs in your eyes, Randy."

"Sweetheart, we need each other, and you know I will work my little cholesterol-clogged heart out to get you the best out-come."

"I suppose I can't argue with that."

We traipse into a small café in an arcade, give our orders, and grab a booth away from the door.

Like a bottle of champagne, fizzing at the cork, I'm ready to pop with excitement at the insurance company's offer. Even sitting at the table, I release a burst of energy by dancing my feet up and down on the floor.

"Two million dollars. They've offered me two million dollars! I can do it. I can go to New York and still have money over for a new start." Neither Randy nor Jason seem to share my elation. "What's wrong? Why aren't you happy? That's more than enough." Then a thought hits me. "I forgot about your fee. Will I have enough left over after you take your fee?"

Some No Win, No Pay lawyers will charge up to fifty percent of the payout but we have pre-agreed an amount, regardless of the size of the final amount, so I know the answer to my own question.

"Of course I will."

The waitress arrives with our coffee and cake and without another word, Jason digs into his tiramisu. My chocolate and beetroot cake waits expectantly, but I don't pick up my fork. I'm looking at Randy, who seems to be deep in thought.

"What, Randy?" I ask.

He sucks the froth off the top of his cappuccino. "Don't panic, nothing to do with the fee. Although, as you know it's not small." He jiggles his eyebrows. "They jumped up from five hundred thousand too quickly. They must know if it went to court they'd pay at least four million, if not more. I think we can get them higher. I think we can get three million."

I stare at the cake, my appetite gone. "I don't know if I want to do this anymore. Be the freak exhibit that shames people into throwing money on the table to absolve themselves of guilt. I've got what I need. Why can't we be happy with that?"

Randy breaks apart his chocolate croissant, placing pieces into his mouth. "We've got a week. Why don't you sit down and work out what you could do with another million dollars and how different it would make your life, then come back to me with what you want to do. I still think we can keep it out of court. Now eat up and enjoy our small victory."

He pokes Jason, whose eyes are scanning the cafe. "Any suspects?" Jason, his mouth full, shakes his head.

"You're disgusting. Both of you." I shovel a forkful of the cake into my mouth. I can't wait to phone Clyde and tell him what's happened.

And then I remember.

"Can you get back to me by Friday morning? I want to work on my argument to double their offer if you come to your senses," says Randy.

My next session with Jarrod is on Thursday. Perhaps we'll unearth information which will make my decision clearer.

CHAPTER 27

"**I** HAVE TO ADMIT I'M NERVOUS. Especially after the last two sessions. Do you think it's helping?"

At least Jarrod looks sympathetic as I prepare to mentally strap myself into the recliner rocker for another ride to hell.

"I certainly wouldn't put you through it unless I thought it would help you, Layla." He rolls his chair over until it's adjacent to mine. "By the way, I was very pleased to get your message about the compensation offer. It seems you will be able to go to New York, after all. How are you feeling about that?"

I wriggle in the chair and push back to bring up the foot rest. "Very excited, but scared at the same time."

"How so?"

"Well, of course I hate the scars and want nothing more than to have them removed. But as Dr. Gassner says, there is no guarantee he can help, or even if he can, to what extent he can improve them. So while I was chasing the money, I could hope and dream that they could work miracles with my face and body. But now that it looks like there are no more obstacles, I'm going to know for sure and what I end up knowing might be more than I can bear."

Jarrod leans forward, one elbow on the arm of his chair and his chin in his hand. "You've analysed yourself so well, you might do me out of a job. What you are feeling is perfectly understandable and whatever happens, we can continue with our sessions when you return." He leans back. "Are you okay for us to start?"

"Yes, let's find out what happened."

When I first started my sessions, it would take at least ten minutes for Jarrod to put me into a hypnotic trance. Now I'm so attuned, it takes him only seconds before I'm floating in that safe, peaceful place where my fears and inhibitions drop away, and his soft voice is a familiar drug.

"You are safe, Layla. We are back in your house on the morning of January sixteenth. You've woken early on a very hot morning, feeling hung over and nauseous. You're still in bed and I want you to take me through what happens next. Some of what you tell me will be repetition, but don't stop in case some new detail emerges. Again, don't be frightened. I give you my word I will bring you back before the fire comes near you. I repeat, you are safe."

I'm in my bed. I turn over too quickly, and the ceiling starts to spin. My bladder is full and I'm either going to wet the bed or vomit in it, so drag myself up. Because the floor is tilting, I grip the wall and half crawl to the bathroom, stumble in, followed by Danger, my dog, and push the door shut, even though I am alone in the house—habit, I guess. Also, I have enough functioning brain cells to choose privacy while I vomit. I throw up in the sink and lurch awkwardly onto the toilet seat, emptying my bladder with great relief. I recall somehow shedding my clothes and am now in the shower. But not for long, as the nausea hits again. I wrap myself in a towel and slide to the floor, hugging the toilet pedestal, and throw up until there's nothing but bile in my stomach. I must have dozed off with my face pressed to the cold porcelain. Sometime later, I drag myself out the door, kick it shut, and gingerly make my way back to bed.

Sleep is all I crave, but as I drift, I hear something. A noise downstairs. Like an item falling—a dull thud. I force my leaden eyelids open and try to lift myself onto one elbow, but there is nothing to see and all is quiet. Perhaps the thud is in my pounding head. I fall back onto the pillow. Back into the abyss of sleep.

A sharp crack followed by a blast of heat, spins me back to consciousness. My eyes spring open as the curtains ignite in an explosion of flames. A dull roar and the air is sucked from my lungs.

And I'm back in the nightmare.

"Stay with the memory, Layla, but be assured the fire will not touch you."

His calm voice overrides the sickening vision and floats me to a hazy in-between place. Not the bedroom and not the doctor's room.

"You are safe from the heat, but you are aware of being in your room, of events unfolding and your reactions. Go back to your bedroom. The fire has blocked you from escaping through your bedroom door and you are now trying to unlock the terrace doors."

Yes. The French doors to the small veranda. I'm on the floor, rattling the lock, beating at the glass. Someone might hear me. *Thank God!* There's someone on the street. Someone wearing a bright red shirt. But they're walking away from the house.

"No! Come back. I'm here, help me. Help!" I scream.

The person turns around to look back at the burning house, hesitates for a moment, and then hurries away. A merciless hand squeezes my airways. I can't breathe. My heart pounds like a war drum and the room spirals into a black vortex. I've slipped out of reality and am lost in a weird dream state.

Because as the person turned, a sharp slant of sunlight trapped, for an instant, their profile. A face as familiar as my own.

Firm hands push on my shoulders to steady my convulsing body and then a finger in the middle of my forehead brings me back to the room.

"Speak to me, Layla. You closed up just as you saw something from the veranda doors. It will still be in front of your memory and it's obviously something very significant."

I roll my head from side to side, not sure if I'm denying there was anything significant or refusing to believe what I saw.

He puts one open hand on my forehead and one on my chest to calm both my mind and body, telling me to take deep, slow breaths. The soothing warmth of his hands and my own efforts eventually dim the shocking image, and I open my eyes, orienting myself to the familiar, unthreatening room.

"Come, Layla. It's obvious you've had a breakthrough. Let's work with it."

His measured, monotone voice gives a false impression of indifference, but instead of his usual, relaxed posture, he leans over me, his hands now gripping the arm of my chair, giving him away.

But I can't speak of it. To say it gives it substance, makes it real.

"I don't think it was anything new, I think I panicked without reason."

The narrowing of his eyes tell me he's too seasoned to be fooled by my words.

"Jarrod, is it common practice for the imagination to play tricks while in a hypnotic trance?"

"Are you saying you saw something which you find hard to believe?" I nod. "Hypnosis is not a truth serum, Layla, and there may be times the imagination creates something that will match a strong belief or opinion, but normally that won't be the case. Based on our sessions so far, I would be more likely to think what you saw was real. If you tell me what it was, we might be able to understand it together."

I shake my head. "If it's all right with you, I might sit with this for a bit. It was such a ridiculous picture, I'm sure my imagination was working overtime."

He doesn't push me further. "You need time to process our session, but please call me immediately if you think we need to talk more. Don't deny yourself an opportunity to find the truth and heal this trauma, otherwise everything you've worked through so far will have been for nothing."

He hands me a glass of water, which gives me an opportunity to break eye contact, before his canny intellect breaches my thin barrier of denial. I nod between swallows.

Even as I escape from his office, his stern gaze, heating my back, tells me I've somehow failed to honour the trust established between us.

The automatic doors slide open, and as I step onto the footpath, it's as if someone upturns a water tank and the rain buckets from the sky, thick as drapery. Within seconds I'm soaked through. Of course I brought no umbrella.

Despite my issues with Clyde, do I dare run to The Black Hole where I can sit out the storm wrapped in a dry towel? The only other alternative is to run into a department store, buy dry clothes, an umbrella, and head off home. But I'm so accustomed to penny-pinching, I discard the idea. I'm not a millionaire yet and after what I've seen today, may never be.

While these thoughts zoom around my head, my feet make their own decision, and by the time there is a break in my anxious head chatter, my hand has pushed open the door to my favourite bar.

A low whistle snakes up the stairs. "I always wondered what that body looked like unclothed. I need wonder no more."

Confused, I look down. Every item of my saturated clothing clings to my body, leaving nothing to the imagination. With wet, suction sounds, I pry the front of my shirt away from my skin and do the same with my trousers.

"If you were a gentleman, Gavin, you'd have rushed to get me a dry towel by now, instead of enjoying watching me shiver like a drowned rat," I retort, my arms now squashed across my breasts.

"Right. Onto it." He jumps up from his chair and prances, to the pulsing beat of James Brown's "Sex Machine," out to the back room, and grabs two of the long bar-top towels. By this time, I've followed him to the bar, scanning the room. "He's out in the alley, unloading some cartons from a truck."

The heat rushes up my neck and I make a show of dabbing my face and rubbing the ends of my hair.

"Who's out back?"

"Oh, come on, Layla. You haven't been in for weeks and every time I ask Clyde how you are, he snaps at me to go and ask you myself. I might look a bit like a dickhead but I'm not," says Gavin.

"Of course you are and don't you believe it if anyone tells you different." Clyde's voice rolls through me like a swallow of rich, hot chocolate, but instead of losing myself in a strong Clyde hug, I keep my head lowered. "Didn't expect to see you here today, Layla. Any port in a storm, hey?"

"It was raining," I mumble. "I was really wet." *What, am I a moron?*

"I can see that."

He hefts a keg into place and turns to walk out the back again. At the door he indicates for me to follow him. When we enter the small back room, he touches my damp sleeve.

"You shouldn't stay in those wet clothes, especially in the air-conditioning. We've got a washing machine and dryer here and I'm pretty sure I've got another shirt in my car." I hesitate, only because I don't believe I deserve this kindness, but he misunderstands. "You don't have to worry. I won't look at you."

What? That stupid comment changes my mousey shame to pit

bull indignation. "Forget the dry shirt. I think I'd rather catch pneumonia."

I spin around to walk back into the bar and his hand grips my arm. Without a word, he pulls me to his chest and the missing him, combined with the shock of my earlier revelation, dissolve my obduracy. The stupid tears well and run down my cheeks onto his shirt. With that and the wet towels pressed against him, his shirt is nearly as wet as mine. Relieved Clyde wants me again, I lift my head, eyes closed, waiting to be kissed. A slight pressure on the top of my head as he plants a platonic kiss on my scarf, tells me I've misunderstood his actions.

Mortified, I step back from him, choking on my blunder. He gestures for me to remove my blouse and winds the bar towels around me.

He leaves me with a mug of hot coffee and the rhythmic whirr of the clothes dryer. He also leaves me with the certain knowledge we are friends and nothing more. I swallow the lump of grief lodged in my throat and wonder if he's done me a favour. It was on the tip of my tongue to blurt out what I'd seen in my hypnotic trance. And once I say the words, they can no longer be denied.

Dad is the one I have to speak to. He'll tell me what to do.

The sound of Clyde's voice wafts through the door as he chats with a patron, and I need him with a yearning so strong it almost strangles me. Or do I want him only because he doesn't want me anymore? Whatever it is, I have to smother it for now. The image haunting my mind is of far greater importance. I need to know the truth about the fire.

I'm counting down the minutes on the dryer timer when I hear a familiar voice.

"Where is she?" The door bursts open and Lavender strides across the room and wraps me in a perfume-scented embrace. "What the fuck is the matter with you two? At my party I thought we'd have to chuck a bucket of cold water over the two of you, and now I hear you're hardly speaking to each other." She notices the towels and steps back with one hand on her hip. "Bar towels, darling?" She throws her hands in the air in dismay. "Give me strength."

Perversely, her brusque confrontation relaxes me.

"It was a mistake. Us being together as anything but friends."

"Rubbish—"

I sigh. "No, it's true. But it's all my fault. I couldn't go through with it and now he's angry…"

She juts out a hip, lips pursed. "What, your scars, his weight or something else?"

I close my eyes. "Oh, God, when you put it like that it sounds so…"

"Stupid? Childish? Superficial? Take your pick, darling. And while you're choosing, listen to Auntie Lavender." I open my eyes as she rolls over a stool and sits next to me. "That man out there," she waves a gold talon at the door, "is one of the best, and do you know why?" I shake my head and then nod, as I know he's the best. "Because he only sees the heart of the people he meets, not their wrapping." She undulates her hand down her body. "Although some of us are wrapped magnificently, darling." She winks.

I manage a slight grin. "To tell you the truth, I'm really not sure what happened. I think I'm scared and there are so many other things for me to deal with at the moment. Things I have to sort out before I even think about my feelings for Clyde. Anyway, I think that's a moot point now, as he's made it clear we're no more than friends."

"Well, darling, you sort out your *things* and know that whatever happens, we're here for you. I might be just a crusty old queen, but I'm a good friend and that fat bloke out there will always be your friend too."

I throw my arms around her neck, regardless of the towel unravelling from my chest.

"You're not a crusty old queen. You're a gracious lady with a big heart and I'm proud to have you as a friend." And there it is. Lavender and the others are not just fellow freaks to hang out with until I can do better. They are true friends.

I give up trying to clutch the towel and, tossing it over the chair, reach up to the dryer to retrieve my clothes.

"A gracious lady, eh? Best compliment I've had in years. Even Lancie hasn't called me that and he worships the ground I teeter on." She watches as I button up my shirt and reaches over to straighten the collar. "You're very pale, *Sourcil*. You almost look like you've had a shock of some sort. Or are you pining after our lad out there."

I jerk my head up, caught in her unblinking scrutiny.

"Yes."

"Yes, what?"

"Yes, I've had a shock and as much as I'm screaming to share it with someone, I can't. And I do miss Clyde, terribly." Suddenly the urgency of it all envelops me and I scramble to finish dressing. "And I have to find my father right now," the tears start drifting down my cheeks, "he's the only one who can help."

Lavender asks no more questions, and as I head for the bar, she grasps my shoulders, turns me around, and pushes me towards the back door and into a side alley.

"You don't need to walk through that rabble, they'll only ask questions. It's stopped raining, now go. Go and fix this, whatever it is."

On tip toes, I kiss her foundation-packed cheek and run out the back door and into the alley.

Please, Dad, have a rational explanation for me.

CHAPTER 28

Too AGITATED TO SIT STILL, I pace up and down Dad's
office, waiting for him to finish with his client.

The conversation I need to have with him couldn't happen at
home, so when I left The Black Hole, I'd phoned his accoun-
tancy firm in North Sydney to ask his secretary to have him wait
for me. My intense preoccupation made me impervious to the
usual stares as I hurried towards his office.

"What a wonderful surprise," he says, striding through the door
and capturing me in a bear hug. "A dull day just got brighter."

Still snuggled against his warm, safe chest, I try to speak but
what emerges is a muffled sob.

"Hey, my darling girl, what is it?"

I lift my head and through another choked sob ask if we can go
somewhere to talk. One arm holding me against him, he presses
the buttons on his phone and leaves a message on my mother's
answering machine to say he'll be late tonight and will eat out.

"I know a great little Japanese restaurant where we can have a
private space. Sound all right?"

I nod.

He ushers me out of the office building, down one block and
across the road. We're the first customers at Sakuro Restaurant
and when we walk through the door the Japanese waitress sees
my scars and smacks her hand over her mouth. After which all
communication is nervously directed towards my father.

With surreptitious glances at me, she leads us into a private
space where bamboo slats provide a see-through division. Draped
green cloth warms the ceiling and colourful ottomans give a
relaxed, homey feel. I direct my order to the sleek, bent crown of

the woman's head—green tea to start, followed by Okonomiyaki pancakes, when we're ready. My father raises two fingers to indicate he'll have the same.

Dad thanks the bowing, kimono-clad waitress and sips his green tea, waiting for me to speak. The problem is, I'm starting to seriously doubt what I saw. How can I speak about something so incriminating unless I know for sure. *God, what if I got it wrong?*

Dad nudges me. "What's this about, pumpkin?"

I open my mouth to tell him, but the words won't form. Instead, a deep moan of grief gouges its way from the pit of my stomach, searing my throat as it escapes my mouth. No, it can't be true. It's a fantasy built on years of resentment, rivalry, and dislike. I'm a bad person, and putting this fantasy into words will confirm it in everyone's mind.

He holds my face in his hands, stroking my cheek. "Good God, Layla. You're as pale as a ghost. You're frightening me. Please tell me what's happened."

"I don't think I can," I whisper. "You'll think I'm a terrible person and you'll probably be right."

"There's nothing you could possibly tell me that could scare me as much as you are right now. Why don't you tell me and then together we can work out where we go with it."

I nod, my face still in his hands. My father has always been my safe haven, the place I go when I need comfort and validation... and I know I must tell him.

"I had another hypnotherapy session today with the psychologist. You know he's been trying to help me remember what I saw the day of the fire?" Dad releases my face and nods. "I saw something that would mean it wasn't an accident. It would mean someone deliberately tried to hurt me."

His harsh intake of breath and the tremor in his hand as he grasps mine, match my own shock at this possibility.

"Are you sure? Did you tell the police? God, my darling, darling girl." He pulls me into his arms, thinking he's heard the worst of it. Then he sits back and takes my hand. "Did you see who it was? Did you know them?"

I nod to each of his questions. "I know who I think I saw. But now I'm scared to say anything, because I might have made it up. It can happen apparently. During hypnotherapy the imagination can manufacture things. Although Jarrod doesn't think it was my imagination, he believes I saw what happened."

"Who was it?" His voice is now harsh, a lion protecting his cub. "Tell me."

"I was beating on the veranda doors, screaming for help, and she was crossing the road. She turned to look back at the fire and I caught a glimpse of her profile...Oh, Dad...I think it was Corinne," I blurt.

He snatches his hand away as if my fingers seep poison, his face a mask of despair. "No! You can't be sure. It must be a mistake."

Stung by his reaction, I rush from the room, barricading myself in the ladies' restroom. Perhaps he's right—I have made a terrible, unforgiveable mistake and should never have said anything. Ten minutes later, I hear a tentative knock on the door.

"Layla? I'm sorry, please come out." His voice breaks with emotion, and the guilt of even suggesting his daughter is capable of such a heinous act, tightens my chest in a vice grip. "Please, Layla."

When I shuffle out, Dad is beside the door, his shoulders slumped and head lowered. I babble an apology, but he puts a finger to his lips.

"Shhh."

But I can't be quiet, the guilt chokes me. "I'm so ashamed of accusing Corinne. Of course she wouldn't be capable of something like that. It was just a figment of my imagination. Oh, Dad, I'm so sorry. I can't believe I told you that."

His cold hand reaches for mine and we walk back to our seats.

He is so still, I fear my words have instigated a state of semi-catatonia. When I finally dare to look at his face, his eyes are dull with pain and his mouth droops—a bitter, desolate look. I can't bear to think I've been the cause of this and silently beg him to forget what I've said, to come back to me. As I feared, I've released a demon which may not be easily subdued.

Although he hasn't released my hand, he also hasn't scooped me into his arms and told me everything will be all right. He stares off into the distance, his shoulders stiff and his jaw clenched tight, as if he is fighting an internal battle. Finally, his shoulders drop and a look of defeat flickers across his face. A loud exhalation indicates his decision to speak.

"Do you remember when Matt was eleven and he had a terrible accident on his pushbike?" he asks, his voice low, monotone.

I nod. "That scar across his forehead."

"Yes. The brakes didn't work on his bike and he lost control going down the hill near the park." Why is he reminiscing about childhood accidents? "Luckily, he wore his bike helmet, otherwise there would certainly have been brain damage. I remember crying for days after seeing his bruised and battered face in hospital," I say. "I don't think I'll ever forget that."

"Do you remember any other events around that time?" asks Dad.

It was not long after my ninth birthday, and I dredge my memory for anything significant.

"Didn't Matt win a debating competition sometime around then?" The memory grows. "And wasn't it against a high school team captained by Corinne and that's why it was such an achievement? Because Matt's team was so much younger? Wait. I remember Corinne was livid that her little brother had beaten her."

Every hair on my body stands on end as I start to connect the dots. But I won't say it. He has to.

"Corinne warned Matt he'd be sorry he made a fool of her in front of the whole school," says Dad.

"But that doesn't mean…"

"Corinne told her closest friend, Susie Ward, she was going to sabotage the brakes on his bike. When Susie heard Matt was in hospital, she panicked and told me. We convinced Susie he had already been having trouble with the brakes and it wasn't Corinne's fault, that it was an empty threat. She said she believed me, but she never came to our home again."

There's nothing to say. Besides there isn't enough air in my lungs to form words. To think my parents have carried such knowledge about their child all this time and now my discovery has made it ten times worse. As these thoughts spin around my head, I feel nauseous, and I also understand Corinne is not just mean, she's dangerous.

Other childhood memories flood my mind: of nasty, vindictive acts against Matt and me when we were kids. Things which may have had a far more sinister motivation than sibling rivalry.

"All those other things she did… when she cut off all my hair… When she ripped the head off my Barbie doll…" I raise my eyes to my father's face. "Dad, do you think she could have lit that fire?"

He drops his head into his hands. "My God, I don't know."

"Why, Dad? Why has she got this capacity for hate and violence and no one else has? We were all raised the same; it doesn't make sense."

"There are things you don't know—"

"Then tell me," I urge.

"I can't. It's not my story to tell—it's your mother's. Don't ask any more."

My shock and sympathy turn to anger at all Corinne has put this family through.

"For God's sake, Dad, we're talking attempted murder here. Not only that, I'm about to accept a huge payout based on this whole thing being the landlord's fault." I force his head up. "Look at me!" I point at my face and down my body. "Look what she's done. You can't keep protecting her. She's poisonous."

Tears pour down my father's cheeks and when the Japanese waitress appears at the door, she slides the pancakes onto the table, bows, and scuttles away.

"Give me time to speak with your mother first, prepare her."

"Tomorrow, Dad. She has to tell me everything tomorrow. I'm running out of time."

"We don't even know if she's done this thing, Layla. Don't jump to conclusions. We have to give her the benefit of the doubt."

He's right. But even as I accede, the image of her unflinching profile as she turned back to the house sends shivers crawling up my spine.

The aromas of seafood, egg, and soft-textured pancakes waft from the plates. Normally, Okonomiyaki is incredible comfort food, like coming home after a long absence. But today, all I can do is poke at the food with my chopstick, releasing waves of steam from the stack.

My dad glances from his plate over to mine. "Try to eat something. You'll feel worse if you're hungry later."

Even in the midst of this shock, he's being a parent.

I force a mouthful of cabbage and shrimp into my mouth and

for a moment my senses focus on the flavours saturating my taste buds. I even manage to swallow it. I gesture to his plate and he follows my lead, and I watch the muscles in his throat ripple with the struggle to swallow. Like a two-person relay we push in a mouthful, gesture to the other, who does the same, until we have eaten at least half the meal.

Dad pushes his plate away. "Good enough." Gratefully, I lower my chopsticks to the plate. "Do you want to stay with us tonight?" he asks.

"No, I think you and Mum might need to talk without me there. Besides I have Bennie to feed and walk. But tomorrow I'll come over. Is Mum working in the morning?"

He gives me a sad smile. "I think work will be the last thing on her mind. We'll both stay home. I'll let you know in the morning when to come. Get Rubes off to school first."

The waitress peeks around the bamboo slats and nods at our plates. We gesture for her to take them.

"You do not like Okonomiyaki?" she asks.

"It was great," says Dad. "We weren't very hungry."

She smiles and bows twice, takes out the plates, and within seconds reappears with the bill.

Dad insists on driving me home and I feel like an abandoned child, as I watch his car disappear down the street.

C

For the first time in my life, I'm nervous walking into my childhood home. This place where I grew up, made all my childhood memories, and from where I entered adulthood, harbours a dark secret. A secret that once told, will change all our lives irrevocably. Or am I being melodramatic? Have so many bad things happened to me in the last couple of years that I see the devil lurking around every corner?

They asked me to come at ten. It's only a few minutes after. I wander into the kitchen, but it's empty. There is a subdued energy and the normally noisy, vibrant house seems flat, morose, as if the life has been sucked from it. As I steal through the portentous rooms, a flash of realisation comes to me. The reason Corinne insisted on being part of the legal battle over the fire, was so she could ensure she was not suspected. Sly and dangerous.

I find my parents hunched together on a couch in the living room, hands clasped, waiting for me, as if I'm their executioner. In a way I suppose I am.

I hesitate a moment at the door and my emotions spill over, wrenching my gut. I rush over, go down on my knees, and place my head in my mother's lap, gripping her skirt.

"I'm sorry. I'm so sorry. I don't want to hurt anyone."

My mother raises my head, her beautiful eyes, glassy with tears, gaze at me. "My God, Layla, the last thing I want is for you to blame yourself for any of this." She grips my face with her hands, her eyes now fierce. "This started a very long time ago and all I've done is try to protect all my children." Her lips tremble and the tears wash down her cheeks. "But I failed. Miserably."

"I don't understand, Mum. You need to tell me."

At first she can't speak, then with her hands safely back in my father's, she tells me their secret.

"None of this will be easy to hear, darling, but I ask you to listen until I've finished." I nod and sit back onto the floor.

"I was in my second year at university and one night when I was coming back from the library late, I was assaulted and raped. He held a knife at my throat."

Icy chills shaft through my body. I've misheard. I must have. But a glance at my father's clenched jaw and rigid posture tells me it's true. I shake my head, still wanting to deny what she's saying.

I clasp her skirt in my fist. "Did they… did they get him?"

Dad leans forward. "They got him, pumpkin. But only after he'd done it again. They locked him away. He's dead now. We found out later he had a mental illness—bi-polar affective disorder. He committed suicide in prison."

My mother closes her eyes, the lines of pain on her face deepening as she speaks. "The thing is, I got pregnant. From the rape."

"And you had an abortion? Is that what happened?" I ask, knowing how taking a life would violate all my mother's personal beliefs.

She shakes her head. "I couldn't. The child was innocent."

"So, somewhere out there, I have a half sibling I've never met."

She shakes her head again. "I didn't put her up for adoption."

Her. She can't possibly mean…

My father takes over. "I was already deeply and irrevocably in love with your mother and made the decision to take the child on as my own, so we married. Corinne is your half-sister."

Corinne. My vicious and hostile sister—correction, half-sister—the child of a violent rape. The blood roars in my ears and if my mother is still speaking, I can't hear over the tumult.

"Does she know?" I finally ask.

Dad nods. "We told her when she turned fifteen. She had a right to know who she is." Dad pulls out his hanky, blows his nose, then dabs at his eyes. "She was angrier than I have ever seen her—smashing everything in her bedroom, screaming at us, saying she knew she didn't belong, and saying how much she hated you and Matt. Ruby hadn't been born then."

Mum interrupts. "It was heartbreaking. She said she knew she was polluted, that you were the perfect, untainted ones. There was nothing I could say to make her believe otherwise. Nothing," she says.

"Matt had his bike accident three months later," I whisper. They both look at each other without answering. But Mum nods, her head dropping lower with shame.

Her voice almost devoid of emotion, Mum continues. "We took her to a psychiatrist who told us she had an underlying genetic predisposition to mood instability from her father. These mood fluctuations meant she had a warped view of life, a borderline personality disorder."

I've been raised to understand the myriad deviations of personality and behaviour from my mother's experiences, but I'm still confused.

"So you're saying she's inherited her father's mental illness…" my tongue trips over the words 'her father', "and she's unstable; has the capacity to hurt us."

My mother's face crumples. "Oh, Layla. Please don't put it so bluntly. It's not that simple…"

"Then explain how it is, please, Mum."

She swipes the back of her hand across her nose, a most unlikely action for my mother.

"She has a tendency to be impulsive, take risks, and when she feels threatened or sidelined, to do things to pay back those who threaten her."

Such careful words to protect Corinne.

"You mean things like loosening the brake cable bolt on Matt's bike? Or setting fire to me?"

As my memory thrusts incident after incident at me, anger boils in my belly at the injustice of three children being at the cruel mercy of one. And Ruby—now I know where her fears and nightmares must have come from. What did our sister do to her that made her turn to drugs? For the first time in my life, I want to lash out at my mother. And my father.

Out of pity for her violent conception, they have been Corinne's enablers all these years. To stop myself, I lurch drunkenly to my feet, stumble to the closest wall, and vent my fury by beating at it with my fist.

Dad pulls me away from the wall and holds me tightly in his arms, but I struggle, trying to punch his chest, screaming incoherently.

"Stop it! Stop it, Layla. We didn't know how bad it was. We thought the accident with Matt's bike was Corinne's reaction to hearing about her real father."

"It wasn't an accident," I yell.

"Alright, it wasn't. Don't you think we would have done something to stop her if we'd realised how angry she was?"

His face is a blur, and I swing my head away to face my mother and rage builds again.

"You didn't protect us. You must have known what she was capable of. It was all staring you in the face—Ruby's nightmares, her fear to have an animal in case it was drowned like the kitten." My mother's face registers disbelief. I want to keep hurting her. "Yes. That's why Ruby never allowed you to buy her an animal. And you didn't know she was using drugs, either, did you? To numb the fears and stop the nightmares caused by Corinne's cruelty."

My mother falls to her knees on the floor, and my father lets go of me to gather her into his arms, rocking her back and forth as she keens. But I'm not finished yet.

"And Matt. Why do you think he's married a woman who acts like she's his mother? Because he needed to experience a mother who could protect him. Corinne made all of our lives hell. Don't tell yourself we haven't all suffered. The others' scars are on the inside; mine you can see."

I stop, my chest heaving from such emotional release, combined with shock at my own savage tirade. Before me I watch my parents, broken and grieving, locked in each other's arms, and I am finally empty.

I turn to leave and Corinne is standing in the doorway, her face pale but impassive.

"How long have you been there?"

"You don't know how it was for me."

What? I don't know how to answer such a narcissistic remark. I glance at my parents, but only my father has noticed Corinne, my mother is lost in her grief. Then it hits me that everything I've accused her of is based on circumstantial evidence, assumption and a vision I had while under hypnosis. Nothing will change unless we know the truth.

"You're right, Corinne, I don't. Please, tell me how it was for you."

"I always knew I was different from you others. *She* kept denying it," Corinne jerks her head at my mother, "but I have eyes. No one else was miserable like I was and I knew it was because you had everything that I didn't. I had to even the score."

"Like when you ripped up my homework or cut off my hair or drowned Ruby's kitten? And sabotaged Matt's bike? Do you mean those things?" I ask, hardly daring to breathe in case she realises I am trying to trap her into confessing.

"Your precious hair? You're still going on about that? I was sick of always having to hear what beautiful hair you had. And why should Ruby get a kitten? I was never given one. No, poor Corinne was just the ugly by-blow of a rapist and didn't deserve anything."

"And the fire. Why would you try to kill me?" I whisper.

The colour rushes up her neck and into her cheeks, and her eyes dart from left to right, like an animal seeking an escape route. My parents are watching. Corinne's face crumples as my mother holds out her arms to enfold her unbalanced daughter.

From the protective circle of our mother's arms, Corinne defends her actions.

"I didn't know she'd be home, Mum. She was supposed to be at her friend's house. I checked downstairs and in the bedroom and she wasn't there. I didn't want to hurt her, only to take away what she had," she howls into my mother's shoulder. "It was a mistake. You have to believe me."

It's done. Over.

I linger another moment, staring at Corinne sobbing her remorse in my mother's arms, and walk out the door.

CHAPTER 29

EVEN AFTER THE FIRE, WHEN my world shattered around me, it was the immutability of my parents' love that gave me a trellis on which to creep back up into the world. I knew they would never fail me: they were paragons of truth, honour, and right. Now I find that it is all an illusion and reality is a dark, slithering entity. It's as if I have stumbled onto the set of a Steven King horror movie and become one of the characters. The thing is, I really *am* one of the characters and turning away from the movie won't make it stop.

When I arrive home, I throw Bennie out the door to fertilise Mr. Bacik's garden, then sink, exhausted, onto the couch with a cup of calming chamomile tea. The answering machine is flashing with messages. I know it will be my father making sure I'm all right. I'm not. I can't talk to either of them yet.

Hours later, I wake to Bennie's gritty tongue across my closed eyelid. A nibble of guilt makes me leave a message on Dad's mobile phone. I tell him I need some time to deal with everything and don't want to discuss it.

Too agitated to stay indoors, I head down to the beach. It's dusk, feeding time for sharks, and a vicarious shudder of fear ripples through me for the board riders scattered like toys on the pewter waves.

My hand closes over a small rock and I draw my arm back, grunting as I pitch it into the sea; not a playful, skimming action but an angry, smash-the-wave action. Then I throw another and another. Bennie tilts his head and barks once as if to tell me to ease off. When I can find no more small rocks, I hurl handfuls of sand at the water, in a continuous motion until my arm shakes and I can no longer ignore the rock lodged in my gut—a conglomerate of self-pity, self-hatred, resentment and white hot anger.

Today's revelations have taken me to an all-time low. And before I can resist, the tapes begin to play in my head in full technicolour. First, there is a close-up of my face the day the bandages were removed, then Tom's cringing horror. The polite tiptoeing out of my life of friends, the loss of my job, my rejection of Clyde, and now the lie of my childhood.

With forced blinks, I attempt to erase the images and lick at the salty tears as they drip into my mouth. Through the blur, I watch a string of orange, fluffy clouds hover above the horizon, sending muted light across the water and I ponder the possibility of sinking deep into the incurious ocean and not resurfacing.

A streak of gulls flies low over the waves and then arrows up into the sky, jogging a memory of a D.H. Lawrence quote about self-pity. "I never saw a wild thing sorry for itself. A small bird will drop frozen dead from a bough without ever having felt sorry for itself."

I sigh, a heavy, dented sound. He's right—self-pity is a purely human emotion, a destructive narcotic which devours our souls and freezes our potential. But only because we let it.

Pfft, what noble sentiments. It would take nothing less than Clyde's wisdom and irreverent humour to slough off the self-pity generated by all I've endured.

How I miss him. Like a physical ache inside. He alone could make this seem less than it is, show me a way out of the skulking darkness, into the light. And as the memory of Clyde's strength and the words he would say permeate my mind, they become my words and thoughts; my solutions.

I jerk upright, tipping Bennie from his position draped across my arm. I won't do it, I decide. Self-pity is for wimps. I am a warrior. I stand, dust off the sand, and order a startled Bennie to arm himself, ready for action.

First, I call Randy at home. The words tangle in upon themselves as I try to deliver a coherent, intelligent explanation. He keeps asking me to repeat my story. The story that my sister is an arsonist. We only have her word that attempted murder was not on her agenda. Randy's thin veneer of sympathy does little to hide how pissed off he is with this new piece of information, which complicates a case we had already won.

"I can't blame the landlord anymore. It doesn't seem right," I say.

"He still bears the blame for the faulty fire alarm, Layla. But this new information certainly limits my negotiating capacity. Damn! I can't believe we've been hit with this at this stage of the game."

"*You* haven't been hit with anything," I say, trying to keep my voice steady. "*I* have discovered my own sister tried to kill me. The money is the least of my concerns."

"Layla, I can't even imagine how this news is affecting you. But if you back down now, she will win because you won't ever have the funds to undo the damage she's done."

Even though I recognise his slick sales pitch, I also know he's right. Without the money for surgery, Corinne will always know she succeeded.

"You can't ask for more money. What they've offered is enough." I hear him draw in a breath and I continue before he can argue. "I don't want you to call them before Monday. I have to work this out with my parents."

"As your lawyer, my opinion is we should still ask for more, based on the culpability of the landlord. The matter with your sister is a criminal matter to be dealt with separately."

When he says *criminal matter*, a chill, like someone running an ice cube up my spine, reminds me I am at the edge of an under-world sink hole, being sucked down along with all my family. I can't stop now.

Next, I phone Ruby. She's so relieved to hear from me, I wish I'd phoned her earlier.

"Everything is so weird here, Layla, and no one will tell me what's going on. Mum and Corinne are locked in her bedroom and Dad is on the back patio, staring at nothing and not giving me any answers when I ask him what's wrong. What will I do?"

"Pack a bag for a couple of days, jump on the train, and I'll meet you at St. Leonards Station. Tell Dad you're going, but also leave a note on the kitchen table because he probably won't hear you. Message me when you're on the train, so I know what time to be there."

"But what's happening? I'm freaking out," she says.

"I'll tell you everything when I pick you up. Get yourself to the train now."

I'm kicking myself that I didn't pick her up from school, but it was the last thing I had on my mind at the time. I check the freezer and pull out a container of vegetable soup—that's dinner—and make sure I'm ready to leave as soon as I get her message. No, on second thoughts, I'll give it another fifteen minutes and head off anyway as it will take me longer to get there than it will take Ruby on the train.

❦

"Well?" Ruby throws her bag onto the back seat and tugs at her seatbelt. "What's going on with this family?" She pulls Bennie onto her lap and buries her face in his neck.

"Why don't we wait 'til we get home and have something to eat?"

"Enough with the bullshit, Layla. I want to know right now why my mother and Corinne are locked in the bedroom muttering and moaning, my father has turned into a zombie, and now you're acting like the Secret Keeper."

Spiriting Ruby away seemed like the best idea at the time. To save her from the drama at home. But now I'm faced with having to be the one to destroy her happy family picture.

"Rubes, can you remember any weird stuff Corinne did when you were a kid? I mean, were you ever a bit scared of her?" Her head jerks up, eyes wide, and a shadow passes over her face.

"Maybe sitting on the street outside the station isn't the best place after all," she says, turning to stare out the window.

A hot, sweaty anxiety crawls through my body and my hands are clammy on the steering wheel. I pull out from the curb into the traffic and once we're on Military Road, I reach over to squeeze Ruby's hand. She squeezes back, but doesn't turn away from the window. Now I want this drive to last forever. Because I suspect when it ends I will hear something I will never be able to unhear.

Of course, the drive does come to an end, but neither of us

raises the subject. Together we heat dinner, make toast, and take it out to the table. The slurping of soup, punctuated by the muted roar of waves crashing on the beach, are the only sounds which break the thick silence.

Without my asking, Ruby clears the table. I then hear water splashing into the sink, and the clink of cutlery against china as she washes up. The unmistakable sound of the kibble bag being opened jettisons Bennie from the chair, and he careens around the kitchen door before his bowl hits the floor. Rather than feeling grateful to Ruby for all her domestic assistance, the worm of anxiety embeds itself deeper into my gut.

When my sister finally walks out from the kitchen, her gaze meets mine and I know she's ready to tell her story. We move over to the couch, where she snuggles under my arm. Then, at her own pace, she tells me what she can remember.

"There aren't a lot of memories from when I was really young, just feelings. Even as a toddler I knew if Corinne was around, not to run to Mum all the time, only to Dad. I can't even remember why, but knew I needed to pretend I wasn't looking for Mum's attention. Corinne was already eighteen when I was born, so she seemed very powerful to me as a little kid. When I found my kitten drowned in the pool that time, I knew it was her. So many things happened whenever she was around that I knew she'd done it."

I had always wondered why Corinne never left home until she was well into her twenties. Knowing what I now do, I can only imagine her obsessive and desperate desire for our mother's love and attention must have kept her there.

"If you knew she'd done it, why didn't you tell anyone? You must have only been about five years old at the time. It doesn't make sense that you didn't talk to one of us."

Bennie crawls onto Ruby's lap and she strokes his head, eyes lowered. "Because she grabbed me that morning and told me she'd done it. Drowned my kitten."

The breath catches in my throat at this blatant display of power. And then I remember my dog, Danger. The kitten was not the only animal who died at her hand.

"She said that was a taste of what she'd do if I ever told Mum or Dad, or you guys about this or anything else."

I battle with whether to raise a subject, which always seemed innocuous. But I now have no doubt it was a symptom of something darker.

"And the bedwetting?"

She flushes at the mention of it and makes a show of searching through Bennie's fur for stray fleas. This was a subject we always steered clear of out of respect for Ruby and the embarrassment she suffered when the bedwetting continued, even after she turned twelve. Sleep-overs caused her days of anxiety and she'd wear plastic pull-ups just in case. A mortifying indignity for a pre-teen.

"Around my sixth birthday she started to come into my room, taking stuff that she couldn't possibly want because she was so old. I never told you but she took the butterfly hair clip you gave me for my birthday and would often wear it in her hair to tease me."

Oh God, the butterfly clip. That's how it got to my house in Balmain, that's who was wearing it.

My bag is slung over the arm of a dining chair and I lean over from the couch and reach in, searching the deep folds until my hand closes around something thin and hard. Ruby watches me, frowning. I open my fist.

"This one?"

She takes it from my hand. "Yes. I loved that clip. How did you get it? And why is the plastic melted?"

I shake my head. "I'll tell you later. Keep going with the story."

Ruby continues to groom Bennie. "I was sick of being scared of her and one day I told her I didn't care what she did, I was going to tell Mum everything I could remember, especially about my kitten. I expected her to be worried or, as she was an adult, to apologise to me, say it was all a mistake and she should never have done those things. But she smiled and warned me how sorry I would be if I told anyone."

"And so you didn't tell."

Ruby shakes her head, stroking Bennie so firmly, he squirms away and drops to the floor.

"A couple of days later she came in with a parcel for me and stupidly I got quite excited, thinking she liked me after all. I ripped the wrapping off and it was a big male doll; one that looked like that monster Chucky doll from the movie, remember?" I nod, grimacing at the memory. "She told me this doll was her spy and he would watch me all the time and report back to her. If I told anyone what she'd done, he would come for me in the middle of the night and hurt me."

"And that's when you started wetting the bed?" She nods, looking past my shoulder. "We always wondered why it only started then, not when you were an infant."

A sudden memory resurfaces of Ruby stuffing a doll into the garbage bin and one of us chastising her and pulling it out again. It must have seemed we were all complicit in Corinne's little scheme. I pull her into my arms.

"I'm so sorry, Rubes. We all missed it. She was too clever for any of us."

We cling to each other, but there are no tears, as if the situation defies emotion, as if it's a barren, dead place.

Eventually I speak. "I figured the other day the drugs were a part of it. A way to numb the years of fear and confusion she caused."

"I didn't actually work that out at first," says Ruby. "But after talking to Anna, I wondered why I had jumped so easily into the drug scene." She lifts her head to look at me. "What made you figure it out? Why now?"

For a moment I'd forgotten she knows nothing about Corinne's role in the fire. But that's why I brought her over here, wasn't it? To explain what was happening at home.

"Before I tell you, do you want a cup of tea or hot chocolate?" I ask, stalling.

She purses her lips, shaking her head. "I wouldn't be able to swallow it anyway."

I take a deep breath and slowly exhale while Ruby watches me, fear of what I'm about to say stripping her smooth cheeks of colour. When I tell her about Mum's rape and Corinne being our half-sister, she grips my hand.

"Oh, shit! That's horrible. Poor Mum." Then she looks at me, her lip trembling like a small child. "But why didn't they protect us from her? Why was she allowed to do such terrible things to us?"

I lean over and kiss her forehead. "They didn't want to know.

They made themselves believe we were normal siblings fighting amongst ourselves. And I guess they had to love her harder than us because of how she was conceived."

"And… the fire, Layla?"

"It was Corinne who lit the fire because she was jealous of what I had: the house, the job and I guess, the fact we all belonged and she didn't."

Ruby stares at me, her hand on her throat. She pushes herself up from the sofa, and leans out the window, gulping mouthfuls of fresh air.

"She tried to kill you?" she asks, her voice high pitched.

"She says she thought I was over at Tegan's." I move over to stand next to Ruby and stare out the window, grateful for the sting of the salty wind on my face. "I had told Mum I was staying the night with her, but came home instead. So I don't think she meant to harm me, only destroy my things."

"But she never told the truth, even afterward. Even when you were in hospital in a coma. When we thought you were going to die."

"Especially then. It had all gone so horribly wrong and if I died she'd be alienated by everyone, locked away in prison, unloved and unwanted. She's sick, Rubes. Her father had a mental illness and it appears she might have as well." Ruby mouths the words, *her father*. Like me, she can't relate to our dad not being Corinne's father. "She's unstable and needs help."

Ruby stiffens and her hands clench into fists as she turns to face me. "How can you stand there and defend her? She set fire to you, for God's sake. Unstable? Damn right she's unstable and she needs to be locked away." Ruby pushes her fist against my chest. "Why aren't you angry? Why don't you hate her?"

I grab her wrists to hold her steady. "I am angry. I do hate her. I've always hated her. I want to smash her ugly face and pull out her thin, greasy hair. I want to rip out that nasty tongue and wrap it around her fat neck."

Ruby's eyes flare as she joins in. "And hold her smug face under the water until she drowns like my kitten, and rip up that horrible floral skirt, tie her to the chair and let the Chucky doll torture her all night."

Still gripping each other, we slide to the floor and dissolve into hysterical laughter. The kind of laughter that massages the brain, ejects all the dark stuff eating away at the psyche, and leaves you exhausted and relieved.

"God, that felt good," I say, brushing tears off my cheeks.

"I know. Pity Matt wasn't here to play. I'll bet the evil witch did bad things to him too."

"No doubt, Rubes. Maybe he'll talk about it one day."

Ruby gives me a quizzical look. "Do you think that's why he married the awful Maureen? He was so used to evil women?"

We both giggle again.

"Well, funny you say that. I've given it a bit of thought over the last couple of days and she might well have saved him. She's like his protective bulldog, making sure no one can get near enough to hurt him. I know she makes us feel excluded, but it might be the first time he's felt safe, so maybe we should appreciate her a bit more."

"Yeah, well when you put it like that. Maybe I'll try being nicer to her."

I force a grin to my lips. "When you think about it, it must have been so hard for Corinne. She didn't resemble anyone in the family, she never really belonged, and didn't know why. And it would have been even worse after they told her the reason." Ruby frowns, tilting her head. "I guess you don't know. But when she turned fifteen, Mum and Dad told her everything. About the rape and the fact she's not our dad's daughter, only our half-sister. Pretty shocking stuff hey? The most stable person probably would have slipped off the rails let alone someone who was already not quite steady."

"Ah, shit."

What?" I ask.

"Now I feel sorry for the evil sister."

I give her a rueful smile, rubbing her shoulder in sympathy. "Yeah, I do, too. Even after this." I gesture at my face.

We remain on the floor, looking at the legs of the dining room table, both lost in our own thoughts.

"Layla? What are you going to do? I mean about Corinne."

I blow out a puff of air. "That's the three million dollar question, Rubes, and I'll have to have the answer by Monday morning.

CHAPTER 30

IT'S AFTER MIDNIGHT AND I stare at the ceiling, unable to stop the storm of thoughts roiling in my head. Before I can change my mind, I reach for the phone and dial.

"Can't sleep?" asks Clyde. No, 'why haven't you called; what makes you think I want to speak to you;' or even, 'piss off.'

"No, I can't. I was looking for Scheherezade. Is she there?"

"Sure. And ready to tell the story of the swashbuckling young sailor known as Sinbad. Handsome as the devil and sexy as sin."

I release a nervous breath. "It's really nice to talk to you."

"Yeah, you too. What's keeping you awake? The legal stuff?"

"I guess. There are complications." Damn, I need to talk to him. I swallow the lumpy chunk of pride in my throat and plunge in. "Are you busy tomorrow morning? Do you want to have breakfast or brunch down the front?"

He hesitates; enough for me to know I've stepped over some barrier. "Sure. If you need to talk."

"You don't have to, Clyde."

"I know that. Nine o'clock?" I mutter my assent. "Okay, snuggle down and turn off the light while I unfurl the sails and steer the ship away from Basrah. Into the seas off Africa to dangerous adventures, unimaginable treasure and strange, magical lands inhabited by mythical creatures."

How safe he makes me feel. Ruby's soft snuffles reverberate through the wall, and I pull up the covers and close my eyes. I switch the phone to speaker as his deep, melodic voice spins a tale of fantasy.

☾

Something hard presses into my ear as I roll over. I shift my cheek off the phone, rubbing at the indentation. Cautiously, I open my eyes and slam them shut as the sun, now high in the sky, shoots laser beams at my eyelids making me dizzy with the bright, swirling spots dancing across my eyeballs. *Shit.* I sit upright in bed and slide my finger across the phone. *Eight-thirty!* Bennie usually wakes me at seven or earlier.

I lurch into the lounge room to find no sign of Ruby or Bennie. The front door's unlocked and I fling it open, check if the coast is clear, and run down the stairs to see if they're in the front yard.

"What's the rush, *kochana*?" Mr. Bacik looks up at me from his crouched position in the garden. "Ruby and Bennie are walking and maybe you should put some clothes on."

I wrap my bare arms across my flimsy cami.

"How long ago did they leave? I have to meet someone in about twenty-five minutes, and I don't want to leave Ruby on her own."

The old man sits back on his heels. "She tells me our boy, Levi comes today. Your Ruby's face is very sad. Something bad has happened to her, I think." I open my mouth to speak, but he shakes his head. "This, I don't need to be told. Levi will help her. But she asks me if I think you would mind if she is alone with Levi."

"Oh? She doesn't want me around?"

He shrugs.

"No. That's good," I say, "because she won't mind if I meet my friend, will she?"

"My Helena, she will give her breakfast. Already she is cooking for Levi. So you go meet your friend, and I tell Ruby you will be back in…?"

"Um, in a couple of hours. I'm going down to the coffee shop, Bean There, on the Corso."

He claps with satisfaction. "See, everybody is happy with this arrangement. Go. Go." He waves me back inside.

After a quick shower, I waste precious time selecting the right outfit. Does that mean I am trying to impress Clyde? This strikes me as ironic, because the first time I saw him at Bean There I tried to avoid him. I go for tight jeans and a light, flowery cotton top with loose sleeves to the elbows, glance longingly at my drawer full of earrings, before wrapping a blue scarf around my head.

Galloping down the uneven steps to the beachfront, I pass Ruby coming back from Shelly Beach with a wet, happy Bennie. She assures me it's fine if I meet Clyde and adds she wants to be alone with Levi while she works through everything I've told her. A small pinch of guilt at leaving her makes me look back as she clambers up the steps; but I know she has to find her own way through this, as do I.

☾

Clyde's bulky form creates a silhouette against the window and he glances up, shading his eyes when I run across from the beach path. His smile seems genuine and I relax a little. It could be my imagination, but he looks like he's lost a small amount of weight, especially from his face. Whatever it is, he looks well. He half stands and with one hand on my shoulder, pecks me on the cheek. A friend's greeting.

"I haven't ordered yet. What would you like?" he asks.

I glance at the menu. "I think the mushroom omelette with toast and a soy latté. What about you?"

By this time, the waitress has approached our table. Clyde looks up and gives her my order, before studying the menu once more.

"I'll have muesli with fruit salad, plain yoghurt, and a long black."

I raise one eyebrow, the one not painted on. "No eggs Benedict, toast with lashings of butter, or a croissant dripping with cheese?"

His shoulders slump. "Had to have a medical check-up and the doctor says, despite my feeble attempt to lose weight, I'm still borderline diabetic. He said I had two options: get serious about the diet and lose a significant amount of weight, or look forward to a life time of stabbing myself with needles." He grins. "Of course, I took the needle option."

"Who wouldn't?" I ask. I take another look at him. "I thought you'd lost a bit of weight. You look well for it."

He looks down at himself. "Yeah, well a long way to go yet, apparently." His gaze moves over me. "You look nice. Blue suits you."

I feel myself blush like a schoolgirl, pleased he's noticed.

We chat about The Black Hole and its inhabitants, his mother, and the two million dollars offered by the defendants in my suit. Time fillers until we've both eaten our breakfast. Me, hungrily and Clyde, with a pained expression as he chews his muesli, while glancing with envy at my omelette. At last our plates have been cleared and we both sip our coffees. I try not to look like I'm enjoying the froth from the top of the latté.

"What did you want to talk to me about?" he asks.

Even before I say a word, the tension drains from my body at being able to share this with him.

"What I'm about to tell you is shocking and a huge moral dilemma for me. I need some perspective on it and don't know anyone else I would trust with it."

I shift in my chair and push my glass into three different positions on the table, unsure how to start the tale of my damaged family. Clyde stands up and scrapes his chair around the table until he sits adjacent to me, rather than opposite. Then he reaches for my hand and holds it in his.

"Talk to me."

An hour later, I have relayed the wretched story of the Danforth family. Well adjusted, upper middle class professional family with four privately educated, privileged children who, apart from a few unfortunate accidents, had the world at their feet. But under the pretty rolling waves on the surface ran a dangerous rip which quietly dragged each member of the family down by their feet, soundlessly and without struggle. Until now. When in a quest to regain my memory, I exposed the secrets and the pain suffered by every member of my family. And the *piéce de resistance*: that my sister's jealousy and instability led her to burn down my home. With me in it.

"More coffee?" asks the waitress, startling us back to our surroundings.

I nod and she clears our plates.

I look down at my hand, still caught in Clyde's. I've gripped so hard my nails have left crescent shapes in his skin. Grimacing, I release my grip and pull my hand free, shaking out the stiffness.

Clyde has not spoken. The shock plays over his face, as he breathes through his mouth—deep intakes of air. As if this will dissipate the information I've just thrust at him.

I barrel on, regardless. "So, I have all these decisions to make. Knowing the landlord was in no way culpable for the fire itself, although he must bear blame for the faulty fire alarm, do I take the two million dollars and be done with it? Do I let Randy push them for more without letting them know there is now a criminal aspect to the case? And what do I do about Corinne? Do I run to the police and break my mother's heart? Do I let her stay free with her twisted mind and know that our family and maybe others could still be in danger from her? If I don't go to the police am I breaking the law by covering up a crime?" I drop my head into my hands. "I don't know what to do."

Clyde shakes his head, his eyebrows knitted in a deep frown of disbelief. "Good God. I...I don't know what to say. How have you remained sane after all that?"

The waitress returns with fresh coffee and I pick up the glass, staring at the steam rising from the surface.

I release a shaky laugh. "You think I'm still sane? I don't feel it."

He leans towards me, and I think he's about to hug me. Instead, he lowers his eyes and grasps my hand again.

"Phew! Okay, it might be easier to separate the money and the Corinne situation, otherwise you tie yourself in knots." He looks at my face. "Into more knots then. What's your first instinct with the money?"

I slurp at my coffee and lick the frothy moustache from my top lip. "First response is to grab the two million dollars and run. But this is my only chance for compensation and maybe it's smarter to go for more. You know, just in case."

"Okay, so not feeling comfortable with the three million he wants to go for, but thinking you might need more than the two million?"

"I guess you could say it like that."

"What about something in between? Gives you some leeway for the things you're thinking might come up."

"I guess. Yes, he could push for two and a half million, and it won't be a big deal if they turn it down. Shall I ring Randy now and tell him to do whatever he has to do in the time he's got?"

"As good a time as any, I guess, and then you can put that one aside and not think about it anymore."

A tremendous sense of relief washes through me and I dial Randy's number. Five minutes later, I place the phone on the table; it's now down to Randy's negotiation skills.

I lean towards Clyde and kiss the dimple on his cheek. "Thanks. And now for Corinne."

He takes a gulp of coffee. "From everything you've told me about your mum and dad, I can't believe they won't do the absolute best thing for all of you, including Corinne."

I snort. "Well, they haven't for the last thirty odd years. Why should they now?"

My stomach churns again in anger at what they sat back and allowed all these years. I now don't trust them where Corinne is concerned.

"Sounds like you're clear you want to take some action. What are the options? I imagine if she was tried for arson, there's a chance she might be found not competent to answer the charges. So she'd be sent somewhere for treatment. Maybe a criminal facility."

"A criminal facility. God, that sounds awful. How would Mum ever get past that?"

"I can't imagine they won't be at home doing the same amount of soul-searching as you," he says. "Maybe give them a day or two and then let them know you intend to press charges and see how much they'll support you."

"What if it splits the family apart? What if I don't have a family after this?"

Clyde reefs a paper serviette out of the holder and dabs at the tears trailing down my cheeks.

"There's always me… and Lavender, and Gavin, and the professor, and don't forget Mrs. Crompton." I hated that he added the others onto the list, but I have to get used to the fact he's my friend and nothing more. "Anyway, your parents might surprise you. And you know, if you can't find a way to get past it all, forgive them, keep your family intact, these…" he indicates my scars, "these will be the least of your heartaches."

I'm too angry and hurt to flip to forgiveness yet, but my parents are so important to me, I can't imagine them not in my life. All I can manage is a half-hearted shrug to his statement.

I don't want our morning to end, but I need to get back to Ruby and make sure she's all right. When we hug each other goodbye, I'm sure Clyde holds me longer than necessary. But then again that could be my imagination.

"Let me know how it goes with your parents and don't abandon The Black Hole. Lavender misses you." Not, *I* miss you.

I dash, without looking back, through the Corso, over to the beach, and onto the path that will take me home.

☾

Late in the afternoon, I pick up a call from Dad. The first contact I've had with either Mum or Dad since I left them comforting Corinne. His voice is hoarse as if he's cried his throat raw. I try to maintain my anger, but know he's no more to blame than anyone else. In fact the man to blame for the destruction of my family has already taken the easy way out and committed suicide.

"I'm so sorry, pumpkin. I'm at a total loss to know what to say. We were blind. Both of us. My heart breaks thinking of what you kids went through, and I'm sure we haven't heard even the half of it."

I can't tell him it's all right; I can't even tell him I forgive him, so I don't respond.

"I wanted you to know we want to put this right. I'm not sure how yet. I hope you'll be able to love us again one day."

That did it for me.

"Daddy, I could never stop loving you. Or Mum. I do need some time to forgive you. For her sake as well as ours, she has to pay for what she's done."

I don't need to say who *she* is.

"I know, pumpkin. I love you." We both hang up.

I clutch my phone, staring into space and breathing down the emotions of anger and blame. I suddenly understand whatever we do about Corinne has to be done as a family. I look over at Ruby and feel a surge of protective love for her. I am so conflicted.

Levi has gone home, and Ruby is glued to her iPad reading up on Jewish practises. She seems more relaxed from whatever support Levi has provided.

"Hey, Layla. Did you know a Jew can't eat a goat cooked in its own mother's milk?"

"Ah, no. Good to know, though."

"And," she continues, "when you light the Hanukah candles, they have to be lit from right to left."

"That also will be useful, Rubes."

Her innocence loosens the tension gripping the sides of my head and I slump into the cushions of the sofa.

Ruby's doing a crash cyber course on everything Jewish. When Levi arrived today he brought news which has the Baciks in a state of frantic excitement. His mother wants to meet these new surrogate grandparents. They're coming for lunch next Sunday, so the flat has to be spring cleaned, the garden weeded and replanted, and baking started immediately.

To stir the hornet's nest even more, Ruby, the non-Jewish girlfriend, has been invited to meet them for the first time. She's terrified she'll do something blatantly goyish and Levi's parents will 'cast her out'—her words, she's been reading too much dramatic Jewish history. Although I strongly suspect Levi would not obey an order to ditch Ruby.

☾

Minutes after I return from walking Ruby to the bus stop on Monday morning, there's a knock at my door.

If my father wore a hat, he'd have been twisting it nervously in his hands. As it is, his fingers tap unceasingly against his car keys until I reach over and remove them. His gaze holds mine and the chill up my spine tells me he's about to say something which will publicly destroy the fantasy of the happy Danforth family. I hold my breath, as if this will freeze the moment, but when he reaches over and strokes my cheek, I crumble into his arms. He eases me backwards and closes the door behind him.

"I've spoken to the police."

"About Corinne?" I splutter, shocked at his words.

"Yes. We're going in this morning to make a statement. We want it to be as a family. Me, your mother, Corinne, and you. It's important we're united in this. It will go better for Corinne."

"Better for Corinne? This is all about Corinne?" I ask.

I can hear the whiny sound in my voice, but at this moment, I don't care.

Dad puts his arm around my shoulder and leads me out to the front room where we both sit at the dining table.

"No, darling, definitely not just about Corinne. We want the truth out there. All of it. Her admission of guilt on paper. Then we get the lawyers and doctors involved."

"But wouldn't it be better to have a lawyer there at the beginning?" Better for Corinne. And why would I care about that?

Dad nods slowly. "Yes, a lawyer would be able to throw obstacles in front of a police interrogation, but we know what happened and we owe it to you to have the story told straight. Besides, it's not a matter of guilt or innocence, it's about what comes after."

Clyde was right. My parents have undergone an agony of soul-searching over how to meet the needs of all their children. It's a white flag and I'm too emotionally exhausted to reject it. Besides, after such a total annihilation of my ideal family, it's time to build a real one.

"I'll get ready."

CHAPTER 31

New York - Six months later

IT'S UNVEILING DAY. BANDAGES OFF forever day. Dr. Gassner never gave me false hope. He said a lot of the scarring was so deep, it couldn't be erased, just improved, and he'd do his best.

So, he warned me months ago not to have unrealistic expectations.

"Ready, Layla?" he asks.

Ready to see the face I will wear for the rest of my life? I nod, swallowing my fear.

It seems to take a month to unravel the bandages.

Holding my breath, the drumbeat of blood pounding in my eardrums, I open my eyes. A thousand emotions churn through my body. Despair, disappointment, resolve. But I won't avert my eyes from the mirror he holds.

The face that stares back at me is not clear and smooth, with gentle contours. This face is still scarred. The gnarly tree vines have been reduced to pigmented patches of raised skin—some dark, some lighter. My twisted mouth has been straightened and when I try it out, I manage an embarrassed, lop-sided sort of grin. The grimace is gone.

No-one speaks to tell me I'll get used to it, or how much better I look. They respect my need to get to know this person. To accept this is as good as it will get.

On the upside, I now have an earlobe on my left ear. And they have even transplanted hair into my bald patch. I glance down at my arm and leg. The scarring is less aggressive and not as raw as when the operation was first done two months ago. Still there, though.

"Layla?" says Dr. Gassner.

I raise my eyes. My gut feels hollow. Hell, my whole body feels hollow.

"Thanks, Dr. Gassner. It looks much better." I give him my new half-smile.

"I understand your disappointment. I know you were looking for a miracle and I wish I could have given you one. Although, I think if you look back on photographs taken before these operations, you'll notice a huge difference. Personally, I am extremely pleased with how well everything went."

After the staff leave my room, I crumple like a discarded puppet. Then, with the sheet over my head, I sob the heartbreak of my shattered dreams.

Somewhere, in the midst of my grief, I run out of tears. I even run out of grief. As if this final burst of despair is unfinished business and now I can dust off my hands and get on with life. The space, previously filled with misery and regret, is now empty, washed clean, and ready for my new reality. I poke my head out of the sheet shroud and hear a peal of laughter from the nurses' station.

A young girl—a burns victim like me—giggles with the nurses as she parodies a mummy for their amusement. By her size, she must be no more than fourteen, although it's hard to tell. Her hands and most of her face are bandaged, as is her torso. One eye is covered and as she squints at me through the un-melted eye, she waves and smiles, before continuing down the hall. My mind is tempted to paint a dark, dismal picture of her future. Then I recall her smile and the sparkle in her eye. Her story will be different from mine. Why? Because that's obviously what she's decided. And at that moment, I understand that my life, despite the injuries, has always had the potential to be whatever I want it to be.

The sound of metal trays clanking tells me it's late. Dinner time, in fact. I drag myself up the bed as a lady in blue places a tray on my table, says something unintelligible, and leaves.

"Welcome to your imperfect life, Layla," I murmur.

Between mouthfuls of salad, I roll that word, imperfect, around in my head. What exactly does it mean? Terrible? Different?

Or extraordinary.

I chuckle. Maybe that's going a bit far.

If I can learn to accept my 'imperfect' self, what about my 'imperfect' family? My mother was the victim of a rape, for God's sake! My heart twists as I imagine her as a twenty year old, having her dreams and her innocence ripped from her by some psychopath. And still, she and my father lavished love on Corinne, this man's child, and gave her the best life they could.

It hits me square in the face that the happy family façade wasn't ever about my parents weaving lies and deceit, it was about love and protection. They might have got it wrong, but that was never their intention.

I heave a long sigh, a release of hard held beliefs. So, I'm not perfect; Mum and Dad aren't perfect; Corinne's not perfect, and bloody Tom's not perfect. The world's not perfect. Where does that leave me? I pick up the mirror again and stare, unflinching, at my face. And don't mind what I see. Life has brutally exploded my long-held myths around what constitutes perfection, success, and happiness. It seems the me I'd yearned for these past few years was just an empty vanity, a pretty vessel with no substance.

Perhaps, like the poster says, this is the first day of the rest of my life. I scrunch my nose and grin at her. The woman I am.

*

It's early evening and I've come in from buying Indian take-away, or 'take-out', as they say here. I settle on the window seat in my Harlem apartment-sit, courtesy of one of Dad's clients, and gaze out at the city skyline. I know nothing about how the trial is progressing or how my parents are coping. Whenever we speak, they use upbeat voices and tell me how well everything is going and I'm happy to believe them. It's easier that way. Besides, I'm so far away, not much I can do to help.

I shove a mouthful of vegetable Biryani into my mouth, and frown at the woman reflected back at me in the window. What a load of rubbish, I tell her. Of course you can help.

I push the food away, pick up my phone and check the time in Sydney. Then dial home.

"Hello… Layla, darling. How lovely."

"Hi Mum. How are you?" A tingle of warmth flutters through me at the sound of her voice. The sound of home.

"We're alright, darling. Did they remove the bandages?"

"Yes."

"And?" Her voice is tremulous. "I hope it's everything you wanted, darling."

"It's not what I'd hoped for, but it'll do. I'm actually okay with the results."

She releases a relieved breath. "That's all that matters. Can't wait to see you. Are we still skyping on Saturday?"

"Sure. But I called tonight as I wanted to find out how everything's going there. You know, with Corinne and the trial."

She hesitates and I hear Dad mumble something in the background. The phone's on speaker and he can hear the conversation.

"We're not that happy with the lawyer. He doesn't seem to have any experience with defending someone with a mental illness."

"Why don't you find someone else?"

She hesitates again. "I'm sure he's doing his best, darling. It'll be fine."

My mother would leave no stone unturned to find the best defence for one of her children. So the fees must be horrendous. They probably don't have the cash up-front and need time to liquidate assets. I have more than enough for Corinne's legal fees. I take a breath and tell her why I phoned.

"No, it won't be fine," I say. "You need to get rid of him and hire the best. A team of lawyers if necessary. I want to pay for it. I've got the money and that's what I want to spend it on."

There, I've said it. That I'll use the compensation payout from the injuries inflicted by my sister to save her from prison. Something I could not have conceived of doing a few months ago. But with this new acceptance of myself, the anger at Corinne has waned.

My mother gasps. "Layla. That money is to ensure you can have a decent life and ongoing medical care, if necessary…you're in this position because of Corinne. We'll be alright, honestly."

"I think I'm doing it for me as much as for you, Mum," I say. "Please, you need to let me do this."

Besides, I'm now aware the money won't be a factor in determining whether I have a decent life.

After much discussion, she agrees, and when I end the call, I feel lighter. As if layer by layer, I am peeling away the weighty coats of self-inflicted misery and shame from my shoulders.

CHAPTER 32

OVER TWENTY-TWO HOURS STRAPPED INTO a space the size of a broom cupboard thirty-three thousand feet in the air, gave me even more thinking time. Especially seated next to a zit-covered youth with a Gameboy and zero communication skills.

For months I'd envisioned Doctor Gassner, miracle worker, inspecting my face, smiling, and with a flip of his wrist, telling me it would be no trouble putting me back together again. I would float out of the hospital, all anger and self-pity erased, and when I got home, everyone would comment on my shining beauty, inside and out.

Not even close. The New York trip was lonely, challenging, and unexpectedly life-changing. A bit like someone swanning off to an ashram in India expecting an experience of cross-legged bliss, with a gaunt, turbaned guru showering blessings on you as he encourages your best self to emerge. And instead, your body aches night and day from the coarse, horse-hair mattress and the hours of sitting on the floor. The food gives you constant diarrhoea and stomach cramps. The other inmates are all nutters and the Guru yells that you're not understanding the truth, no matter how many ways he explains it.

That's what New York was like.

In fact, I think that describes my journey since the fire. As if I've been thrown into a washing machine to be agitated, tossed against the sides, and wrung dry until I've crawled out, bedraggled, chafed, weary, and clean. So stain-free and squeaky clean, I can see myself clearly for the first time in my life. Stripped of the paraphernalia I've collected since birth. But more importantly, stripped of the dark, destructive crap I've dragged around since the fire. The flotsam I erroneously believed defined who I was.

And I've had time to get to know this new self—the one I've become. The one who's broken through the scarred exterior to discover, with arcane understanding, how transient surface beauty is, and how loosely it connects you to others. I may even have come to believe I'm as worthy of love as the perfect Layla was. In fact, I believe this Layla has more to offer as she's had to dig deep to find the truth of herself, rather than relying on a pleasing exterior.

I shift in my seat to peer out the window, where luminescent shafts of pink and orange pierce through the clouds, sparkling off the silver wing, as night morphs into day. The belly of the plane rumbles with waking passengers, and the rich aromas of eggs, hot bread rolls, and coffee drift from the small galley kitchen. Normally, I don't drink coffee this early in the morning, but there's something about the altitude that makes me crave caffeine, even at five a.m.

As the flight attendant bends forward to take my breakfast order, her gaze flicks to my scar. Instead of the heat of anger and shame churning my gut, I smile and nod, acknowledging her curiosity. When she turns away, I trail my fingers down the scar. It's still conspicuous, but everything is relative, and this I can live with.

My laptop is open and I re-read a Facebook message from Lavender. We've skyped, emailed, and messaged but I've still missed them all so much. Even goofy Gavin. Apart from my family, the Black Hole gang will be the best part of my homecoming.

After gobs of gossip about everyone, Lavender had slogged me with the news Clyde has left—not only the job, but the country, and says without him the bar is truly a black hole. She explains he's being interviewed to take on a position lecturing at the University of London.

No matter how many times I read this information, I can't believe it's true.

Or that he didn't tell me.

Actually, he did tell me about the job opportunity, and how interested he was, but I convinced myself it wasn't a serious consideration. I think I even made a joke about it being an extreme measure to take just to avoid Wretched Wednesday with his mother. He'd laughed and changed the subject. My shame at how I'd treated him the night of Lavender's birthday stopped me from digging deeper; made me keep our interactions light and superficial.

It also stopped me from saying, 'Don't go.'

Lavender's email implores me to come to the bar when I return. But I can't imagine descending those stairs without Clyde's dimpled smile welcoming me. There is so much I want to share with him. After all, I'm here because he believed in me and taught me to do the same. It was Clyde who also showed me I could embrace my future, rather than clinging to the ghosts of my past.

I move the laptop, so the smiling attendant can place my breakfast on the tray. Despite the enticing smell, the scrambled eggs are pre-cooked and there is a dangerous looking sausage lurking at the edge of the plate. I butter the roll, heap eggs onto it, and avoid eye-contact with the sausage. At least the coffee attempts to live up to its promise. As I eat, my thoughts drift back to Clyde.

A gritty lump forms in my chest. Of remorse and regret, at being so self-involved when we first met, I never truly appreciated the qualities of this man. Of course, I believed I could remedy all that when I returned, but life has decided otherwise.

*

The wheel on my luggage trolley rattles sideways, sending me careening into other passengers as I battle through the doors of the airport arrival lounge. Everything is a blur as people jump up and down screaming names into the jumble of tired travellers. Out of the corner of my eye I see someone rush towards me with a delighted squeal, and my face is buried in Ruby's silky hair. She finally releases me and commandeers the recalcitrant trolley, shoving it towards the hesitant, loving faces of my parents. Wrapped in their arms, I know I'm home.

Mum steps back from me. "My God. You look amazing. That doctor's made a huge difference to the scars. Skype didn't do your face justice."

I grin, enjoying the compliments. "It's not amazing, but at least it's better. And you'll be pleased to know I'm finally done with plastic surgery."

Mum rolls her eyes and wipes nonexistence sweat from her forehead. "Well, thank goodness for that."

I push up the sleeve of my jacket so they can see my arm. "See how much smoother the scarring is here as well?"

"You did the right thing, darling. Going over to that doctor." She steps back and gazes at me. "You're different. But I'm not referring to the scars. It's as if you've come home to yourself."

She links her arm through mine and with Dad now pushing the trolley, steers us towards the exit doors.

Much later, after a frenetic reunion with Bennie, a few hours' sleep in Ruby's bed, and a bowl of chunky minestrone soup, I'm finally ready to acknowledge the elephant in the room.

Mum passes me another shortbread biscuit and I pause with it halfway to my mouth. "So, how's Corinne doing in the group home?"

The air is sucked from the room at my question. Mum glances at Dad, and Ruby pushes her face into Bennie's furry head.

"Not as good as we'd hoped. As you know, her insistence that she never intended to harm you helped. Also the psychiatrist believed her symptoms were sufficiently subdued; that's why the court placed her in a supported group home with two other girls. On a forensic order."

"That's good. Isn't it?" I glance from one to the other.

My mother shakes her head. "Unfortunately, she lost her temper with one of them and threatened her. There was nowhere else available, so she's in the mental health unit for now." Her voice catches with emotion as she speaks.

"Oh. Do you see her?"

"Yes, Dad and I go regularly, but Ruby and Matt aren't ready to visit yet." I glance at Ruby, who bites her lip. "At least we know we gave her the best defence, thanks to the money you contributed, sweetheart."

This was more a gift for my mother than Corinne. To ease the heartache of watching her child struggle in court without the best defence, but I said nothing. My sister had faced charges of arson, grievous bodily harm, and attempted murder. The money I sent home gave her an expert legal team to effectively argue that her cognitive, volitional, and moral capacity were impaired at the time. Her team also presented the past psychiatric reports. A re-assessment confirmed the initial diagnosis. She did spend time in prison, but that was only until the trial.

"What's it like? The mental health unit. Is the treatment making a difference?"

Ruby puts Bennie down and slips onto a chair at the table. "Matt and I want her looked after too."

Like the others, I'm not ready to see her yet, but the anger and hatred have gone and it seems we all want to see her have a better life.

Mum leans over and puts her arm around Ruby and, at the same time, grasps my hand.

"Thank you for still caring. A group home was a better alternative, but she's where she needs to be. Besides we all need time to do some healing. I know some good support groups—"

We all groan and Mum's shoulders relax as she gazes at her family of survivors.

In the midst of our joking, Matt walks through the door. He crushes me in one of his bear hugs and we cling to each other in more than just pleasure at my return. Maureen is behind him and with a warning look at Ruby, I disengage myself from my brother and for the first time, give her a genuine hug. The tension in her face relaxes and her tight, thin lips soften into a wary smile. Out of the corner of my eye, I see Ruby move from her chair and join me. The shock on Maureen's face at Ruby's sudden embrace has Matt chortling while he throws his arms around the three of us. It's all a little too much for Maureen and she wriggles free from the group hug.

&

Dad fires up the barbecue for dinner—fish, garlic prawns, and fresh salad. It's good to be home. We're shovelling creamy vanilla ice cream and strawberries into our well-satisfied bellies when Ruby's phone rings. She squints at the number and shakes her head, not familiar with the caller.

"Who is this? Stephen?"

She walks away from the patio, into the house. After a moment we hear a cry of anguish. Both Mum and I run inside. Ruby is slumped on the sofa, sobbing. I only know one Stephen and can guess at his news. I unlatch Ruby's fingers from the phone, clutched to her chest.

"Stephen? It's Layla. What's happened? Is it Anna? "

"Layla." The relief in his voice is almost tangible. "I'm so glad you're there. I would have phoned you first, so you could tell Ruby, but I only had her number from the day she came to the rehab centre. And I haven't been able to raise Clyde yet to get yours."

At the mention of Clyde's name, a hundred questions pop into my head about where he is and whether he's coming back, or even if he wants to see me, but I push them down. Wrong time and place.

"Tell me what happened."

"She died from an overdose yesterday." I crumple to the chair next to Ruby. The loss of the beautiful young woman to that ugly drug twists my gut, birthing a violent urge for vigilante justice against the drug dealers who mete out destruction and death to the young and innocent.

"Layla, Anna left a note in her bedroom drawer. It wasn't suicide," he adds quickly. "Well, not consciously, anyway. I think she knew the time would come and wrote it in preparation."

"What did the note say?"

"It said some things to her parents, but it also said she wanted to tell Ruby how grateful she was for her friendship and that whatever happens, Ruby gave her something precious."

"I'm passing the phone back to Ruby. She needs to hear this. When is Anna's funeral?"

He gives me the details and I wrap Ruby's hand around the phone and support her arm while Stephen reads her Anna's note.

CHAPTER 33

WE AGREE NOT TO WEAR black.
Although the only Anna we knew lived a life of anguish and despair, we want to wear bright colours in honour of the light this drug extinguished. It's the three of us—Ruby, Levi, and I—who make our way into the chapel, slipping into seats towards the back, behind a sea of heads, all facing the tragic evidence of death.

I think the presence of a person-sized box in pride of place at a funeral, is a diminution of the deceased. As if someone's entire life has been reduced to nothing more than this wooden box. When loved ones read their eulogies: lists of words and deeds to describe the person, your eyes are drawn back to a crate which screams over the platitudes, 'Look at me, I'm not any of those things anymore, I'm simply a corpse in a casket.' Even after a joke is thrown in to a speech, you laugh and then swallow it back, admonished by the sight of a severe box glaring at you in judgement.

But not this box. Rather than a sedate, polished walnut coffin, Anna's resting place is a simple pine box alive with dancing murals and ringed with flowered leis. Each image depicts a personal memory of this fairy girl. There are wattle trees in blossom, rolling surf, mountains, fantasy creatures peeping around tree trunks, and animals in mid-frolic. Balanced on the lid of the box are symbols of her life: her favourite scarf, best loved books and her guitar.

Around the coffin are photos of a happy, healthy Anna. Before she sold her soul to the drugs, and was forced to live her life in the shadows. Ruby claps a hand to her mouth, smiling through tears at the joyous display. I press a kiss onto her shoulder and turn back to the proceedings. She nudges me and gives a thumbs up as the upbeat sound of The Wanted's "I'm Glad You Came" booms through the speakers.

If I crane my neck I can see part of Stephen's profile; he sits a couple of rows from the front. Patricia, the woman we met in the kitchen, is next to him and Colin sits beside her. A man on Stephen's other side looks familiar. Without warning, my stomach lurches with a mix of excitement and apprehension. Then he tilts his head to the side and hunches one shoulder as he leans to hear a whispered comment from a teenage boy.

It's him. Clyde.

A young man walks up to the lectern and I reluctantly slide my gaze away from Clyde. The man must be Anna's older brother, he is so like her. He smiles at the painted coffin and speaks.

"My little sister was like a fairy, but her life wasn't all rainbows and butterflies. We lost our brother, Anna's twin, a few years ago and it seemed like small fragments of her peeled away from that day. The drugs numbed the pain, but diminished my sister until she was empty, had no substance, and was certainly no match for Crystal Meth."

My mind flashes to the thin, waif of a child in the garden.

"You might say Crystal Meth won the battle with Anna. Or you could look around, even in this room today, at a sister, brother, friend, who may not have been here if not for her. Even while in the relentless grip of this drug, she dredged up a small spark of defiance, enough to frighten others into refusing this drug or making the decision not to try it a second or third time."

Ruby and Levi glance at each other and I squeeze Ruby's hand. He's right, I have my sister because of Anna's bleak honesty. Her brother shifts to anecdotes of happier times with his sister and then we are invited to make our way to the front to say goodbye as The Band Perry sings, "If I Die Young."

The aftermath of a funeral is awkward. People gather outside the chapel not sure what conversation is appropriate, nervous of approaching the family, whose grief can't be acknowledged in mere words, but who also can't be ignored. Colin grips Levi's shoulder and they do a man hug. When Stephen wanders over, I glance behind him, but don't see Clyde. After chatting for a few minutes, Ruby and Levi indicate they're going back to the car and with a final scan of the crowd, I turn to follow them.

"Layla. Wait a minute."

His deep voice sends a thrill from my stomach to my brain and I suck in a breath before turning.

I opt for wide-eyed surprise. Which is not hard as he's lost more weight and looks fit and healthy. "Clyde. I didn't know you were here." The lift of his eyebrow tells me he doesn't buy it. "I thought you were in London."

"I was, but flew in two days ago. How's Ruby handling this?"

I glance over to the car-park. "Distraught. Shocked. Disillusioned. She believed Anna was doing well. That they had a friendship worth more than the drugs."

His eyes glisten with compassion. "She loved Anna and believed in her. Anna would have taken that with her. She's special, your Ruby."

I nod, too emotional to answer. There is an awkward silence.

"The surgeon did an amazing job with the scars," he says. "You look good."

I smile and gesture at his new look. "Not looking too bad yourself. Bet your mother's pleased."

He chuckles, holding my gaze for a beat. "She says it's a good start."

"So, did you get the position?"

I hold my breath, praying for the god of job interviews to favour me.

"Yes. They want me to start in two weeks. I came back to pack up."

My heart sinks and when I try to swallow a lump of disappointment is lodged in my throat.

I stretch up and kiss his dimpled cheek. "I hope you'll be really happy there. You deserve a great life."

Before he can answer, I turn and hurry to the car-park where Ruby and Levi wait in the car.

CHAPTER 34

SCHUSTER AND BEASLEY'S GOTH RECEPTIONIST leans against my office door, scowls and pops her gum. Her way of asking if I need her for anything more today.

"Another coffee would be great, thanks Brenda." I love calling her by her un-goth name and watching the scowl deepen. She rolls her eyes and saunters down to the staff kitchen.

This is my third month managing the new Contracts Division at the law firm. Randy offered me the position by email while I was in New York and I accepted immediately. He's let me run it the way I want and we're doing well, with the client base growing consistently. My idiosyncratic colleagues make me feel quite at home. Even Jason Crane has grown on me.

Since returning from New York, I've become an irregular regular at The Black Hole. Mainly to keep an eye on the professor. It's not the same with Clyde gone and poor old Gavin mopes around as if he's lost his best friend. Probably has. I know I have.

As if thoughts of the bar have conjured her, Lavender's familiar ring tone bounces my phone across the table.

"*Sourcil,* darling. It's me."

"Yes, I know. I was just thinking about you guys. What's new?"

"What you're really asking is, what's new with Clyde."

Busted. "No. I want to hear about you. How's Lancie?"

"You don't fool me for a moment, *Sourcil.*"

"Alright. Have you heard from him?"

"Yes."

"Stop it," I groan. "Don't leave me hanging. What's he up to? Is he seeing anyone?"

"He wouldn't say, darling. That either means he is and he

doesn't want me to tell you, or he isn't and he doesn't want me to tell you." She rasps with laughter, at my moan of frustration. "For fuck's sake, you two are as bad as each other. He's too far away for me to shake down, but you I can pin down with a stiletto to the forehead until you spill. So, what *do* you feel about our sweet leviathan?"

What a question. A well of emotion churns up to my throat, blocking the words.

"That silence is a bit ominous, darling."

I blow out a hard breath. "I…well…look I'm at work so can't really talk much."

"Enough with the mealy-mouthed excuses and game playing. Spit out what you feel, and admit it was real."

She hits a nerve. Prods the old angry Layla. The part of me that can't forgive my actions that night. Or my silence after. "You bloody push 'til I snap, don't you?"

"Go girl!"

"If you must know, there's not a damn day that goes by when I don't think about him. There's not a man I meet that measures up to him." Lavender giggles. "Stop it, you heartless queen. You know I'm not talking about his size."

"Of course not, darling, couldn't help myself. Now tell me why he's under your skin."

This is so hard to put into words. But I want to; I need to. "I think Clyde taught me about love. That it's not all about violins and stars-in-the-eyes. It's about being stripped naked with nowhere to run; it's about struggling with your demons; being shaken to the very core of your being, and through it all, knowing you are worth being loved and respected." My hands are shaking and my heart feels like a drum behind my ribs. Lavender is unusually silent, waiting for me to continue. "When I saw him at Anna's funeral, I wanted to jump on his back and hold him down so he couldn't leave."

"And still you let him go," she says.

"Yes, I still let him go," I whisper. "It was too late."

Lavender draws in a deep breath. "So, are we done with the love lament, darling?" I grunt. "How about lunch next week? Wednesday? At our fave down at the Rocks?"

"I'll be there."

"Done. Mwah, mwah, darling."

❧

Today we are visiting Corinne. Ruby, Matt and me.

When we arrive, we're led to a common room with a view of a garden courtyard, and Corinne is brought out by an orderly. After a palpitating silence, Matt asks how she's doing. This elicits an eye roll and a sound somewhere between a snort and a grunt. It's excruciatingly uncomfortable and Corinne has no intention of making it less so.

Of course, she's wary of her siblings. The last time she saw any of us was in court. We each gave testimony about her mental instability. Mine was by video from New York and included all details of the fire and its consequences.

When, after fifteen minutes, it becomes clear she's not interested in communicating, by unspoken agreement, we rise to leave. It's then I see the tears gather in her eyes. As we've been told it's unlikely her delusional view of us will change, I'm taken by surprise at this display of emotion.

In my new spontaneity, I put my arms around her, holding on even when she squirms and turns her head away. Matt takes my cue and embraces us both, and Ruby, hesitant at first, hugs her from behind. Despite the tears, Corinne's body is an unyielding board and her gaze remains fixed on the wall behind us.

But, for the three of us, at least, the healing has begun. Perhaps in the future, somewhere inside Corinne's fixated mind, there will be a small shift.

CHAPTER 35

A SHARP BARK PUNCTURES THE SILENCE. I turn, jolted from my wardrobe reverie to see Bennie smiling at me. A slight twist of his lips and a baring of his teeth. Definitely a smile. His is the only voyeurism permitted in my bedroom and I nod, acknowledging his choice of my outfit.

My social outings are infrequent, by choice. A few blind dates: one which was quite bizarre. Dad set me up with an accountant at his firm. The man seemed so quiet and unassuming until he had a few drinks. With a lascivious grin, he told me how turned on he was by my battle-scarred face and pawed at me until I peeled him off and sent him packing. I nearly farewelled him with a piratical 'Arrrr' but didn't want to risk his ardour re-igniting.

Tonight will be fun, though. Lavender has organised a party at the Black Hole for Gavin's thirtieth birthday. And all the gang are coming along, with several of Lavender's birthday cowboys and any others she can pressgang into attending. Gavin has closed the club to the general public and hired some live music. This will be a test for me to see how much I have moved on from Clyde. My goal will be to enjoy the night with no more than a passing salute to Clyde's absence. Lavender regaled me at our lunch a few weeks ago with descriptions of all the single men she's inviting to 'get my juices flowing'. The visual doesn't bear thinking about.

I do a twirl for Bennie in my new black dress: tight bodice with boat neck and elbow-length sleeves, and short, slightly flared skirt. I pull on black tights and red, ankle boots and top it off with a red jacket. All the vital bits are covered. Old habits die hard. My dark hair is longer now, sitting below my shoulders and just for fun, I plait a strip of hair down one side.

I pick up a bright red lipstick. Am I ready for such an audacious display? The mirror reminds me my mouth is still a bit lopsided, and I reach for the softer nude shade when a quote from Anais Nin chimes in my head: 'Life shrinks or expands in proportion to one's courage'. The hell with it, no more shrinking for me. I slash the luscious colour across my lips and smack them together.

A deep thud of bass vibrates through my body as I push the heavy black door open and descend into The Black Hole. The tables have been pushed back to expose a dance floor and Gavin is poised in the centre dressed in a white suit, flared trousers and black shirt. His right index finger points to the ceiling, his legs are wide apart and his head is down. The falsetto trill of the Bee Gees singing 'Stayin' Alive' moves him like a go button; his hips thrust from side to side and his arm points to floor then ceiling, in time with the music. Two steps into that place and I'm already laughing.

"Dahling, over here!" shrieks Lavender.

I clap a hand over my mouth to restrain my mirth. A huge, blonde afro wig balances on Lavender's head and her muscled thighs bulge under the grip of tight green sequined flares.

"What's this?" Lavender flicks a wrist at my outfit. "Gavin's birthday, darling. Automatically means seventies. Do I have to spell everything out for you?"

"Apparently." I grin, grateful for my ignorance.

She squints at my face. "Ooh, love the red lippy, darling. I think you might finally be growing some balls."

I stretch up and plant a red imprint of my lips on her cheek and wander over to the bar to order a drink. Lancie leans on the counter with one foot resting on the rung of a stool. His hairy chest leers at me from his open-fronted gold satin shirt. It takes all my self-control not to look down when I glimpse matching gold satin trousers.

"Hey, Layla!"

Gavin calls me onto the floor and giggling recklessly, I run over to grab his hand. He pulls me into his chest and spins me out in a jive turn. We spin and kick and hop; our arms cross, he does a shoulder slide and then picks me up and throws my feet out in a swing. The man is not just a pair of tooled boots and flared pants, he can dance. After watching us for a few minutes, others are spinning, turning and sliding in a crazy, sweaty frenzy, while the preposterous silver disco ball twinkles and spins above our heads.

Exhausted from my gyrations, I stumble back to the bar and request a glass of cold water. As I suck a long mouthful into my parched throat, I glance over to the booths which line the far wall. A lone drinker lifts his glass to me and I push my way through the dancers and minglers until I reach the booth.

"Professor!" I throw my arms around his neck and kiss his bristly cheek. "You came. How have you been?"

The old man seems smaller than when I last saw him and his skin has a yellowish hue. Red-veined eyes peep out above pouches which sag like water balloons. He takes a breath to respond but has a spasm of dry coughing, then wipes his mouth with a grey handkerchief and places it into his pocket. He clears his throat and finally speaks.

"Never better, dear Layla." I slide into the seat opposite him and reach for his hand. It's clean, but the fingernails are dirty. "Please excuse my fingernails. I haven't had my manicure today." I swallow the emotion which churns up my throat at his shame. "This is the loveliest surprise to see you here. It's worth enduring such stentorian music and Gavin's pitiful imitation of the great John Travolta."

"Gavin knows how to jive, though," I say.

"Yes, I saw the two of you out there. And dear God, I also saw Mrs Crompton doing a bizarre version of the funky chicken dance." He snorts and we both dissolve into laughter until he has another coughing fit. I rub his back, not sure what else to do. Finally, he regards me with watery eyes. "You know, I used to tear up a dance floor myself at one stage."

"Really? Would you like to—"

"Good heavens, no. That would not end well, I fear. No, I only came tonight because such a special person was going to be here."

"Oh Professor, you're so sweet."

"I think he means me."

My heart stills, then with a thump it jumps in my chest like an overjoyed puppy. I turn, my eyes squeezed shut in case it's an illusion.

"Open your eyes, crazy girl."

"It's you," I squeak. He grins and nods. "Why aren't you in London?"

"I was forced to come back."

"Oh. Why?"

"Because you weren't there."

It takes a moment for his words to penetrate my dull brain.

"You came back for me?" I ask.

"Sure did. It was too cruel to have all those young men measured against such perfect manhood."

"It was Lavender, wasn't it? She told you."

"She might have mentioned something about you being stripped naked and cavorting with demons."

I gurgle, a burst of joy, and he opens his arms.

"I missed you," I say, launching myself into his embrace.

As he crushes me to his strong, warm chest, there is a roar of cheering and clapping, led by Lavender and Gavin. I chuckle, my mouth squashed against the soft fabric of Clyde's shirt and a warm rush of gratitude swirls through my body for this new family, who love me as I am. With stunning clarity, I realise the fire I thought had destroyed me, has instead revealed me. A shinier version of myself, worthy of Clyde, my friends and, more importantly, worthy of me.

Lavender steps up to the mic. "My job is done, darlings. Anyone who needs a matchmaker, I'll give you my card later." She cups her silicone prosthetics. "Now, come on up here you gorgeous man and make my tits vibrate to the throb of 'Proud Mary'!"

Clyde presses a soft kiss to my lips and pulls away. I grasp his sleeve, needing to ask him a question I asked someone else a lifetime ago.

"Clyde, when you look at me what do you see?"

"I see you."

I smile. It is enough. It is everything.

ACKNOWLEDGEMENTS

So many people came on this writing journey with me and I will try not to leave anyone out. First of all Cathy Yardley – writer, editor, mentor – who shared her "Rock Your Plot" course with me and turned me from a panster into a plotter. Her wonderful developmental editing polished the manuscript and made it so much better. My good friend, Kassey Gardiner, the grammar nazi, spent many hours with me, discussing scene outlines and characters, as well as late nights reading and editing. Also, Jill Knell for her constant encouragement, plot ideas and beta reading. Thank you to Deborah O'Neill Cordes for her critiques and her tireless assistance in navigating the technical confusion of self-publishing. To Téa Cooper, who gave me valuable feedback, honest critiques and who braved a nerve-wracking pitch session on my behalf. Thanks to my dear Mum who loves everything I write (honestly, she's not at all biased) and my friends, Trish Murphy and Robin Ward, who read each chapter and stroked my ego. Thank you to Peter McAllister, whose bizarre sense of humour created the nightclub scene at The Silk Purse.

Heartfelt thanks to the wonderful Dean Morzone, QC, DCJ, who patiently gave me legal information about compensation cases and how these are negotiated by the lawyers out of court. Gratitude to the generous and informative Officer In Charge of the Fire Investigation Unit in NSW who gave me information about how the case and exhibits would be handled. Any mistakes or deviations in either of these areas above are entirely my own. Thanks to various medical professionals for their invaluable expert information on the treatment of burns and special thanks to Courtney Lee who shared her personal and harrowing experience as an ice addict, giving me a deep emotional insight into the devastations of this drug.

Finally, as always, thanks to the readers who will make this all worthwhile by taking the time to pick up my book and read it. You are why I write!

ABOUT THE AUTHOR

Joanna Lloyd was born in Papua New Guinea, before moving to Sydney, Australia, to attend high school. After thirteen years in Sydney, she gravitated to the warmth of Far North Queensland where she attended university to study psychology, trained as a mediator and spent many years conducting workplace and family law mediations. She writes historical and contemporary fiction.

www.ingramcontent.com/pod-product-compliance
Lightning Source LLC
Chambersburg PA
CBHW032142190626
46814CB00005BA/1800